Last Request

LIZ MISTRY

H Q

ONE PLACE. MANY STORIES

This novel is entirely a work of fiction. The names, characters
and incidents portrayed in it are the work of the author's
imagination. Any resemblance to actual persons, living or
dead, events or localities is entirely coincidental.

HQ
An imprint of HarperCollins*Publishers* Ltd
1 London Bridge Street
London SE1 9GF

This paperback edition 2019

First published in Great Britain by
HQ, an imprint of HarperCollins*Publishers* Ltd 2019

Copyright © Liz Mistry 2019

Liz Mistry asserts the moral right to be
identified as the author of this work.
A catalogue record for this book is
available from the British Library.

ISBN: 9780008358358

MIX
Paper from
responsible sources
FSC® C007454

This book is produced from independently certified FSC™ paper
to ensure responsible forest management.

For more information visit: www.harpercollins.co.uk/green

Printed and bound in Great Britain by
CPI Group (UK) Ltd, Croydon, CR0 4YY

To my family, for all that you do and all that you are.

Prologue

1983

Her hand, scaly and trembling, reaches out. The flash of shocking-pink nail varnish that I'd applied with painstaking care whilst she'd been sleeping is incongruous against her yellowy skin. The stench of death hangs heavy around her, as if she's rotting from the inside out. I take her hand, careful not to grip too tightly. Every worm-like sinew, every frail tendon, every arid vein a braille pattern against my palm. Still, she flinches, the pain flashing in her milky eyes. A sheen of sweat dapples her forehead. Her night-dress is soaked with perspiration that mingles with fetid pus and piss, creating a cacophony of odours that make me want to retch. Her pink scalp shines through matted hair. Her cheekbones, jutting against paper-thin skin, bear raw scabs.

The room is dire – stinking and filthy. I should clean it, but I don't know how. That was never one of *my* jobs – cleaning up, keeping things neat, tidy. That had always been her job. Her eyes look heavy. Soon, once the morphine kicks in, she'll doze off. The dim light from the bedside lamp illuminates the layer of dust that covers the cabinet top. We don't use the main light anymore. It hurts her eyes. With the curtains drawn against the

1

outside world, we are cocooned in this hell hole together … slowly disintegrating … decomposing like two worthless corpses thrown on an unlit pyre.

The carpet's gross. I've spilled more piss on there than has made it into the bedpan and that's not mentioning the stains where she's thrown up. No matter how much Dettol I use the overwhelming stink of vomit still hangs in the air.

When she drifts off into an uneasy sleep, I switch the television on. Casting anxious glances her way, I wait. Today's the day. The court hearing. It's like the entire country is on tenterhooks waiting for the verdict. I've tried telling myself I'm imagining things – the looks, the surreptitious glances, the whispers every time I go to the shops – each one a piqueristic experience of both pleasure and pain. Each one grounding me in the reality of what *he's* done to us. Deep down I know that everyone – the postman, Mr Anand at the corner shop, Mrs Roberts two doors down – everyone in the entire fucking world is waiting, holding on to their bated breath, with the heightened anticipation of an illicit orgasm.

They barely noticed me before this. Now it's as if, in the absence of my mother's presence, I've been thrust into minor celebrity status, my every move scrutinised. At least the paparazzi have slung their hooks, for now. Not before Mum had to face them though. When the story first hit the news, she was forced to run the gauntlet, her head hung in shame, her eyes swollen and red, her gait unsteady. It took its toll. Well, that and the shit that he'd infected her with. It all combined to drag her down, drain her.

The recording I've seen so many times, the standard one they played on endless repeat when the shit first hit the fan, flits across the screen. He looks so suave, sophisticated. All spruced up in his suit, beard trimmed, sleazy smile playing around his lips. Like he'd done nothing. Like none of this was *his* fault.

I daren't put the volume up so I flick to subtitles …

'Three more students under the care of Professor Graham Earnshaw have come forward, with accusations of rape. This brings

2

the total number of victims to fifteen. Professor Earnshaw's solicitor still maintains his client is not guilty and as the trial enters its fifth day, the court heard how Professor Earnshaw is alleged to have infected not only his wife, but four of his victims, three male and one female, with the HIV virus. It looks like this case could run into its second week, if not longer.'

The camera flicks to the front of Leeds Court and after a quick glance to make sure Mum is still asleep, I pull forward to hear what the Dean of Social Sciences is about to say about my father.

'... and the department has responded to student concerns as quickly as possible. We are doing our best to support our ...'

A groan from the bed and I press the remote. The screen goes dark and I look round. She's holding her hand up in front of her, a slight smile tugs her thin lips into a toothless grimace. 'Thank you. I like pink, always have.'

I lean over, tuck the sheets around her emaciated frame, ignoring the wafts of decay that hit my nostrils. Her frail hand grips my arm and I pause, turning my head towards her. 'What, Mum? What is it?'

Her smile widens, and I try not to flinch at the bloody cracks at the corner of her mouth and the gaps inside. She nods once and swallows. I go to lift the half-filled glass from the bedside table but she shakes her head – a painful movement that pulls a frown across her forehead. When she speaks her voice is low and raw. 'Promise me.'

I lean closer, hardly able to hear her words.

'My last request – you've *got* to promise that you'll do it. Live your dream. Do *everything* you always planned to do before this.'

Her hand gestures towards the TV. She saw it. I haven't been quick enough.

I bow my head and promise her. I'd promise her anything right now, but still, I keep my fingers crossed. I curse my careless-ness but there's no point, for when I glance back her eyes are closed. She is on her final journey and, as if on cue, my entire

3

body responds to the smash of a train hurtling through my core, pummelling me to the ground and, as she gasps her last breath, I cower on the floor hugging my knees tight to my chest. My heart shatters into a jigsaw of fragments that can't ever reconnect; a sense of relief coddles me like a woollen blanket and guilt and anger swamp me.

*

Days pass with those whose slurs had previously scorched us, now offering platitudes. Each false word drips like acid, as I take in the detritus that is my life from here on in, and all the time her last request plays in my mind like an annoying jingle.

There's nothing else for it. I'll have to do something about that.

Monday 15th October
2018

16

Chapter 1

Dour rain pummelled the cobbles that ran between the two rows of houses on Willowfield Terrace, making them sleek and dangerous underfoot. Except for the oppressive, grey clouds that promised more of the same, the alleyway was deserted. The air hung heavy, waiting to embrace the latest drama involving the Parekh women as Detective Sergeant Nikita Parekh flung open the back door and stormed out. Anger emanating from her every pore, she flew down the steps into the yard and out the gate, followed by her daughter. Leather jacket flying loose, she ignored the spatter of mucky water that her trainers kicked up the back of her jeans. With a plastic bag looped over one wrist, she raked her waist-length hair back into a ponytail and slipped a scrunchie round it. She was on a mission and nothing would deter her.

'Mum ... Mum! Wait up.' Charlie, a foot taller than her mum, ran behind, hitching her schoolbag onto her shoulder. Unlike her mum, she tried to avoid the puddles created by the worn cobbles.

But Nikki was already pushing open the back gate of the neighbouring house and striding up the steps. Using her fist, she brayed briefly on the door before turning the handle and pushing it open, not waiting for a reply. Entering the kitchen, she glanced at the hijabed woman cooking a fry-up in a huge frying pan on the cooker. 'Where's Haqib?'

The woman puffed her cheeks out in a 'what's he done now?' expression and, shaking her head, pointed her spatula towards the kitchen door. 'Front room.'

Stopping only to grab a bite from a piece of buttered toast on a plate on the worksurface, Nikki marched out of the kitchen, through the small hallway and into the living room. The room was in semi-darkness, with just the light from an Ikea tabletop lamp and the TV illuminating the area. She went straight over to the large bay window and swished the curtains open, allowing the scant light from outside to penetrate.

'Oi!' All angles, acne and attitude, Haqib, slouched on a bright red leather sofa, TV blaring, remote control in his hand, bare feet balanced on top of a glass-topped coffee table. 'What d'ya think you're doin'? Can't see the telly, can I?'

Nikki turned with her hands on hips, and glared at him, the spark in her eyes forcing him to back down.

Charlie panted into the room, the knot on the top of her head wobbling as if it might fall off, her cheeks spattered with raindrops. 'Mum, if you'd just hang on a minute.'

Nikki extended her hand, one index finger raised to her daughter, just like her own mother had always done, '*Chup kar.*' She rounded the bulky couch and positioned herself right in front of the TV.

Charlie folded her arms under her boobs, one hip extended towards her mum, pure sulk dripping from her pursed lips.

Haqib bobbed his head, first to one side and then to the other, trying to see the TV, his tone a little less confrontational this time. 'Can't see.'

Nikki bent over and swiped his feet off the table.

'Hey.' He glanced from his aunt to his cousin, his hands splayed before him. 'What's up? What've I done now? You can't just come in and do that, you know?'

Nikki snorted before tipping the contents of the plastic bag she was carrying onto the table where Haqib's feet had been. Haqib stopped, mouth open. If Nikki had been in a better mood she'd have laughed, but right now she was fuming. Really fuming. Haqib's eyes moved from his aunt's stern face to the bags filled with multicoloured pills, then up to Charlie. The pills with their smiley faces, love hearts and winky eyes incensed Nikki. Over the past few months she'd seen umpteen cases of kids in the city taking E and landing themselves in Bradford Royal Infirmary. This new batch was potent – three deaths and a brain damaged kid testified to that. It made Nikki's piss boil. She snatched the remote from her nephew and switched off the racket that boomed from the speakers. 'Spill!'

Haqib clipped his mouth shut, then opened it, before once more closing it like a minnow about to get swallowed by a shark. That analogy appealed to Nikki. All she wanted to do was to swallow the lad up, chew him till he squealed and spit him out.

'I ... erm, I ...' He looked at Charlie as if expecting her to bail him out.

Nikki moved closer, breathing heavily, her anger exuding from every pore. 'You selling MDMA to my 14-year-old, are you? Got a death wish, have you?' Another step and Haqib was trying to mould his body into the leather couch.

'You all right in there?' Nikki's sister, Anika, called from the kitchen.

Nikki glowered at Haqib. 'You'd better start spilling before your mum comes through.'

'For God's sake, Mum.' Charlie, her face perfectly made up, eyeliner on point and her school skirt too damn short, flounced forward and flung herself onto the sofa beside Haqib, sliding her schoolbag round till it rested on her lap. 'If you'd give me half a chance to explain. Haqib didn't *sell* me it.'

Nikki glared at the lad, eyebrows raised. 'You *gave* them to

9

her? You *gave* your 14-year-old cousin E? That's no better. In fact, that's bloody worse.'

He ran the back of his hand across his nose and glanced at Charlie. 'I didn't. I wouldn't – she ...' He glanced at Charlie and shrugged.

Charlie elbowed him in the ribs. 'Tell her then – you might as well ...'

Head bowed, looking like a 2-year-old in trouble for stealing the Easter eggs, he mumbled something.

'What?' Nikki's voice was sharp. She'd thought Haqib knew better than to bring drugs of any sort near her family, near her home or even onto the damn estate. What the hell had he been thinking?

Clearing his throat, Haqib tried again. 'She' – he jerked his thumb towards Charlie – 'confiscated it.'

'You *what*?' Nikki looked at her eldest daughter who was all sulky indignation and 'I told you so'.

'What? So, you thought I'd *buy* Es? I'm not a loser, you know!'

Nikki grinned and scooped the bags up. Charlie wasn't a loser. Definitely not. Nearing the sofa, she leaned over and kissed the top of her daughter's top-knot head. 'No, *you're* not.' She leaned over further and cuffed Haqib's head. 'You, on the other hand, will be, if you don't stop with the damn drugs. Now I've got to bail you out, yet again. Not good enough, Haqib – not fucking good enough.'

She could just about put up with the weed that was rife on the estate – turn a blind eye and all that – but *this*? Once this shit got a grip on the estate it'd spread like wildfire bringing with it crime and violence and despair. She'd seen it all before on other Bradford estates and she was buggered if she'd allow it on hers. But what was she to do about Haqib? She was tempted to turn the little scrote in – let him see what it would be like – but deep down she knew she couldn't do that to her family or to this runt of a boy.

10

Haqib rubbed his head. 'I don't take them, Auntie. It's just …' He sighed.

Charlie broke in. 'What he's trying to say is that Deano's back.'

A talon curled its way round Nikki's heart and squeezed, hard and sudden. If Deano was back, then that meant his drug lord boss Franco was too … and he was an evil sod. 'I'll deal with this.' She hung the bag back over her wrist and chucked the remote control at Haqib, making sure it whacked his head. 'Don't be late for school, you two.'

When she re-entered the kitchen, Anika handed her a mug of steaming coffee. 'Weed? Again?'

Nikki sighed. Anika took a pragmatic approach to her son's weed consumption. Personally, Nikki would rather he didn't smoke the stuff, but then she knew how many alternatives there were out there, so she let it pass. She could tell her sister the truth, but what purpose would that serve? Anika would wail and moan and threaten to ground him and Haqib would do what he always did and ignore her.

She'd deal with it and they'd move on with her keeping a closer eye on the little turd. 'Yeah, summat like that.' She shrugged. 'Deano's back … and Franco. Don't worry, I'll sort it though.'

Anika nodded and went back to the fry-up she was cooking. 'He's trouble, that lad, but I've heard Franco's worse. Sort it before it gets out of hand – like last time.'

Nikki munched the remains of the toast she'd started on her way in. She enjoyed spending time in her sister's kitchen. It was homely. Filled with clutter and love. Kids' schoolbags by the back door, shoes kicked off in a huddle next to them, well-tended plants on the windowsill, a series of sentimental 'There's No Place Like Home' plaques and cutesy pictures of cats. Her own kids were always telling her to get some plants and put some pictures on the walls. Truth was, Nikki was as green-fingered as weed killer and the only plant that had been able to flourish in her home was the cactus Charlie had given her three Christmases ago. As for the sentimental crap? Well, that was *so* not Nikki. She liked things streamlined – no clutter. That way she knew if her space had been infiltrated. That way she felt safe and in control. As she watched her sister, something niggled at her. Something was different. When she realised what it was, she smiled but her heart sank. Why did Anika have to be so needy? 'You can't have it both ways, Anki.'

Anika frowned. 'What you on about?'

Taking a sip of coffee, Nikki pointed at her sister's head. 'You can't wear the hijab on one hand and fry bloody bacon and sausages on the other, now can you?'

Anika's face broke into a grin. She flung her head back, laughter bubbling out of her like warm fuzzies on a winter's day. 'Just as well I'm not wearing it on my hand then, innit?'

Covering her sigh with a smile, Nikki nursed her coffee, observing the warm flush across her sister's cheeks. Anika was happy … for now. 'Take it *Yousaf's* back an all.'

'Aw don't be like that. I love him. Maybe he'll stay this time.'

Nikki wanted to shake her. Make her wise up. 'You know he'll never leave his Pakistani family. 'Specially now he's a "councillor".' Nikki made air quotes round the last word and crossed her eyes for effect, pleased that her silly actions seemed to have taken the sting out of her words when Anika laughed.

'He loves me and he loves Haqib.'

Nikki groaned and stuffed more toast into her mouth, chewed, swallowed and then spoke. 'Come on! When's the last time he bought Haqib owt – or you for that matter? Yousaf's a loser. You keep taking him back every time he turns up for a booty call and he'll get you up the duff again and leave you. The likes of us – working-class, dual heritage and Hindu to boot – are *not* good enough for well-off businessmen-cum-councillors and especially not for married ones. He won't leave her.'

Anika's eyes welled up and Nikki could have kicked herself. Maybe sometimes she should just learn to shut her big mouth.

She jumped to her feet and moved round to put her arms round her sister, hugging her tight. 'I'm sorry. I know I'm bitter and twisted, but I just don't want you getting hurt again.'

'Not everyone's like you know who, Nikki.'

Nikki sighed. Anika was right. Just because she'd had a bad experience didn't mean Anika would. But the truth was Yousaf just was not good enough for her sister. She only had to convince Anika of that fact. The sisters hugged until, smelling something beginning to burn, Nikki wheeled round, turned off the cooker and yelled through the house, 'Breakfast's ready.'

Haqib and Charlie appeared from the living room as Nikki knocked on the wall that adjoined her house and yelled. 'You two, Auntie Anika's got breakfast ready. Shift it.'

Faint yells of, 'I'm starving' and 'Hope it's a fry-up' filtered through the walls and within seconds, Nikita's younger two children, dressed in school uniforms, faces all rosy and clean, ran into the kitchen and plonked themselves down at the table, grabbing their cutlery and looking like they'd never been fed in their lives. As Nikki grabbed another slice of toast, she felt her phone vibrate in her pocket. Pulling it out, she saw it was a text from her boss, DCI Archie Hegley. She circled the table to drop kisses on each of the kids' heads in turn. 'Work. Gotta run. Be good and, Charlie, change into trousers. Your skirt's too damn short.'

Driving down Legram's Lane in her clapped-out Zafira, windscreen wipers going like the clappers, Nikki wondered if she had transferred her wellies from the pool car back to her own. She had a sinking feeling she hadn't. Every so often a drop of water landed on her head and Nikki cursed. She really needed to get a new car, but the kids seemed to have an endless stream of requests for stuff that was never free. The car would have to wait. A new drip splatted on her head, rolled down her forehead and landed on her nose. She wiped it off with her sleeve. Maybe after she'd done her Inspector's exam and got a promotion, she could treat herself to a car that didn't leak – or maybe she'd have to repair the leaky tap in the bathroom and the thermostat on the central heating and double-glaze the kitchen window before its old wooden frame rotted and released the pane.

After taking a right at Thornton Road, Nikki joined the trail of commuters. A few hundred yards and she could already see the telltale police vehicles and crime scene vans. She abruptly took advantage of a gap in the traffic and bounced her car onto the opposite kerb. Ignoring the hoots from cars travelling in the opposite direction, she got out and turned her collar up against the rain. Typical! Weeks without a suspicious death and then you choose the day when it's pissing down to reveal yourself. She jogged the last few hundred yards, hoping the crime scene tent would be up and she could get some shelter.

Chapter 2

The Odeon building was all domed shapes and scaffolding. It dominated the landscape from City Park where it was situated next to the Alhambra. Work had recently begun on renovating the building with a view to making it a concert venue. Nikki hoped it would be a success. Bradford could do with the revenue a building like this could bring in. She had fond memories of visiting the cinema as a child with her mum and Anika and … but that was a thought for another day. She wasn't going to go there.

The site behind the Odeon was a disused car park on Quebec Street facing a Cantonese restaurant that served the most delicious buffet Nikki had ever tasted and had occasional karaoke nights. Behind that was the Renault car dealership, outside which she'd parked her car. As she approached, she saw that the old car park and entry to Quebec Street was cordoned off with crime scene tape. Inside the taped area, a series of diggers and cement mixers had signed a deal with the weather to create a quagmire of khaki-coloured slime that looked as runny as slurry and smelled almost as bad.

'There's been a leakage,' a drenched uniformed officer in a police-issue poncho informed her. Lowering his voice as if he feared a bevy of journos would appear in a puff of smoke to nab his quote, the officer added, 'Sewage.'

You don't say? Nikki took the proffered clipboard, signed herself into the crime scene and ducked under the tape. There were no stepping stones and the crime scene officers were busy, so Nikki took a moment to survey the area. Towering above the machinery, the green cupolas of the Odeon surrounded by its protective framework looked angry against the hovering rainclouds. Uniformed officers were dotted round the cordon, chatting to passers-by and drinking coffee from takeaway cups. The crime scene van, back doors open, had parked inside the cordon, as close as possible to the site. A few builders in yellow hats and T-shirts and high-vis tabards hovered near the edges. One of the men was talking to a figure in white that Nikki assumed to be Gracie Fells, the crime scene boss. She'd just decided that there was no option but for her to brave the swamp and join them when a hand on her shoulder made her jump. Shrugging it off, she swung round, a sharp retort on her lips. It was Detective Constable Sajid Malik. 'Fuck's sake. What you playing at?'

She glared up at the six-foot-two officer, who held his palms up in a placating gesture. Dark gelled hair was splattered across his forehead, with rain pouring down his aquiline nose and dripping off the end. Not right that even in the pissing rain he could look so bloody handsome. Pity he knew it too.

'Sorry, Nik. Thought you heard me approach.'

Nikki doubted that was true. Saj was nothing if not an annoying little, or rather, big shit who would take great delight in making her jump. But now wasn't the time to address that. 'What we got?'

'Not sure, think the builders found summat.'

'Duh, you don't say?' Nikki belted him sharply on the arm. 'For God's sake get a move on, Saj. Let's see what we got.'

With a quick glance down at her shiny DMs, Nikki stepped into the slurry, ignoring the grin that the DC sent in her direction. Trust him to have his wellies with him. Maybe she'd just have to make sure she splashed a bit of muck on the trousers of his too-bloody-suave suit as she traipsed to the scene. The sludge was like walking through quicksand. Not that Nikki had ever walked through quicksand but, hey – she had an imagination, didn't she? The rain dribbled down the back of her neck and she wished she'd had the foresight to grab her parka before she left home. Sajid of course was in an ultra-smart raincoat – probably Armani as opposed to her Primani.

Shoving her fists into the pockets of her jacket, she squelched forward, Sajid following behind, like they were on a bloody bear hunt or something. Nikki saw that at last they'd managed to erect a tent. God only knew how that was going to stay upright in this weather. On reaching it, Nikki stuck her head in. 'Boiler suits? One small, one extra-extra-large with a doubly big hood for Sajid's over-inflated head.'

Gracie laughed and gestured to a lidded plastic box that stood by the tent flap. 'Help yourself. Not that I think it'll do any good. Doubt we'll find owt forensically usable in this weather. Bloody crime scene nightmare, this is. Body's in that hole there.'

The hole was about four foot by four – a little shorter than a grave and a little wider. Rivulets of mucky water seemed to be forging into the hole from all directions. That would be a problem for the crime scene techs. A criss-cross of muddy boot prints were rapidly being filled by the rivulets pouring towards the hole.

Gracie grimaced. 'It's on a slope – gonna be a nightmare to contain the water. We'll need to keep everything we drain just in case there's any evidence. Bloody weather!'

Nikki felt something soft slap her back and turned to see Sajid had thrown a suit to her. 'Hobbit size – just for you.'

'Yeah, Troll size for you then or Orc – whichever's the biggest and ugliest.'

Even before they'd managed to struggle into their suits, Nikki's was damp with mucky streaks all over the legs. A quick glance told her that, as expected, Sajid had managed to get his on over his dirty wellies and still had only a little bit of muck around the ankles. The man was a bloody contortionist. How the hell could he do that?

As Nikki took a couple of steps towards the hole, Gracie grabbed her arm. 'It's slippy. We're not sure if the sides are going to hold. Don't get too close.'

Heeding her warning, Nikki stood her ground, but leaned forward and peered into the rapidly filling cavity. Inside she could see the telltale shape of a skull and what might have been an arm, sticking out. 'It's a skeleton.'

'Nobody tell you that? The bloke who found it did say that when he phoned it in.'

Nikki wasn't surprised that a key detail like that hadn't made its way to her ears. 'Who've you called?'

'Langley Campbell's on his way.'

Beside her, Nikki sensed Sajid tense and then a voice said, 'No, he's not, he's here.'

Nikki turned around to see the pathologist shimmy through the opening, already wearing a Tyvek suit and carrying his bag of tools. Sajid shuffled his feet and edged behind Nikki, avoiding Langley. Ignoring Sajid's rudeness, Nikki smiled at the pathologist. 'Don't think this'll be yours for long, Langley. It's a skeleton and it looks like it's been there for ages. What do you think?'

Langley edged as close to the hole as he could, peered over and then exhaled. 'Got owt to put down over this bog, Gracie? I'll lie on my stomach – get a better look that way.'

Gracie and one of her team, with Sajid and Nikki's help, managed to slide a plastic sheet over the mud and Langley knelt on it before stretching his body along the sheet so he could examine inside. 'Hold my feet, someone. Last thing I want is to slide into this morass.'

Nikki nudged Sajid, who reluctantly leaned over and held on with his huge hands circling the pathologist's ankles whilst everyone else waited for Langley's opinion.

'Look, visibility is rubbish. But there's a huge crack in that skull – whether it's peri or post-mortem, I can't say for sure yet. But I can tell you that the skull looks to have been there for at least ten years and it's human and I can see metacarpal bones, an ulna and a radius. You'll be needing to get in a forensic anthropologist.'

Nikki uttered a silent, 'Yeah!' to herself. Thank God! This one was someone else's business, not hers. They had a cold case team for this sort of thing and she'd be happy to hand this over. She had more important things to deal with on the Listerhill Estate and a decade-old murder, for that's what it surely must be, wasn't going to detract from her little discussion with Deano Gilmartin.

Chapter 3

Who'd have thought it? For years they'd been banging on about doing up the Odeon. Years! Now they've finally started – and I've been waiting, wondering when they'd get round to that car park. Wondering how far down they'd dig, how far they'd need to go. Some days I convinced myself they'd leave the foundations – the ones they put in fifteen years ago. Other days I was certain that they'd pull the lot up. Made sense really. They'd need to go deep if they were going to extend their plumbing and their electrics – stood to reason, didn't it?

It's been grand watching them, waiting to see when they'd hit gold. When they started near the building, I knew who they'd find. I nearly pissed myself though when I saw who rolled up from the constabulary. Couldn't have planned it better if I'd tried. Nikita Parekh! I've seen her loads over the years. 'Course I have. Bradford's not that big a place and of course, she hit the news a few years ago. Got her that jammy promotion on the back of it.

They all mouth off about the Yorkshire Ripper and the Crossbow Cannibal, but they're amateurs compared to me – abject amateurs. How fucking sick of them to go for women – prostitutes. Disgusting really. Sexual motivation makes me sick, makes me want to vomit. I can feel the hatred surging in my stomach. I knew a man like that once but he's where he belongs now If you're gonna rid the world of scum, make it the right sort, eh? Them that deserve it – not just so you can get your rocks off.

Wonder when they'll realise though. Wonder when they'll expand their horrid little narrow minds and see what's really going on here. Don't think I've owt to worry about for now. Don't think they've got the brains. They've already let one slip through the crack – bet they'll do the same this time. They've got no imagination, that's their problem – no imagination at all.

21

Chapter 4

Listerhills was a strange estate. A combination of terraced houses backing onto one another and worn cobbled alleyways like moats winding between them. Running at either end, like the top and bottom strokes of a capital I, were two Seventies-style ex-council-housing estates. As a whole, the area was known as Listerhills despite the fact there wasn't a hill in sight and Lister – presumably he of Lister woollen mills fame, Samuel Lister – was long dead. What made Listerhills so notable was that unlike many of the Bradford estates, it was a hotchpotch of races and cultures. Bordering the university and being within spitting distance of the city centre, it was unique. In Bradford, the word *estate* was often considered a mucky word. Nikki hated it. Folk used it as an insult and, once branded an estate kid, it was a difficult label to shift.

Nikki often wondered which jackass had thought that nobody would notice that Listerhills was missing a botanical garden, a boat pond, a pavilion and a manor house, when they'd categorised it an *estate*. Did they think snotty-nosed kids forced by economics and unemployment into wearing wellies in summer and sandals in winter would grow up to have high aspirations? Nikki snorted. Who was she kidding? That was *her* childhood, these kids faced other challenges. Poverty only changed its face, it never went away.

She stood on the corner of Lister's Front Terrace, leaning against the wall, waiting for Deano to emerge from his mother's house on Lister's Avenue. In the shadows, she was barely visible, although the flicker of lights in the houses opposite kept her company. The rain had persisted throughout the day and it seemed that most people had been driven indoors for the road was almost deserted. Cars lined the streets, half of them mounting the kerbs, and standing like sentries along the pavements were a series of wheelie bins. *Must remember to put the bins out tonight.* On a different day, Nikki would have got out her supply of police notices, to tell people to park properly. Not that it did any good. Within days, they'd be back to their old tricks, blocking the pavements making it impossible for wheelchair users or mums with pushchairs to pass. She'd swapped her leather jacket for a parka and had replaced her mud-soaked Doc Martins for her old pair. She reckoned she'd be lucky to salvage them, but she'd bunged them in the washing machine on a quick low-temp wash, in the hope that she might be able to eke out a few months of wear in them.

Even from across the road she could hear the TV from Deano's house. Anywhere else there'd be a noise complaint within minutes, but not here and *definitely* not now Deano was back. Deano's house was like a cold sore between two perfectly manicured premises. The gate was hanging off its hinges and someone had wrapped a rope round it in an attempt to stop it clattering to the pavement. The garden was more weeds than flowers with an old sofa, its arse hanging out as if it had evacuated a volcano of yellowing foam from its innards. Three old crates, two burst black bin bags and a broken coffee table completed the ensemble. Deano's wheelie bin lay on its back, lid half detached, and with the house number 38 scrawled across it in black paint. An enormous tabby cat sat on the windowsill observing the proceedings indoors like some sort of feline *Gogglebox* character.

As she waited, Nikki scrolled through her texts. One from

Charlie saying she needed twenty quid for some school trip or other and five, no six texts from Marcus. She responded to Charlie's, telling her to tidy her room and help the younger two with their homework and maybe she'd consider it. The others she deleted, squashing the pang of guilt that she was becoming more and more used to of late. Marcus sensed she was pulling away and she *knew* she was. The one thing she didn't know was *why*. And that was something she'd analyse sometime in the future when hell froze over.

If the little rat didn't come out soon, she'd be forced to head over and knock on the door. Last thing she wanted, though, was to stress Margo out. Poor woman had enough on her plate with an abusive husband and now her runt of a son was back. If Nikki turned up on her doorstep, she could guarantee that Margo would be sporting a black eye at the very least, next time she saw her. No, best to get Deano on his own and exert her own kind of threat if his mum got hurt.

The cat stretched its front paws out on the windowsill and yawned. The roof overhang was keeping him dry, unlike Nikki who was beginning to feel like a damn fish. The door clattered open, sending the cat in a yowl of meows skittering over the rubbish and into the next-door neighbour's garden. Deano, all five-foot-one of sheer unadulterated nastiness, hunched over on the doorstep, lighting his cig. He took a few hard drags before stepping out into the rain, designer hoodie pulled up over his shaved head so that the swastika at his left temple was covered. Nikki was familiar with the artwork on his arm as well: a St George's cross with the slogan *Pakis Out* underneath. What made it worse was that the stupid arse was half-Pakistani himself.

When he was younger – hell, he was only 18 now – she'd wondered if his stunted growth had made him a victim. If it was the bullying that had pushed him to the dark side. Now, though, she didn't care. She just wanted him and his puppet master, Franco McNally, off her estate.

He walked down the path, phone held to his ear. 'Come on, Kayleigh. For fuck's sake pick up, will you? Need to know you're okay.'

He flicked his half-smoked cigarette into the neighbour's garden and kicked the gate, before dragging it open. It grated against the cement slabs as he walked onto the street, with a quick glance up and down the road.

Watching with interest, Nikki wondered who this 'Kayleigh' was, who was causing Deano such stress. If she ever met her, she'd be sure to buy the girl a drink. Stepping forward into the gleam cast by the streetlights, Nikki waited. He stopped, lit another fag, took a quick puff and then, using his thumb and index finger, he flicked it through the drizzle, to land in the gutter in a flicker of orange embers. 'Aw for fuck's sake. If it isn't piggy, piggy, oink, oink.'

'That the best you got, Deano? Losing your touch?' She crossed the road, one hand stuffed in her pocket and gestured for him to walk with her. At five-foot-two, Nikki just topped the lad by an inch, but the way he walked, the way he held himself, still had her wary of him. She'd turned her back on him to show him she wasn't cowed by him, but her entire body was on alert, her shoulders tensed, ears straining for any rush of activity behind her. Inside her pocket she gripped her Mace. In the other hand her car keys protruded from her knuckles ready to blind the little bastard if he chanced his luck. It was the only way to go with thugs like Deano. In fact, it was that same attitude that had earned Deano his reputation. His inability to back down, the way he bulked his small frame up to its maximum – Nikki used the same strategies in her professional life. It was the only way *she* knew to survive. Sometimes she wondered if she had that same look in her eyes too. The one that made people quickly glance away and cross the road. The one that looked like his soul had been ripped out through his throat and all that was left was a mulch of dark, bloody gore. 'Having girlfriend trouble, are we?'

'Eh?'

'Kayleigh? Giving you a hard time, is she?'

Glancing round, Deano hesitated and then fell into step beside her. 'You stalking me now, Parekh? Got an obsession with me, eh? Want a bit of my meat, do you?' He thrust his hips out and cupped his groin with his hand as he walked.

'Your meat still come with a side helping of chlamydia and crabs, does it? Think I'll pass, if it's all the same.'

At the end of the road, she stopped and leaned against the post box that stood on the corner. Cars drove by, their headlights sweeping past them, bouncing off the puddles and sending up a thin spray of water as they passed. On the opposite side of the road a Chicken Cottage was doing a roaring trade and Deano, if his glances in that direction were anything to go by, had been heading there.

'Say what you gotta say and then fuck off back to your pigsty.'

'Oh, Deano, Deano, Deano … originality isn't your strong suit is it?'

'Eh?'

'Thing is, *you're* not welcome here.' Her tone was conversational, tired, bored almost. As if she couldn't quite bring herself to be overly concerned with him. Of course, it was all an act. A squirm of emotions, like maggots on gone-off meat, wriggled inside her chest. Deano was only a kid, yet he was toxic and she would never forgive him for the things he was responsible for. Never. His presence on her estate was a scab that she couldn't avoid picking.

'Just visiting me mum. Nowt wrong wi' that.'

Nikki shook her head and took a deliberate step forward to invade his space. A glance over the road told her Sajid was parked up in his car, as arranged. She relaxed a fraction. Not even Deano would knife a police officer in full view of CCTV and, if he did, Sajid would have him within seconds. 'Thing is, Deano. That's where you're wrong. You being here puts Margo in danger.'

'Humph, I've never hurt me mum.'

'No, *you* haven't, but your stepdad has. He doesn't like you, does he, Deano? What with you being of dual heritage and all.'

In the streetlights, she saw his face flush, then his bottom lip curled, eyes darkening. Her grip on her Mace tightened and she released her keys from her other hand and pulled her hood down. Sajid would recognise her prearranged signal and be on high alert.

'I'm not a fucking Paki – not like you, Parekh.'

'Not sure your stepdad sees it that way, but hey ho, that's neither here nor there. He'll take it out on your mum and you know it. So, you need to shimmy back under whatever rock you've been living under and stay there. We had a deal, remember?'

'You can't make me go. This is my home.'

Nikki took another step forward, her chin jutted up, her face distorted in a scowl that betrayed her feelings. 'You are a poison that we don't need here. You will go. And you'll go tonight. Tell Franco we won't accommodate him here. Not then, not now and not ever.'

Bluster fading, Deano stepped back off the kerb, landing in a puddle, with a 'For fuck's sake.' He jumped back onto the pavement, his mouth open in a snarl. 'You can't do this to me, Parekh. You just fucking can't. I can't move till Franco says.'

Nikki stepped back and twisted her mouth into a smile. ''Course I can. You know I can. But I'll give you the benefit of the doubt. Maybe you just forgot what I have on you, eh?'

Deano kicked the post box. 'He'll kill me. Franco will kill me.'

'Really? And I care about that because …?'

'Give us a break.'

'No bloody way. You had your chance. You blew it when you brought ecstasy and MDMA to our streets. Then you did something even more stupid when you double-crossed Franco. Wonder what he'd do if he found out you'd been skimming off the top, eh? So …' Nikki smiled. 'You pay the price. Get off my fucking

27

estate and take your drug-dealing boss with you. This is non-negotiable.'

She turned to cross the road, pulling her hood back up over her sleek dark-brown hair, then, as if in afterthought, she turned back. 'Or of course I could make sure that package is delivered. Up to you, Deano. Up to you.'

Chapter 5

'Why do we always need to come here?' Sajid waved two fingers in the air signalling to Gordon, the owner, that they'd have their usual and followed Nikki over to a booth with worn but clean seating. Nikki grinned. He said this every time they came to The Mannville Arms, but the truth was he loved it – Saj just liked to moan.

The gleam from its buffed wooden walls caught the light from the vintage glass lamp that cast a yellow hue over the equally well-polished table. The faint smell of beeswax contributed to the old-fashioned feel of the pub. Nikki slid into the side facing the doorway. 'You know you like it here. So stop moaning. It's one of the few pubs left in Bradford where you can get real ales.'

'The Fighting Cock, The Sparrow ...' Sajid began counting them off, one by one on his fingers.

'Yeah, I know. But I'm a creature of habit and Gordon and Nancy need all the trade they can get.'

Apart from Nikki and Sajid there were only five others in the entire bar. Old Stevie who propped up the corner most nights and the regular Monday night dominoes tournament in a table in the snug. As Nikki positioned a beer mat before each of them, Gordon ambled over, a tea towel draped over one shoulder, his rotund belly preceding the rest of him by a good couple of feet and two pint glasses of Cannonball, one in each hand. Nikki often wondered how he maintained balance. Gordon was a man of few words and most of them were unintelligible grunts which seemed to signify anything from, 'hallo' to 'goodbye' to 'nice to see you' to 'fuck off, you're barred'. His wife Nancy was his opposite in every respect. Almost as short as Nikki, and skinnier, she could and would, given half a chance, talk the proverbial hind leg off any four-legged creature that deigned to enter her domain. Her saving grace was that she was an expert reader of human nature and seemed able to gauge exactly what each of her customers wanted, whether it was a sympathetic ear, a babble of meaningless tittle-tattle or a serious confab over one of her rare whiskies, reserved only for her favourite customers. Nikki had partaken of said whisky a fair few times in the past.

With a grunt, which Nikki took to mean 'enjoy your drinks', Gordon placed both glasses on the mats, took a packet of salt and vinegar crisps out of his pocket and tossed it on the table, before beating a slow and rolling retreat.

Sajid took a long sip, wiped the froth off his mouth with the back of his hand and grinned. 'Can't stay long. Langley's got a surprise lined up. It's our anniversary. A year.'

Nikki's lips twitched. He looked so damn proud of himself, which was more than he'd looked at the crime scene. 'Yeah, well, you could've fooled me earlier, Saj. Poor Langley, he must be a saint to put up with the huge wedge you drive between the two of you in public.'

Sajid picked up his glass and had another sip. 'Well, truth is he is getting pissed off with me. Says I'm ashamed of him.' He looked at Nikki a slight frown marring his forehead. 'I'm not ashamed of him, no way. It's just like … complicated.'

Complicated family life was nothing new to Nikki, but she really felt for Sajid. He was clearly in love with Langley – they'd been living together for a year now, but he still kept their relationship secret, in case his family found out. Every so often, the strain of that reared its ugly head. She nudged Saj's arm. 'God! Surprised he managed to put up with you for so long. *You* should be the one treating him.'

'Ha bloody ha.' He took another swig of his beer. 'Langley's spitting. Springer and her sidekick Bashir caught that skeleton case we were called out to earlier. Turns out it's a murder, skeleton had its head smashed in. Lang says Springer's being an arse already.'

Nikki snorted. She'd had run-ins with 'The Spaniel' before and always tried to give her a wide berth. Thankfully, cold cases and current investigations rarely overlapped. 'Now why doesn't that surprise me? The woman's a bitch.'

'Yeah, well, they found a passport on the body, so it looks like it'll be all tied up soon.'

'Lucky Spaniel. She'll be wagging her tail at that, won't she? She doesn't like to get her hands dirty, that one.'

Stuffing a handful of crisps in his mouth, Sajid studied her. 'So, you gonna tell me what all that was with Deano?'

Nikki sighed. She trusted Saj. They'd worked together for years now, since before he'd met Langley, and they'd been through a lot together, but this thing with Deano and by extension, Franco, was personal. Of course, Sajid knew about the E on the streets and it was a pretty fair assumption that Franco and his cronies were behind it. Sajid was aware that Nikki had evicted both Franco and Deano from Listerhills the previous year and, if the details were a bit sketchy, he wasn't going to complain. He probably thought she was just cleaning drugs off the streets.

However, her reasons for keeping schtum about the whole Franco and Deano thing were nothing to do with her job – no, it was personal. This was about her family and she kept family matters close to her chest. Now though, she couldn't decide whether to trust him with Haqib's involvement. Maybe that was pushing his loyalty a step too far. By rights, she should have taken

Haqib in for carrying the amount of shit he had, but then Charlie had been the one in possession, not Haqib. 'Got a load of Es and they link back to Deano. Needed to make him aware we didn't want his shit here. I'll get a couple of uniforms on him tomorrow, hassle him a bit, make it hard for him to deal.'

'Franco back too?'

Nikki drained her glass, plonked it down and rolled her shoulders. 'Yep, looks that way.'

Sajid studied his half-full glass for a few seconds, then, 'You gonna tell me where the Es came from?'

'Got a lead. Some local lads, but they ran before I got them. At least they're off the streets, eh?' She knew her partner didn't believe her, but that didn't matter. What mattered was that she didn't make him complicit in anything dodgy.

Draining his glass, Sajid stood up. 'When you're ready to give me the full story, I'll be here.'

'Aw piss off, Saj. Go and get wined, dined and laid. It won't make you any prettier, but it'll make you better company tomorrow.'

Sajid grinned and with a wave to Gordon and Nancy, he was off.

Nikki stayed where she was, using the time to text Marcus. With everything that had gone on, she needed to touch base with him. He was looking after the kids and she should really have told him she'd be a bit later. Truth was, she was reluctant to go home. Marcus had proposed yet again and just as she'd done every other time, Nikki had refused. Why couldn't he understand that they were fine the way they were. Their relationship worked. If they moved in together … got married … whatever, it would all go tits up. Nobody knew that better than Nikki.

When Nancy came over ten minutes later, Nikki put out the feelers about the Es. Despite its quietness tonight, when the weekend rolled round, The Mannville Arms perked up with both university and college students as well as locals. Nancy was one of the many eagle-eyed landlords that the Bradford police approached to keep their eyes open for possible dealing. The latest batch of MDMA, or Es as the kids called them, were particularly potent and Nikki wanted everyone on alert.

Chapter 6

How many years have they been blind? The thing is, they all think they're so smart – so damn smart – but they're not.

Every one of them I killed deserved it. Time and again they proved that they're not only stupid, but weak too. At first, I wanted them to prove their superior intellect – show me how they were better than me. Show me they deserved what I was denied, that it was more than just privilege. That they'd earned it through hard work and dedication. Then, I wanted them to pay for the way they'd let themselves down. Taken opportunities and then just fucked it all up. One by one, despite my best efforts they failed and at some point – maybe after the fourth or fifth – I realised that this was something in which I excelled. I'd found my forte – my calling, if you will.

I'm not inhuman though, not at all. Despite my social experiment I gave them something before the end. Some little salve as they realised what the end was going to be. Each of them got their last chance – each of them bared their soul and made their last wish. Whether their last request was ever granted though is a different matter. That's how it is. That's life.

The police finding the remains has made me a little anxious. Need to soothe myself. I run my hands along the shelf. Which one shall I choose? November 2003? No not that one. That one I'll save for when I've got more time. No, I'll opt for this one. With the tip of my finger I remove the DVD case and insert it in the player. I settle down with my glass of Glenmorangie on my sofa. I have half an hour. This will be enough time for Day One, more than enough.

The date is 6th March 2008.

Day One and this is the first recording.

The scene is set – a backdrop of fabric, spotlight shining across the stage. Props at the ready. Each knife sharpened – metal glistening as the light bounces over them. A single chair centre stage. A figure waits in the wings, shadowed and grim. My voice rings out over the tape. 'Bring the captive through,' I say. 'Bring the captive through.'

I love listening to my voice narrating as if I am a mere bystander and not an active part of it all. Everything up until that point is enjoyable – of course it is – but it's doing my David Attenborough bit that really makes my blood fizz. Homing in on small details, analysing the scenes – that's what I love best. And if I'm right, this one is a particularly well-produced cinematic performance. Here we go …

We see the figure, dressed in black – oh, how spooky! Arms under the captive's arms, he is dragged through and flopped with all due finesse onto the chair.

In this wide-angled shot, we see the figure exit stage right, returning within seconds. Rope is wrapped round the captive's arms, legs and chest. Things are hotting up now.

Note how the captive barely reacts – no resistance. No awareness of his surroundings. No understanding of the basic premise of this experiment. His privilege sets him above us mere mortals. His sense of worth lends him an arrogance, an entitlement denied the hordes that flock here. Tonight, as on previous nights, his true worth, his true character, will be ascertained and he will ultimately get his just desserts.

Sound-over – clapping hands and gleeful chuckle.

Now to wake him up – bring him out of his stupor.

The figure slaps our captive – once … twice … three times across the face. Our captive groans, his eyes flicker – open briefly then close, keeping his audience on tenterhooks.

The figure, hooded drape trailing the floor, leaves in silence, returning within seconds carrying a bowl. With an agile twist of the hands, the bowl's contents are thrown over the captive, eliciting a frenzied jolting movement. It has the desired effect. The ice-cold water wakes the specimen up, makes him focus and … ah – he speaks, in the bewildered tones of a baby deserted by its mama.

'Wh – what the f …? Where am I?'

Zooming in for the close-up we can see his pupils are dilated – pulse increasing, thrashing around. We've got ourselves a lively one. Wonder if he's as clever as he is lively. Time will tell. We'll soon see. Now for the main event. Ha ha! Fingers crossed he lives up to expectation.

The figure speaks. 'Have you earned your place here? Your position? Have you earned it? Or is it all about Daddy's wealth – privilege – entitlement?'

Do tell. Indeed, do tell.

The captive glances round the space – sees the table and the knife. Begins to struggle against his constraints and, at last, he speaks.

'What are you doing? Let me go. What the fuck you doing?'

The figure's response is low but if we strain, we can hear it 'Ascertaining your worth. I thought that was clear. That's the purpose of this. Why should you be here with all your privilege and not Joe Bloggs from down the road in Holmewood or Tyresal.'

'You're fucking mad – mental. Let me go. Right now – just let me fucking go.'

Note the heightened colour on his face, the flush of rouge over his cheeks as he struggles. His fingers fisted, held tight. Observe the whitening across his knuckles. This one's a fighter.

Let's see if he also has a modicum of intelligence.

'We have rules. Easy rules. Rules an imbecile can follow. I expect you to comply. Will you?'

Alas, our captive continues to struggle, displaying an abject inability to correctly analyse the situation. His head shakes rapidly from side to side; his upper body, though trapped, strains against the rope. With the sad desperation of a failing man, he makes a vain attempt to wrench his tied hands apart. In his increased state of tension, the pitch of his voice rises, higher and higher to a shriek of desperation.

'Fuck off. Let me go. Fuck off or I'll kill you.'

Note the figure's placatory response – soothing, yet with the promise of a reprimand implicit in the delivery. 'Really? That's the most intelligent thing you can say?'

Watch closely, for things are going to pick up speed now and you don't want to miss anything. See how the figure picks up the item from the floor. Did you notice it lying there? Never mind, it was easy to miss in the muted lighting. But wait for this bit.

As the camera pans out, the figure approaches the captive. The long slender metal, glinting beneath the subdued stage lights.

Still, the captive is oblivious to the threat that approaches him so slowly. The figure slaps the bar against the palm of one hand causing the captive to glance up. With lightning speed, the figure strikes, jabbing the cattle prod onto the captive's thigh.

The captive jerks back and screams.

'Are you ready to listen to the rules?' The figure raises the prod, waves it in sight of the captive. The specimen's eyes water, a single stream of liquid rolls down his right cheek. He nods.

Bravo! Specimen is under control.

Sound-over – clapping and cheering.

Watch now as we find out the rules of play.

'That's more like it. Rule one – you must answer every question. Rule two – you may not pass on any question. Rule three – if you get five questions in a row right, you will be released. You will have earned your freedom. Rule four – for each incorrect answer you will be punished. Rule five – your fate is in your own hands. When you have had enough and don't want to play anymore then we will move onto your last request. Do you understand?'

Ha! Now we see the typical response of a captive in denial. See how he shakes his head.

No matter. That will change. For now, enjoy his simple mistakes.

'No, no – 'course I don't. I don't get it, not at all. Let me go. Let me go.'

You see what he's done, don't you? His rookie mistake? Now for the consequences.

'Wrong answer number one.'

Watch the concentration as the figure picks up a knife, studies it. Runs his finger along the blade and then approaches the captive. It's all about care and precision …

I hear a sound outside the door and quickly turn off the DVD. Never mind. There will be plenty of time later. Plenty of time.

Chapter 7

'Oy, Deano, get your arse over here, right now, ya tosser.'

Deano's heart sank as the Ferrari pulled up to the kerb outside Chicken Cottage. Last thing he needed right now, when he didn't know if Kayleigh was all right, was to have a convo with her old man. He burped, took a last swig from his Vimto and tossed the can into the gutter, before stuffing the last of his burger into his mouth and throwing the polystyrene food container after the can. Wiping his hands down the front of his joggers, he approached the car. Shoulders hunched, big-man glower on his face, he ignored the passenger and spoke over his head to the driver. In situations like this, the only thing you could do was brazen it out. He'd find out soon enough if Franco knew. 'Y'aright there, Franco?'

Franco – tall but skinny, cap on backwards, pockmarked face and ice-cold eyes – cast a sideways look at Deano. He shook his head and tapped his fingers on the steering wheel twice. As if on some sort of preordained order, the prick, Big Zee, thrust the passenger door open, crashing it into Deano's legs and jumped out, quickly repositioning himself in the back seat, beside another one of Franco's goons. Deano wanted to slam his fist into the idiot's sneering face, but contented himself with hoiking a gob of phlegm into the gutter. It was pushing it for Franco to come back to Listerhills. Thing was he didn't get it – too arrogant. Didn't he realise Parekh would never let him get away with supplying to her nephew?

'Get in.' Franco's words were an order and Deano had no option but to obey. He was in too deep and Franco knew it … but did he know about him and Kayleigh? With a quick glance along the road, Deano wished that Nikki hadn't disappeared off with that big Paki dick. He slid into the front seat, next to Franco and tried to angle himself to the side, out of arm's reach of Big Zee and his sidekick in the back. Deano had been in too many similar situations in the past not to be aware of what was coming. How many times had he been the one to move to the back seat, ready to slip a chain round the neck of the idiot Franco was grilling in the front seat if he didn't deliver the goods?

'Little bird told me you were talking to that Parekh bint?'

Fuck, word travelled fast! Deano laughed, tried to look nonchalant, hoping his face wasn't giving owt away. He was caught with his balls between a rapidly closing vice. On the one hand, Parekh had made her threat clear and Deano couldn't risk Franco finding out about him skimming. No way did he want to end up as pig food on one of them farms in the Dales. He'd seen too many end up there. On the other, Parekh was no pushover. She'd made her intentions clear. The only option open to him was to strike some sort of deal with her. What the hell was he going to do? 'Yes, frigid bitch. She needs a good seeing to, to loosen her up a bit.'

He sensed Big Zee leaning forward at the ready and, from the corner of his eye, he saw Franco glance into the rear-view mirror. His hands grew damp with sweat and relief swept over him as his next words gushed from his mouth. 'She wants me to keep an eye on my stepdad. Tosser's been beating up my mum. Had her in hospital twice. I told her I'd deal with the fucker.'

'That all?' Franco's eyes honed right in to his soul, red hot like a soldering iron.

Deano ignored the sounds from the back of the car – the rattle of metal, the squeak of leather as Big Zee edged forward. Deano could feel the big man's breath on the side of his face, and the smell of his aftershave made him want to choke. He shrugged. 'Yeah, that's all. Cow think's that cos she's a copper she's got the right to sort everyone out. Don't worry, my man, I'll keep her sweet. I'll keep her out of your hair.'

Gaze razoring Deano's face, Franco leaned towards him, encroaching on his space and then, slapping the steering wheel, he laughed and jerked his head to one side – presumably the signal for Big Zee to step down. 'You better, D. We don't need some half-caste whore messing up our plans now, do we? This estate's gonna be mine this time and *you're* gonna help me.'

As Deano watched the streaming rain splatter down the windscreen, every fibre of his being screamed a warning. Franco could give the order and anything could happen inside the car without anyone outside noticing. Even if they did, chances were they'd ignore it. Franco was just that little bit too unpredictable, that little bit too dangerous for folk to risk annoying him. No one here ever volunteered a witness statement! 'We did all right in Oldham, didn't we? Ousted them Pakis and took control. Listerhills will be a doddle. Don't worry, I'm on it. I've got my ears to the ground. Like you say – get the kids with us and the rest follows on. Parekh won't fuck things up this time.'

Franco lifted his hand and angled it palm upwards, finger moving in a 'gimme it' gesture to Big Zee and Tyke in the back seat. A bit of rummaging and then a package wrapped in a plastic bag was given to Franco who passed it to Deano. 'Here, go do your job then.'

Taking the package, Deano stuffed it up the front of his hoodie. No point in advertising what he had to everyone. There was always some tosser waiting to grab your stash, and that wouldn't go down well with Franco. The man expected returns on his produce and Deano would have to make sure he paid up. 'Usual rate?'

'Yeah, keep the cost down, get 'em hooked, then, BOOM!' Franco laughed like he'd cracked the finest joke ever – head back, furry yellow rabbit teeth on show. 'Right, piss off then. I'll be in touch.'

Deano slid out of the car, his legs shaking, and watched as Franco squealed off down the road towards town. Fuck! That had been a close one. All he'd wanted was a lousy Chicken Cottage and what did he end up with? Fucking Nikita Parekh on his case and then Franco. He glanced round. Who the hell had told Franco about his meeting with Parekh? Shit, he'd have to be extra careful now. Seemed like Franco had eyes everywhere.

Huddled over against the rain, Deano retraced his steps back to his house, wondering as he went how long he could keep his secrets hidden from Franco. He suspected it wouldn't be for much longer. Shit, why did he have to do the dirty on the toughest drug boss in the north? As he neared his mum's house, he slowed down. There was nothing else for it, he'd have to go to Parekh – cut some sort of deal. What with Franco involving Parekh's nephew, Deano hoped she'd be only too willing to back him against the psycho. He shuddered, his back prickled as if a million pairs of eyes were scouring it. How the hell could he get to her without Franco finding out?

Tuesday 23rd October

Chapter 8

Sun speckled the walls through the blinds in Nikki's bedroom and sent little specks of shimmer like a kaleidoscope over the carpet. The room wasn't spacious, mainly because one corner was stacked with large cardboard boxes, each with a year scrawled in black marker pen on the front, dating from 2000 onwards. A bed, bedside table, wardrobe, chest of drawers and a chair took up most of the remaining space.

The radio blared some funky feel-good song from the Nineties. Nikki didn't know the title or the name of the band, but she didn't care. Having the house to herself for once, meant she could prance around and get rid of some of the pent-up energy that had built in her recently. Sajid had suggested she go jogging with him, but she'd made it clear that she'd rather go trekking through Bradford's rat-infested sewers covered in cheese than do that. He'd laughed, finding it funny that her aversion to any member of the rodent family was compounded by the ongoing battle with her youngest child Sunni who, with his tenth birthday approaching, was adamant that a hamster was all he wanted. Nikki shuddered. The mere thought of their ratty tails and clawy-like feet and gnawy teeth brought her out in hives. Their pittery-pattery scritchy-scratchiness, their scurrying, all made her skin crawl.

Sunni was going to be disappointed. Poor kid, he never asked for anything, but this was just too much for her to cope with.

The track changed and, breathless, Nikki flopped on the end of the bed wondering if she maybe should take Sajid up on his offer after all. The only thing was Marcus wouldn't like it. He was already jealous of Sajid and the last thing she needed to do right now was fuel his stupidity. Of course, she could just tell him Saj was gay, but then that would seal up that escape clause and even after eleven years in some semblance of a relationship with Marcus, she couldn't quite bring herself to fully commit to him. *What is wrong with me? Maybe I should go jogging with Saj.* Maybe that would be enough to knock Marcus over the edge and into ex-boyfriend territory, and the best thing was she wouldn't even have to do a thing. *Aw, Nikita, what are you thinking?* Marcus was great – the perfect boyfriend: good with the kids, reliable and shit hot in bed. Still, it was too intense for her, too much to handle.

She studied her face in the mirror opposite. She was in her early thirties with three kids by two different dads. Didn't that tell her she was no good at relationships – that she was better on her own? Her face was smooth, her mix of Indian and Scottish genes giving her a healthy bronze complexion. Her eyes were like her Indian mother's; dark brown and intense, like thunder on a balmy day. Her cheekbones were high, her nose bent from when that drunk had broken it when she was in uniform three years earlier and then there was the scar – five inches long, ropey, fading right across her throat. She didn't hide it. Kept it exposed to remind her that she was a survivor and, if she was honest, to make her look scarier on the streets. Most women would cover it up with makeup and shit, but not Nikki. When she was stressed or anxious, she stroked it, getting reassurance from its raised uneven surface. It was a reminder that she was strong – she'd *always* been strong.

'*Breaking news on Capital Radio Yorkshire. Whilst police in*

Bradford have identified the skeletonised remains discovered last week in the Odeon car park, the shocking revelation that the remains are more recent than was previously thought and the nature of the death has led them to announce an active historic case investigation. Relatives have been notified, but as yet the victim's name hasn't been publicly released.

'And on another front, schools in Bradford are getting set for the October break …'

It looked like the Cold Case Unit were going to have their work cut out. She was glad to be well rid of that case. Nikki much preferred current investigations. They were always a bit easier to coordinate. She yanked her heavy wardrobe doors open. *What to wear?* Like she had a lot of choice. Jeans, jeans and more jeans. Half a dozen T-shirts in a variety of colours and a couple of crewneck jumpers. Three pairs of DMs and a single pair of strappy flat sandals were lined up along the bottom shelf. Then there was that one black suit for interviews and the like and her uniform, both in crinkly plastic clothes bags. On a shelf to the side were a rainbow of saris, again in clear bags.

Nikki couldn't remember the last time she'd worn one. Probably for her cousin Reena's wedding last year. That had been an affair and a half. All posh, with more gold and sparkle than Liberace, she'd hated it. Her Gujarati was rubbish, but everybody had insisted on speaking to her and Anika and the kids in mother tongue. Anika had been on edge and whilst Nikki tried her best to convince her sister that nobody was talking about her, she knew fine and well that they were. The sidelong glances and mumbled conversations that stopped abruptly as soon as she and Anika came near testified to that. They'd committed two of the biggest faux pas they ever could have done. They'd both had a child out of wedlock … with Muslims. *Hai hoi!* Not content with that, Anika had chosen to give her son a Muslim name. Despite her uncles' pleas and her aunties' tears, Anika had dug her heels in. Nikki had never been prouder of her than at that moment.

Not that she liked Haqib's dad, Yousaf, she didn't – but it took a lot for Anika, the shy one of the two sisters, to assert herself. Nikki and their mum took her side and protected her from the worst of the gossipmongers.

'*Weather in the north set to remain sunny if cold, with winds of forty ...*'

It wasn't often that she had a late start and she was determined to take advantage of it. She'd pampered herself for once. She looked down at the boxes scattered on her floor; her ongoing hobby – the 'Stalk the Stalker' project as she liked to call it – could wait. The last three weeks had been hectic, with three murders and a suspicious death to contend with, and now she needed to unwind and recharge her batteries. So, instead of her usual quick shower, she soaked in a bubble bath, turned the radio up full volume and used some of the smellies Charlie had given her for Christmas. She got dressed in her usual jeans and T-shirt – *an upmarket whore with downmarket tastes!* – and was just beginning to brush her still-damp hair when the faint echo of the doorbell disturbed her. She rolled her eyes at herself in the mirror and ignored it, studying her split ends. Maybe a trip to the hairdresser's was in order.

There it was again, the damn doorbell. *Couldn't they take a damn hint?* She stood up and walked over to the window, parting the blinds with her fingers and straining to see who was at the door, but the angle was wrong. Whoever was ringing the bell with such persistence was standing too close to the door. She backed away from the window and waited. If they didn't ring again, then she'd ignore them. She didn't want her valuable time eaten up by one of her neighbours with their never-ending problems or one of the men from the mosque wanting donations to some Islamic charity or another. She'd just about decided that her would-be visitor had given up, when the ringing started again – longer and louder and more insistent. *Gonna have to disconnect the damn thing!*

She ran down the stairs, nearly tripping on a pair of trainers placed halfway up. *Ruby!* That child was going to be the death of her. Reaching the bottom, she could see a male shadow behind the frosted glass of her front door. Not recognising the figure, she hesitated. Maybe he'd give up now. But no. The buzzing was really doing her head in. In two strides she was at the door, wrenching it open, not bothering with the safety chain, her mouth open to tell her visitor to take his damn finger off the bell.

Gripping the door handle, she glared at the man. Pale skinned. *Middle Eastern?* In an instant, she was transported back fifteen years. Her breath caught in her throat. *This couldn't be.* Nikki blinked, her mouth closed, her words dried up, ashes in her throat. Her fingers left the handle and flitted up to her scar, fluttering over it briefly, before re-establishing their grip on the door. She tried to swallow but couldn't. Heart thudding like a stampede of wildebeests, she eyed the intruder. How long had she waited for this? How many years? The plastic edge of the door dug into her hands, sharp and real. It was like seeing a ghost, an apparition. She wanted to yell, to rage, to raise her fists and hit him. All the frustration she'd experienced before incapacitated her again now and she hated herself for it. Just for a second, she'd tricked herself into seeing what she wanted to see.

A gaggle of thoughts drifted through her head, trying to make sense of this situation. And then it hit her. *Khalid!* Something had happened to him.

With eyes the colour of a burnished chestnut, the man on the doorstep held her gaze. His brow furrowed, creases spreading out from the corners of his eyes like a shattered window. His skin, wizened, his body hunched and skinny. He leaned with both hands on a walking stick, positioned between his feet. The urge to jump to her feet and push him backwards down the three steps was strong. Ignoring the prickles all over her skin and her sweaty palms, she returned his stare.

The old man took one hand off the walking stick and wobbled

a little as he rummaged in his pocket. Nikki's hand went out to steady him and then she snatched it back, her shoulders tensing. She needed to be on her guard. Khalid had always told her how devious and manipulative his dad could be.

Pulling out a cloth handkerchief, he raised it to his face with a liver-spotted hand and wiped his eyes, one at a time.

For fuck's sake, is he crying? Nikki exhaled, long and slow. Whatever he wanted, this meeting was not going to go his way. Ignoring her wobbly stomach, she straightened her back and pursed her lips. Was it her imagination or had it got darker, chillier? She was being fanciful, yet her entire body was reacting.

'I am surprised you weren't expecting me, Nikita.' His voice was weak, but his English was good. Almost as good as Khalid's had been, but still there was that telltale accent. The slight hesitancy over some of the consonants. 'Especially when what you did all those years ago has come to light. You didn't expect that, did you? Well, you've been caught out.'

Nikki strained to catch the words. It was as if they floated on a puff of air that snatched them away as soon as they left his lips. Each word seemed to be delivered on vibrato – shaky and tremulous. What was he on about? What she'd done all those years ago? His frailty should have softened Nikki's heart, but she wasn't giving an inch. After what he did, what he plotted … He could say his piece here on her doorstep and then be gone. It would be as if she'd never seen him. She'd push it to the farthest, darkest corners of her mind and leave it there to fester beside the memories of his son.

'I'm in a rush. Say what you have to and then go and never, ever come back.' Her voice barely wobbled, her words clipped. Saying them gave her a surge of power. She had this. It would be over soon, but she *was* in control.

The old man's lips trembled and he wiped his eyes again. For God's sake, he was crying. It must be something bad. Her resolve splintered. Did she really want to deal with this on her doorstep with Mrs Shah earwigging from her garden next door and Mr Khalifa from opposite twitching at his curtains? She stepped back from the door, pulling it wide. 'Come in.'

Her voice couldn't have been any more unwelcoming if she tried, yet the old man lifted his stick and placed it on the doormat, using his other hand to grip the door jamb as he manoeuvred himself inside. Nikita, wanting to avoid touching him, pressed herself against the wall until he had moved far enough into the cramped hallway for her to close the door, with a little wave to each of her nosy neighbours. It'd be all round Listerhills by lunchtime that Nikki Parekh had entertained a strange man in her house whilst the kids were at school.

Aware that he was looking at her home – judging it too, no doubt – Nikki turned and slipped past him. Why did the kids have to leave all their shoes heaped at the bottom of the stairs and why hadn't she spent five minutes hoovering instead of spreading smelly lotion over her feet?

Without uttering a word, she marched down the hallway and into the kitchen, leaving the door open for him to follow. She walked straight over to the sink and filled a glass of cold water. As she gulped it down, she heard the tap, tap of his stick on the wooden floor. She turned and leaned against the sink, cradling her glass in both hands. Again, his eyes flitted round the room, taking in everything, scouring her life. *At least the breakfast dishes were done.* Nikki followed him with her eyes as he edged closer to the table and, with an enquiring glance in her direction, pulled out a chair and flopped into it, a heavy sigh leaving his mouth as he took the weight off his feet. He seemed in no hurry to speak, his eyes continuing their survey, until they landed on the fridge.

Nikki's heart sputtered. *The photos!*

He pulled himself to his feet again and stepped over to study the magnetic photos that hung on the fridge door. He reached out a hand and with one finger traced Charlie's face. 'She's his,

51

isn't she? Khalid's? She's got his eyes. How *could* you do that to him when he has a daughter? How *could* you?'

Do what? Nikki wanted to snatch the photo away from him, hide all evidence of her daughter and send the old man away. 'She's mine.'

Favouring his right leg, he hobbled back to his chair. He was so much older than he'd looked in the photos Khal had shared with her. Older, shrunken and somehow diminished.

'Can I have some water?' He nodded to the glass she was holding.

Nikki grabbed a glass from the drainer, filled it with water, plonked it down on the table and pushed it towards him, spilling some as she did so. 'Look, Burhan, you don't want to be here and I certainly don't want you here, so why don't you just say whatever it is you've flown over two and a half thousand miles to say and then go.'

Khalid's dad lifted the glass and took a long drink, gulping the liquid down as if it would give him strength. Was he playing for time? Was Khal poorly? Didn't matter to her, she couldn't care less. He could be *dead* for all she cared. Fifteen years and no word from him. Barely married and then he fucked off back home to Palestine. No, Khalid Abadi, meant *nothing* to her.

'I've come about what you did to Khalid.' His voice was strong as he spoke, each word staccato. 'I want you to know that I will *personally* make you pay for what you did. If your British courts won't provide justice, then *my* promise to you is that you will still pay and *I* will take your daughter. You don't deserve her.'

What was the old man talking about? What she'd done to Khal? He was the one that had left her. Her breathing was beginning to hitch in her chest and a flutter at her temple told her that her eye was twitching so she took refuge in anger. How dare he come into her home and start accusing her of doing something to Khal when she hadn't even seen him for years? 'Oh, sod off – you can't come in here and talk to me like this.'

The old man's eyes sparked and the hand on the top of his cane shook. '*You* killed him. You *killed* my son and you will pay. Like the worthless whore you are, you took my boy and then when he wanted to come back to *us*, you killed him.'

The words hammered into Nikki's chest. Was he deranged? What was he talking about? Khal wasn't dead. She thought her heart would stop. Was he saying Khal ... her Khal ... was dead? Was he saying he'd died because she'd driven him away? None of it made sense ... none of it.

'Khal's dead?'

'Hmph ... you know he is. Don't pretend.'

Dead ... Khal ... dead. For all she'd told herself she didn't care, it was still a shock. Khal had always been so alive, so full of fun, so vital and now he was dead. She was a widow? She turned around, stretched her arms out and leaned on the sink, head bowed. Burhan was still speaking, but she couldn't hear his words. Her brain was filled with buzzing, her vision distorted. She'd gone through hell when Khal left. She'd moved on, put him to the back of her mind – except when she looked at Charlie who was so like Khal. The last thing she'd expected was to feel this scorching pain, this squeezing, wrenching agony ... but none of what the old man was saying made sense. Was grief making him insane?

His other words filtered into her consciousness. He was saying she'd killed him? How could she have? He'd left Bradford fifteen years ago. Khal's dad was acting as if *she'd* murdered him.

Her phone rang, breaking through the fuzz. Still not looking at Burhan, she slipped it from her pocket – the boss, Hegley – and silenced it before tossing it onto the table. No sooner had it landed than it started ringing again. *Fuck's sake, can't it wait?* Then the doorbell was ringing, echoing through the house. She lifted her hands to her head and covered her ears. *Shut up, just shut the fuck up!*

'Nikki, Nikki, open up, come on, let me in. It's important.'

Sajid! Just go away, let me think.

Her phone started ringing again, DCI Hegley flashed on the screen. It rang a few times and went to voicemail. They must have caught a case. *Why now?*

Burhan, with effort, pushed himself upright and made to approach her but Nikki extended her hand, palm up. 'NO! Just go.'

The voice from the door came again. 'Nikki, Nikki. Open up, Come on. I can hear you're in there.'

Fuck off, Saj!

The phone started going again. Nikki wanted to smash it through the kitchen window. *Just let me think!*

Almost conversationally, Burhan continued as if they were completely alone. 'Khalid had responsibilities at home, but he was adamant he would stay here with you. We thought when he stopped contacting us, answering our calls, that he'd divorced himself from us.'

Nikki frowned. What was the old idiot talking about, Khal divorcing himself from *them*? It was Nikki he'd left.

Straightening his spine, Burhan slammed his palm on the table and yelled at her. 'Did you not think they could identify him from his remains. You should have taken his passport.' Spittle flew from his lips and his frail body shook. 'They told me how you went there, saw my son excavated. How you never gave a hint about what you'd done. Cold as ice. They've come to arrest you. You will either rot in a British prison cell or *I* will kill you.'

Nikki stilled. Anger tinged with sadness flashed in his eyes and her shoulders slumped.

'They contacted me. You see all they found to identify him was his passport, with me as next of kin.'

What? Nikki reached out her hand to the worktop. *What is he talking about?*

'All these years we thought he was with you and all these years he's been dead … murdered. We *will* have our revenge. You *will* suffer for this. How could you discard him so thoughtlessly – like rubbish – in a car park?'

The Odeon car park.

The skeleton?

Khalid?

Fifteen years.

Like an electric shock, it all slotted into place. He'd been here all along. *He'd not left them … he'd not left her.*

With everything ringing in her ears, Nikki turned and vomited into the sink.

Chapter 9

The wind whistled lifting empty crisp packets and yellow takeaway containers, dancing them further down the weed-ridden alley which skirted the recreation ground. On the one side was the rear of a row of shops, their backyards fenced off with black painted metal topped with barbed wire. An old settee wobbled on top of a skip. Rain-swollen grease-spattered worktops and a dozen metal ghee cans stood next to a line of industrial-sized bins. The stench of decaying meat hung strong in the air. On the other side was a six-foot concrete wall sectioning off the kids' playground. Overgrown grass skirted the bottom of the wall – a coarse browny-green fringe that stank of piss and hid a conglomeration of syringes and bent spoons. The alley was a shortcut between the terraced houses at one end and the main road. It was rarely used now, except by drug dealers, prostitutes and the occasional rough sleeper.

The lad, in his school uniform, spotty and ghostly pale, was sprawled on the wet ground, a rolled-up sock in his mouth, one foot bare. His gelled hair rippled in the breeze, the contents of his schoolbag scattered all around him. Textbooks soaked up the damp from the floor, a few pages fluttering, making a strange whirring sound in the air. Pencils and pens, trampled on, jotters covered in blood and muddy footprints surrounded him. His shoe floated in another puddle, laces dangling in the water. One hand, held away from his body, trailed through a mucky pool of water, his fingers twitching. Blood trickled down the back of his hand and dripped into the slurry, sending small waves over the surface. Beside it, on the cobbles by the watery rut, lay his little finger, blood oozing from the stump.

With his two mates, Tyke and Big Zee, standing behind him, Franco glowered down at the boy, a satisfied smirk on his face. Tyke had his phone out, taking photos of their handiwork – moving around, getting the angle just right – whilst Big Zee snapped the pliers open and shut, his gaze fixed on their victim as if daring him to provoke more action from the pliers.

'You deal with me, you make sure you get your payments in on time. This was a warning, okay?' Franco kicked the lad on his leg. 'I said, okay?'

Whimpering, the lad nodded. His lower lip trembling, his eyes wide and staring. Tyke had held him down whilst Big Zee did the deed. He'd tried to yell but all that had come out was a muffled noise.

'You take my stuff, you sell it and you pay me. Them's the rules. You fuck up, you pay the consequences.'

The boy moved his head a little to see the damage and groaned, spitting the sock from his mouth as he did so. A stream of vomit flooded from his lips, mingling with the stagnant water on the path. With his good hand he wiped his mouth, his chest heaving. As Franco moved closer, the boy curled his legs up, to his stomach, preparing himself for more pain.

Franco kicked him on the thigh once more for good measure and then jerked his head to his mates, 'Come on. Let's go before someone sees us.'

As they passed, Tyke and Big Zee too kicked the boy. Big Zee snapped the bloody pliers in front of the lad's nose, laughing as he whimpered and tried to push himself away from them.

They walked up the alley towards the main road and then paused. Franco yelled back down the alley. 'Get up to BRI with that – you never know, they might be able to re-attach it.'

*

Haqib waited till their voices faded into the distance followed by the sound of a souped-up car engine as they roared off, before moving. His hand throbbed and when he looked at his severed finger more bile gushed into his mouth. Weeping, he pulled his phone from his pocket with his good hand and dialled. Relief surged over him when it was answered and great sobs rent the air as he told Charlie what had happened and where to find him. Keeping his eyes averted from his injured hand he shoogled himself into a sitting position and leaned against one of the wheelie bins.

Why the hell had he been so stupid? He should have known better than to trust Deano, but it seemed easy. Deano had promised it would be easy. Just sell a few pills. Set up a supply in Listerhills and he'd be quids in. And it had been easy till Charlie had swiped his stash so he couldn't sell it. She'd been going to give it back to him on pay day so he could return it to Franco. Trust his aunt to find it. It was all Auntie fucking Nikita's fault. She should've minded her own damn business and he could've returned it and everything would be sorted.

He heard Charlie before he saw her, 'Fuck's sake, Haqib. What did I tell you about getting mixed up with that lot? Bloody stupid you are.'

As she got closer and saw his hand held out away from his body, she gasped. 'Shit. They cut your finger off?'

'Nowt like stating the obvious, Charlie. Just help me up. I need to get it sewed back on.'

Galvanised into action, Charlie rummaged around in her schoolbag for tissues, before loosely wrapping his stub. Displaying

58

less aversion than Haqib, she picked up his pinkie with two fingers and after placing it in another tissue, she put it in her bag and helped her cousin to his feet. 'You know you're a damn idiot, don't you?'

Every bone in Haqib's body seemed to protest as he shuffled along the alleyway to the waiting taxi, his injured hand held out to his right so he didn't have to look at it. 'Gimme a break. I'm in agony here. Need to get this fixed before Mam finds out.'

Charlie stopped and stared at him. 'You what? You think you can hide this from your mam? Don't be a dick, 'course she's gonna notice. Anyway, I'm phoning my mum soon as we get to BRI. I'm not risking being grounded till I'm thirty just cos you're a knob.'

Chapter 10

So, they've identified the remains – fools! Sheer negligence, lack of attention to detail. They don't know what's ahead of them and when they find out they'll be the laughing stock again. I wonder when they'll release the name. Can hardly wait. That's when the shit will hit the fan. Until then I'll have to content myself with reminiscing. I flit through the DVDs. Which one shall I choose? Who is worthy of my attention today? Ah yes 8th May 2010. Yes, that's the one!

I fast forward the first bits to get to the main event. It's always the last bit that shows their mettle. I could watch them all again and again – makes binge watching take on a whole new meaning. I settle into my routine, whisky in hand, settled on the only comfy chair in the room and watch as the scene unfolds. My voiceover begins.

Time in captivity: six days, one hour and twenty-five minutes. Note how our captive has deteriorated.

The past days have not been kind to her. Her own fault, of course. If she'd been worthy, she'd have been allowed to proceed with her life. Observe as the shadowy figure enters from the gloom and hovers behind the specimen. It's the captive's reactions that are so intriguing. Her hands are tied and clasped in her lap, with rope binding her chest to the death chair, so her responses are restricted. However, take note of how her right leg judders up and down, up and down. As she nears the end, she holds her head high, stares at the blinking light, eyes dull, yet focused. A fascinating study of the human meeting his maker.

Note how the wounds across her chest have scabbed and crusted. Each one at a different stage of repair, each bearing testament to her valiant struggle to prove her worth. She lasted well. Tried so hard – harder perhaps than the rest. She has surpassed all the others before her – yet still she has failed. More than seventy cuts – one for each failure. So many opportunities, so many failures. If it wasn't so necessary, I'd almost feel sorry for her. Note how she, unlike those who have gone before, has carried herself with dignity. Pride – spirit even. We're in the home stretch. Watch and learn. Bear witness, for you are privileged to be party to this.

As the camera zooms in, focusing on the captive's face before cutting away to sweep downwards, we see despair etched across her forehead in rivulets of blood and sweat. Visible as we pan down over her body are each of the punishments she has endured and yet, still, she is unable to justify her entitlement … or indeed her inability to fulfil her potential. One is bad enough, the two together are unforgivable.

Watch as the figure, like a bird of prey, circles the captive female, prodding her on the thigh with a live cattle prod. The captive's response is sluggish, her groan half-hearted, a sure indication that her strength is dwindling. Alas, my dear audience, I feel her time with us will be short. However, pay attention to her final moments, as she is challenged for one last time. I guarantee, you will not regret your dedication.

'Look at the camera. You have proven time and time again that your privilege is stronger than your brains. That you are lacking – undeserving of the opportunities that have been offered you at the expense of those more deserving. You have one last thing you can do. One last thing you can leave behind – a last chance, if you

will – to redeem yourself in the eyes of those who matter to you. A chance to prove that there is more to you than unearned advantage.'

The detail we are privy to has never before been recorded. You, my dear audience, are witnessing history in the making. As we zoom in, we can focus on her open eyes with their pinprick pupils. Panning down, we see the pulse at her neck, weak and erratic. Ha! Observe her stare. I wonder if she too senses the importance of what is about to unfold. These last few special moments have a significance all of their own. Let them not be in vain as the captive is released to her death aware that her last request is recorded for posterity. Closure at the end of a long struggle which so nearly ends in victory.

'Are you ready to relinquish your privilege and admit your short-comings?'

Ouch! As the cattle prod engages with her thigh, she barely reacts – a single jolt of the head, no more.

Oh dear, don't judge the figure, after all his hard work indulge him his enjoyment. It's good to be happy in your work. After all, this is what all of this is about – a commitment, a dedication to your life choices.

'You can do better than this? No? Show your audience some strength.'

Despite his plea, and the added incentive of the cattle prod, you can see our captive refuses to respond. Look at the way her mouth tightens. Her defiance is admirable, if ill placed. Let's see if she can be tempted.

'Right. The floor is yours. Your chance – your final chance – what is your last request? Make it count. This time you won't get a re-take.'

Look how our figure moves into position behind our captive, lifting her almost lifeless head, making sure you, his captive audi-ence, miss nothing.

The figure's words ring out. 'Your turn. Make it good – make it clear. You only have one shot at this. It's your final-night production. What is your last request?'

See how her eyes flicker. Her mouth opens, her tongue flicks out, *licking her lips. I'm sure you agree. Her final performance – her swan song has, to date, been inspirational. Let's hope she makes it count. I can feel you willing her on, wishing her the strength to complete her last request. But only a gurgle of unintelligible words reaches our ears.*

'Noo ... my ... mmm ...'

You can see how much she's trying. How much she wants to do this. This is her legacy. Her final chance. I'm sure we've all got our fingers crossed that she doesn't stumble at the last hurdle. She's tried all the way along the trial – given a stellar, almost successful performance. Let's give her a round of applause to spur her on. Come on now, don't be mean. Applaud her efforts.

Sound-over: raucous applauding.

Our figure leads the clapping and the sound of our encouragement seems to have the desired effect. Our captive starts, and her eyes flicker again.

Come on, you can do this, lass. You can do this. You need to do this. You know you do.

'My mum – love my mum – tell her – love her.'

Didn't she do well? Her last request duly recorded. Now for the finale. Focus now. Watch as with all the gravitas fitting such an auspicious occasion, our figure lifts the hammer above her head.

Game over – last request denied.

Last request recorded and denied: Julie Katch 03.22.

63

Chapter 11

Nikki stumbled to the front door and yanked it open, leaving Khalid's father standing in her kitchen. She had a vague recollection of Sajid marching in and directing both her and Burhan into the front room. At some point he must have made tea, for she was cradling a comforting mug that smelled sugary enough to cause instant tooth decay. She took a tentative sip and looked over at the old man – Khalid's dad. Sitting in her oversized favourite chair next to the fire, he looked to have shrunk in this short space of time and he was shivering. Sajid must have given him a fleece because Charlie's leopard skin one was draped round his shoulders and Burhan was pinching it beneath his chin. She wanted to speak, but no words would come. What could she say? She was still trying to make sense of it. How could the bones under the Odeon car park belong to Khal? Plonking her mug on the coffee table, Nikki began plucking at the elastic band she wore round her wrist. It soothed her, calmed her, made her feel a little more in control.

Sitting beside her on the sofa, Saj angled his huge frame towards her, the slight frown across his forehead the only indication that he wanted answers from her. Nikki closed her eyes and sighed. Of course, he'd expect an explanation. Why wouldn't he? They'd been partners for nearly three years and she'd never mentioned Khal to him. Not even once. She'd never told him she'd been married. Never told him about Charlie's dad. Now that it appeared to be out in the open, he'd expect her to confide. But Nikki was determined to closet her emotions away. Nobody would ever know just how deep the scars from Khalid's disappearance had gone. Few people would ever see the emotional wounds that stayed with her and she was not going to bare all to a work colleague – not even one who was a friend.

Steeling herself, she placed her cup on the stained old coffee table next to the sofa, folded one leg under her bottom and willed herself to ignore the dull ache that mangled her heart. If she stopped to analyse her feelings too closely, she'd be lost. That was something for later. Removing all emotion from her face, she gestured towards her father-in-law. 'How did they find *him*?'

Sajid shrugged and settled himself more comfortably in the chair, making it dip with his weight as he moved. 'They found Khalid's passport in with his remains. It had his father's contact details and the Cold Case lot contacted Mr Abadi here. He flew straight over and it was only when he mentioned you, that DS Springer realised that Khalid was your husband. Thank God she passed that onto Archie or ...'

Yes, Abadi had said that earlier, hadn't he? Nikki knew exactly how things would have panned out had Springer been the first to land on her doorstep. No doubt Springer would be en route on her broomstick. God only knew what she made of Abadi's accusations against her. She was glad Saj had got here first. She could do with a friendly face in her camp. She risked a quick glance at her friend. The look in his eyes told Nikki that Sajid was upset that she hadn't shared this with him. *Why should I though? It's private.* When Khalid had gone off, everyone assumed he'd gone home to his family – chosen them instead of her. She hadn't talked about Charlie's dad to anyone outside her immediate family.

That's why Sajid was here. That's why Archie had been phoning her. Then, the real reason for Sajid's presence hit her. She wasn't being treated as a grieving widow, she was a suspect and she guessed Abadi had been only too keen to fuel that speculation. He'd already accused her, hadn't he?

'They're coming for me?'

Sajid had the grace to avert his eyes as he nodded. 'Yes, Hegley wanted to give you a heads-up, but bearing in mind Mr Abadi hasn't left Ramallah for the past twenty years, you're their next best suspect.'

Her phone started to ring – Charlie's ringtone. She answered, keeping her voice low, hoping Charlie wouldn't pick up on her distress. 'Yep.'

As Charlie explained what had happened to Haqib, Nikki stood up and walked into the hallway, closing the door behind her. Once sure that she couldn't be overheard, she said, 'Charlie, wait there. I'm coming. Don't move and don't let that stupid little turd do owt else daft.'

She crept along the hallway. Sajid's jacket was on top of her leather one, so, with all the dexterity of the Artful Dodger, she rummaged in his pocket and took his car keys. Her car was parked on the main street, so she hoped they'd assume she'd left in it and she'd be able to buy herself some time. Shuffling into her trainers, she grabbed her leather jacket and eased the front door open. Closing it gently behind her, she stepped outside. If they wanted to interview her about Khalid, they'd have to wait – she'd family things to deal with first. *You've waited this long, Khal, you can wait another few hours.*

Without considering the consequences of her actions, she ran down the stairs, vaulted over the neighbour's fence to keep herself out of sight of the living-room window and headed down the path. Taking a second to remove the battery from her phone, she placed it behind a plant pot in Mrs Shah's garden. Sajid's Jaguar was parked a few hundred yards up the street and without hesitating she opened it and started up the engine, savouring the roar as it sprung to life … She was off, hotfooting it to Bradford Royal Infirmary. Her boss and Sajid would both be pissed off, but sometimes you just had to crack on with life. Khalid would still be dead in a few hours, but Haqib was alive and she needed to make sure the stupid little sod stayed that way.

Chapter 12

'I don't know how she managed it. Her daughter rang and she went into the hallway to take the call.' Sajid grimaced and held the phone away from his ear as Archie Hegley yelled at him.

'You were supposed to get her side of things before Springer pounced. For fuck's sake, Sajid, couldn't you keep her in sight for five minutes?'

Hegley was all bluster and fat rolls and Sajid could imagine them wobbling as he paced the office, his face becoming redder and redder with each step. The man was a heart attack waiting to happen. What Sajid had told him wasn't exactly true either. He did know how Nikki had managed it. She'd managed it because *he'd* cut her some slack. He'd let her have privacy to take a phone call and had compounded his error by being slow to notice she'd gone. But in fairness, sometimes those calls with Charlie could go on for half an hour or more. Besides, he'd been sent to break the news about her husband's death – the husband *nobody* had realised she even had until a few hours ago – not to apprehend her.

It was suspicious that when Khalid Abadi had disappeared off the face of the earth, Nikki hadn't even registered a missing persons report. 'Course it was, but hell, they were talking about *Nikki*. She was no murderer. At least he hoped she wasn't. 'Yes,

yes, I've sent out a BOLO, first thing I did, Sir. No sightings of her car yet.'

'And the father-in-law?'

'Well, in the circumstances I thought it best to have him taken back to his hotel. He's at the Midland Hotel in town, so I got a uniform to drop him off and stay with him. He's been mouthing off, accusing Nikki. Didn't want him here when Springer landed.'

'The Cold Case lot not there yet?'

'CCU are on their way.'

'Keep me updated.'

Sajid took a deep breath. Hegley's bark was worse than his bite, but hell, it was ferocious nonetheless. *What the hell, Nikita? What are you playing at?* Picking his phone up, he dialled Charlie's number, but it went straight to voicemail. Pissed off now, he brought up the tracking app he and Nikki had on their phones. Nikki's app was inactive, but the last registered position was right here. Shit, she'd clearly ditched her phone in the street. What the hell was she up to? She needed to get her ass back here pronto before Hegley burst a gut.

The back door opened and a small Indian woman in jeans and a T-shirt, black hair falling to her shoulders, came in. Aw no, why did Nikki's mum have to turn up right then? Hoping she'd leave before the CCU officers arrived, he smiled. 'Hallo, Mrs Parekh, you all right?'

Lalita Parekh had her daughter's height and her down-to-earth Yorkshire accent. The two women were clearly mother and daughter. 'Don't you Mrs Parekh me, Sajid. I've told you before, it's Lalita. Nikita nipped out, has she?'

Pleased that she'd provided her own reason for her daughter's absence, Sajid nodded, 'Yeah, something like that. She'll be back in a bit.' Well, he hoped she damn well would.

Lalita proceeded to dump a couple of Morrisons' bags-for-life on the table and began putting groceries into cupboards. 'Pop the kettle on, love. I'm gasping for a tea.'

Sajid hesitated. What was he supposed to do? If he could, he'd rush Lalita out of the kitchen and into her own house down the street, but that was out of the question. This wasn't his story to tell. Nikki would *kill* him if he told her mum, but what other option did he have? He shrugged his shoulders, trying to shake the tension out of them.

If that's what she wanted, then she shouldn't have pissed off like she was guilty of something, then should she? Picking up the kettle, he walked to the tap and filled it. 'Lalita, something's come up. Maybe you should sit down. Leave the shopping for now. We need to talk.'

Lalita froze, her dark eyes studying his face, and then without saying another word, she put the tins she was holding on the worksurface and sat down at the kitchen table, resting her clasped hands on the brightly coloured plastic table cover. 'What's she done this time? Is she okay?'

Sajid put the kettle on, flung a tea bag in one mug and a spoonful of coffee in another before replying. 'She got some …' He frowned, trying to think of a suitable word to describe the information his colleague had been confronted with a couple of hours earlier and settled with '… troubling news.'

A small frown pulled Lalita's eyebrows down. Unlike Nikki who was full of anger and passion and activity, Lalita possessed a calm stillness that instantly reassured. The pressure across his back diminished a little. Lalita Parekh had not had an easy life, but here she was exuding soothing vibes, ready to face whatever he had to tell her. He filled the mugs, stuck a teaspoon in Lalita's tea and took a carton of milk from the fridge. Before he had a chance to pour it into his coffee, Lalita stretched out her hand, a smile teasing her lips. 'I wouldn't risk that. Knowing Nikki, it's three weeks out of date. There's some fresh in the bag.'

Sajid sniffed the milk, grimaced and poured it down the sink. He settled opposite the older woman and studied her face. Nikki hadn't told him anything about her mother's past, but police stations were notorious for gossip and Trafalgar House was no different. It was funny how the fact that Nikki had been married and somehow misplaced her husband, had passed the gossip-mongers by completely.

According to the rumour mill, Lalita Parekh had been through a lot and yet, despite her own trials and tribulations, she'd raised two daughters single-handedly. Okay, Anika was a bit loopy and Nikki carried a chip the size of Concord on her shoulders but, all in all, she'd done all right. Shame neither of the girls had inherited her serenity.

Conscious that time was running out, Sajid blew on his coffee and then told Nikki's mother about the Odeon remains, the passport identifying them as belonging to Khalid Abadi, and his dad flying over from Ramallah and accusing Nikki of killing his son.

As he spoke, Lalita's grip on her mug tightened. Her face paled, her frown deepened and a tear trickled from the corner of her eye. He wanted to put his arm round her shoulders and hug her, take away the pain that had dulled her eyes. Sniffing, she wiped the tears from her cheek with the back of her hand and wiggled her nose as if that would stop the onset of more tears.

'Fifteen years.' Her voice was a whisper. 'We thought he'd left her, gone back to his family. His dad put pressure on him, you see? We thought he'd chosen his family, the business, everything they could offer and … all the while …' Her breath hitched in her throat and she stood up, scraping the chair back and began pacing the room. 'Oh, my poor beti, my poor Nikita. How is she?' As if noticing her daughter's absence for the first time, she looked round the room, apparently expecting her to materialise.

Sajid wished to hell she would! Time was running out. Springer would be here soon and there was no love lost between her and Nikki. The last thing Nikki needed, was to give the other woman more ammunition.

'Where is she? Is she next door with Anika?'

This was the tricky bit. How could he explain to Nikita's mum that her daughter was a suspect in her husband's death *and* that instead of waiting to be interviewed, she'd run? *For fuck's sake, Nikki!* 'That's just it. I don't actually know where she is. But that's not all. Khalid's dad's accusing her of having something to do with his son's death. She's a person of interest.'

'Phuh! Person of interest indeed.' Lalita, her eyes reproachful, glared at him. 'If you'd seen her when Khalid disappeared you wouldn't be standing there telling me that. She was devastated – broken.'

'Aw, hell. I don't think she did it, Lalita. But I'm not the one investigating. She never filed a missing persons report – it looks suspicious. The Cold Case Unit will be all over her till they can prove either way. She dumped her phone and took off. We've no idea where she is, none at all.'

Lalita moved over to the sink and began washing up her mug. 'Well, she can't have gone far, can she? Her car's up the street.'

Sajid paused, processed that thought, then it dawned on him. This was Nikki they were talking about. She'd have been one step ahead of him. Slamming his cup on the table, he ran to his coat, rummaged in the pockets. 'Aaaagh.'

He wrenched the front door open, jumped down the steps and onto the pavement. The space that had been filled by his Jag was occupied by a bashed-up Mini Cooper. *Fucking hell, Nikki. You better not have damaged my car!*

Chapter 13

Nikki parked Sajid's car on Toller Lane and jogged down the hill to BRI, pausing only to nip into the hardware shop that, for some reason, also sold cheap mobiles. At least now she'd be able to contact Charlie and possibly Sajid, under the radar. Mind you, she might leave Saj for later, he was prone to being a bit possessive about his Jag and she'd enough to worry about without getting beef from him.

Every so often, a sharp pain, like lightening, jabbed her heart. Khal! How many times had she parked in that car park? Passed by? Visited the Chinese buffet? And all that time Khal was there … buried under there. What had happened to him? How had he ended up there? Everybody loved Khal. There was just no explanation for it. Unless, of course, his dad had orchestrated something from Ramallah. He'd plenty of money – more than enough to order a hit on his only son. The question was, would he? If the stories Khal had shared with her were true, then she would put nothing past the old bastard. Of course, if he was guilty, what better way to exert a little more revenge than to point the finger at Nikki. But he had seemed upset, hadn't he?

If she thought about it, her breath started to clog up her throat, and her heart hammered. She *had* to keep it under control, had to sort out Haqib and then she could go back and talk to them about Khalid. That old bastard had told them she'd done it to stop Khal returning to his family. *Surely* they wouldn't believe that. She was a police officer. Niggling at the back of her mind was the fact that she hadn't reported Khal missing. That would play against her big time. However, she'd known he was conflicted. Known he was anguished by the pressure from his family. That was why she hadn't told him she was pregnant.

Turning into BRI, she steered clear of the ambulances, pulled her hoodie up over her hair and the collar of her leather jacket over her lower face. Keeping an eye out for any officers accompanying those with drink- or drug-related injuries, she skirted the Accident and Emergency Department and entered the hospital. Despite it being early in the day, the corridors were bustling with patients, visitors and staff. Hopefully, she'd blend in.

Haqib, according to Charlie, was on Ward Two and Nikki made her way there as quickly as possible. She couldn't blame Charlie for contacting her instead of Haqib's mum. Anika had always been useless in an emergency. Nikki had lost count of the times she'd had to break off from work in order to sort out something to do with Anika's kids – broken arms, split heads. Anika had deferred responsibility to her older sister and Nikki had, as usual, taken it on. She owed Anika a lot. It was because of Anika and her mum's childcare that she'd been able to focus on her work. Sometimes though, an aching tiredness suffused her body. Sometimes, all she wanted was to curl up in her huge double bed, wrap the duvet around her and block out everything for a week. But she also realised that *that* was a luxury she couldn't afford. If she stopped for a minute, let her control slip for even a nanosecond, then perhaps she wouldn't be able to bring herself back from the brink.

To survive, like a well-trained soldier, she compartmentalised things. Put Khal in his box – the big dusky grey one towards the back of her mind. That one was slightly in front of the ridged

74

black one with the lock and hasp that contained her dad, but behind the rainbow-coloured one that stood, lid ajar, with all her family stuff spilling out, its colourful entrails intertwining in a buzz of love and exasperation and responsibility.

She entered the ward, giving Haqib's name and identifying herself feloniously as his mother to the busy nurse on the desk. As she moved towards the bed where Haqib lay, all his usual bravado dissipated, face pale and right arm elevated, Charlie got up to meet her. Her *beautiful* Charlie. Her heart contracted. So like her father, her skin a lighter brown than her own, her eyes the exact same shade as Khal's, more than a touch of her mother's drive but tempered with Khal's patience and ability to reason. She'd protected Charlie from the moment she was conceived, but *nothing* could protect her from the fallout surrounding the discovery of her father's remains. How could it? Charlie thought he'd deserted them before she was born and, in self-preservation, Nikki had pretended not to have known him well – a one-night stand. For nearly fifteen years she'd deprived her eldest child of being acquainted with the essence of her dad. His humour, his loyalty, his care and joy. How could she ever square this with Charlie? Feeling the unwelcome tickle at the back of her eyes, Nikki swallowed hard and smiled. 'You all right, Charlie?'

'FFS mum, what's with all the cloak and dagger stuff? "Take your battery out, don't phone me back" and all that shit?'

Nikki shrugged. 'Less of the "shit", Charlie.'

Charlie, lips pursed, hand on hip, harrumphed. 'Like you don't swear.'

'Do as I say, not as I do.' Nikki mimicked her mum's words making Charlie grin.

'Now you're here I can go get a drink or summat, yeah? This bloody radio station is doing my head in.'

Nikki became aware of the muted sounds of some dated music drifting from the next bed. 'Don't be so mean, Charlie. The radio's keeping the old bloke company.'

With an exaggerated sigh, Charlie plopped herself on the side of Haqib's bed eliciting a 'watch my bloody hand, Charl,' from her cousin.

'… *Now, here on Bradford Radio Royal we have a news update. It seems that the skeletonised remains found in the Odeon car …*'

Nikki held her breath. Now, she too wished the old man would switch off the damn radio. Would they release Khal's name – or worse still link it to her? She glanced at Charlie and wondered if she should take the time to tell her what was going on now.

'*The police have not released a name, although the victim has been identified …*'

Thank God for that! It would take far too long to explain everything to Charlie, and she couldn't just rush off, leaving her daughter to process everything on her own. No, they hadn't released a name so she'd sit her daughter down later, just the two of them, and take the time to make her understand. Why the hell was there always so much drama in her life? Bloody Haqib and his eye on making a fast buck. *Idiot!*

She turned her attention to her nephew. His pupils were dilated and his bandaged hand was held at an angle as if he didn't want to have to look at it. Nikki would have hugged him, but suspected that would make the tears shimmering in his eyes start. This had all the hallmarks of a Franco hit on it. He was a heartless thug and he had it in for the Parekh family. Yet another reason that Nikki wanted to keep her sister out of the picture for now. Not that she'd be able to keep it from her for long. Anika would need to be told about Haqib's stupidity and Franco's part in it. But she'd deal with that when she had to. Instead, she hardened her tone. 'For God's sake, what the hell did you *not* understand last week when I told you to steer clear of Franco and Deano? You really are a stupid little turd, you know that?'

'Mum!' Charlie's tone was sharp.

Haqib's lower lip trembled and he looked down at the bed sheets. Sighing, Nikki plonked herself down on the seat Charlie had vacated. He was just a kid trying to grow up too damn fast. She blamed the useless piece of shit he called his dad. Yousaf only showed up for the odd booty call and Anika had spent sixteen years kidding herself that he was going to leave his wife to settle down with her. He was the worst sort of role model – all sexist shit and bravado. Nikki couldn't stand him. Nikki's kids might have different dads, but Marcus was active in his kids' lives and he treated Charlie as if she was his own. Okay, so recently Marcus had been getting a bit clingy, a bit too keen on making their arrangement more permanent. That was something to think about another day. Besides, how the hell could she explain about Khal to him? For now, she had Haqib to sort out. 'What happened?'

Voice shaking, Haqib outlined how he'd been grabbed from a street near school, bundled into Franco's car and transported to the back alley. As he spoke, Nikki's heart sank. The school cameras didn't reach as far as there. Despite their frequent moaning about drugs being sold nearby, the police hadn't acted on advice to extend their camera footage to cover the streets adjacent to the school. As a result, rather than deal right outside the school, the dealers hung about at the end of the road where they weren't recorded. So, Haqib's abduction wouldn't be recorded and as for the back alley – again no CCTV footage.

'It weren't Deano, though. He weren't there. Just Franco and two of his men.'

Deano might not have been there, but he was the one who'd brought Franco and his little shitbags back into their lives. He'd pay for that – she'd make sure of it. 'You been given pain relief?'

He nodded once.

'It working?'

Again, the nod. Nikki turned to Charlie. 'What are the doctors saying? Can they re-attach?'

'Yeah, if you sign the consent, they'll take him up in a bit.'

'Right, I'll do that on my way out. You stay with him for now, Charlie.' She leaned over and ruffled her daughter's hair, earning herself a grunt. 'Once he's in surgery phone Auntie Anika … on second thoughts, phone Aji-ma and let her know what's happened.' Having her mum break the news to Anika would make things easier in the long run.

'What d'ya mean? Are you not staying?

'No, I've got something to do. Get Auntie Anika to come over and get Ajima to watch the other kids.'

She should really go back home and face the music. The longer she left it, the worse things would be and she and DS Springer had history. However, right now, she wanted to find Franco. Nobody did that to one of her own and got away with it. Keen to put distance between the BRI and herself before Sajid got wind of where she was, Nikki got to her feet. 'Right, I'll be in touch when I can.'

About to leave, Nikki saw a familiar figure strutting down the ward. And she turned to her daughter, her tone accusing. 'You called Marcus?'

Charlie rolled her eyes. 'Duh, 'course I did. You were acting all weird, so I called Marcus. Chillax.'

Chillax? Nikki wanted nothing more than to barge past Marcus, avoid a repeat of last night's argument. As he approached, she studied his face. Sculpted cheek bones, lashes to die for and a grin that many women, and a lot of men, swooned over. But Nikki wasn't observing his prettiness, she was more concerned about whether he knew about Khalid. He loped down the ward, all loose-limbed ease, and dropped a kiss on her lips before she could protest. Seemed that, so far, Marcus was out of the loop which meant she really needed to escape before Saj had the bright idea of involving him.

'Gotta go, Marcus. Work. Glad you're here. Keep an eye on these two, yeah?' And with Charlie's indignant 'Muuuum!' ringing in her ears, she was off down the ward, intent on chasing up Deano and Franco. *Living family stuff trumps decease husbands every day of the week.* Well, at least that's what she told herself.

Chapter 14

The Midland Hotel might not have been up to Burhan Abadi's standards, but it was the best hotel in Bradford and was ornate in an old-fashioned English sort of way. As the lift whisked him up to his room, Burhan thought about Nikita Parekh. Why his son had chosen that woman over his family was beyond him. Not only was she an infidel, but she was a police officer – a half-caste police officer at that … and ugly with that scar round her neck. What power had she exerted over Khalid to keep him here in this freezing, dull, drab city? She had seemed shocked to hear about the identity of the body, but she was a police officer and, in his experience, they were prone to lies and deceit when it suited them. He'd been told that she had been the attending officer when they first discovered his son.

Surely, even that cold-hearted bitch would have revealed something had she been responsible. He had wanted to push her. Make her pay for the divide she'd caused between Khalid and his family. Make her pay for Khalid's death. He was sure she had killed his son – who else could have? She had the perfect motive. Khalid was coming home and rather than allow it, she'd killed him and buried him. And now she had escaped. He should have known better than to trust the police. He should have employed someone to come with him. Someone who could control that whore. Then she wouldn't have escaped. He suspected that the DC, Sajid Malik, had turned a blind eye – let her go on purpose. So what if he was Muslim? His loyalties clearly lay with Parekh.

Also, there was the daughter, Charlie. There was no doubt she was Khalid's daughter and although he would have preferred a grandson, he'd make do with a granddaughter. One thing was certain, he would not leave his kin, half-caste or not, with that woman. She was out of control. One of the more gossipy officers had told him that she had three kids and wasn't even married. No way could he leave his only progeny with a slut. *Khalid, what were you thinking?*

The lift doors swished open and Burhan exited. *Inshallah, they've got the central heating on.* Limbs throbbing, heavy overcoat slung over one arm, he leaned heavily on his walking stick. An aroma of lavender tickled his nostrils as he dragged himself along the thick carpeted corridor to his room. The cleaners' metal trollies clanged along the corridors along with their light-hearted chatter as they worked. Eastern European, he supposed.

His luggage had been delivered to his room earlier and when he opened the door, the first thing he saw was the king-sized four-poster bed and immediately an overwhelming desire to lie on it without removing his clothes or showering or praying flooded him. Instead, he crossed the room, his leg dragging slightly as he moved, and tossed his coat onto a cushioned seat near the window and stretched his shoulders, trying to alleviate the tension that coiled his muscles as tightly as a spring. He stood for a moment looking out the window.

The rain speckling it marred his view and was typical of this godforsaken city. Through the raindrops he watched the people on the pavements beneath, huddled under umbrellas, hoods up, scurrying like sewer rats about their business. The buildings opposite were a mismatch of eras from concrete Seventies' buildings to the older, more traditional sandstone. What attraction had this city held for Khalid? He'd been used to more than this – *better* than this. A lifestyle with servants and ease. His every whim catered for, the sun, his family, his home ... and he wanted *this* ... and that whore?

He loosened his tie and flung it on the bed before undressing and taking a quick shower. He'd ordered a light snack – some eggs and toast. Who knew if the hotel really catered for halal? Ablutions done, he prayed like he'd never prayed before – for the strength to cope with what was before him. The strength to show to these English that he was a better guardian for Khalid's daughter than a promiscuous whore who'd killed her husband and buried him.

*

Dressed in pyjamas, the hotel's fluffy robe wrapped round him for warmth, a plate of half-eaten scrambled eggs and coffee discarded beside him, he took out his laptop and started the first of two Skype calls.

Abubhakar Husayni had been recommended to Burhan by his own business solicitor. Husayni dealt with more delicate family issues and was based in London. Not having the time to visit the barrister in person, Burhan preferred Skype. He liked to get the measure of the person on whom he was placing such faith. Husayni was expecting his call. Burhan knew he would be. The amount of money he was offering made that a certainty. First impressions played an important part of Burhan's business negotiations. He'd been known to pull out of major deals, solely because he took a dislike to one of the negotiators. A lot rested on this for Husayni, although he didn't realise that ... yet.

He was younger than Burhan had expected, but he was courteous and took notes as they talked. Like Burhan's, his suit was Western and of the highest quality – *Armani? Versace?*

'As-Salaam-Alaikum, Mr Husayni.'

'Wa-Alaikum-Salaam, Mr Abadi. What can I do for you?'

Bhurhan explained about his son's death and his desire to bring his granddaughter back to Ramallah, no matter the cost.

'From what you have told me, Mr Abadi, the best *legal* solution would be for us to prove this Nikita Parekh to be an unfit mother. I think you would have many grounds for this, particularly if she was found guilty of your son's murder. She has a proven track record of promiscuity which we can play on – three children and not married. Hmph, I understand exactly why you would not wish her to influence your grandchild. I also took the liberty of looking into her background and it seems that this promiscuity runs in her family. Her mother was known for having a countless number of partners and Nikita and her sister are the result of this activity.'

Bhurhan already had an inkling of this. Loose tongues at the police station had told him Parekh, whilst respected by some, was not popular with others. A bit like sheep's brain curry – you either liked it or you loathed it. Husayni was still talking, so Burhan tuned back in.

'Then there are the demands of her job, the area she lives in – all in all, I think we can pull this your way.' He paused and steepling his fingers together, he tapped them on his lips. 'Of course, there are *other* options available should you so choose.'

Husayni instinctively understood what his client wanted and was prepared to take great lengths to remove any barriers that stood in Burhan's way. By the end of this, inshallah, Nikita Parekh would be imprisoned for murder and Khalid's daughter Charlie would be under his guardianship, where she would learn how to be the heir her father couldn't be. The knot of anger that had pressed against Burhan's chest eased. He was happy to pay whatever Husayni needed to gather the evidence. He had his eye on the end goal and cared not a jot about Nikita. She had brought this on herself and if he needed to play dirty further down the line, then so be it.

'Keep me informed. I want regular updates. At the moment she is "in the wind" as the British say. I suppose even the Bradford police will be able to find one of their own quickly.'

Bhurhan leaned back in his chair, stretching his legs out before him. The damp weather made his muscles ache and he desperately needed to sleep. His doctor had advised against the trip, but how could he not come ... regardless of his own health. First though, he had to call his wife.

Enaya, scarf covering her head, looked at him, her eyes wide and expectant. Burhan could see the hope still burning in them and hated that he would have to dash it so completely. For years, she had prayed that her only child would return and forsake the infidel. She was a simple woman and Khalid's betrayal had hit her hard. She, like Burhan, had been sure that when given the ultimatum, Khalid would choose his family, his privileged life in Ramallah over the drudgery of life in a Yorkshire city with a woman who neither understood nor took steps to embrace their religion and culture ... but worse than that, was the fact that she was of Hindu descent. Both he and his wife had been severely wounded by Khalid's actions.

Wishing he was with her to comfort her, Burhan shook his head. 'It's him, Enaya. They took DNA and there is no doubt, our Khalid has gone.'

Enaya began to recite Qur'anic script, rocking back and forth as she did so. A wave of tiredness rolled over him, drowning him, pushing him under a suffocating quagmire. He could do nothing but watch as tears flowed down her cheeks, dripping from her chin, unheeded.

'She killed him, Enaya. That woman killed him to stop him coming back to us.'

Enaya stopped crying, straightened her scarf over her hair and looked straight at her husband. 'You will deal with this. Make her suffer as I have done for the last fifteen years.'

'I am working on it. Trust me, she *will* pay. Now, I have some better news.' He picked up the photograph he'd taken from Nikita's fridge and held it to the screen. 'This is your granddaughter. Khalid's daughter.'

Enaya's lip trembled, her hands clutching at a tissue as her eyes scoured the picture. 'Khalid's girl?' Her hand reached out and her fingers touched the screen, stroking the face of the girl. 'She has his eyes. She looks like him. Her name?'

'Hmph, Charlie. Her name is Charlie.'

Enaya frowned. 'When you bring her home to us, we will call her Aadab.'

Burhan smiled 'Hope. That's a good choice. Aadab. I like it. Respect and politeness.' Whilst Burhan suspected the girl would have neither in abundance, he supposed the name was a good omen.

'You *will* bring her home, won't you?'

Burhan nodded. 'That is the plan. To bring her home and make her mother pay.'

Chapter 15

It is strange to sit here whilst outside the consequences of my choices so long ago are causing chaos to many. Strange, but dare I say it, quite thrilling. Time on my own is always a welcome thing, but time shared with my memories is second to none. In this time of crisis, I find myself eking out more 'me time'. Not sure that what I do in my 'me time' is exactly what they've got in mind but nonetheless, I derive great pleasure from it. There's something particularly satisfying in knowing that whilst I am indulging myself in my homemade production, others, in more clinical surroundings, are trying to work out what happened. Perhaps one day they'll be able to compare their findings with these recordings. I wonder how well they'll match up.

I've already inserted the DVD and fast-forwarded to near the end. I love the way my voice sounds through the speakers. Many hate their own recorded voices, but for me it is like music. I love seeing myself too. I look powerful, strong, but more importantly dependable. I am dependable! Unlike my targets, I am fully committed to whatever decisions I make. I don't give up, don't opt out. No matter how difficult things become, I dig my heels in and crack on. Maybe it's that Yorkshire grit in me. Off we go …

10th November 2003. Time 00.45. Time in captivity: four days, one hour

As we watch, the shadowy figure looms over the captive man. Hands tied behind the death chair, feet tied to the legs, his head droops. It's nearly time – time to lose all hope. Time to face his maker. Notice the number of cuts, the frequency of the slashes. Each bears testament to his failure to prove his worth. You won't be able to count them, but I can assure you there are more than fifty. Fifty chances he had and fifty chances he blew. Note how he fails to flinch now. Resigned to his failure. Just one more indication of his readiness to submit – to admit defeat. We're in the home stretch. Watch and learn. Bear witness!

As the camera zooms in, the figure circles the captive, prodding him occasionally with a cattle prod. Watch how our captive flinches, half lifts his head and groans. Watch as the figure pulls his head up and directs it towards the camera.

'Focus! You have proven time and time again that your privilege is stronger than your brains. That you are lacking – undeserving of the opportunities that have been offered you at the expense of those more deserving. You have one last thing you can do. One last thing you can leave behind – a last chance, if you will, to redeem yourself in the eyes of those who matter to you. A chance to prove that there is more to you than privilege and entitlement. Answer the question. Why are you here?'

Note how the captive remains inert. Is he bluffing? I fear not. His exhaustion is clear, his weakness apparent. Take heed how the figure deals with this. Watch how he teases the captive back to consciousness. Smelling salts and an injection of adrenaline, that's all that's needed.

See how the captive's head slumps backwards, his eyes, although open, keep rolling back in his head before refocusing. For now, he is alert. Witness the care taken to make these last few moments special – momentous. The captive can go to his death safe in the knowledge that his last request has been recorded. Closure at the end of a long struggle which has ultimately resulted in the same abject failure that has plagued his life's choices.

Listen to me. 'Have you had enough? Can you not answer? Why are you here? Are you ready to relinquish your privilege and admit your shortcomings?'

'Aaah.'

Is that all he can muster? It is his final opportunity and his only utterance is a strangled pathetic cry. Can you blame the figure for sniggering?

'Oh, come on now, surely you can do better than this? No?'

The captive's lack of response necessitates a punishment. I am directing this show, not him. The figure uses the cattle prod and then speaks in a voice both melodious and compelling.

'Right. The floor is yours. Your chance – your final chance – what is your last request? Your message to someone you love. Make it count, Khalid. You don't get a re-take.'

The figure moves into position behind him, arms raised, hammer at the ready and says, 'Your turn. Make it good – make it clear. You only have one shot at this. It's your final-night production. What is your last request?'

The captive's eyes flicker. His mouth opens. He licks his lips, tries to lift his head. He's trying hard. I'm sure you'll agree. His final performance – his swan song – is poignant. Let's hope it counts.

As the camera zooms in to the captive's face, we can see tears pouring from his eyes. In a final show of bravery, he looks directly into the camera. 'Let her know …'

You can see how much he's trying. How much he wants to do this. This is his legacy. His final chance. I'm sure we've all got our fingers crossed that he doesn't stumble at the last hurdle. He's tried all the way along the trial – given a stellar, if ultimately redundant performance. Let's give him a round of applause to spur him on. Come on now, don't be mean, applaud his efforts.

Sound-over: raucous applause and cheering.

Come on, Khalid, you can do this, lad. You can do this. You need to do this. You know you do.

Now, at last, the part we've all been waiting for. Listen in now.
You don't want to miss a word, do you?

'Tell Nikki, I saw the test. I saw it. Tell her … love her … bril-
liant mum … brilliant.'

What a finale! What a last request. Watch now for the last scene.
The figure steadies, then in one fell swoop brings the hammer down.
Curtain!

Last request recorded: Khalid Abadi, 10th November 2003

Chapter 16

They brayed on his door – for a second Deano thought it was the police, and then Big Zee's guttural voice echoed through the letterbox and up the stairs. 'Come on, Deano. Get your arse down here. Franco wants to see you.'

Fuck! This was the last thing Deano needed right now. He was still trying to finesse his plan. Trying to work out a way to get Parekh on side. It was the only way he could see to cut free from Franco and now Franco wanted to see him. A prickle like a lion's claw scraped up his spine. The less he had to do with Franco the better. He looked in the mirror, took a few deep breaths and straightened his back.

Downstairs the letterbox clattered shut, but Deano could still hear them laughing on the doorstep, Tyke's voice higher than Big Zee's but just as stupid. He looked round his bedroom. On his return to Bradford he'd kicked his stepbrother, Bailey, out of it. The perennial whiff of weed, sweat and stale socks still hung in the air. Despite him spraying Lynx every day, the spray hit against the stench-wall and bounced back, catching in his throat, making him cough, before dissipating, leaving the original pong. His own clothes were packed, folded neatly in his sports bag. When he'd first claimed the room, Bailey's discarded clothes were strewn all over the place. It made Deano's skin crawl, so he'd braced himself and bundled them all up into black bin bags and chucked them into the hallway. The bed sheets had been another trauma, filthy and crusty to the touch with enough DNA to implicate a whorehouse. Again, he'd bagged them up, turned the mattress and remade the bed with clean bed linen. He hated being home, but he had no choice. Right now, he was stuck here until he wangled a way to escape Franco's clutches.

They were kicking the door, now. Deano took a deep breath, pulled up his hood and headed downstairs. His mum cowered in the hallway, eyes wide, trembling against a backdrop of fried bacon and burnt toast. 'Dean, sweetie, make them stop. If they damage the door, your dad will kick off.'

'He's not my dad.' This was Deano's automatic response, one he'd repeated many times, but it seemed his mum still lived in hope of a happy family. He tried to dredge up an ounce of sympathy for her but failed. It wasn't her fault, she was weak – weak *and* stupid. She'd not had it easy, but every time he looked at her, all he wanted to do was smash his fist into her face. Her weakness had landed them all in this shithouse, landed him in this situation.

Through the frosted glass, Deano saw their silhouettes. Two thugs jostling with each other, voices raised, brains dormant. Just out of view, he waited, timing his next move. Just when he sensed they were about to recommence their kicking, he yanked the door open. Tyke, following through with his size elevens, barrelled into the small hallway. Behind him Big Zee clicked his finger, chortling. 'Good 'un, Deano, good 'un.'

Stepping over Tyke, Deano brushed past Big Zee and down the outer stairs. He was halfway down the path before he turned round. 'Come on then, you two. Where's Franco?'

Tyke picked himself up, his face scrunched into a scowl, eyes blazing as he glared at Deano. 'Tosser.'

Deano shrugged. 'Yeah, and what you gonna do about it?'

Big Zee, still laughing, jumped down the stairs and caught up with Deano. 'Just ignore him, Tyke.'

Placing a heavy arm round Deano's shoulder, Big Zee opened the gate and guided him through, leaving Tyke to bring up the rear. Deano was under no illusions that this was a friendly gesture. The weight of Big Zee's arm pressing down made it a struggle not to let his knees buckle. Perhaps he shouldn't have asserted what little bit of authority he had. Perhaps he should have kept his head down and followed on like a meek little lackey. *Aw well, no point in worrying about that now – what's done is done.*

Franco was waiting in his black Ferrari, head bobbing to some hip hop beat that he played loud enough to cause permanent brain damage. No problem for Big Zee and Tyke, but Deano thought Franco could've been a bit more careful with his own brain function. Big gold rings like some rapper's, glinting as they tapped against the steering wheel.

Sliding into the front seat, a familiar tension gathered at the nape of Deano's neck. Spreading out across his shoulders it made his entire upper body tense. By his sides, his hands curled into fists. Tyke and Big Zee took up their usual positions behind him, and the entire car trembled as Big Zee's frame settled. Tyke was still chuntering 'knobs' and 'tossers' and suchlike under his breath. Everyone ignored him.

Franco turned the earache down and leaning against the door, angled his torso towards Deano. 'We gotta problem, bruv.'

The gangsta shit would have been comical if not for the look in Franco's eyes. Deano had always thought he was one loop short of a double helix, but this coldness just confirmed it. Franco was definitely missing something the rest of the world would describe as humanity.

'Whassup?'

'Haqib Parekh.'

Deano schooled his face to remain impassive, but inside his heart had started to thump. What the fuck had that stupid little

91

turd done now? Last thing he needed was more hassle from the little fucker's auntie. Not until he'd worked out his next game plan and he couldn't do owt with Franco breathing down his neck.

'Haqib?'

'Yeah, you and Tyke gave him some kit to offload, yeah?'

The hammering in Deano's chest was like a dinosaur trampling inside him. In his head he recited his mantra, *Show no fear! Show no fear!* It had little effect, his stomach was roiling, his insides threatening to make a bid for freedom up his throat and onto Franco's lap. *Not a good move.* Franco wouldn't have dragged him in if something hadn't gone off with Haqib. *Why had he targeted that little scrote?* He knew why. Haqib was easy prey – a bit gullible, trying to act the hard man. Deano'd taken the easy option and now it seemed like he was about to pay. He should have known better than to meddle with any of Parekh's clan. She was a bitch and when it came to her family and her estate, she was worse ... *and* she was a pig. *Let's hope Franco hasn't gone over the score.*

'Yeah, gave him some. He'll come up with the goods.'

Franco snorted and raised one finger off the wheel. Recognising the signal, Deano lunged forward, but was too slow. Big Zee's big hands flicked the chain over Deano's head and yanked it backwards. Deano's head slammed against the headrest, his fingers up, gripping the chain trying to release the pressure. He struggled for a minute and then stopped, relaxing his body, feeling the chain relax a little round his neck, he gulped in small mouthfuls of air, his eyes on Franco's.

The other man studied him, then his face broke into a grin. From the corner of his eye, Deano could see Tyke squirming and giggling like a schoolboy. *Getting his rocks off, dirty little fucker!* Franco slammed the heel of his hand onto the leather steering wheel, making a slapping sound, then nodded at Big Zee. At once the pressure around his throat alleviated.

Deano coughed and hoiked, before opening the door and

spitting into the gutter. 'What the fuck?' Rubbing his neck, voice hoarse, eyes watering, Deano closed the door and, mantra still running through his head, glared at Franco.

Franco only laughed. 'Just a bit of fun, Deano boy, just a bit of fun. Your Haqib hasn't come up with the goods, so ...' He shrugged. 'Me and the lads paid him a little visit.'

Deano wanted to scream 'No!', but apart from his aching throat, he was in no position to nail his colours to the Parekh mast, so he remained silent.

With a laugh brittle enough to splinter glass, Franco flung back his head, releasing a waft of garlic into the car. 'Let's just say Haqib's having a few attachment issues.'

Tyke and Big Zee's sycophantic laughs made Deano's hand itch to slam their heads together. He needed to get away from them, needed to think. He knew exactly what the attachment issues would be. He'd worked with Franco for long enough to know his methods. And this had just escalated things for him with Nikita Parekh. *Stupid fuckers!* All he could hope for was that power tools hadn't been used.

Chapter 17

Charlie's moans about the muted hospital radio station playing crap music, and the uncomfortable chair still niggled Nikki, as she stopped at the nurses' station to sign Haqib's parental consent form for his operation and braved the disapproving frown from the male nurse, as she left her burner phone number in case of an emergency. She noted but ignored the nurse's expression and hurried down the hall.

His 'Some mother, that one. No wonder the kid's got on the wrong side of a drug gang' fell on deaf ears. Nikki was used to the casual racism that sometimes reared its ugly head and she was also aware that *her* idea of maternal was different from most people's. She'd fight ferociously for any of her kids, and Anika's kids too for that matter, but what she wouldn't, or couldn't, do, was sit idly by, weeping into handkerchiefs and soothing the little prat when she could be going after the thugs that had done this. In her opinion, wiping *them* off the face of the universe was infinitely more of an act of love than mollycoddling her stupid, spoon-fed nephew.

Her one pang of regret was that she was leaving Charlie to deal with it all. As usual, Charlie, head screwed on right, was taking on a responsibility that her Aunt Anika would indubitably fail at. With Marcus there though, Charlie wasn't on her own. Squashing the thought that with Marcus around, *she* wasn't on her own either, Nikki tried to be annoyed. Marcus always jumped at the chance to get under her defences. She recognised that she was being unfair, but right now she couldn't handle anything more – anything that would complicate things. First, she had to try to fix Haqib's mess, and then maybe she'd be able to sort out her own feelings. Thrusting the thought aside that she was risking Charlie finding out about Khalid from someone else, Nikita steeled herself and gave into the adrenaline that courtesy of her rage, now surged through her body.

She'd warned Deano and he'd chosen to ignore her warning. He'd brought this onto their heads and now she was determined to force his hand. Listerhills would be a better place without him. Tossing her head, ponytail swinging, Nikki left the ward and with her usual impatience avoided the lift, choosing instead to whiz down the stairs. Weaving her way past wheelchairs, drip stands and mothers with kids, Nikki headed for the main entrance. It was far enough away from A&E to minimise her risk of being spotted by any duty officers and it had the added benefit of having a payphone nearby. She could phone Ali Khan, her taxi driver friend, without leaving a trace back to her or her burner. Ali would come for her, no questions asked, and while she waited for him, she could grab a coffee from the BRI café and plan her next moves.

Nikki, a cappuccino cradled in her hands, tried to focus. Thoughts of Khalid kept intruding, squeezing her heart, distracting her. Cursing herself, she took out her wallet and opening it, she wiggled her fingers into the slit at the back pulling out four small squares. With an unfamiliar lump in her throat, she studied each of the photo booth snaps, one at a time. Khalid and her, fifteen years ago. He was so handsome, his arm round her neck, holding her close, kissing her cheek, whilst winking at the camera. The pair of them blowing raspberries. She was laughing, her head thrown back, her scar visible, but she knew Khalid didn't care about that. How long was it since she'd been so carefree? How long since she'd belly laughed the way she used to with Khal? He'd brought out the best in her. Diluted the bitterness, infected her with his optimism, made each nerve ending tingle with passion and life … and then it had been yanked away from her – ruthlessly, with no explanation, no fond farewells. She'd hated him. Hated him with a vengeance. How could he have done this? She wished she'd never met him. Wished he hadn't opened her heart, made her trust again. For when he'd disappeared, it had been so much worse – so bad that she'd almost not been able to pull herself back. Her mother, she acknowledged, would argue that she still hadn't managed to pull herself back.

That initial irrational relief that flooded her when she realised that he *hadn't* left her, had soon been replaced by a whole plethora of emotions that she'd had to stash away. With her finger she traced Khal's face on the one photo where he was looking straight at the camera. His high cheekbones, his sparkling eyes, his full lips. She'd give anything to feel those full lips on hers again, to hear his sexy accented voice teasing her, to feel the warmth of his arms around her. Now here she was dodging her colleagues, under suspicion of his murder, and not knowing how to tell her daughter that everything she believed about her father was a lie. For the first time in a long time – in fifteen years to be exact – Nikki felt out of control.

Bradford Radio Royal segued from a jaunty Bob Marley track to a news bulletin;

'*In a local news update, Khalid Abadi has been identified as the ophthalmic student whose remains were excavated from the Odeon car park last week. In a shocking twist, it appears that at the time of his disappearance fifteen years ago, Abadi was married to one of Bradford's golden girls. Detective Sergeant Nikita Parekh, better known for infiltrating a child grooming ring in the district and bringing her superior officer, Jacob Kowalski, to justice ten years ago. Sources close to the investigation into Abadi's suspicious death say they are interested to discover why Parekh didn't file a missing persons report in 2003. DS Nikita Parekh is unavailable to comment at this time.'*

Where the fuck had they got that from? Somebody had leaked sensitive information to the press and when she found out who, they'd better insure their balls for big bucks because she'd rip them off with her teeth. Her first thought was to dash back up to the ward in case Charlie and Marcus had heard. Nikki stuffed the photos back in her wallet, and glanced around her. Was there anyone around who recognised her? She pulled her hood up, and began to slide out of the corner booth when a huge hand plonked itself on the table, making her barely touched drink slosh over the sides.

'Going somewhere?'

Sajid! She should've known he'd manage to find her. 'Charlie told you, I suppose?'

He shook his head and slid into a chair, indicating that she should sit down. 'Ali, actually. When I worked out you'd jacked the Jag and ditched your phone, I reckoned you had limited options. You couldn't hold onto the Jag for long, so you'd need wheels. Didn't take me long to realise you'd phone Ali, so I camped out in his taxi office and monitored all the calls.'

Sitting on the edge of her seat, shredding a napkin, Nikki leaned forward, 'You need to let me go, Sajid. Just for a couple of hours.'

He leaned back, making the chair creak so much that Nikki feared for its fate. He raised an eyebrow, but said nothing.

Shit, he's going to make me work for this. 'I *know* I've got to come in. I know it looks bad, but I've got to do something first.'

Sajid sighed. 'Thing is, Nikki, you've always got something to do. Always on the move, always doing more than the rest of us put together. Now, you need to slow down. They'll crucify you if you don't.'

She frowned and stared at the table. He was right, of course, but that didn't make it any more palatable. She tried again. 'Just two hours. That's all. Two hours and then I'll come in.'

Sajid frowned. 'Look, Nikki, I know you've nothing to do with your ex-husband's death, but even knowing that, I find it hard to balance your innocence with your current behaviour. Think how it looks to CCU. Not only didn't any of us know you'd ever been married, but now we've discovered your murdered husband's remains, you think it's okay to head off in my Jag instead of helping with the enquiry? Instead of eliminating yourself so the CCU can focus on the real suspects. *Especially* when old man Abadi's very vocally accusing you.'

Everything he said was true, but that didn't help Haqib, nor did it get rid of a more imminent threat – that of Franco and his crew. But she knew Saj wouldn't get it. He was from a well-off family, who'd never lived in fear, never wondered if they'd be hurt, tortured, sold out to the nearest pervert for the price of a packet of fags and a pint.

'When he disappeared, why didn't you report it?'

Realising she'd have to give him something, Nikki exhaled, the vice around her heart pulsing. This wasn't her. She didn't do the big 'confide'. She didn't lay her soul bare for anyone – not since Khalid anyway. His eyes held hers, a slight smile tweaking the corners of his mouth. 'Go on, *Nikita*. I'm your mate. I've got your back. You're going to need to trust me.'

With a brief nod, she began. 'I was a kid back then. Nineteen and in love. We got married to prove to the world that they were wrong about it being a brief fling.' She shrugged with a rueful smile. 'Three months into the marriage and Khal was getting hassle from back home. Threats to disown and disinherit him. It was ...' She paused, flashing back to the rows they'd had, Khal's moody silences, the heated phone calls in Arabic with his dad. 'The first flush of our love was tainted by reality, I suppose. When he disappeared with his passport, I assumed he'd chosen his inheritance, and his family, over me.'

Sajid waited, but Nikki was done. She'd given him more than she'd shared with anyone for years. He could fill in the blanks for himself. Her soul was hers.

'So you didn't think to check?'

Nikki stood up. 'Pride. Now, I've got to go.'

Sajid stood, his chair scraping across the floor. 'Not so fast, Nikki. You're coming in with me. Right now. Whatever other stuff you need to sort out, you need to do it later. This is important.'

Shoulders tense, she raised her chin and, eyes narrowed, she all but growled at him, 'You arresting me, Saj?' She snorted as if to say, 'As if'. 'You do realise that *I'm* the sergeant here, don't you?'

Sajid held her gaze, kept his voice low. 'Yes, but one who's been accused of murder. Think I'll swing it all right with Hegley, don't you? But I'm hoping you'll see sense and just come with me – like a sensible, sane person.'

Cheeky bastard. She nodded and took a step towards the exit. When she felt Sajid's hand on her arm, she jerked away, 'Personal space, Malik, personal space.'

Smiling, he backed off, hands in the air in an 'okay, okay' gesture and followed her out the main entrance and down the steps. He'd parked a pool car right at the entrance, but Nikita, eyes alert as ever, saw that Ali Khan was idling in one of his taxis at the bottom of the car park. Nikki waited till Sajid moved round to the driver's side and then ran down towards the waiting taxi. She'd got twenty yards when she felt strong arms round her waist, lifting her up and swirling her round. 'Really, Nikki? Really?' Sajid raised his voice and bellowed down the car park 'Fuck off, Ali. You can do a Thelma and Louise another day.'

The last thing she saw as she was deposited in the back of the pool car and locked in was Ali disappearing with a big smile and a wave in her direction. *Fuck, fuck, fuck, fuck, fuck!*

Chapter 18

The annoying DJ had been getting on Charlie's nerves. Old-fashioned songs, old-fashioned gags and an annoying laugh that grated. Haqib, on the other hand, had found it funny and insisted they tune into it from his bed too. Like it hadn't been bad enough with it drifting from the old bloke in the next bed. Realising it was his way of distracting himself from the operation he was waiting for, she gave in. What the hell was it with her mum, though? Why couldn't she just have stayed with Haqib? He needed her right now. Not later on. Typical of her mum to leave it up to Marcus to pick up the pieces. Charlie suspected that her mum was heading off to do some damage to Deano or Franco or both, and much as she relished the thought of them getting their comeuppance, she wished for *once* her mum would get her priorities right and not leave her, yet again, to be 'mum' in one of the crises the Parekh family seemed to find itself in with such regular monotony.

'*... In a local news update, Khalid Abadi has been identified as the ophthalmic student whose remains were excavated from the Odeon car park last week ...*'

Haqib was happy slagging off the newsreader whose heavy Yorkshire accent seemed to amuse him. In truth, Charlie thought it was very similar to their own accents, but she was happy to go along with it if it kept his mind off his missing appendage. Marcus just ruffled Haqib's hair and told him to stop being an arse. That was the thing with Marcus, he didn't get all het up about stuff … not like her mum did, anyway.

'… *was married to one of Bradford's golden girls, Detective Sergeant Nikki Parekh, better known for infiltrating a child grooming ring in the district and bringing …*'

'Shh!' Charlie's voice rattled out cold as ice and Haqib froze mid-sentence and they both turned to stare at Marcus as the reporter droned on about her mum. Charlie slumped in the uncomfortable plastic visitor's chair, trying to work out what she'd just heard. 'Did you …?'

But Marcus was already shaking his head. *Typical fucking Mum.* Charlie took shallow breaths, her stomach twisted into a ball of fire. Flames flickered, licking and lapping at her insides, sending painful sparks up her body into her throat. *My mum was married?*

'… *discover why Parekh didn't file a missing persons report in 2003. DS Nikita Parekh is unavailable to comment.*'

Charlie understood what that meant. They thought her mum had done it. Murdered this bloke … her dad? The one she'd been told her mother barely knew. Her mum had always made out he was little more than a sperm donor. Her mum had been *married* to him? *What the hell?* The importance of the second part of the story kicked in at the 'no missing persons report'. Shit! Had she done it? Had her mum killed this man, and more to the point was he her dad?

She glanced at Marcus again. 'You sure you knew nowt about this?'

His fingers rasped over his stubble, his eyes filled with pain as he shook his head. She turned to Haqib. 'And you? Did you know?'

'Fuck no. 'Course not. I'd have told you, girl. Shit, you know I would.'

Charlie nodded. Haqib would never have been able to keep

something this important secret. The slightest bit of pressure and he'd spilled everything about the MDMA and Deano. No, this was clearly an 'adult' secret. The thing was, this must be *her* dad – it had to be, the timing was too close. She sat up straight, extinguishing the fire in her gut with a layer of ice. She put up with a lot from her mum. Looked after the kids, gave her the freedom to crack on with her job. Hell, she was proud of her kick-ass mum, who'd overcome all sorts to get where she was. But *this*? This was something else. She didn't think for one minute she'd be able to forgive this. All those years of thinking it was her and her mum and the Rubster and Sunni against the world. All these years of thinking she didn't have a dad and now she found out her mum had been married. Nikita Parekh, the most independent woman she'd ever come across, had been married to her dad. That meant something.

For a second, she debated dialling her on her burner phone and then she shook her head. No point. Over the phone her mum could just spill out the lies she'd fed her for the last fourteen years. No, she was done with that. Done with the lies. Done with her mother.

Rubbing her arm across her face, she looked at Haqib as a porter and nurse arrived to transport him down to surgery. She managed a wobbly smile and patted his arm. 'You'll be right. I'll be here when you come back and so will your mum.'

He grabbed her hand. 'You know she didn't do owt wrong, Charlie, don't you? Your mam, she didn't do owt wrong. I don't care what that bitch on't radio says, she didn't do owt wrong. She wouldn't, not Auntie Nikki.'

Summoning up a smile she didn't feel, Charlie nodded, 'I know that Haqs. Now off you go and get your pinkie sewed back on.'

He laughed. 'You mean my brownie, don't you?'

It wasn't funny – not really, but Charlie felt a gurgle of laughter splutter up her chest and out of her mouth. 'Idiot.'

Chapter 19

'You're kidding right? You're gonna traipse me through my police station like some sort of criminal?'

They were parked in the off-road car park dedicated to the police station. Trafalgar House was situated on Nelson Street just up from the city centre. It was a huge four-storey sandstone structure trying unsuccessfully to blend in with the surrounding buildings, but looking too much like a newer, brawnier, more powerful fortress on the top of the hill in contrast with its more weathered neighbours.

Sajid grinned. 'If you act like an idiot, then I'll have to, won't I? If, on the other hand, you walk in like a normal officer, then we can do this low key. Choice is yours.'

Nikki scowled. 'Et tu, Brute?'

Throwing back his head, Sajid released a rumbling laugh. 'Always the drama queen. Just get out the car, Nikki, and we can walk in like we do every day. Guilt-tripping isn't gonna work on me.'

With bad grace, Nikki climbed out of the back seat and, resigned to her fate, shrugged her shoulders and strutted towards the entrance. 'Come on then, let's get it done.'

As soon as they were inside the station, she headed, without being told, to the interview rooms on the second floor, Sajid trailing behind like a hulking great bodyguard. *Waste of damn time, this.* Nikki wanted to get in, get it done and get back out on the streets again. Whilst she was wasting her time on this, who knew what Deano and Franco and his thugs were getting up to? She hadn't expected to bump into The Spaniel until she reached the interview room, but there she was, like a miserable guard dog waiting for her, hackles up, tail between her legs. 'Well, there she is. Nikita Parekh, Bradford police's golden girl for diversity and closing her cases quickly. Look at her now – reduced to being a murder suspect in her own station.'

A sergeant for years with little hope of promotion on account of her acute laziness, DS Springer was a pillock of the most massive proportions. Nikki turned and, unable to stop herself, raised her middle finger.

Springer started a slow hand clap. Nikki was mollified to observe that most of the other officers scurried about doing their business, ignoring her. Nikki wasn't the most gregarious of officers. Something that came up with annoying regularity on her professional development aims. But Nikki didn't see the point in playing nice for the sake of it. Wasted time in her opinion. Not that she was rude – well, not all the time anyway. Just not up for meaningless idle chit-chat. Still, it was reassuring to see that not everyone was taking gratuitous enjoyment from her current predicament. With it hitting the local news, Nikki was well aware that the grapevine would have disseminated the information through Trafalgar House quicker than a dose of the shits through a muslin cloth.

Saj told her Archie wanted to see her before her meeting and Nikki hoped her colleague would keep his trap shut about her little altercation with Springer downstairs. She was sure antagonising her accuser wasn't something Archie would be overly impressed with. The lifts were those silent ones that, in the absence of rumbles, made Nikki think she was in some sort of *Back to the Future* meets *Star Wars* themed contraption. That was the reason she usually took the stairs.

'You gonna tell me where the Jag is, then?' Saj was persistent.

Nikki snorted. Why should she? They were supposed to be partners. Partners didn't do this shit to each other. She'd make him sweat a bit more. 'Think I've forgotten, but I seem to remember there were metal crushers and car wrecks all over the place. Maybe I'll remember later.' She marched out of the swishy lift doors, flinging over her shoulder, '… maybe not.'

DCI Archie Hegley was standing outside his office, arms folded across his chest, floral pink tie flipped over his shoulder, bald head gleaming in the overhead lighting, the two strips of greying hair at either side sticking up like devils' horns. 'Where the bloody hell dae ye think you've been, Parekh! This is no damn time to go prancing off on yer own like bloody Calamity Jane.' His Scottish burr was more pronounced than usual as he spoke. Another sure sign that he was off kilter.

As she strode towards him, Nikki saw Springer and her sidekick enter the interview room further down the corridor, so she kept her expression bland. 'Afternoon, sir. Lovely to see you.'

'Pht, don't gie me that "lovely to see you shit". I ken damn fine when ye're taking the proverbials and I willnae hae it, Parekh. Get your damn butt in that room and get yerself off the CCU's suspect list, right now.'

Nikki was well used to Archie's 'proverbials'. They covered a multitude of sins that were left open to interpretation. She gave a single nod and made to enter the room but as she passed him, he grabbed her arm. 'Would've been good to ken in advance you were married to a deid man.'

Nikki stopped and looked up at her boss. His ruddy face was strained, lines around his mouth and across his forehead told her he was concerned, so she moderated her response. 'Would've been good if I'd realised the man I'd married hadn't done a runner …' She shrugged. 'My bad, eh?'

Hegley squeezed her arm and nodded. 'We're with you on this, Nikki lass. Me and Sajid have your back.'

Sajid murmured something that sounded a bit like, 'Not if there's so much as a scratch on my Jag.'

Hegley turned and tutted, making the younger man grin. 'Only kidding.'

The byplay between the two men relaxed Nikki. Her shoulders lowered and the tightness across her chest eased. She wasn't on her own and that was a good, if unfamiliar, feeling for her.

'Just be nice, won't you? Don't back chat like you usually do, eh? Answer their questions and then move on,' said Archie, biting his lip.

Not sure how to answer that, Nikki managed a reluctant half smile. Did Archie really think she was going to give her account and then back out gracefully? Did he expect her to just hand this over to the CCU? For fifteen years she'd lived with the understanding that she'd been ditched and left to bring up her child single-handedly because the love of her life chose his family's money over her. Now she realised what a cock-up she'd made of things. How her mistake had impacted every decision, every choice, every action she'd made since. How the brittle, untrusting person she was now had been as a result of Khalid's disappearance and her skewed analysis of it. Every layer he'd unwrapped in their short time together had been rewelded with a soldering iron so hot, her heart had become untouchable. No way would she leave this to the CCU. No damn way!

With Sajid and Hegley following, she walked along the corridor, pushed the door to Interview Room One open and went in. The room wasn't used very often. It was one of the ones used for more sensitive interviews and Nikki was grateful for that. That fact alone told her that either Hegley had insisted or the CCU were prepared to offer her some latitude on account of her rank and history. A faint citrus smell mingled with the aroma of coffee and aftershave was welcome – reassuring. No body odour and

106

vomit undertones. They were, it seemed, not going to drag her over the coals. Springer, wearing a beige suit, hair tied in a bun, ready smile on her face, sat beside a younger, skinny man with a combover and a large nose. Nikki's previous optimism drained away from her. For some reason Springer seemed to feel personally affronted that Nikki had blown open DCI Jacob Kowalski's sordid history. At the time Nikki had wondered if Springer and Kowalski had been more than just colleagues, but that suspicion had never been proven. Nevertheless, Nikki suspected this interview might not flow as smoothly as Archie wanted.

Hegley and Nikki sat on the opposite side of the table with Sajid taking up position on a plastic chair by the wall behind them.

Springer's smile was easy – a fact that set Nikki on high alert. 'We'll be recording the session.' She signalled to her colleague to set up the recording and Nikki sat straight backed until they were ready to continue.

For the tape, Springer introduced them before continuing. 'You waive your right to a solicitor at the moment or a union representative?'

Hegley butted in. 'I'm representing her for now. If necessary, we will terminate and get a solicitor then. Shouldn't be necessary though, should it?'

Nikki glanced at Hegley. Despite his admonishment to her not to be arsey, his tone had been pugilistic. It was then that she realised he was more concerned about this interview than he'd let on. Maybe it wasn't going to be as straightforward as she'd thought.

Springer smiled. 'If DS Parekh can satisfy us, then of course it shouldn't be necessary.' She turned to Nikki. 'Shall we begin? We need to clarify a few things about your husband.'

Her smile this time seemed less friendly as she pushed a photograph across the table. 'Can you confirm that this is your husband, Khalid Abadi.'

Nikki glanced at it, refrained from reaching out to touch his face. It was a picture she'd taken of Khal on Haworth Moor. He was laughing, head thrown back, throat exposed, eyes sparkling – 'Doing a Heathcliff'. There were two copies of the print that she knew of. One he'd sent to his parents and one she kept in a locked box in her bedroom. She assumed Khalid's dad had given this one to the police. 'Yes, that's Khal.'

'Your husband?'

Nikki's eyes narrowed. 'Yes, my husband.'

Springer pushed a copy of a marriage certificate over the table. 'This is your marriage certificate?'

'Yes.'

'When did you last see Khalid … alive?'

The slight pause between his name and the word 'alive' wasn't lost on Nikki, but she wasn't going to rise to the bait. 'The last time I saw Khalid, was when he left to go for a drink at the Mannville Arms on 5th November 2003.'

'That's very precise?'

'Well it would be, wouldn't it? It was the last time I saw him.'

'He didn't return that night?'

Biting down a frustrated sigh, Nikki took a second before replying. 'No. I think I've now said that in three different ways. Can we move on? I've got work to do.'

Springer exchanged a glance with Bashir that clearly held some significance for the pair of them, but was lost on Nikki. She didn't play mind games and she couldn't be arsed with them pussy-footing around the bushes. Why couldn't they just get a move on?

'You're keen to get off. Doesn't it concern you that the husband *you* failed to report as missing, has now been discovered to have been murdered and dumped, fifteen years ago? You weren't worried about him?'

'No, Khal had many friends. He sometimes stayed over with them when he'd had a bit to drink.'

'But he didn't come back the next night or the next?'

'No.'

'You didn't search for him?'

Nikki slapped her hand on the table. Hearing Hegley fidget beside her, she took a deep breath. 'Of course I looked for him. I phoned round his mates, asked at college. Nobody had seen him. Nobody knew where he was.' From her pocket, she took out a scribbled list of names she'd made in the car on the way to the station and pushed it across the table. 'These are as many of our friends as I can remember from then.'

Bashir took it, flattened it with his palm and inserted it into the back of his notebook with barely a cursory glance.

'You were married only three months before Khalid disappeared?'

Nikki knew exactly where she was going with this but could do nothing about it. 'Yes, that's right.'

'So, your new husband disappeared after being married to you for a scant three months?'

Springer had managed to imbue the word 'disappeared' with a sinister implication and it took all of Nikki's willpower not to slap her face. So much for the good vibes she'd felt at the start of the interview. 'Yes.'

'You didn't think it was strange that he just disappeared?'

'No.'

'After only three months of marriage you didn't think it strange that your new husband had disappeared without trace?'

Nikki bit the inside of her cheek hard, to stop her letting fly with a venomous outpouring. She tasted blood and somehow its bitterness calmed her. 'His family were unhappy with his choice of wife.' Nikki spoke through gritted teeth. 'He was torn – unhappy. They'd chosen to disown him. To cut him out of their lives completely. I thought he'd chosen them. His passport was gone.'

'His father says you were the one who wanted him to cut ties with his family.'

Nikki inhaled sharply, her face pale. 'Never. *Never* in a million years would I have asked that of Khal. Never.'

'Still, you weren't concerned enough to remain at your house until we came to interview you? Getting to the bottom of your husband's murder wasn't of concern to you?'

Nikki's fists tightened on her thighs, her heart beat a tattoo against her chest bone. 'Of course it concerns me.'

The words 'you idiot', although left unuttered, hung implicit in the pause before she spoke again. 'Khal is the father of my eldest child. I need to be with her. I need to speak with my mother and my sister. All of us thought Khal had given in to pressure from his family and gone back to Ramallah. Speak to the people on that list I've given you – they all thought the same. Do your job instead of hounding me because of a bitter and twisted old man who also didn't report his son missing, and can't let go of the fact his son loved someone who wasn't of his choosing.'

Nikki stood up. 'I'm leaving. If you need me, you have my number.' She scraped her chair back and headed for the door.

'Nikita.' The word left Archie's mouth like pistol fire. 'You need to sit down. Listen to DS Springer.'

Nikki ground to a halt. A quick glance at Sajid told her all she needed to know. The big man couldn't meet her look. They'd set her up. Fists bunched, jaw tight, she turned and glared at Springer, enjoying the slight power she gained from her elevated position.

Springer waved a hand at the chair opposite. A tic fluttering under her eye, the only indication of her annoyance. 'Sit.'

Pure venom spewed from Nikki's eyes, holding the other woman's gaze, challenging her to escalate things. Archie cursed under his breath and then growled. 'For fuck's sake, Parekh, sit down and stop this pissing contest. There's more testosterone from you two than in a rugby scrum.'

Nikki spun the chair round and straddled it, leaning her arms across the back, glaring at Springer. 'Well?'

Despite her prickly demeanour, her legs were shaking. This wasn't going well and she was anxious to get going.

'You are suspended from duty until this investigation is complete. You're lucky we're not detaining you.' Springer sniffed, a hoity-toity sniff that grated across Nikki's cheek as if she'd been slapped.

'You're kidding, right?' Nikki looked from Archie to Sajid and then back to Springer again. 'You're suspending me? On what grounds? You think I offed Khal, buried him in that car park and then jollied on with the next fifteen years of my life? When I was called to the scene did you see me run? Was there any indication whatsoever that I knew the identity of that skeleton?'

Her chest was heaving and her words were spilling out. She couldn't stop them if she tried. 'It's this sort of incompetent detecting that lets the criminals run rough-shod over the police in Bradford. This sort of *pick on your own* mentality is ineffective. It's so damn easy to focus on us whilst the real criminals are out there. So safe to do your investigations from inside Trafalgar House – never getting your Jimmy Choos sullied by treading in the shit on the streets.'

She stood up and marched to the door. 'Suspend me all you like, but let me just point out something to you, because with your Spaniel nose so far up your own arse you won't see it. Two years ago, when the Sunbridge Wells tunnels were first being excavated, a skeleton was discovered then too – possible link, eh?'

Archie lumbered to his feet and shook his head. 'Well done, Springer. You dealt with that nicely.'

He turned to Nikki. 'Should've bloody muzzled you. Now get out. I want a word before you go.'

Cheeks hot, adrenaline fizzing like acid in her veins, Nikki barely managed an abrupt nod before she yanked the door open and stepped into the corridor and nearly banged straight into a uniformed officer who was clearly unsure whether to interrupt the heated argument he could undoubtedly hear from just outside the door.

Nikki made to sidestep him just as he stepped in all red-faced and flustered. 'They've found another one.'

Springer, voice cool, with only a slight tremor to indicate that Nikki had rattled her, questioned, 'What?'

Nikki stopped and spun round. 'Another skeleton? Where?'

The young officer's face became redder as he glanced hopelessly between his superior officer and the rather indignant Parekh. Nikki saved him the trouble of deciding who to answer by throwing her hands up in the air and backing off a little. No point in intimidating the lad when she could just listen to what he told Springer.

'It's at the opposite end of the car park. Nearer to the Chinese restaurant. Builders say that area was last dug up around eight years ago.'

Nikki, unable to keep quiet, said. 'So, more bones. This time buried only eight years ago. You still suspending me?'

She raised her chin and straightened up, her expression one of gloating superiority.

Springer glanced at Bashir and gave a slight nod. He picked up Nikki's warrant card and held it out to her.

Stepping forward, hand outstretched, Nikki made to take it, just as Bashir dropped it on the floor, with an exaggerated 'Oops'.

'Tosser.' Nikki bent over and picked it up, then, stuffing it back in her pocket, she wiggled a few fingers at them and said, 'ta-ra', before turning to leave.

Springer placed her knuckles on the desk and glowered. 'Steer clear of my investigation, Parekh. This is off limits to you. Understood?'

But before Parekh could respond, Archie hustled her out of the door, saying over his shoulder, 'Understood.'

Once outside, he took off striding down the corridor. 'My office.'

The set of his shoulders told Nikki her day was about to get even worse.

112

'Come on. Don't make things worse than they are.' Sajid nudged her.

Nikki jerked her arm away. 'Fuck off, prick.'

With an exaggerated sigh, Sajid headed along the corridor after their boss, leaving Nikki to take up the rear like a dog who'd been whipped into submission as she did the walk of shame through the large room leading to Archie's office.

Chapter 20

Deano was rattled. He hadn't shown Franco just how rattled he was, but now that he'd been allowed to leave the car, his entire body throbbed. His limbs shook, his throat ached, his head was fuzzy and his thoughts were slow and dream-like. Could you get brain damage through lack of oxygen even if you never lost consciousness? It was like someone had injected him with a fizzy drink and it was surging through him like wildfire.

When he went to light his fag, he could barely flick the lighter. His thumb wouldn't stay still until finally it did. He inhaled the smoke and immediately began to cough as it stung the back of his throat. He rubbed his neck, wincing as he tried to swallow. Swollen and dry, he looked at his roll-up and then threw it in the gutter where it fizzled out. Things were desperate for him. He needed to distance himself from Franco. Needed to get some protection in place, but how? Nikki Parekh could help. But of course, she wouldn't. She hated him almost as much as she hated Franco. She'd told him to leave and she meant it. There was no way back once you'd earned Parekh's disapproval.

He needed to find a way to speak to her without Franco, Big Zee or Tyke finding out about it and *that* was a near impossible task. They had so much on everyone in the area, those lot.

Everyone was scared of them. Everyone scrambling over each other trying their best to wangle favour. Piling the shit on someone else and watching them wade through it was sometimes the only way to survive. As long as Franco's eyes were on some other poor sod, you'd be okay.

The rain was starting up again, slapping in great big globules on the pavement, soaking Deano as he walked, shoulders hunched, hands in pockets. This was shite. Why had he come back? Why had he let himself get embroiled with Franco again? All for a quick buck or two. Thing was, the shit they were putting in the streets wasn't pure. Who knew what it had been laced with, but kids throughout the district were ending up in hospital on the back of Franco's MDMA. Not that Deano cared. If the brats were daft enough to OD on ecstasy, that was their problem. All he worried about was trying to distance himself from Franco so that when *he* went down, Deano could come out smelling of the proverbial roses. Franco wouldn't go down without a fight, but Deano had stuff on him. The trouble was he couldn't end up in the nick. Not Armley or Wakefield. He huffed. Probably not anywhere. Franco's contacts were all over the shop.

All Deano needed was a bit of leeway. A chance to get Franco locked up for long enough for Deano to slip away somewhere hot with the money he'd siphoned off. But, to do that, he had to get Parekh on board without Franco finding out. He neared his mum's house and glanced around. There were eyes everywhere – behind curtains, in a car just along the street, the two lads hanging near the ginnel. All of them were in Franco's employ and none of them would think twice about sending him down. He'd already been far too near the edge with Franco. He ran his fingers along the swollen welt that decorated his neck. He wondered if Parekh had got her scar the same way – if so, she was lucky to be alive. His bruising would go in a week or ten days tops. If what Franco had said about Haqib was true, Parekh would be even more enraged and she'd blame him. He *knew* she would.

Dipping his head to the 16-year-old in the souped-up Honda and waving his hand at the kid on the corner, Deano opened the gate and slouched up the path. He'd just have to be inventive and already an idea was forming. There was one sure way to get Parekh here and make it look like he'd nowt to do with it. All he needed to do was set it up. Abruptly, he spun round on his heel and retraced his steps down the path. First things first, he needed to make a wee visit to the offie's – get in some of the hard stuff and then hopefully his stepdad would do the rest.

Chapter 21

Archie gestured to his office door as Sajid and Nikki entered. 'Shut it.'

Sitting behind his desk, his face was marred by a ruddy scowl as he tapped his fingers on the desk. He leaned over, picked up the photo of his wife and kids, studied it for a few seconds and then replaced it, before standing up and walking over to the larger window wall that looked out into a large open-plan office space beyond.

The room was packed and Nikki didn't need telling that the 'busyness' on the other side of the glass was due to office gossip about her. She shrugged it off. She was used to it. Mixed-race working-class women didn't usually hit the giddy ranks of sergeant so young. She'd earned it though. Nearly lost her life earning it in fact, so she was damned if she'd apologise to those who resented her success. She worked hard and got results, so as far as she was concerned, they could sod right off. She did wish that Archie would shut the blinds though. Last thing she wanted was that lot to see her getting a rollicking, and Archie's rollick-ings, although few and far between, were notoriously loud and pithy, with plenty of 'proverbials' in them.

She was on edge. Her left leg kept jiggling and she was aware of Sajid glancing at it. *Trust him to notice!* She needed to be out there sussing out what had happened to Khal, talking to her daughter about her dad, facing her mum and sister who wouldn't understand why she'd run off like that. And, of course, there was Haqib's little problem to fix. Why did she always have to be the one to sort everything out? Huh, who was she kidding? It was her that sorted stuff because Anika was unable to and her mother had been through too much already. But before she could be there for her family, she had to sort out Deano and Franco.

Glowering, she shrank into the chair, shoulders hunched, head forward. She pressed her hand on her leg and willed it to be still. While she focused on it, the jiggling stopped, but as soon as she moved her hand, it started up again.

Archie began pacing the room, his gaze periodically landing with a scorching scowl on Nikki. When he spoke, his voice boomed out and reverberated around the room making both Nikki and Sajid jump. 'Right, Parekh. You nearly got yersel suspended. We were hoping for a "confined tae desk duty" but *yer* damn temper put paid tae that, so now you've made yersel subject to intense scrutiny. It's only by the skin of yer teeth that you managed to avoid being out on yer proverbials. But, hear me now, loud *and* clear.'

Nikki suspected they could hear him in City Hall. His voice crashed into her with all the power of a lorry, hammering each point home, making her want to flinch. Instead she held firm, her chin lifted, accepting each hurled word with no expression.

'This means yer off this case completely. *Nae* crossing paths wi' Springer and Bashir. *Nae* fancy footing around thinking ye can dae stuff under the radar when we all know yer idea of subtle involves flying mallets and luminous Lycra. Got it?'

Nikki, still reeling after her encounter with Springer and Bashir and with her head full of thoughts weaving and interweaving around, just wanted the barrage to stop, but Archie wasn't finished.

'You need to take some gardening leave, Nikki. Regroup, refocus and realise you need to rein it in sometimes.'

Gardening leave? Archie was sending her home. Her cheeks were warm and she knew this would be reflected in their colour. She dreaded leaving the room and moving through the officers waiting with bated breath outside – enjoying the side show. Some of them – a few of them – would be sympathetic but some of them would relish this, savour it and dine out on the tale of Parekh getting her *proverbials* from Auld Man Hegley.

Hegley puffed out his cheeks like a blow fish and exhaled. He marched back to the window, glared at the sea of faces peering inside not wanting to miss any of the drama and with a flick of his wrist dropped the blinds. Why the hell couldn't he have done that earlier and saved her some embarrassment?

More leisurely now he wandered back to his desk and allowed his heavy frame to fall onto his chair making it roll backwards with the impact. Propelling it forward till his legs were under the desk and his elbows resting on top, he laid his head in his hands before speaking in a whisper. 'Right. I'll give ye Sajid – off the record. You see what ye can dig up on your ain about Khalid's disappearance. But I dinnae want to see yer skinny arse in Trafalgar House.'

Nikki frowned, what the hell was he talking about? *Sajid? Off the record?* Then she got it. It had all been an act … a show for the rest of the station. At that precise moment she could have kissed him. The stain of humiliation faded. Archie not only had her back, but he was giving her permission to investigate Khal's death too. She nodded and ignored Sajid's mumbled, 'Maybe I'll get my damn Jag back now, then.'

'You won't be sorry, Archie. I promise you won't be sorry.'

'Hmph, just keep your heid doon and keep yer proverbials away from Springer, okay? I'm not getting my bollocks in a vice because of you. Clear?'

'Crystal.' Nikki was on her feet and heading to the door.

'Hey, wait a minute. What's that about another skeleton at Sunbridge Wells?'

Hand on the door, Nikki turned back to her boss. 'It was a couple of years ago. Was put down as death by misadventure, I think. Yardley dealt with it. At the time it looked like a student had got pissed and fell into a hole when they were doing the first part of the City Park excavations around ten years ago. The hole got filled in but the body wasn't discovered till they were doing · re-excavations. It just occurred to me when Springer was mouthing off in there. That woman wants to tie things up in a bow. She's not going to put herself out for this.' She paused and sniffed. 'Think it warrants another look now, in light of Khalid's death and the discovery of more remains. Might be nowt, but we can't be too sure.'

She pressed the door handle down and pretended she didn't see the look that Archie and Sajid exchanged. It was a 'keep an eye on her' sort of look and it irked her. Archie meant well but she could look after herself. She didn't need Sajid to watch over her. Especially as he might get wind of Haqib's involvement with Deano. He'd turned a blind eye to Haqib's weed possession in the past, but this was a completely different ball game.

Walking into the outer office, the room fell silent. A quick appraisal of the situation told her that her earlier summary had been accurate. The few that were revelling in her fall from grace stared her out, grins on their arrogant faces, whilst the ones she could count on as friends kept their heads down or offered sympathetic smiles.

Refusing to interact with either camp, Nikki straightened her spine and marched down the middle of the room, with Sajid following. The bastards wouldn't see her look weak.

Chapter 22

A part of him had been ripped out – all hope doused like a candle snuffed – and Burhan Abadi wasn't used to that sensation. Apart from when Khalid had flouted his authority regarding his relationship with Nikita, he'd always been in control. In control of his wife, his business, his family and now, no matter how difficult, he had to rise to the challenge again. Despite being in another country with all its strange customs and ways, Burhan Abadi had the means at his disposal to pay for anything he wanted. Right now, he was praying for guidance from Allah. Should he allow the British authorities to deal with Nikki Parekh or should he take matters into his own hands?

His gut told him to inflict every punishment imaginable on the woman. Make her pay for robbing him of his son. Springer and Bashir had said that they'd released her. The discovery of new remains near to where they'd discovered Khalid's remains led them to believe they had a murderer with multiple victims and that didn't, at the moment, implicate the whore.

What he had to decide was how responsible she was. If not for her, Khalid would have returned to Ramallah, and taken over the business from him. Instead he'd remained in Bradford, insistent that he would not leave Parekh, would not return to his obligations. His absence had forced Burhan to rethink his plans for the family business. He'd been left with no option but to try to groom Khalid's cousin, Omar for the role. A decision that he regularly had cause to regret. The boy was lazy and, worse than that, he was stupid. More eager to spend money than make it – a key failing in a financial business, and one that Burhan was constantly having to navigate around.

Then there was Enaya. Because of *that* woman, Enaya had been tortured. She'd taken to her bed for months when Khalid refused to leave Bradford and even now, all these years later, she suffered with her nerves. Didn't he owe it to his wife to seek revenge?

He rolled his prayer mat up and propped it by his suitcase before taking out his phone. Just one phone call could set things off in one direction. The question was, should he or shouldn't he? If he chose to, there would be no going back and he'd have to live with that for the rest of his life. Could he do that in all conscience? He closed his eyes, the weight of the phone heavy in his palm. The only positive thing he could offer Enaya was a grandchild – Khalid's child. If he presented her with Charlie or Aadab perhaps that would be enough to help her recover from the loss of her son. He would make sure that Nikita Parekh was followed. He'd find out everything he could to disgrace her and he'd take Charlie away. That was his plan … the only way forward that would satisfy his thirst for revenge. However, if the British courts looked like they would not apply a harsh enough sentence on Parekh, then it would only take a single phone call to make sure he got the sort of revenge he thirsted for.

Chapter 23

Sajid was happy to let Nikki lead the way as she left Trafalgar House and made a beeline for the car park. Sandwiched between the lights from the offices on her left and the white LED street-lights on her right, Nikki beat a determined path towards the pool car they'd parked up earlier. It was easy to tell that, despite the reprieve she'd been given and Archie's unexpected bending of the rules, she was still in a mood. Her shoulders were up, her head down with her ponytail bouncing as she trudged through puddles uncaring that they splashed up and speckled her jeans.

To those that didn't know her well, it could seem like Nikki could stay in a mood for hours. Sajid, however, was well aware that her mood would be short-lived, replaced almost impercep-tibly by an intensity that only those closest to her would correctly identify as resolve. The trouble with Nikki was she took everything too damn seriously. She couldn't take even a momentary step back from something. No, Nikki tackled each and every problem head on and with a ferocity and drive that left others wondering how she coped. Sajid, on the other hand, knew exactly how she coped. It was through sheer grit and determination, often at her own expense.

Thinking about Marcus and Nikki's domestic issues made him

remember his own. Langley was still pissed off that Saj found it difficult to be open about their relationship. If Langley had been brought up in a traditional Muslim household like he had, he'd understand how difficult it was to be up front about being gay. Last thing he needed though was to fuck this up. Langley was his rock and he didn't want to push him away. A small nagging voice whispered in his ear, 'Why do you do it then, Saj?' He pushed the thought away and focused on Nikki.

In light of the recent discovery that she'd once been married, Sajid wondered if perhaps he'd worked out the root cause for her single-mindedness, her obsession with being in control at all times and her inability to let her feckless sister's family fend for themselves. Archie gave Nikki a certain latitude. She'd proven herself and Archie was keen to give his detectives the opportunity to work in the way best suited to them. Which was why Sajid often ended up with Nikki. Their pairing was a match of opposites. His calm dogged perseverance tempered her impetuosity. Saj was well aware that his bulk also meant she could push buttons a lot harder with him around – he had her back, always.

'Hey, Nikki, you gonna tell me wh—?'

Before he had the chance to finish his sentence, she rounded on him, eyes flashing, mouth curled. 'You think I'm telling you where your Jag is after all that?' She wafted her hand towards the police building. 'Judas!'

She spun round on her heel and skipped past two other pool cars to reach the one they'd used earlier.

Sajid shrugged. 'Actually, I *was* going to ask why you were at the hospital, but since you've brought it up, where is my damn Jag?'

Yanking the driver's door open, Nikki tutted, before sliding into the seat and slamming the door shut. She adjusted the seat so she was pulled right up to the steering wheel, her chin practically touching it. *She could do with a kid's car seat!* Climbing into the passenger side, Sajid took his time getting comfortable and slipping his seat belt on, before crossing his arms in front of him and staring out the windscreen.

Nikki twisted towards him. 'Well?'

'Well, what?'

From the corner of his eye, Sajid saw her exaggerated eye roll, and smothered a smile. Sometimes she was like a damn schoolkid.

She extended her hand, palm upwards, 'Keys. Unless of course you want to bundle me into the back like a damn criminal again.'

Unfolding his arms, Sajid scrabbled in his coat pocket for a minute and then dangled them just out of her reach. Nikki scowled, but made no attempt to grab them.

'You want the keys, Parekh, you gotta start sharing. We're investigating this under the wire. So, where are we going?'

Nikki tapped her fingers on the steering wheel and fidgeted. When she spoke her tone was flat, almost robotic. 'I've got stuff to do. I'll drop you off by your precious car and then we'll meet up with fresh eyes tomorrow.'

Sajid thought about that for a minute. 'Nah, that's not gonna work for me. Don't want Archie to string me up by the proverbials now, do we?'

A smile flashed across Nikki's face and then vanished. 'You really want me to answer that one, do you?'

Sajid threw back his head and laughed. Thank God the tension was broken. Now he and Nikki could talk. 'Look, me and Archie know you haven't got anything to do with Khalid's death – goes without saying really. That's why he's letting you have a free rein – for now.' He let the words 'for now' hang between them before continuing. 'We need to sit down and work through a plan of action, but I get the feeling you've got your own agenda. You need to let me in, Nik. Need to play nice with me.'

Nikki nodded, exhaling a breath as she did so, her fingers gripping the steering wheel as if to ground her. Sajid stretched out a hand and squeezed her arm. 'This is a lot to take in, Nikki – too much. You've had a shock. I say we go to the Mannville

Arms for a drink and you tell me all about your Khalid. He's Charlie's dad, isn't he?'

Tight lipped, Nikki nodded once. 'Yes, he's Charlie's dad.'

He handed her the keys. 'Right, let's go.'

But Nikki shook her head. 'I can't.' Her voice was strained. 'I've got summat to sort out first. I'll drop you at the Jag and then do my thing. We'll meet up tomorrow.'

There it was! Sajid had been waiting to find out what had been so important as to make Nikki hot tail it out of her house instead of staying to clear her name. 'Uh uh, no chance. I can do without my Jag for a bit longer. We'll do whatever you have to do first and then you can take me to my car where we *will* do a microscopic examination of the bodywork. So, spill.'

Nikki slotted the key into the ignition and started the car, but instead of driving off, she put it in neutral, fiddled with the heater and pushed her seat back. 'It's that bloody little idiot Haqib.'

The words Haqib and idiot in one sentence together were no surprise to Sajid. Nikki often used such descriptors for her nephew, but this time it was different. Her tone was different and the way her leg kept bobbing up and down told him it was serious. Injecting a calming tone to his voice, Sajid said, 'I repeat, spill!'

Nikki directed her gaze out the side window as if she couldn't bear to meet her partner's eyes. 'It's that toerag Deano's fault. He never should've brought Franco back here. Never! The pair of them should have stayed in Huddersfield or Halifax or Manchester or wherever they'd gone to.'

Sajid allowed her words to settle. Deano was a thug – a cocky little thug – but Franco was a different game altogether. When Nikki had exposed her boss years earlier, Franco had been on the periphery of the investigation. 'I thought we dealt with Deano, and by extension Franco, last week?'

Nikki shrugged and turned to look at him. Her dark eyes flashed, her brow was furrowed. 'Seems like we either didn't

126

express ourselves strongly enough or Deano doesn't have as much pull with Franco as we'd thought. I thought he'd go the extra mile for us, bearing in mind what we have on him.'

'But he didn't?'

'No … he didn't. They hacked off Haqib's little finger.'

'What? Fuck! Really?' That explained it. Nikki always put family first. 'That was what Charlie phoned about?'

A single nod was all she gave, but that was enough. 'He all right?'

Nikki wiped her nose with the back of her hand and sniffed. 'Yeah, they're sewing it back on. I signed the consent form and then left Charlie in charge.'

'God's sake, Nikita, you can't keep expecting Charlie to take up the slack while you head off into the night like some sort of vigilante cleaning up the streets of Bradford. She's only a kid.'

'Sod off. Not like you have kids, is it? It's fucking hard. I didn't want to leave her, did I? I wanted to be there for both of them, but I did the best I could and Marcus turned up anyway. I need to sort out this Franco/Deano thing before Haqib comes home – he owes them money for MDMA.'

'Yeah, I worked that one out for myself. Kinda realised he didn't owe them for a couple of tenners bags. How much?'

'A thousand maybe.'

Sajid blew out a long low whistle.

'Think he was making an example of him.'

'Nah, you don't say? So, where's the money or the drugs.'

'Idiot hadn't sold owt. Charlie found them and confiscated them and then I found them and confiscated them again. That's why I dealt with Deano. I warned him off.'

'So where are they now, the MDMA?'

'In my knicker drawer.'

'Your *knicker* drawer? You mental, Nik? For fuck's sake.'

'Well, I was waiting till there was a drug raid and I was going to add them to the take.'

'What if Springer or Bashir decide to search your house? What then?'

'All right, all right. Keep your hair on. I'll get rid of them.'

'Just get Haqib to come clean to the police – to us, to uniforms. Say he had second thoughts. He'll get a slap on the wrist that's all.'

'Yeah right. He's Asian. He's from Listerhills. Yeah, he'd get a slap on the wrist but he'd *also* be on the wrong side of one of the gangs on the estate. You know as well as I do that he'd be top of the list every time they needed to hound someone or get information about drugs in the area. I can't do that to him.'

No, Nikki couldn't do that to Haqib. The kid was an idiot, but he was her nephew and that meant something. 'So, what *are* you going to do?'

'Thought I'd apply a bit more pressure on Deano. Franco keeps his nose clean, but Deano must have shit on him. Last time he was a bit reluctant, but who knows, maybe I can change his mind. After all, if Franco's so into amputations, who knows what he'd do if he found out Deano was diddling his baby mama.' She said the last words in a mock American gangster accent.

'Okay, let's go, but you better phone home first.'

'Duh, no phone.'

Sajid rummaged in his coat pocket and brought out Nikki's phone. 'Found it where you left it. Knew you wouldn't damage it, so I had a poke around till I found it.'

Nikki took the phone off him, and turned it over in her hand. 'Who knows?'

'Your mum. She turned up not long after we took Khalid's dad back to the hotel. She's worried about you. She told Anika, who went to pieces as if she was the principal mourner in all of this.'

Nikki nodded. 'Typical really – that's Anika all over.' She looked at her friend. 'Just before you found me, they reported the incident on the hospital news. Named me and Khalid. Charlie and

Haqib were listening to Radio Royal when I was there. What if she heard it?'

Sajid sighed. 'You need to leave Deano for now and sort out your family. That's your priority. Phone your mum to get the heads-up on what's awaiting you at home and then deal with Deano tomorrow. Meanwhile what can I get on with regarding Khalid?'

Nikki handed him a crumpled list from her jeans pocket. It was longer than the one she'd given Springer. 'These are all the folk we hung around with in those days. I don't do social media so I've no idea where most of them are. Apart from Jacko, of course, he's still around ... him and his loopy sister. Locate them and arrange to see them tomorrow. Also, get the post-mortem report on Khalid and access the investigation file on the Sunbridge Wells skeleton and get it printed off – photos, interviews, the lot. We'll go through it all tomorrow from my house.'

Sajid shook his head. 'Uh, huh. No way am I dodging my way round your chaotic family life, leaving sensitive files around, etc. I've cleared it with Langley. We're working from mine and ...' He raised an eyebrow at her. 'I want no smartass comments about the "upper classes" or any of that shite, got it?'

Nikki's lips twitched. 'Okay. Look, I need to drop by BRI anyway, I'll drop you at your car on the way.'

'Good plan. Give my love to Haqib, won't you? Though he'll take that as more of a threat than anything. Still the little toad deserves a bit of hassle for being such an arse.'

'Eh?' Nikki frowned, then nodded. 'Yeah, Haqib – I'll tell him.'

That momentary hesitation spoke volumes and Sajid realised that Nikki wasn't going to BRI to see her nephew. Chances were she was going to the mortuary.

Chapter 24

When I first saw them digging up that area down by the Odeon, I wondered if they'd find the others ... and they have. I'd disposed of them at different times over the years and in slightly different spots – there were always a lot of water leaks and suchlike necessitating a bit of heavy digging. Not that I'm claiming responsibility for all of them – no – some I confess were purely coincidental. First Khalid ... I knew it was him before they released the name. Knew exactly whose bones were deposited where. For years, I'd been pondering how it would make me feel when they found the first one.

Of course, there was that muck-up at Sunbridge Wells a few years back, and the one at the ice rink, but the dozy fuckers didn't seem to make any links. Now though, with finding so many so close together, it's inevitable that they'll realise. Oh, what I would give to be a fly on the wall right now. Looking down at them, seeing them kick themselves when they realise that the Yorkshire Ripper was the least of their worries. All these years and they didn't realise they had me.

Suppose they assume I'm dead or something. Those CSI shows on TV always seem to think that a lengthy break in crimes means the perpetrator is either six foot under or serving a lengthy spell at her majesty's pleasure. Well, I've broken that mould for sure. The thing they don't realise is that some of us are in control of our impulses. Not many, granted. But I am one of those few who keeps everything on a tight rein.

After my dad died a few years back – rotting to death in a prison hospital – the urge hadn't been so strong anymore. His passing had settled things … for a while at least. Maybe now is the time to resurrect my vocation. There's been a fair few I've been tempted to target over the years, but right now I've got my beady eye on someone in particular. My motto has always been 'Why do things by halves and make tiny ripples when you can do things full force and create a tsunami?'

Watch out, Nikita Parekh, the pressure is about to explode. Big time.

BOOM!

Chapter 25

'Do you really have to examine every square inch … it's peeing it down!' Nikki had dropped Sajid beside his car on Toller Lane and was now suffering the humiliation of standing in the rain whilst he did a detailed survey of the entire bodywork using his pencil torch. Getting edgier by the second, she was on the point of storming back into the pool car and tearing down to BRI. However, guilt at swiping Sajid's car in the first place, made her allow him his five minutes of revenge. Sajid always had her back and she'd nicked his precious baby. He deserved a short period of making her suffer.

Once he was done and she was out of Sajid's hearing, she made a quick phone call, so that she was expected and then, with Sajid's various messages for Haqib ringing in her ears, Nikki diverted from her original plan of finding Deano – that could wait till the next day – and instead headed to visit her nephew. When she'd spoken to her mum earlier, she'd been told that the operation had been successful and that he was back on the ward. Her mum's annoyance with Haqib's dad, Yousaf, had crackled over the phone like a firework ready to explode. He'd pleaded commitments with his 'other family', once again leaving Anika to cope on her own. Not that Anika coped very well with life's curve balls either. Earlier, her mum had told her that Haqib, embarrassed by his mum's gushing tears, had sent her home to look after the kids. Charlie and Marcus had stayed for a while, but then been evicted by the nurses at the end of visiting time.

Poor sod. How was Haqib supposed to keep on the straight and narrow when his prime examples were an absent father who doted on his 'other family', a neurotic loopy mother, an auntie who was on his case all the time and a grandma who tried to smooth all of the above over?

Good job he had Charlie.

By pulling her warrant card, she gained access to the ward and headed straight to Haqib's bed. His curtains were half-closed around him so he was invisible from the main walkway between beds. Nikki wondered if she should try to get him into a side room – maybe organise a uniform to stand guard – and then quickly reconsidered. Franco had sent a message – end of. He'd even had the audacity to tell Haqib to head up to BRI to get his finger sewed back on. No doubt he'd already lost interest in Haqib Parekh. Besides, how could she explain to the drug squad about the drugs that she hadn't handed straight over? Haqib was safe here in a busy open ward and he was asleep.

She slid into the plastic chair beside him. His cheeks had a slight glow to them and his bandaged hand was elevated in a slingy type thing. In the floral hospital gown, he looked younger than his fifteen years. *Didn't Anika even think to bring the lad some PJs?* She reached over and smoothed his hair down over his forehead, grinning at the thought of his indignation if she tried that move when he was awake. When he recovered a bit more, he'd be cursing the lack of hair gel to spike his hair up. If she remembered, she'd pack some in a bag for her mum to bring tomorrow.

Standing up, she bent over and kissed his warm forehead, again taking advantage of him sleeping to demonstrate her affection. No point in letting him think she'd gone all mushy. Next time she saw him, she'd be back to her brusque self, back to giving him a hard time and trying to rein in his wayward tendencies.

As she turned to leave, she saw his eyelids flutter. *Little sod was awake!*

'Love you too, Auntie Nikki.'

Nikki shoved her hands in her jacket pocket and, voice gruff, said, 'Yeah, right. That why you keep getting yourself in bother, is it?'

Haqib, still half asleep, grinned. 'You're getting all soft in your old age. Kissing me and smoothing my hair and that.'

She prodded him gently on his good arm. 'Less of the "old age", you little shit. Now get some rest. Someone will be by tomorrow to drop off some more toiletries and stuff.'

'Aw, not me mam. Please not her. She stresses me out. Send Aji-ma, eh?'

'I'll see what I can do.' But he'd already drifted back off to sleep.

Walking back up the ward, Nikki bumped into one of the nurses she'd seen earlier. 'You still here?'

'Yeah, no rest for the wicked.' The nurse smiled but she looked weary. 'Got another hour and a half left. Somebody pulled a sickie, you know how it is.'

Nikki knew exactly how it was. In her line of work, you too stayed on duty till the job was done.

The nurse walked with her towards the door. 'I don't know what's going on out there, but your lad's the third in two weeks with the same injury. They tell us all sorts of crap – got it caught in a car door, dog bit it off and so on, but we know damn fine they're lying. Just thought I'd let you know, you being a copper and all.'

Frowning, Nikki paused. 'Don't suppose you can give me any names?'

The nurse tightened her lips. 'Sorry, patient confidentiality and all that.'

'Yeah, I thought so, but could you at least let me know if any other injuries like that come in? We need to monitor it.' She handed the nurse a card.

134

Leaving Haqib's ward, Nikki made her way downstairs to what she called the bowels of the hospital. She'd phoned Langley Campbell, who'd agreed to meet her in his mortuary. As far as she was concerned the smell down there was worse than any intestinal odour she'd come across – but then she was biased. It wasn't the bodily smells that disturbed her anyway. It was the bleach – that too-clean smell that made her want to vomit. It conjured up all sorts of memories that she worked hard to quell.

As she approached the autopsy suite, Nikki's steps slowed. Did she really want to do this? Wouldn't it be best to remember Khalid how he'd been? So vital, so alive, so passionate and full of love for her. He'd rubbed off all her edgy corners, smoothed them over, got under her defences. She should remember him like that, yet the compulsion to see him for one last time was too strong. She'd misjudged him. Had been too quick to assume he'd betrayed her. She should have known better. She should've known *him* better and now it was too late. For fifteen years she'd allowed her edges to grow back – sharper and more vicious than ever, bitterness and distrust her constant companions. She'd erected a higher, more invincible barrier – higher than the one surrounding The Wreck, deeper than the sewers of Bradford.

At the door, she hesitated. She could walk away, of course she could, but she wouldn't. Khal deserved better than that. Khal deserved her apology. Langley had told her she wouldn't be able to recognise him from the bones, that seeing them wouldn't convince her they belonged to Khal. So, he'd gathered all the other evidence – the DNA, the dental records, the height measurements, the ethnicity measures – everything. Nikki could have told him not to bother. As soon as Khal's dad had turned up accusing her of murdering his son, she'd known. She didn't need science to tell her that Khal lay behind that door. It was as clear as day. He would never have left her, and he certainly would never have left her without a word to let her know he was all right. She *should've* known that. She should have kept faith with the essence of her husband. His love for her and his honesty wouldn't have let him slip away, leaving her in distress.

She pushed open the door and stepped through. Her eyes were drawn immediately to the trolley in the middle of the room … to Khal.

Langley was waiting for her, worry etched across his forehead. 'I'll stay with you, if you like, Nikki.'

But Nikki shook her head. 'Got to do it on my own.'

His voice was quiet but firm when he responded. 'Actually, Nik, you don't. You don't need to do anything on your own. We're here for you, Saj and I.'

Nikki took a deep breath. Langley was always so sensitive. Not that Sajid wasn't, he was. It was just that Langley was a little bit older, had seen a bit more of the world and wasn't scared to express his emotions. Saj on the other hand was always there with a quip and a laugh to lighten any situation. The two of them were a good match. Both handsome in their different ways. Langley was tall and slender. He carried himself with a degree of authority that didn't rely on being muscly.

Langley squeezed one of Nikki's shoulders and turned to the back door that adjoined two separate post-mortem suites. 'Well, I'll leave you to it, but I'm just next door if you need me.'

With heavy steps, Nikki approached what remained of her husband.

He was laid out, all his bones intact. Langley had given her the details of his injuries, so putting her detective's hat on, she let her gaze run down the skeleton. It could have been anyone, but it *wasn't*. It was Khal – her Khal. He was diminished. No matter how delicately he'd been placed, no matter how respectfully he'd been looked after, all that was in front of her now was a pile of bones.

A wave of caustic liquid seared her throat. She swallowed it down, feeling the secondary nipping.

Breathing in through her nose, long and slow, she settled

herself. She could almost pretend it wasn't Khal, that it was some other poor sod … almost, but not quite. It took everything she had to study what was left of him. Moving closer, she focused on picking out the marks and etchings Langley had outlined. As she studied them, she tried to imagine what could have made them. Khalid must have been terrified. Did he cry out for her? Did he beg for mercy? The assumption was that they'd been made when he was alive – what else could they assume? That's how most sick fuckers got off. They'd documented at least twelve puncture sites, but, when pushed, Langley admitted there could have been more – many more –that hadn't hit the bone.

Leaning over she whispered, 'Hi Khal, it's me.'

Raising her hand, she traced her finger over his forehead, his eye sockets, across his cheek bones and his grotesque gaping mouth. They were cold and hard to the touch, yet as her fingers moved, she thought back to the times she'd done this in the past. He'd been warm and vibrant then – full of life – living and breathing. Who had reduced him to this?

Inside her, the angry vat of acid erupted again and hot tears rolled down her cheeks. She lifted a hand and roughly wiped them away, but the gesture was futile, for no sooner had she done so, than they were replaced by more. 'I'm sorry, Khal. I should've known. I should've fucking *known*.'

Her legs wobbled and, scared that they would no longer hold her weight, she slumped onto the chair that Langley had placed next to the trolley. Fifteen years she'd believed he'd let her down. For fifteen years she'd betrayed him by accepting his deceit so readily. What sort of wife had she been? For weeks, he'd been struggling – she'd been all too aware of it. The pressure exerted on him by his father had taken its toll, left him looking gaunt and drawn. The shouted conversations in Arabic, followed by periods of withdrawal, made him distant. His need to find work to supplement their income after his father withdrew the financial help Khalid had been so used to, left him exhausted.

Restaurant work till the early hours of the morning followed by full days struggling to complete his final year dissertation meant there was little time to discuss things.

Nikki had delayed her entry to police training when she discovered her pregnancy, yet she hadn't told him the real reason. Instead, she'd taken a job as front of house staff at the National Media Museum. Things had been strained. They were keeping secrets from each other and look what it had led to.

She pulled her chair closer and rested her hand on his arm. 'I promise you that I *will* find out who did this to you. Whoever deprived you of your life, of seeing your daughter, I *will* make them pay.'

Sitting quietly in the dimmed lights, Nikki allowed her thoughts to drift back to their time together. For so long she'd denied herself the memories, forcing them behind a locked door in the recesses of her mind. Marking them out of bounds. Now, she opened the door and they tumbled out like a flash flood.

'You've got a daughter, Khal. She's beautiful and smart. She's got your eyes – she looks so much like you it hurts. You'd love her. She takes no shit from anyone and she protects her family. Don't know yet who'll get to decide what happens to you now, Khal, but if it's me, I'll do what we always agreed. I promise. You'll stay here, close to me and Charlie. I won't let you go again.'

Afterwards Nikki sat with Langley, sipping coffee. He hadn't commented on her red cheeks or smudged mascara; a fact Nikki would be eternally grateful to him for – she hated fuss. Langley wouldn't share this with Sajid, she was sure. Nikki took a deep breath. She couldn't lose focus now. Couldn't be distracted by imagining things that might never have happened. She needed to lock those thoughts away for now. She could drag them out one night when this was all over – in the relative security of her bedroom, on her own. Instead, Langley just sat with her, inputting information into his computer, answering emails and the like.

The regular tap of the keyboard and the sounds of the building settling down for the night, quiet now most of the staff had gone, were therapeutic. It allowed Nikki the space to regroup. Had it only been this morning, just a few hours ago that she'd discovered that the husband she thought had deserted her was dead? So much had happened. Haqib, the Springer and Bashir incident, Archie – and she hadn't had a chance to touch base with the only person who really mattered in all of this: Charlie. As usual she'd left it for her mum and Marcus to take up the slack, whilst she went on trying to fight the world. Why were things always so damn hard? Why did she always find it so hard to deal with the emotional side of things? Khal had always teased her about that – about how she'd rather brood than talk, sort it out for herself. He always said she internalised too much and that was why she was so loyal to her family and the few friends she had. He'd stayed for longer than first impressions, looked deeper, saw her strength. Nikki thought that was a load of romantic old bollocks; she, the moody cow, just didn't like many people and that suited her. Khal had laughed and shaken his head.

Why was it that she missed him more than ever *now*? Why, after all these years was it as if her heart were a pomegranate being squeezed with every emotion popping out, seed after blood-red seed? This little hiatus in the morgue was bittersweet. Khal was nearby. She could think without the constant noise and chaos that was her normal life, yet guilt plagued her. Guilt about Khal, guilt for Charlie. She reasoned that giving herself the time to adjust would mean she could be there for her daughter. She had a lot of explaining to do. But the puddle of curdling milk in the pit of her stomach told her she was being selfish – was putting it off because of her own weakness, her own inability to be the mother that Charlie deserved. She'd just about got herself in the right frame of mind and was ready to leave, when her phone went and within minutes, she had left the morgue. One day she would slow down and draw breath.

Chapter 26

Parked in the street outside Jacko Dyer's house in Wyke, Nikki considered her options. She could march along the road and up the crazy-paved path and hammer on the door, hoping all the while that Jacko's sister was at the bingo or she could do what her conscience told her she should and turn the car round and head home. *This* could wait till morning, but Charlie couldn't. Even as she considered this, she was half out the car, ignoring the rain that drove, almost horizontally, against her body. She half jogged, half shuffled forwards, head dipped against the wind. The lights were on in both the living room and the kitchen. Peering past the bedraggled window pots with the last of the summer's blooms inside, she tried to see through the slight chink in the closed curtains. No use. Short of going right up and gawping through, she wouldn't be able to see a thing.

Oh well, I'll just have to risk it. She stepped up and hammered on the door before taking a single pace back and waiting. She was wet through. Her jeans clung to her legs and her hair in its ponytail dripped onto her leather jacket. From inside the sound of whistling – Jacko's trademark – approached and it wasn't long before the door was flung open.

Jacko yanked the door open wider. 'You took your time. I expected you hours ago.'

Nikki frowned as she stepped inside, then the furrow on her brow cleared. 'The news?'

'Yep. Looks like we all got it wrong about Khal.'

For some reason, his words pulled at Nikki's heart and a prickle jabbed at the back of her eyes. She sniffed and shrugged out of her sodden jacket, handing it to Jacko, who wordlessly took it from her shaking hands and draped it over a radiator in the hallway.

'You okay, Nik?'

Standing in the middle of Jacko's lobby, she allowed the warmth to seep back into her body for a second. She raised her head and saw that he was staring at her intently. His eyes were narrowed slightly, and his weathered face was wrinkled in concern. 'I'm okay. A bit numb if anything.'

Jacko nodded, stepped forward and pulled her into his arms in a bear hug. 'You look like a teenager, Nikki. Just like you did when you and Khal got it together.'

Nose pressed against his jumper, she laughed. 'And the rest. I'm too old and tired and jaded to be that teenager again.'

She heard the smile in his voice when he replied, 'You were always jaded, Nikki. Always just a little bit distant – always a little bit unobtainable. You had that faraway look in your eye, as if you had secrets that would pummel the rest of us – as if you held the weight of everything in your head.'

She laughed and pulled back a little, tipping her head backwards to look into his eyes, 'You're being fanciful. I was just a kid just like the rest of us – no more, no less.'

'Aw, Nikki, Nikki, Nikki. You were never *just* like the rest of us – you were never *just* anything, you were always *more*. That's why *we* loved you and the girls hated you.'

'You mean Tess, don't you?'

Jacko nodded to the door and Nikki took that to mean that Tess was out. 'She never forgave you for Khal, that's all.'

'Tess fancied Khal?' Nikki shook her head and exhaled. Why was she just being told this now, after all these years? 'That's why she hated me? Because I had Khal? Well – I didn't have him for long, did I?'

Her phone vibrated in her jeans pocket and with difficulty she extracted it. It would be Marcus again, telling her to come home. He was always so sensible, so responsible. But he never quite seemed to get Nikki's passion – her need to keep active. *If you keep moving, the bastards can't mow you down.* Khal used to say that to her and she'd never stopped moving since he left – she couldn't, for if she did, then she'd have had to address her emotions. Now? Well, things were different now. The stakes had changed.

Jacko pulled her back into his body and she allowed his warmth to heat her. His coffee, minty scent was familiar as his strength seeped into her frozen bones. For once her stomach stopped jangling. She wasn't being fair to Jacko. He loved her – always had – and she loved him too. Just not in the way he wanted. 'I'm sorry …'

He pushed her away from his chest and placed a finger on her lips. 'Ssh, Nik. I know. You don't need to say it.' He smiled. 'I don't expect anything from you. I know it's Marcus you love. He's great, I like him too and he's a lucky man.'

Nikki frowned. He thought she loved Marcus? It was almost laughable. She was incapable of loving anyone, bar her kids. Just showed how wrong someone could be. She tightened her scrunchie and shook her head. 'Nah. Marcus isn't Khal. He could never replace him.'

Shaking his head, Jacko's eyes clouded, his brows pulled together. 'What? You mean now you've discovered Khal didn't piss off back to Gaza at his dad's bidding, you're going to elevate him to sainthood?'

He jumped to his feet. 'This isn't all about you, Nikita. He was *my* best mate. You're not the only one who doesn't know what to do with themselves. I fucking don't. I've spent fifteen years cursing him on your behalf, on Charlie's behalf *and* on my own behalf. I feel like a dick. I should've known he wouldn't do that. *You* were his world – his universe. But Khal was only human. He had secrets. Things he kept quiet about.' His eyes sparked when he glared at her. 'Regardless of all that though, *we* should've been better than we were. *We* should've fought for him.'

Nikki massaged the bridge of her nose between her finger and thumb. What secrets? About his family? That wasn't a secret. She was well aware of the pressure Burhan Abadi had placed on his son. She thrust the thought aside and concentrated on Jacko. He looked distraught, not quite meeting her eyes. If she didn't know him so well, she'd think he looked guilty. After Khal disappeared, Jacko was the one who'd been there for her. He'd been hurt, upset, but she'd been his priority. Sometimes Nikki wished she could love him the way he wanted. 'We let him down *then* – I'm damned if we let him down now, right?'

Jacko nodded. 'I'll get my jacket. Last thing you need right now is to face Tess. She's …' He shrugged and cast a quick glance at the door as if expecting his sister to materialise there. '… a bit unpredictable at the minute. This'll set her off on one. You know what she's like. We'll go to The Mannville Arms and talk things through. Maybe Gordon and Nancy will remember something.'

Squashing the thought that this wasn't about Tess, it was about Khal, Nikki sighed. She doubted the pub landlords would remember anything more. Fifteen years was a long time and a lot had happened in the intervening years. It was worth a try though.

After grabbing his jacket, leaving a note for his sister and locking up, Jacko followed Nikki to her car and slid into the seat beside her. 'Hell, don't you ever clean this cesspit out? It's vile. I'm sure I'm sitting in something sticky. Aw for God's sake – it's toffee sauce. You been eating those bloody Maccie D's chocolate fudge sundaes again?'

Nikki put the car into gear and drove off. 'Nothing wrong with a chocolate fudge sundae.'

'There is when it ends up slathered all over your passenger seat.' Jacko grabbed a tissue from a box in the footwell and tried to wipe the gooey mess off, but instead, big clumps of tissue stuck to his fingers. 'Bloody lethal.'

Nikki's response was to switch the radio on.

'*Capital Radio News. And in Bradford, in a shock new discovery, it appears that more bones have been discovered at the site of the Odeon car park on Quebec Street. A source close to police say they are now linking the gruesome discovery with the skeletonised remains found during the Sunbridge Wells excavations in 2012. Bradford it appears has yet another serial ...*'

Tutting, Nikki switched it back off. 'If we ever find the tosser who keeps leaking news of ongoing investigations to the press, then I'll happily lead the lynching mob.'

'If I ever catch the fucker who did this, Nikki, I'll kill him.'

His quiet tone had Nikki risking a quick glance at her friend. Jacko was staring straight out the window, his eyes narrowed, his chin thrust out. Nikki had never seen him look so ferocious and it calmed her. Whatever happened, she wasn't in this entirely on her own. Releasing the wheel for a nanosecond, she squeezed his knee. There was no need for words.

Driving past the ice rink and through the traffic lights, Nikki pulled up outside the Mannville Arms.

'You sure about this? You could just head straight home to Charlie.'

Despite what her heart was telling her, Nikki shook her head. 'No, my mum's got her. This is more important. Besides, after the day I've had, I could do with a pint.'

They walked through the puddles – Jacko dodging them, Nikki storming straight through them – and entered the pub. If Nikki closed her eyes, she could almost imagine the heavy fug of smoke, the taste, the smell. Khal had smoked. She'd hated it but had given up nagging him. She ate chocolate fudge sundaes, he smoked. They both had their weaknesses. When they'd come here in a group of friends and later as a couple, the bar had always been busy; busy, smoky and loud. Khal would have hated the smoking ban that followed a few years after his death. He'd have moaned, but he wouldn't have given up. Maybe Charlie's appearance would have been the catalyst for him breaking the habit.

The night he'd not come home, he'd come here to get away. To think, he'd said. None of their friends had been here. Jacko had flu and was in bed and Tess was looking after him – their mum already too much of an invalid herself to care for her grown-up lad. Amar and Samir were at a Bhangra gig in Huddersfield and Cindy and Sally had gone to the pictures. It wouldn't have mattered to Khal. He'd have bought his pint and sat in a corner, brooding into it. He'd been doing a lot of that in the weeks leading up to his disappearance. Thinking of her friends from that time, Nikki realised she'd pushed them away. She'd neither seen nor heard from any of them in years. Jacko was the only friend from then that she'd kept in touch with. Actually, it was Jacko who insisted on keeping in touch with her.

In the early days, she'd have been happy to let the friendship slide. It was he who persevered, wouldn't take no for an answer, insisted on turning up and demanding she interact with him. Over the years, she'd grown to accept it, to rely on him. As she glanced round the pub, she could almost imagine Khal hunched over in the corner, nursing a pint. *Oh, Khal, who did this to you?*

She was brought back to the present by Jacko nudging her. 'A pint?'

She nodded and seeing Nancy at the end of the bar, edged her way towards her. The landlady's concerned, sympathetic smile told Nikki that the other woman had heard the news already.

'Oh, sweetheart. Are you okay? Oh, what am I saying?' Her hand fluttered up to her chest, 'Of course you're not. Who the hell would be? I'd nearly forgotten you'd ever been married and then I heard it on't news. What a shock for you – and that little girl of yours too. I was just saying to Gordon that it was a real bolt out of the blue.' She turned to her husband and raised her voice. 'A right bolt out of the blue, I said, didn't I, Gordon? You know about young Khal – Nikki's husband? You remember – dark lad, always one for a laugh. We thought he'd pissed off back to his folks in India, remember?'

'Palestine. He was Palestinian, not Indian.' But Nancy was paying no attention to Nikki.

'That's who them bones down by't Odeon belonged to. They're saying there's more down there too. Saying it's a serial killer. You heard it on the news, didn't you, Gordon?'

Gordon, who was serving Jacko, nodded, his eyes flicking over Nikki and then back to the job in hand.

'Man of few words, my Gordon.' Nancy shrugged and smiled. 'Means I get to blether on as much as I like though, dun't it?'

Experience told Nikki that the best way to get a word in with Nancy was to wait till she'd wound down. Her heart was in the right place but with every new visitor she was like a steamroller – full speed ahead with a load of inconsequential rubbish until she ran out of steam. That was the time for a more equal conversation to commence, so Nikki nodded and smiled and kept her hands in her pocket in case she was tempted to use them to strangle Nancy into silence. At last, the older woman rolled to a gradual stop and looked at Nikki as if she expected great things.

'I know it's been years, Nance, but now we know Khal didn't just go back to the Middle East, I need to find out what happened. Someone did some bad things to him and he's lain down the road all these years and we've been none the wiser.'

Nancy's hands fluttered about her chest again, her eyes full of concern. 'Of course, my dear. You want to work out what happened to him. They said on the news they've found more bodies – must be a worry for the police.' She leaned over the bar till her head was almost touching Nikki's. Her breath was sour with a faint alcohol tang as she spoke. 'We've already had two of your lot in today.' She turned to her husband who was now ringing up Jacko's order on the ancient till and raised her voice, negating her previous subtlety. 'Who were them coppers came in earlier? What were their names?'

Gordon mumbled something that Nikki couldn't make out. His wife, however, seemed not to have such trouble, 'Springer and Bashir. Yep that's right. Bloody hoity-toity young madam she was. Don't hold out much hope of her finding her shoes in the morning, never mind finding a serial killer.' She patted Nikki's arm. 'Good job you're on the case, lass. You've got a bit about you, you have.'

Much as she was pleased to hear this, Nikki really wanted to get to the bottom of things. 'What sorts of things were they asking?'

Nancy began to spiral a tea towel into a tall glass and shrugged. 'Just if we'd noticed your lad that night. If he'd been with anyone, that sort of stuff.' She began to hum the tune from the jukebox under her breath and again Nikki's fingers itched to throttle her.

Keeping her tone measured, Nikki asked, 'And?' When she received a blank look, she schooled her mouth into a smile. 'Did you notice Khal that night? Was he with anyone?'

'Oh, lass, I wish I could say I had. I wish I could tell you who he'd left with, but the truth is, I just can't remember. I think he was in, right enough – we thought that at the time – but who he was with, I don't know. Who he left with – again, I don't know. Might not even have been that night, I told you that back then, Nikki.' She raised her voice, 'We don't, do we, Gordon? We don't know if he wur in or who he left with, do we?'

With his standard shrug, Gordon mumbled something as he disappeared through the door to the back and down the stairs to the cellar. From the corner of her eye Nikki saw Jacko approach carrying two pints and ignored the smile that played across his lips as Nancy, seemingly unperturbed that Gordon had escaped, continued. 'It wur a Tuesday night, you see?'

Nikki didn't see so she shook her head. 'You've lost me.'

'Pub quiz night.' Nancy looked affronted that Nikki had failed to register the biggest social event of The Mannville Arms' weekly calendar. 'Town Versus Gown. That's what we called it back then. The teams were either from the university or from the town. Winning team got a free beer each and we worked out whether the Towns or the Gowns won overall according to their total scores. Bit of fun, but they loved it, did the kids in them days – pure loved it. Now we're lucky if we get four teams on quiz night and half of them are on their phones, Googling this and Googling that.'

Sensing that Nancy was set to go off on a rant, Nikki interjected with a quick, 'Thank you' and went to join her friend. Jacko motioned towards a bench table and Nikki, trying not to imagine banging her head against a brick wall, joined him. 'Anything from Gregarious Gordon?'

'You mean other than a grunt and a moan … oh and a rather loud cheese 'n' onion flavoured burp? Not a lot. Old Bertie at the bar was a bit more forthcoming. Said he remembered the night Khal disappeared because we all came in asking about "Young Khal" later in the week. Nothing more than that, although he has a notion that he left before Khal – not exactly positive evidence is it?'

Nikki sipped her beer, allowing the smoothness to flow down her throat, soothing her. After this, she'd really have to go home. She couldn't put her responsibilities off any longer. This trip to the pub had been a complete waste of time if nobody remembered anything concrete.

Chapter 27

Nikki had been well aware, before she'd even left the hospital, that she was remiss in her maternal duties. Even another quick nip in to see Haqib, who was still sleeping off the effects of the anaesthetic, didn't salve her conscience. How could it? She was a crap mother. She couldn't count how many parents' evenings she'd missed for one work-related reason or another, leaving her mum or Anika to pick up the slack. How many family meals had had to be binned because she was tied up at Trafalgar House or on the streets? Finding out that Khal wasn't alive and thriving in Ramallah but had been tortured to death and buried here in Bradford had set a fire in her gut and she needed to keep going until she'd found who did it.

Now, driving home, the rain battering the car had an almost soporific effect on Nikki. Physically she was spent – moving on adrenaline which was gradually wearing off – but her mind kept wandering. Last year she'd even missed her cousin's wedding because she and Sajid had to attend to the murder of a Polish woman whose neighbour had hit her on the head with a brick because she didn't want some immigrant living next door. The fact that the victim was a registrar in paediatrics at BRI hadn't seemed to matter to the neighbour. The victim's children had seen the attack and would no doubt be traumatised for life. Nikki's mother had been irate, accusing Nikki of deliberately taking on the case to avoid the wedding.

True, Nikki hated getting into a sari, yet her mum had insisted. 'It's part of our culture – *your* culture. Grab it with both hands, Nikki, embrace it, enjoy it.' Her mum had looked so sad as she'd matched jewellery to the sari and helped Charlie and the Rubster to choose theirs. Nikki had put her hand round her mother's waist and squeezed tightly before promising to be there.

It was only in the last twenty odd years that Lalita Parekh had been reunited with her family. Some of her Indian relatives had long memories – not the ones that mattered, though. Despite her mother's brave face, the three Parekh women were still pariahs in the eyes of some of the family. So, she had to admit that the Polish woman's death had provided an ideal excuse.

This was different though – Khal turning up dead was different to the Polish woman. Her mum would understand what drove her onwards. The question was, would Charlie?

She still hadn't eaten, and driving along Ingleby Road she debated whether she could take the time to grab a McDonald's drive-thru on her way home. A faint nausea lingered in her gut, her eyes were gritty and every bone and muscle protested as she engaged the clutch at the traffic lights.

Approaching Listerhills, her thoughts ran to Khal and Charlie. How was she supposed to speak to Charlie about all of this? Maybe she'd be in bed, asleep? Who the hell was she kidding? Charlie was too much like her. She'd be waiting, like an avenging angel, to challenge her mother. Pulling up at the kerb, Nikki's heart sank. Every light was on at the front of the house. She had a welcoming committee. She stumbled out of the car and slowing her steps to a snail-like crawl, she approached the front door, aware that it was too much to hope that it was only her mother awaiting her return. Maybe if she crept in, she'd be able to sneak upstairs and put off the confrontation till the next day.

Pushing the door open, the effort almost too much for her, she saw that the living-room door was ajar and she could hear the heavy silence rumbling along the hallway to greet her. Taking a deep breath, she shrugged off her leather jacket and hung it on the banister before kicking her trainers into the corner beside the kids' schoolbags and walking the short distance into the lion's den. Hovering just inside the doorway, she'd never felt more like a schoolgirl about to be rollicked by the headteacher. Marcus sat on the double sofa with Sunni, his round face flushed, thumb in his mouth, fast asleep on his knee and Ruby leaning against him, her cheek pressed against his shoulder. Hearing the soft purring snores she made as she slept, Nikki's heart contracted. She was blessed to have such wonderful kids and yet half the time someone else was looking after them. That had to change – it just *had* to.

Moving her gaze round the room, she saw her mum, legs folded under her, as she sat on the chair next to the stove which was lit, bringing a welcome warmth to the chilly atmosphere. She looked tired – anguished. Like she had in the early days when it was only the three of them. Nikki risked a small tight smile and was rewarded by her mum's reassuring nod. No matter what, Lalita Parekh always had her daughters' backs and Nikki took that for granted. She needed to stop that too. It was too much to expect.

Exhaling slowly, Nikki lifted her eyes to Charlie who stood in front of the stove, all tall and angular. Her eyes sparked and her lips were set in a thin line. Nikki could tell she'd been crying, although Charlie would never admit it to her. With her chin jutting out and her hands on her hips, she looked ferocious – ferocious and beautiful, and Nikki's heart constricted. She was so much like her dad. So much like Khal and, in that instance, Nikki wished she could wind the clock back. She wished that instead of letting Khal leave the house that night, she'd gathered him in her arms and told him about this precious little bundle that nestled inside her. Perhaps then he'd still be alive, perhaps then things would be very different.

Her gaze drifted to her other two children and she rejected the idea. If Khal was still alive, who was to say she'd still have the Rubster and Sunni. Aware that she was biting the inside of her cheek to stop her face betraying the overpowering emotion that flooded her body, Nikki deliberately pulled her shoulders back and unclenched her hands. She took a step towards her daughter – a step into the silence that thundered around them crashing their entire worlds into smithereens.

Charlie held both hands in front of her warding her off. '*Don't* come near me. How *could* you? How could you *not* have told me? How could you have let me find out from a *stupid* bloody hospital radio station? What sort of a *mother* are you?'

Her strident words sliced through Nikki, and she took a step backwards. 'Oh, Charlie. I'm sorry. I'm so sorry.'

But Charlie wasn't finished. 'That's the story of your fucking life, isn't it? Sorry for this, sorry for that. Always fucking sorry after the event. We'd be better off if it was *you* that was dead.' And, tears streaming down her cheeks, she barged passed, knocking her mother to one side. 'I hate you. I wish *you* were dead. You're not my mother. You're just the piece of shit that turns up to mess things up.'

Charlie reached the door and paused, turning. 'And it's all your fault about Haqib too. Everything you do makes things worse for us. Every sodding thing. Why don't you just leave? Just fucking leave. Marcus and Aji-ma can look after us. We don't need you. Go to your precious fucking job. That's the only place you're happy. That's the only thing you love.'

As her daughter stormed upstairs, her feet hammering on each step, Nikki wanted to take off after her but her mother's soft words stilled her. 'Let her be. She's angry. She needed to vent. She's had a shock. We all have.'

Nikki swallowed, trying to dislodge the spikey lump that was lodged in her throat. Her mum was right, but Nikki knew there was more to it than that. She was only too aware that she'd neglected her family and now she was suffering the consequences.

Her mum got to her feet and perched on the edge of Nikki's chair, gently placing her arms round her daughter's shoulders. 'Never mind Charlie for now. She's young, she'll adapt. She's lost less than you, for she never knew Khalid. I'm more concerned about my own baby. How are you, beti?'

Nikki's lips quivered and her breath caught in her throat as she looked across and met Marcus's eyes. As fair as Khal had been dark, he was handsome in an 'I don't give a shit sort of way'. His hair always a bit too long, his clothes the same ones he'd worn when they first met. He met her gaze with a slight smile on his lips, yet his pain shone through. He was suffering too. Khal's death changed things, altered their relationship in an indefinable way. He smiled and nodded, his expression telling her how much he cared for her. He was a good man. He didn't deserve to be second best. But the question remained, could he ever be first in her eyes?

Nudging Ruby awake, Marcus lifted Sunni up and with a sleepy Ruby trailing behind, he paused, whilst Nikki kissed her second daughter, and took them upstairs to bed.

When he'd left the room, Nikki cradled her head in her hands. 'I've well and truly fucked everything up.'

Her mum smiled and shook her head. 'Tell me everything.'

And with the warmth of her mother's arms round her, Nikki told her all about Khal's dad turning up, about Charlie's call about Haqib and how she'd nicked Sajid's car. The latter brought a smile to her mother's lips.

'Yes, I was here when he discovered that. He was *not* a happy bunny.'

Nikki smiled briefly, rubbed her hand across her cheek and continued her tale about going to the pub with Jacko to talk to Nancy and Gordon. When she was done, she heaved a great sigh and leaned back. 'I'm the worst mum in the world. How could I have let Charlie find out about Khal like that? How could I *not* have been there for her when she most needed me?'

'Hmph.' Lalita got to her feet. 'If my Anika was half the mother you are, Nikita, you wouldn't have to spend half your life looking after Haqib.' She wafted her hands at her daughter. 'As for the rest. You *had* to go to Trafalgar House. You *had* to comply. That nasty little man was making all sorts of allegations and your colleagues had to investigate. Now you are in the clear. Now you can grieve for Khal, whilst others investi …'

She caught her daughter's eye and then shook her head with a sigh. 'You're not going to leave it to the Cold Case Unit, are you?' She tutted. 'What am I talking about, of course you're not. You're Nikita Parekh and you won't stop till you have all the answers you need.'

Pulling the sleeves of her jumper down till she could grip the cuffs with her fingers, Nikki wrapped her arms round herself and gave an inelegant snort. 'I can't leave this to someone else. He was *my* husband. I loved him. He was the best thing that ever happened to me and he was stolen from me, from Charlie and me, by some murderer. I won't rest till I find out who. He was the love of my life – he *was* my life. Now I have to get used to the emptiness all over again.'

A noise at the doorway made her look up. Marcus stood there, his eyes pinned on her, all colour drained from his face. If she'd stabbed him in the belly, she couldn't have hurt him any more. For a long time, they said nothing. Nikki had no idea how to take her words back. She wasn't even sure that she wanted to. Khal had been the love of her life, there was no doubt about it, but Marcus was the father of two of her children.

Finally, Marcus spoke. 'Guess I always knew I was second best, but fuck, Nikki. It's hard to have it slapped in your face like that.'

He made a strange noise that caught in his throat and Nikki realised it was a half-hearted laugh. She opened her mouth to speak and then closed it again. What could she say? How could she make this better?

'Thing is, Nikki. I've had enough. For years, I've put up with you keeping me at arm's length. Not wanting me to move in, putting obstacles in the way, keeping secrets. You've called the shots all this time and ...' He prodded at the hole in his jeans that was there through old age not through trendiness. '... like a fool I've let you. Thought you'd grow to trust me ... to love me.'

He paced the living room. 'Now I see that I've wasted my time.' His lips twitched. 'I'll back off, Nikita. Obviously, I'm still the kids' dad and I'll be there whenever you need me to look after them, but ...' He threw his arms up in the air. 'I'm done. I can't compete with a dead man and I'm fucked if I want to try anymore. I'll stay at my own house tonight, Nikki. Call if you need me.'

And before she could think of what to say, he'd turned on his heel and walked from the living room. Nikki stared after him, her head filled with a jumble of words that wouldn't form into coherent sentences. Her heart shrivelled to the size of a prune and, as the front door slammed behind him, a single tear rolled down her cheek.

She willed herself to run after him, beg him to stay, promise to change ... but she knew as well as he did, that she couldn't. She was too damaged to allow anyone else under her armour. Too independent to compromise and too bloody-minded to beg. As if she was wading through a stormy sea, she made her way through to the hallway, her heart skittering an erratic tattoo against her chest. It was almost like an SOS that nobody could hear: da da da ... doo doo doo ... da da da. A plea for help gone unanswered.

Nikki walked upstairs to the toilet and threw up.

Chapter 28

'She's been here, hasn't she? I can always tell when she's been here. You always look like you're hiding summat.' Tess Dyer flung her bag by the side of the settee and wedged herself between two oversized cushions. 'Suppose she came for tea and sympathy? Like *she* deserves any.'

Jacko turned up the volume on Sky Sports and tried to ignore his sister, but her incessant moaning, sifting over old facts and past mistakes, was too much for him and he gave up, flicking the TV off and trying to hide his scowl. Her venomous words made him anxious and with her in this mood, who knew what she could let slip. If things were to remain sound between him and Nikki, he needed to calm her down. Last thing he needed was her mouthing off in a fit of temper, so he fixed a smile on his face and kept his words light. 'Aw, Tess, give it a rest, eh? What's done is done. Now we need to move on. Khal's been found … but that doesn't mean we need to drag everything up again, does it? Last thing we need is Nikki turning her attention towards us.'

He could tell by the flush that spread across his sister's cheeks and trailed down to her wobbling chin that she disagreed. She had that habit of running the palm of her hand up the front of her nose when she was agitated, slewing off the flaked skin that surrounded her nostrils. He stood up. 'Look, I'll make us a nice cup of tea and we'll talk it all through. We just need to keep our stories straight. Last thing we need is anyone finding out we were lying. We've been in the clear for fifteen years, we can't let those bodies being found spoil things for us … not now. We *need* to keep things quiet.'

Tess clenched her hands into fists and banged them down on her knee three times, setting the flab on her belly undulating like a sea of jelly under a tight-fitting tarpaulin. 'I hate her, I hate her, I hate her. She always got what she wanted … always!'

Moving to the kitchen, Jacko paused and turned, his eyes catching his sister. 'Not always, Tess. Not always … she lost Khal, didn't she?'

Bringing her hands up to cover her face, Tess groaned. 'Aw, don't be mad at me, Jacko. It were an accident. You know it were.'

Sighing, Jacko closed his eyes and exhaled. Right now, at this precise moment, he was barely holding things together. The last thing he needed was for his sister to crack up and spill the beans. He remembered how hard it had been to keep her quiet fifteen years ago. There was no way he was going to let her mess things up for them now. Not after they'd managed to cover up what they'd done for so long. 'Just don't think about it. Keep your head down and don't speak to anyone about it. In fact, why don't you take a trip to Whitby? You can stay with Aunt Jackie till it's all blown over.'

At once, Tess lowered her hands and glared at him, her eyes sparking, her mouth sulky. 'Are you mad? I'm not leaving. Not when things are just getting so exciting. No way. I'm staying right here where I can see what's going on.'

Chapter 29

When she came back downstairs, her mum took one look at Nikki's face and led her to the table, pushing a plate towards her accompanied by a single word. 'Eat!'

As soon as she smelled the omelette, Nikki's stomach curled up and withered. Were any of her internal organs going to be intact by the end of this night? She barely managed two mouthfuls before pushing her plate away with an apologetic glance across the table at her mum.

'Marcus gone?'

Nikki inclined her head. Her mum would have heard everything he said and was probably wondering why Nikki hadn't made him stay. 'I tried to stop him, but I had no words, Mam. The words were all there in my head, but I'd nothing left inside to make them come out.'

Her mum placed her hands on the table and pushed herself upright. 'You need to rest. You're spent. Go to bed. I'll lock up and come back in time to get the kids ready for school.'

'Charlie?'

Her mum shook her head. 'She's hurting, my beti. She'll come round.' She moved over and put her arms round her daughter. 'You are a great mum, Nikita Parekh, and a great person. I am so proud to have you as my daughter. Don't you doubt yourself, not even for a second. You do things your own way but it's always for the good of *this* family.' She turned Nikki around and pushed her gently towards the stairs. 'Sleep.'

By three o'clock in the morning, Nikki's mind was still buzzing. She'd looked in on her children earlier. Sunni was sprawled diagonally across his bed, leg sticking out of the duvet, his shock of brown hair falling over his forehead. She'd promised him a haircut the previous week and still hadn't got around to it. *This weekend definitely!* She pushed it back from his forehead like she'd done with Haqib earlier and dropped a kiss in its place before heading into Ruby's room. The Rubster was huddled under her duvet, only her nose visible. Her room was the neatest one in the entire house. Nothing was out of place; clothes folded, notebooks and pens in orderly piles on her desk, bookshelves ordered alphabetically, schoolbag packed and ready by the door.

Switching off her middle child's light, she pulled the door half closed and moved on to the next room. For a moment, she hesitated before entering Charlie's room. Would she still be awake? But it looked like the day's events had exhausted her, for Charlie was lying, one arm flung over her eyes, snoring loudly. She'd had to deal with a lot today – more than any 14-year-old should have to. More than Nikki had ever wanted her kids to suffer. She'd always promised they'd never face the sort of trials she had. Wasn't this nearly as bad? Sighing, she went to her own room, closing the door fully behind her.

Hours later, still struggling to sleep, Nikki did the one thing that always made her feel safer. She pulled one of the cardboard boxes, the one labelled 2018, onto the bed and lifted off the lid. The last report, which had arrived three days previously, was at the top with a series of photographs taken with a long-range lens.

The subject is working as a bricklayer and lives at the following Craigshill address in West Lothian. As per your instructions, now that we have eyes on him, we are monitoring his activities 24/7.

Nikki knew the report by heart and so she lifted the photos, one by one. Every time she'd done so over the last few days, bubbles of sweat had erupted all over and her hands had shaken. Tonight, she was dispassionate. Her eyes, raking over the photos, studied the man from every angle. The way he stooped. His greying hair. How he held his cigarette with his index finger draped over it like a hook when he inhaled, the stubble on his chin. Before, all of those things had evoked visceral memories. Smells and sights that made her want to throw up. Tonight though, things were different. *She* was different. He wasn't the important one right now. He'd need to be dealt with – 'course he would. Having him a few hundred miles distant from her and her family, didn't reassure her … that was still too close. But right now, she needed to insulate her family from any more hurt. She needed to regroup … dealing with her dad could wait.

She drifted into an uneasy sleep, the photos all around her a kaleidoscope of weird memories flitting in an out of her subconscious mind.

'Come on, Nik, for goodness sake, just put a bit of bleach in the bucket before you mop.'

Khal is laughing at me, waving a bottle of cheap bleach in the air, his brown eyes full of laughter.

'No!' My voice is croaky.

'Let me put the bleach in.'

'Go away, Khal, leave me alone. I'm not putting bleach in.'

But he opens the bottle and pours it into the bucket. As soon as the smell hits my nostrils, I rear back, slamming my head into his nose. Blood spurts out onto the floor. I dive out of the kitchen into the bathroom and am violently sick. My head pounds and my heart hammers against my chest. For a moment, I think I'm going to pass out. Khal's right there, banging on the door, voice thick as if he's covered his face with something. 'Let me in, Nik.'

'Go 'way.' I can taste the sick in my mouth, smell the bleach. Acid refluxes into my mouth and I vomit again.

'*No! Open up.*' *He's insistent, sounds worried.*

Crawling across, I flick the lock open and he's there, holding me, demanding I tell him what's wrong. And there, squashed in the loo of our rented terraced house on Rand Street, I tell him.

I'm sobbing now. Khal's T-shirt's drenched, but still he rocks me, stroking my hair whispering over and over again, 'I love you, Nik. I'll look after you now.'

'Khal! Khal!'

Shit. A dream. Nikki pulled the photos off her sweaty legs and grabbed the glass of water from her bedside, taking small sips. Not those again. Not the nightmares. Not now. Allowing her breathing to steady, she leaned back against the headboard. She had to get a grip. Needed to hold things together.

Hearing a noise, she swung her legs off the side of the bed, listening. One of the kids? Her mum coming back to check on her? There it was again. Someone moving about downstairs. She strained her ears. Was it on the stairs now? As quietly as she could, she leaned over and grabbed the baseball bat from under her bed, before standing up. Gripping it with both hands she positioned it over her right shoulder ready to strike.

Her bedroom door was thrust open and … she exhaled in a loud whoosh, flung her weapon on the floor and ran to the figure standing in the doorway.

Marcus grabbed her as her legs went around his waist and then they were pawing at each other, lips, teeth and bodies writhing and grinding together. The sex was hard, fast and furious – a tension-buster, their bodies familiar, their mating primal.

When they were done – still lying on the floor, half naked – Marcus stood up, straightened his clothes and looked down at her. 'I couldn't sleep. Couldn't bear to think of you here on your own awake looking at those photos of your old man, thinking about Haqib, mourning Khal.'

Nikki swallowed.

'Don't worry. Nothing's changed, Nik. I know my place. We're just friends with benefits. Just the way you always wanted it.' And he turned and left.

Nikki lay there, covered in a film of sweat, her body relaxed in a way it hadn't been all day. *Oh, Marcus. What am I doing to you? To us?*

Wednesday 24th October

Chapter 30

Nikki always thought that Sajid's apartment perfectly reflected the man himself; urban swank with a touch of bijou chic. It was in Bradford's prestigious Lister Apartments right in the heart of Manningham, a stone's throw from the city centre – a gentrification project stalled at first base. Its luxury was in direct contrast to the area in which it was housed. It cost well above Sajid's pay grade. If she hadn't known he'd had an inheritance a couple of years ago, she'd have been suspicious that he was taking backhanders. He wouldn't have been the first, after all. DCI Kowalski, her previous boss, had been taking backhanders whilst coordinating a trafficking enterprise on the side. Nikki had no regrets about exposing his sorry ass. Sajid, on the other hand, was similar to her, albeit with a tad more sartorial elegance, in his dedication to putting Bradford's gangsters away.

She parked her Zafira in the underground car park then spent a few moments chatting to the on-site security guard before heading up in the glass lift to Sajid's apartment on the top floor. Once there, she took a minute to look out the window at the view which never ceased to fascinate her. From here, Bradford's contradictions were never more apparent. From rows of sandstone terraced houses to the splendour of Bolton Woods. From inner-city bustle to the tranquillity of Lister Park. The city's landscape paid homage to its diversity with church spires and mosque minarets – it had its share of greenery dotted around, with a dollop of spice added in for good measure.

As she looked around the opulent hallway with its lacquered glass banisters, well-watered potted plants and polished wooden floors, she smirked. From Listerhills to Lister Mills. No difference – just another one of Bradford's contradictions.

She hammered on the door and waited. She was early – but hell, they'd wasted fifteen years already, time to crack on. She was well aware that yet again, she'd put a penny in the 'bad mum' slot by leaving without touching base with Charlie.

Part of her decision not to wait was selfish – pure and simple. She had no idea how to cope with Charlie – what to say to her. What could she say to the daughter who had until now thought her dad had deserted them, only to find out he hadn't? Nikki's mum had told her that Charlie had been asking about Khal's family and that struck an arrow right through Nikki's heart. She didn't want her precious child to have any contact with Burhan Abadi, yet deep down she was aware that this was something she couldn't prevent. How the hell would that play out? The man was convinced she'd murdered his son. It made it easy for him, made him able to spout venom at Charlie and poison her against her mum. Nikki had no intention of allowing that to happen.

Thrusting these thoughts to the back of her mind, she hammered on the door again and was rewarded by Sajid's voice through the door. 'Hold on, hold on. For God's sake.'

She grinned. Sajid was never at his best first thing and she'd just dragged him out of bed. He would be in a right mood. He pulled the door open wearing a T-shirt that hugged his muscles and a pair of boxers that left little to the imagination. Through half-closed eyes, he glowered at her. 'Christ, Nik, it's barely dawn.'

Nikki pushed past him and made her way through to the kitchen where she plonked herself down at the small white table.

'Hurry up – shower and then we can crack on. Shit and shave can wait.'

Sajid, still with a bemused half-awake look on his face, padded after her in his bare feet, 'You forget something, like?'

Nikki put her head on one side and pretended to think. 'Eh, no. Don't think so.'

With a humph, Sajid walked over to the state-of-the-art coffee machine that took up most of the small worktop in the dinky kitchen – easy seeing where his priorities lay – and flicked it on. 'If you had to come so damn early, you could at least have brought some coffee.'

His tone was petulant and Nikki grinned. He looked like Sunni when he'd just woken up with his hair all ruffled and sticking out. It was rare for Nikki to see her partner in a less than perfectly put together way. 'What – when I've got a barista for a partner? Not bloody likely. Where are the files?'

Sajid sniffed. 'Living room – dining-room table. And keep the noise down, Langley had a late night.' As Nikki stood, he turned to make his way back along the corridor, then turned. 'Grab some cereal or toast or something. We've got a long day ahead of us and you look like the flap of a butterfly's wing could knock you over.'

Talking off her jacket and flinging it on the seat she'd just vacated, Nikki opened the bread bin and took out a loaf. Typical. Sajid had artisan bread – actually, on reflection, the bread was probably courtesy of Langley. She'd seen Sajid wolf down a McDonald's. He liked his carbs white and processed. She shuffled around opening drawers looking for a bread knife, then noticed an electric knife – again typical Langley. Pathologists and their cutting and slicing instruments, she supposed. Apart from the fact that her family had a problem with losing digits, the last thing she would risk in her kitchen was a power tool of any description. Mind you, might come in handy should her dad come calling. So, feeling a rush of excitement, she plugged it in and gave it a few whirs before watching it easily slice through the loaf of brown seeded bread.

In no time, she had four even slices. Definitely an improvement on the straggly ones she'd have produced manually. She placed them into the large toaster, only then noticing that all the appliances were in the same shiny black as the unit doors. Sajid and Langley were such damn posers. Opening the cupboard, she saw that they were better filled than hers at home. No sticky jam and honey jars, no Better Buy peanut butter, no own-brand chocolate spread. Instead her host's supply of organic jams sat pristinely on the shelves mocking her. With a sigh, she opened the fridge, grabbed the butter – not marg – and an opened a jar of Bonne Maman raspberry jam.

When the rich smell of coffee and toast filled the open-plan area, Nikki's stomach rumbled. She really did need to eat and so she slathered butter and jam on all four slices and by the time Saj re-entered the room fifteen minutes later, all spruced and rosy cheeked, she was on to her second cup, had put more toast in the toaster for him, set up her laptop and was poring over the files he'd brought from work.

As Sajid joined her at the large table, she looked up. 'The skeletonised remains uncovered at Sunbridge Wells six years ago in 2012 were found to belong to Mark Hodgson who disappeared thirteen years ago in 2005. At that time the file says that he was presumed to have fallen into the trench that had been dug when a water pipe had burst and hadn't been noticed when they refilled the trench.'

'For heaven's sake, didn't anyone suspect foul play?'

Nikki read on. 'Seems like they put it down to death by misadventure. Would be interested to see what Langley makes of the PM photos.'

Langley, dressed and ready for work, entered. 'Someone using my name in vain? Give me a minute to get some breakfast and I'll have a look.' He wandered into the kitchen, set the coffee machine off and expertly sliced some bread. Five minutes later, munching on toast with gooseberry jam – *who the hell eats gooseberry jam?* Langley studied the photos.

'They should really have picked up on these marks, which bear some resemblance to those found on Khal's bones. Thing is, the victim was homeless and an alcoholic and had been missing for years. This probably wasn't too much of a priority at the time. They found a narrative that fitted and they stuck with that. It's only in the light of the numerous remains found in the Odeon car park, that you're picking up on these now. Which, by the way, is my cue to head off. Got a busy day ahead of me.' He skirted the table, kissed Sajid, and with a wave in Nikki's direction, headed to the door. 'If this Mark Hodgson was buried and if you get an excavation order, I'll happily compare the marks. As it stands, I couldn't testify with any certainty.'

Nikki nodded. Another option to explore, but first they'd need to find something a bit more compelling to encourage Archie to pressure Springer into linking the Odeon bones with the Sunbridge Wells ones.

Chapter 31

He hammered on the door, glancing around as he did so. He'd waited till he saw that Nikki bint piss off out in her car and he was sure that Anika was on her own. Her old man was probably giving it some with his other family.

Anika was an issue for him – she held a strange fascination for him, one that unfortunately appeared not to be mutual. When she opened the door, he groaned. What the fuck was she wearing one of those bloody Paki scarves for? Made her look 50. Stupid bitch. He reached out to pull her hijab from her head and she jerked back. Her face paled and the smile faded from her lips as she tried to push the door shut.

Franco grinned. 'Not gonna ask me in?'

Anika gripped the door tighter and pushed it further closed, sending a quick glance up and down the street. 'Go away.'

'Just wanted to let you know I'm back in the area, like. Saw your Haqib yesterday. Did he tell you? How old is he? Does he know his old man's got another family? His half brothers and sisters all go to Bradford Grammar, you know. Bit of a jump up from Listerhills Academy, isn't it? Anybody would think he was ashamed of the lad, wouldn't they?'

Anika's lips scrunched up and tears formed in her eyes. 'It was you, wasn't it? It was you who did that to Haqib!'

Studying her pallor, the way her fingers gripped the door, knuckles so white, the tear that had begun to roll down her cheek, Franco lowered his hand and adjusted his erection. Even with the scarf on, Anika Parekh was hot – not as hot as her sister, mind. But at least *she* was pliable. That Nikki was a complete ball-breaker and he wanted to stay down-wind of her if he could. Their last encounter, with the help of her Paki friends, had resulted in him being exiled. Not that it had done him any harm in the long run. No, fortunately he'd made a killing in Oldham and Ashton and had enough allies to risk a return to Bradford. Getting his own back on the Parekhs was just an added bonus to his lucrative business deals. Hijabi Parekh was still going on.

'What'd you do that for? He's just a kid – just a kid. You didn't need to do that to him.'

Franco put out his hand to push the door open, but Anika must have been prepared for that, for she pushed back against him and he only just got his foot in the gap before it slammed shut. 'Let me in, Anika. You know you want to. Last thing you need is for poor Haqib to lose another digit, isn't it? Besides, you know we could be good together – really good.'

Anika spat in his face and stamped on his foot, her slippers ineffectual against his boot, all the while shoving hard against the door trying to close it. A voice from behind interrupted their little power play and when Franco turned around, copper Parekh's kid was there, standing at the bottom of the steps, phone in her hand, chin jutting out. Just like a taller version of her mother. Her tits were just starting to sprout, but she was curvy all the same. Franco's erection got harder.

'Everything all right, Auntie Anika? Dialled two nines already. Shall I dial the last one?'

Fucking little whore. Standing there in her school uniform, like butter wouldn't melt. His fists clenched by his sides and he wanted nothing more than to slam one into her face. *Just like her damn mother.* He'd sort her out. One of these days, he'd sort the little bitch out once and for all. He extended his arms, palms upwards. 'No, no. No need for that. Was just checking in on young Haqib. That's all.'

He ran down the steps, and pushed past Charlie making sure he jammed his elbow into her stomach as he passed. Her 'poof' and the sight of her curling over at the waist made him smile. Before he'd finished with her, she'd be screaming, never mind that little noise.

All he'd wanted was an easy lay. Now that he'd fed Kayleigh to the pigs, he was in need of someone else to spread their legs. Anika would have done, but now the girl had put herself on his radar, it looked like Nikki Parekh's daughter would be a better option.

Chapter 32

Nikki's stomach was awash with coffee. It glugged around inside her, making strange gurgling sounds. But worse than that, the excess of caffeine was making a headache blossom, just at her temple. Scraping her chair backwards, she gently dropped her head back and circled it from side to side trying to ease the tension that had settled across her shoulders and up her neck. Sajid's dining-room table was not the best place to work on a laptop. She needed a break and, by the sounds of the huffs and puffs coming from Sajid, so did he.

'Come on. We're getting nowhere here. You need to get yourself into Trafalgar House and find out more about the remains found yesterday.'

Sajid held up a hand. For hours he'd been trawling through HOLMES (the Home Office Large Major Enquiry System). Archie had allowed him home access and he'd been painstakingly adding in search parameters that fit what they knew about their killer. 'Wait. I've just found another body discovered fifteen years ago – in that car park near the ice rink. Only thing is, it really doesn't fit with the other victims – this one was a woman, Stephanie Fields, and she wasn't skeletonised.'

He took a sip of cold coffee, grimaced and continued. 'However, she very nearly went undiscovered. If a young lad on the ground hadn't been keeping an eye on the rubble tipping into the hole, she'd have been covered and buried just like Khal and nobody would have been any the wiser. That was 2003, right around the time your Khal went missing too. Nobody had reported her missing, but they seem to think she was gone for about six days before she was found. Boyfriend was initially in the frame for it, but was alibied out.'

A flutter started in Nikki's stomach – awaking the acid and dispelling the niggle at her temple. Things were beginning to add up. It made so much more sense that there were more bodies out there waiting to be discovered. They had the ones at the Odeon and now two possibles at different locations. Did Bradford have another serial killer? If so, was he still active and how many victims had he claimed? Going by the dates, he'd had at least fifteen years, if not longer, to rack up a horrific number of victims. On the one hand, she trusted her instincts – Khal had been the victim of a serial killer. On the other, she found it difficult to conceive that a killer had managed to go undetected for so long.

She moved across and peered over Sajid's shoulder at the police report he was reading. There were so many things she didn't understand. His victim choice was one of them. This killer didn't seem to have a type; Khal had been a Palestinian student, Mark Hodgson was a white homeless man and the latest one they'd uncovered, if indeed they were linked, was a Jamaican woman. It seemed their killer didn't just cross races, he also crossed sexes. It didn't add up. They were missing something here. 'They never found out who killed her? Can you pull the post-mortem report, see what it says?'

Sajid typed and in seconds the report was on the screen. 'Multiple stabbings – at least fifty. Look, it's easier to see the full extent of them here because Fields's body hadn't decomposed yet. Poor thing was pregnant – eight weeks.

'According to the report, various implements were used,

ranging from a machete to a kitchen knife, possibly a Stanley knife and even a Phillips screwdriver. Again, only some of the wounds went through to the bone. Fields was a 19-year-old kid in her second year of a foundation degree in Art and Design – from Sunderland originally.'

Nikki studied the report for a few seconds. 'The knife wounds add up – deep slices hitting the bone, but …'

'The gender is wrong – all the others we've found were male.'

Dragging the chair over so she could sit next to Sajid, Nikki placed her elbows on the table and propped her chin on her palms. 'Thing is, Sajid – we don't really know what the hell we're dealing with. We could easily be dealing with a serial killer. Who knows how many bodies have ended up buried throughout the city – who knows what gender they might be? He's already targeted cross-racial groups and, if it's the same guy, then both genders, and varying ages.'

Sajid stretched back causing his chair to creak as if his sizable frame would reduce it to a pile of Ikea timber on his highly polished floor. 'We just can't seem to get a handle on this fucker at all.' He slammed his hand down on the table before jumping to his feet and pacing the small living room.

Used to Sajid's sporadic frustrations during an investigation, Nikki waited him out. Once he'd expended some nervous energy, he'd focus again. Sure enough, a couple of minutes of pacing did the trick. He flung himself down on the couch with an exaggerated sigh and closed his eyes. 'You okay, Nik? Don't know how you're holding all this together – really don't.'

Glad that he couldn't see her face as she replied, Nikki rolled her shoulders. 'You know me, I compartmentalise.' No need to share the nightmares that had plagued her the previous night, no need to tell him about waking up covered in sweat, the covers tangled round her legs and tears pouring down her cheeks. No need to tell him about the piercing grief that threatened to saw her heart in two – threatened to knock her over the edge. And certainly, no need to tell him about how pinging the band round her wrist hadn't been enough to stop her fetching the blade from her bedside cabinet. Hadn't been enough to stop her lifting her T-shirt and pressing it into her tanned stomach, just below the line of her jeans. Hadn't stopped her savouring the pressure of it denting her skin until, in slow motion, she sliced it open releasing the bubbles of blood that calmed her – gave her some grasp on herself, on her life, her obligations, and ultimately allowed her to continue – to keep going – until the next time. No, there was no need for Sajid to know that – none at all.

Sajid was the only man, bar Archie she supposed, who didn't want a bit of her 'proverbials' – who didn't crowd her, make her run scared. Khal had been like that to a certain extent. He hadn't crowded her or made her run scared – he'd been her all, her world. He'd given her hope – but no, that wasn't strictly true. Khal hadn't *given* her anything, instead he'd encouraged *her* to grab it, take it, insist on it, take what she wanted – feel like she deserved it. He'd showed her she could be in control whilst still letting someone in. Why couldn't she be like that anymore? Why did she always let Marcus down? There and then she vowed that when she'd got Khal's killer, she'd sort out the rest of her shit. Take control again. Think about what *she* wanted – not what she felt obliged to give.

Shaking off thoughts of her sorry life, Nikki jumped to her feet. The tension in her shoulders gone, she was enervated. 'Get a map of the city centre up and plot the sites of the possible victims. If we can't link the victims at this stage, perhaps the dump sites are significant in some way.'

Saj clicked a few buttons on his laptop and brought up a map that allowed you to see it in real time and then Nikki was looking at a three-dimensional, aerial representation of the sites. The Odeon car park, Sunbridge Wells and Bradford Ice Rink. 'What the hell makes these sites so special?' She leaned forward, pushing paperwork to the side. 'How the hell can you dump this number of bodies near enough in the middle of the city centre without being caught?'

Saj had run his fingers through his hair so many times that it now stood up in spiky peaks all over his head. Despite being dressed for a day at the office, in his shirt and suit, he'd hadn't yet got around to putting his socks on, and his jacket was hung on a hanger near the door. His frustration was clear in the set of his chin. 'To date there are at least six bodies, four at the Odeon site, and one each at the other two. What do these sites have in common? What attracted the killer to them? All of these bodies were dumped at different times, so how the hell did he select his disposal sites?'

'So, I'm the killer ...' Nikki grabbed both her and Saj's mugs and wandered through to put on yet another pot of coffee. 'Why do I choose these dump sites? What makes them so appealing – especially the Odeon one? What do they have in common?'

'Well, the last question is easy. Each site had some sort of building work on it. Presumably the site was unattended over-night, making it an easy place to dump a body ... topple it into a hole. Some of them were waterlogged, but if not, you'd cover it with a bit of grit and the digger does the job for you the next morning – well mostly. Didn't quite work out that way for Stephanie Fields's body.'

'Okaaay.' Nikki walked back to the computer, studying the map, her brain firing on all cylinders. Something was there, she just had to put her finger on it. 'So, evidence suggests that I keep the victims for a period of maybe a week or so – torturing them during that time. Maybe I'm scoping out dump sites from the minute I grab the victim—'

'You'd be keeping an eye on building work that necessitated the digging of trenches big enough to house a body—'

'Yeah, but only nearby. It would have to be local. Couldn't be traipsing a dead body through the streets like a swagman, could I? Maybe—'

'You work for the council or Yorkshire Water. I'll get—'

'Check that out. But okay, that's one possibility for how I identify the sites. Maybe I just keep my eyes open. Maybe I know the city centre area really well.' Nikki went back into the kitchen, slopped freshly brewed coffee into two mugs and returned, handing Saj his. 'Maybe I live there, right in the city centre.'

She studied the map again. 'Still doesn't explain how I've managed to transport those bodies to the different sites. Hell, I'd need to be invisible. To get to the Odeon, I'd either need to drive into the car park, hoist the body out of the boot or the back seat and plop it into the hole or traipse down the back road past the Alhambra and down the ginnel with a body on my back. Fine, except for the fact that that area of Thornton Road and that car park were pretty well used by prostitutes, pimps and punters most of the night. I could see him managing a successful dump once, twice maybe … but four times? No chance.'

'Maybe the tosser is invisible.'

Nikki dug her fingers into her scalp. 'Aww! What are we missing?' Pacing the room didn't seem to help. The confined space wasn't giving her even one iota of inspiration. She was convinced they were close to a breakthrough, but she could see that Sajid was as frustrated as she was. She sat down next to him and in silence they studied the sites. Nikki could sense his increased frustration as he drummed his fingers on the table edge like a tabla player ad libbing. Come on, Nikki! Come on. What the hell are you missing?

She moved closer to the screen and traced her finger in a triangle between the little red flags Saj had added to the map. 'You know what? Maybe he is …' Seeing Sajid's frown, she added, 'Invisible, that is … or as near as makes no difference, anyway. Have you heard of Bradford's underground beck?'

Without waiting for Sajid to respond, she continued, 'There's a beck that runs all the way from the top of Great Horton. If memory serves me right, it meanders around, breaking the surface at different places on its travels towards the city centre. The Theatre in the Mill, near Bombay Stores is one of the places it surfaces. However, after the beck flooded in Victorian times, a series of paved tunnels were fashioned to go alongside the beck. Many of them branched out under buildings to provide access for building works. They follow the beck's trajectory with street-level access points at a variety of locations.'

'You think he's using the tunnels?'

'Might be. Wouldn't hurt to look at a map of underground Bradford that incorporates all the sites we've discovered bodies or remains – you know, basically the city centre.'

Sajid Googled for a while, but became increasingly frustrated when the only maps he could find were basic sketches. 'Right, let's visit City Library. They're bound to have summat or if not, they'll be able to direct us somewhere.'

'No, you go back to Trafalgar House. We need to get someone accessing all missing persons reports going back, say, eighteen years. We're only interested in the still-open cases. If we're right, some of these MPs could be buried around Bradford.'

'What about the interviews with Khal's friends?'

Nikki thought for a moment. She'd intended to interview all their friends from 2003, but now that they had this lead it seemed more imperative to follow it than to duplicate Springer and Bashir's donkey work. 'Leave it. We'll see if The Spaniel and Bashir come up with owt worth following up. Truth is, Saj, I talked to them all at the time – nobody knew owt. None of them.'

179

Chapter 33

Right now, I need to take stock. They've discovered more remains and I'm okay with that, but it has prompted a certain nostalgia. A desire to revisit the origins, the very beginnings of my work. I don't really need my recordings but still, I settle in prepared to enjoy my youthful achievements. In those days I hadn't perfected my craft. I was still honing my skills, but unlike the worthless captives, I was prepared to employ my brain, to finesse my work, to learn and develop, to better myself. I smile as I press Play. This recording is testament to my worthiness. I prepare to enjoy my younger self. Full of promise, full of spirit – worthy of the great things that were to come.

You'll realise by now that things didn't go exactly to plan that first time … no matter. The important thing is, that this does not muddy the waters but rather opens up an opportunity for reflection, consideration and analysis. No point in continuing regardless; not adapting and changing, not assessing the situation and embarking on a course of action that will ultimately be beneficial.

The first time was like a trial run … almost. Hadn't had the time to think things through – to follow everything to its conclusion. Didn't know enough about my craft, the measures necessary to be successful. It wasn't rocket science in the end – not really. Just common sense, but then common sense was in scant supply the first time. If I can learn from that, then why can't the captives? Why do they continue to disappoint not only themselves, but me too? They are given every opportunity possible and still they fail to step up to the mark. I digress ...

The end plan had been to dispose of the body with no chance of it being found. Pick them off one by one – under the radar, no come-backs. I hadn't needed to worry though. Bloody headless chickens that lot. They were too eager to put it down to high jinx gone wrong – students and all that.

I sip the last of my whisky as the DVD goes fuzzy and remember just how much I have achieved. Killing per se, although enjoyable, isn't my thing. For me, it is the orchestration, the manoeuvring – creating the scene – that's where I excel. The intricate planning makes my blood effervesce; my synapses go into overdrive. In implementing each meticulous detail, I become the person I am inside. I am superior to each and every captive, more deserving than they. I am in control of my own destiny, like Dionysus, I hold the sword of Damocles in my hand. Their lives are dependent on their ability to prove themselves. That has always been an essential part of it.

I walk over to my library, run my finger along the DVD cases, each one catalogued ... initials followed by their own unique number. Each DVD pays testament to the many chances each captive had. More than that, they pay homage to the entire production, without which it would all be futile. Each recording bears witness to the skill and art of the recording – hauntingly thought-provoking voiceovers, camera direction, lighting, background music, all used to maximum effect. All of that is equally satisfying – until at last it is complete, my production ready to watch again and again for hours of unadulterated enjoyment. Soon, I will add another one to the collection and, once more, the West Yorkshire Police will be oblivious.

It's time for another captive. The bodies surfacing after all these years have got the old juices running again.

Chapter 34

Charlie left school to head over to Lidl to grab some lunch. That was another damn thing to blame her mum for. As usual there was sod all in the fridge and, after the face-off with that thug this morning outside Auntie Anika's house, she didn't have the stomach to ask her aunt for a sandwich. She'd been near hysterical and, like always, Charlie had been forced to swallow her own misery, pacify her aunt, round up the kids and take them to school. It was doubtful whether her auntie would even make it up to BRI to see Haqib – poor Haqib. At least Aji-ma would go. As she'd turned to leave her aunt, she'd heard the crisp clink of the lock turning. She must be really scared. Charlie couldn't remember a time when her aunt had locked the back door.

Sighing, she'd turned on a smile, grabbed Sunni's hand and escorted him to their primary school around the corner, before she and Ruby headed to the bus stop. She wished Haqib was here. She'd be able to talk things through with him. Stupid idiot! Of course, that was another worry – would he be okay? Haqib was such a knob, but at least she could talk to him about stuff – the crazy stuff, the shit stuff that always seemed to happen to her family. And now there was this other stuff. Her dad being dug up, after her mum had told her a whole load of lies about him pissing off back to Palestine. Made her blood boil. You'd think she'd have had the decency to hang around – talk to her daughter this morning – but no! She'd left a note saying she'd headed off to Sajid's to find out what had happened to Khal – she hadn't even called him 'your dad'.

The thing was, Charlie didn't feel like she had a dad. How could she? For years her mum had shut down any communication about him, leaving Charlie sneaking about the house looking for scraps of information when her mum was out. That's how she'd found the pictures – the ones her mum kept in her knicker drawer. The ones Charlie wasn't supposed to see, the ones with Nikki smiling in a way Charlie had never ever witnessed – looking up with soft eyes into the face of a handsome guy who had a definite genetic link to Charlie herself. His cheekbones, his eyes, his hair colour. Charlie was in no doubt that he was her dad, yet her mum wouldn't talk about him – wouldn't say anything. She'd said her dad was a one-night stand, but Charlie had always wondered about that. She hadn't even had a name for him until yesterday. 'Khalid Abadi' – she tried the name out on her tongue, rolling it around her mouth like a delicious sweet sneaked behind her mother's back, and devoured in licks and sucks.

'Khalid Abadi.' She grinned. It sounded strange to her, so she tried something else. 'Charlie Abadi.' That sounded even stranger and it felt strange too – like a guilty pleasure that didn't taste of chocolate. Better than boring old Charlie Parekh – more exotic, more WOW!

Planning to skip the afternoon class and jump on a bus up to the BRI, Charlie waved to her friends and hustled on her way, ignoring their yells to hang out with them. She walked towards the pelican crossing ready to cross Manchester Road and only then did she fully register the presence of a man behind her. She'd been daydreaming as she left the school gates but still, she'd been half aware of a presence behind her. She flicked a glance at him and was disconcerted to see that he was staring at her.

Oh, for fuck's sake! Why did the weirdos have to hang around outside her school? Like she didn't have enough to deal with. Bad enough the damn drug dealers hassling you, without stinky old perverts. She threw him a dirty look and pressed the button, hoping he'd take the hint. As luck would have it, the green man came on almost immediately. Charlie sped up and headed across the road, leaving the perv hobbling across behind her. Choosing to take the short cut rather than walk round the path, Charlie skipped over the verge and across the Lidl car park, avoiding the muddy puddles that dotted the grass. Tossing a fifty pence piece to the homeless guy who sat by the trolley park, she went inside where the smell of fresh baking hit her nostrils and her decision was made. A pain au chocolat and a can of pop! It was all she had money for anyway.

She skipped the rest of the aisles and joined the short queue at the checkout, not realising until it was her turn, that the perv from earlier was now standing behind her in the queue. The worst thing was that he didn't look to be buying owt. He stood so close to her that Charlie could smell his aftershave – a tangy, musky sort of smell, not unlike the one she'd got Marcus for Christmas. She supposed it was better than the normal eau de piss that she associated with the sick old pervs that hung about the city centre, ogling the young girls or sometimes the lads. She edged forwards, away from him but he also edged forward. She rolled her eyes. The perv was persistent.

Chapter 35

'Shouldn't you answer that?' Sajid looked at Nikki as she glanced at her phone before silencing the call. They were back in his flat and Nikki was buzzing with developments so far.

'It's only bloody Anika. Don't have time for her nonsense today.'

'Might be important.'

Nikki snorted. 'Yeah right. It'll be summat and nowt – as usual. Probably wants me to head up to BRI to see Haqib. Like I've nowt else to do.' Sometimes Nikki wanted nothing more than to shake her sister. Yes, Anika had her reasons for hating hospitals, for wanting to avoid them, but, hell, so did Nikki, yet you never saw her moaning and passing the buck. The thought that she was being a little unfair did cross her mind, but Nikki pushed it to the side. Today was the one day she had to let Anika cope on her own. *She* had to push forwards for Khal's sake. She had to do what she should have done all that time ago. For once, Anika could just brace herself and go and take care of her own kid. For too long Nikki had cushioned her, made it easy for her sister to lean on her. Right now, though, Nikki needed her sister to step up to the mark and just get on with it. She needed her to be an adult for a change, not a dependent younger sibling.

'Tell me what you got from Langley.' Nikki knew that Saj hated having to consult with Langley at his workplace. He hated the thought that anyone might figure out that they were in a relationship. Truth was, most people knew about it already, but Nikki didn't have the heart to tell him that. It was awkward being from a Muslim family and gay. Saj had once confided in her that he lived a double life. When he went back to Dewsbury, he was the traditional Muslim son, but here in Bradford, at least in his personal life, he could be himself. Langley, on occasion, was frustrated that Sajid wouldn't be as open as *he* was about their relationship. Nikki got it though. Families had certain expectations, regardless of culture or religion, and if you fell outside their narrow parameters it could be hell for you – she knew that from personal experience because she was continually on the outside of her extended family's expectations herself.

'They found another three complete skeletons and are now confident there are no others in the car park. Seems like each body was deposited at a different time, which seems to coincide with building or gas and water works in the area. Rough dates are that one was buried in 2005 and another in 2008. The markings are consistent across all three bodies, the same slash marks right through to the bone. The identification process is almost complete. One was a white male student – ID'd from his student card as Martin Black. The other was a white woman who was visiting her friend and reported missing when she didn't return to Newcastle in 2008. Statements taken on her missing persons report say she was a prostitute. The third victim, also male, has not been identified, but may have been buried as recently as 2012.'

Nikki's phone started to ring again and with an exaggerated sigh she pulled it out of her pocket, declined the call and threw it on the sideboard.

'You sure you shouldn't take that?'

'No, let's crack on.' Earlier, after a fruitful visit to an old antique shop in Thornton, Nikki had seen an old map detailing all of

Bradford's underground tunnels. She retrieved the photos she'd taken of them and got them enlarged and printed off. Blown up, they gave a clearer view of the lie of the land. The street names were printed in a cursive script, yet were more readable. The two of them pored over them, identifying landmarks like the Alhambra Theatre, the ice rink and the site of the recently built Sunbridge Wells. Not trusting herself not to smudge, she asked Sajid to mark off the three body dump sites in red and the nearest tunnel exit to each in blue.

By the time they'd finished, it was clear that each dump site had an equivalent tunnel exit nearby. Nikki traced her finger over the glossy prints, tracing the myriad of lanes that meandered under the city centre and off in various directions under the main roads she was so familiar with. This could be huge. If they were right, she and Sajid may have stumbled over something much bigger than she'd previously thought. Perhaps Khal's killer was more prolific than they'd believed.

She moved over to the kitchen and poured herself a mug of coffee, savouring its smoothness, and as she sipped, she used the time to consider her options. Should they tell Springer and Bashir? Was there any point? Judging by Springer's antagonism towards her, the other woman wouldn't believe a word Nikki said. Besides, she'd have to reveal that she'd ignored their explicit instructions to back off. The last thing Nikki wanted, was to get either Sajid or Archie into trouble. Looked like they were on their own on this one. She put her mug down. 'Now we go and check out each of these three exits and see if they are still accessible.'

He nodded. 'Yeah. When we get something a bit more conclusive, we can approach Archie, let him decide what to do.' His gaze moved back to the map, and he tapped a building with one finger. 'You notice this?'

'Yep – The Broadway shopping complex. There's a tunnel leading straight to the construction site. How long was that hole there in the city centre just waiting for some psycho to dump a body? Any word from Missing Persons in Bradford? Let's hope there's not too many with last sightings in Bradford.'

Her phone rang again and seeing that yet again it was Anika, she pointed to it and mouthed. 'Get Archie on that. I'll deal with this.'

She slumped into Sajid's couch, her bones melting into its lush softness, making her ache to remain there, curl up and sleep for a month. She closed her eyes and schooled her voice to neutral. 'Hey?'

Almost immediately her eyes flew open again as Anika's hysterical weeping pushed the weight of her fatigue more heavily down on her shoulders. When her sister got like this, she was almost impossible to console and Nikki couldn't afford the time to calm her. Injecting a calm steeliness that brooked no argument into her tone, Nikki pinched the bridge of her nose, 'Stop. Crying. *Right. Now.*' She waited and soon the sobs reduced just a little.

'Tell me.' Nikki heard a few hiccups followed by a ferocious nose-blowing. She could visualise her sister clearly. She'd be bundled on the couch in her living room, lights out, curtains shut, duvet pulled tightly over her head, tissues and a bottle of wine on the coffee table next to her. It had been a while since she'd been like this and now thinking about it, Nikki realised that it wasn't just the prospect of visiting Haqib in the hospital that caused it. She'd been okay the day before, so what had happened between then and now to result in this melt down?

'Charlie's not gone to school for afternoon class ...'

Nikki's grip on her phone tightened. Little cow was playing up. She'd have words with her later, but no way was Charlie getting away with this crap. But her sister was speaking again.

'Franco came here. At the back door. Tried to push his way in and Charlie turned up. Threatened him with the police ...'

Determined not to jump to conclusions, Nikki bit her lip. '... And?'

'He was looking at her, Nik. That bastard was eyeing her up

188

like she was a piece of meat and now she's not at school or picking up her phone and Haqib's not heard from her. You don't think …?'

Nikki's heart started to thunder and she jumped to her feet. Pacing helped, but not much. 'Did he follow her?'

Fuck, Charlie was near that slimy bastard! Her hand went down and slipped under her T-shirt, worrying at the fresh scab that her previous night's anxiety had created. The slight tinge of pain as she pulled it off, her purposely short nails digging in and yanking the tender skin, calmed her a little.

'Don't know. Don't think so. I'm scared, Nikki, really damn scared.'

Her blood boiling, Nikki wanted to yell at her sister to get a fucking grip. She was more worried about Charlie. Her precious, beautiful Charlie. Why hadn't she taken the time to speak with her this morning? Why had rushing off to be Khal's avenger seemed so much more important than being with her daughter, trying to build bridges with her, trying to make Charlie understand why she'd let her find out via some stupid radio programme, rather than from her? She didn't deserve the beautiful girl she had.

As she tuned back in to Anika, Sajid reached over and dragged her hands away from her belly. She looked down at her fingers. The nails were all clagged with blood, smears trailing along her fingers. She looked up at him and saw the shock on his face. Fuck, fuck, fuckity fuck, fuck, fuck. Now Sajid knew her guilty secret too.

Holding her hand loosely by her side, hating the stickiness, hating that she'd exposed one of her dark corners to her friend, Nikki tried to focus on her sister. 'Where's Charlie now?'

'I don't know. She'll be fine, Nikki. She's strong like you.'

Nikki wanted to slam her fist into the wall. She was a kid. Charlie was just a damn kid. Why hadn't Anika kept Charlie with her, safe? 'Look, I need to go. Need to check Charlie's okay. If you're locked inside, you'll be all right. Why don't you get Yousaf to come over – he's your man, isn't he?'

Her sister's voice took on a whining tone. 'He's with his other family – they need him.'

With no thought for the consequences, Nikki let loose. 'Oh, for fuck's sake, Anika, just grow a pair. *You* need him. *You*, Anika. He's the father of *your* son. If he can't come now when you need him, then just fucking dump him. He's a bloody liar and a cheat anyway – all "I'm a councillor representing my community" crap, whilst all the time he's got a bit on the side. He's a duplicitous snake in the grass, is what he is. I'm fed up clearing up your mess. I've just found out my husband's been murdered. My daughter's found out her dad's dead and she's grieving and *you're* on my damn case all the time. You need to bloody deal with this yourself for once. Just fucking do it, okay?'

Nikki hung up and speed-dialled Charlie. Straight to voicemail. Oh shit, shit, shit. If anything happened to Charlie, she'd never forgive herself. Pausing to take two deep breaths, she dialled the school and after five minutes of waiting was told that Charlie hadn't returned after lunch. Turning to Sajid, hands trembling, Nikki spoke. 'Charlie needs me – I gotta go. The tunnels will have to wait.'

Sajid, who'd spoken with Archie during Nikki's conversation with her sister, shrugged. 'No probs. Archie's sent two constables to check out the exits for us. We might have more on our hands than we initially thought. Archie says a missing persons report came in this morning – a young lad reported missing when he didn't return to his flat last night. It was an anonymous call and none of his friends have seen him. He's a student who's dropped out. Probably gone home and not told anybody and most likely not related, but until we know more, it worries me. Let's hope we're on the wrong tracks here. I don't think Bradford could survive another serial killer and especially not one as prolific as we suspect this one is.'

'It's unlikely that this recent missing person is linked, though. Why would this fucker lie dormant for years and then start up again just when we start to discover remains?'

'We don't know that he has lain dormant all this time though, do we? He could've been active right under our noses for the past twenty years, for all we know.'

'I can't think about that right now, Sajid. I've got to find Charlie. We'll cross that bridge when we come to it.' She bit her lip. 'Thing is, with Charlie, I don't know if she's just punishing me for not telling her we'd found Khal's remains or if I should be really worried. Fuck – kids! Who'd have the little fuckers? With Franco in the loop, I need to err on the side of caution.'

Chapter 36

'Fucking bitch threatened me and no one does that. No one, right?' Franco was on his phone to Big Zee. His car was parked just down from Anika's house where he could see the front windows clearly. The kid had gone – collected the younger sprogs and hustled them down towards the school. Franco had been tempted to teach her a lesson there and then, but a couple of her friends had appeared, so he let her go … for now. The cunt Anika had drawn the curtains and was probably huddled in a pile of piss in the corner. Bitch! He'd get her. It might take a while, but he'd get her. No way was he letting this one go. He'd lost one bint and had no intention of losing another. But that was for later. Right now, he'd other things to be dealing with – Deano for one. No way was that little scrote getting away with what he'd done. The boys were watching his house – keeping tabs on him. That bitch Kayleigh had nearly got away with it. If he hadn't come home early and caught her packing, she'd have got off scot-free. His fists clenched at the memory. It hadn't taken much for her to come clean … and then all he'd had to do was take the bint to the pig farm.

Deano's part in the whole thing was what really got him. He had to send out a message, loud and clear, and it had to be a substantial one. One that would ensure none of his boys would double-cross him ever again. That's why he was taking his time – toying with the little fucker. Making sure word got out on the streets, so everybody would know exactly what Deano's punishment was. A clear and strong message was what was needed and Franco would enjoy administering it. Fingers tapping on the steering wheel, he growled into his phone. 'Bring that little fucker to me. It's nearly time to end him, but I want to make him sweat before I make the pigs squeal.'

Collapsing into gales of laughter, he exchanged his tapping for a couple of hard palm slaps on the wheel. 'You get what I did there? Fucking pigs squeal – get it? The pigs'll fucking squeal all right when I dangle that little scrote by the legs into their sty, especially after we've used the tools on him, yeah? Squeal with fucking joy, they will. Better than that pig swill Sowerby feeds them any day.'

Big Zee's laughter over the phone bolstered him and he was content to let Anika Parekh's reprieve drift to the back of his mind. She'd get her due – dead right she would and then he'd dip his wick. That piss pot of a Paki screw of hers wouldn't so much as blink either. Probably be relieved to get rid of her. Common as muck she were, not like Councillor Yousaf Mirza's missus – the one he dangled on his arm at every social function going. No, she were class, that one. Bit prim for Franco's liking, mind, but pure class nonetheless. He wouldn't mind dipping his wick there either. Cupping his erection, he let his mind wander. The Mirzas were always plastered over the papers, with their 'business enterprise' this and 'charitable works' that.

Fuck, you wouldn't think he was rolling in the green stuff though, would you? Not with the way his slut was living on the side in that crummy terraced house next door to her minger of a piggy piggy oink oink sister. Maybe he'd make that his next aim. Once he'd done Anika Parekh, he'd fuck Yousaf's wife till she was halfway back to Pakistan.

Franco interrupted Big Zee's laughter. 'Bring him to The Wreck – and don't bother about being gentle. Time to ratchet things up.'

'Okay … I'll get on it. Eh, boss …?'

What the fuck now? 'Yeah?'

'You sent Tyke to do a job somewhere?'

'Eh?'

'It's just, I can't find him. He's not picking up his phone. D'you know where he is?'

'Christ's sake, Zee. If the little prick in't turned up that's not my problem, is it? He's probably screwing around or wasted somewhere. Now just get *my* job done and stop bothering with Tyke, got it?'

Sliding the car into gear, Franco revved the engine a few times making a mum with a pushchair crossing the road jump before yanking the buggy back onto the kerb.

'Watch where you're going, bitch,' he yelled out of his open window and revved away up the road. At this time in the afternoon, The Wreck would be quiet. Nobody hung around there when it began to get dark – nobody except Franco and his boys. He'd make use of that.

It still niggled him that Deano had overstepped the mark with his baby mama. What the fuck had she seen in him? Deformed little short arse. Was it worth it? Spreading her legs for him? Fucking bitch.

Parking up by The Wreck, Franco pulled up, got out of the car and slammed the door hard. The sound reverberated round the near silent backyard and was answered by the dogs that roamed freely in the grounds of the junk shop. Franco was well aware that this outfit was a money laundering one – and the presence of the dogs told him that business was good. He'd plans for that too. A bit of poisoned meat, a night-time shimmy over the fence and the business wouldn't be in quite such a good position … economically that was. He'd bide his time though, keep an eye out and wait till he knew their regular payment dates.

The streetlights along the back alley separating the shops from the kids' playground were strategically broken, casting a shadow over the area where he'd now parked his vehicle. He liked the gloom. It made him feel cocooned ... secure. He lit up a spliff and inhaled deeply. He needed to calm down – thinking of that cow with Deano always boiled his piss. But a quick way out for the tosser wasn't good enough. Franco was determined to exact every ounce of pain and torture he could. No point in teaching others a lesson if you went about it half-heartedly. No, you've got to approach these things with an eye on the end game. And Franco's end game was to make an example of the tosser – one that would never be forgotten, one that would elevate his position in Bradford to the top of the pile.

Lights blinked on and off twice at the top of the alley. Big Zee had arrived. He reached in to duplicate the signal and listened to the faint bang as the car doors slammed shut followed by low murmurs and scuffling feet as the trio walked towards him. As they walked under one of the remaining lights, their silhouettes were illuminated – Big Zee dwarfing the man that walked beside him.

Franco smiled. Deano had tried to bulk himself up by poking his elbows out at an angle from his skinny frame. Good – that meant he was running scared. Exactly what Franco wanted, and the turd had nowhere to hide.

Taking a last draw of his spliff, Franco tossed it into the weeds that curtained the bottom of the fence separating them from the playground beyond. 'Glad you could make it, my man.' He purposefully kept his voice jovial. Lull them into a false sense of security and then BAM, hit 'em where it hurts. He extended his arm and gripped Deano's in a gangsta-style hug, pulling him towards him and bumping shoulders.

Deano's mouth split into a grin as Franco released him. His shoulders relaxed and his arms hung loose as he opened his mouth. Before he could utter a sound, Franco drew back his arm, balled his fist and propelled it with force into Deano's stomach.

Deano's response was immediate. He folded over, hacking and dribbling from his mouth. Trails of vomit-spiked saliva drifted to the uneven ground.

In a conversational tone, Franco said, 'You see, Deano, much as I like you, you gotta take your punishment like a man, eh?'

Deano glanced up, eyes narrowed, still hacking, holding his belly.

Franco studied him. Fear lurked at the back of the other man's eyes and Franco was aware that Deano was trying to work out exactly what Franco knew. 'Been a naughty boy, have you?'

Deano glanced round as if hoping that someone would appear from the shadows to protect him. Franco enjoyed toying with him – making him suffer, pushing his advantage. His pulse spiked and a jag of electricity wired him. 'Something you want to tell me, Deano boy?'

The lad tried to straighten, but it seemed the effort was too much for him because he remained in a half-upright position clutching his belly with one hand whilst using the back of the other hand to wipe his mouth. 'You lost me, man.'

Forcing his lips up, Franco delivered his 'empty smile'. The one he reserved to strike fear into his opponents. The one he'd been told petrified everyone, friend or foe alike. The one that said they'd 'reached the end of the road'.

Inhaling, Deano's body tensed and Franco's grin widened. This was fun – so much fun. Almost enough to make him forget about Anika Parekh and her annoying sister altogether.

'You said you'd sort out Nikki Parekh. But have you?'

The flicker in Deano's eyes combined with a slight relaxation of his shoulders made Franco want to grab him by the shoulders, slam him against his car and kick the shit out of him.

Deano raised a hand and tried a smile. 'Got it under control. Give me till the weekend and it'll be sorted.'

Franco backed off, enjoying the fear in the other man's eyes. He opened his car door, looking like he was about to step inside. Instead, he spun on his heel, using the impetus to once more propel a heavy fist into Deano's gut.

Shrieking, Deano, retched and fell to his knees right into a mucky puddle.

'This weekend. Get. It. Sorted.' Franco nodded to Big Zee who shoved his arms under Deano's armpits and yanked him upright. With Deano a dead weight, he dragged him, legs trailing behind, back to their car.

Franco watched them. All of a sudden, he was hungry. He grinned; bacon sarnie – that's what he needed right now, a bacon butty.

Chapter 37

The old man was still there behind her, so close she could almost feel his breath on the back of her neck. The checkout man scanned Charlie's two items and in a disinterested tone told her how much she owed. Before she could get the cash out of her purse though, the perv reached forward, his hand covered in liver spots and wrinkled holding a twenty-pound note. His accent all weird. 'Here, I will pay.'

The checkout guy wakened up now as he looked from the perv to Charlie, suspicion in his eyes. 'You know this man?'

Charlie was on the point of shaking her head, grabbing her stuff and hotfooting it out of the shop and back to school, when something struck her. The accent … the accent and something about the way he held his head. She turned around till she was facing him fully and stared at the old man. Her heart skipped a beat as he held her gaze and then, seemingly realising she'd recognised him, he nodded once. Without looking at the cashier, she said, 'It's okay, he's my grandad.'

Shrugging, the lad took the note and doled out the change whilst Charlie and the perv took turns glancing surreptitiously at each other. Realising she was holding up the queue, Charlie turned and slowing her pace to accommodate the old man, walked towards the exit. 'You know I thought you were a perv, don't you?'

'A perv?' The old man frowned. 'I'm not sure I understand that word, but I take it you're relieved that I'm not one of those.'

Charlie threw back her head and laughed. This was the first time since she'd found out about her dad that she was able to crack so much as a smile. It was good. It seemed to lift the tension that had settled on her shoulders and chase away the headache that throbbed just beneath the surface. Her mum would be mad when she found out that Charlie's grandad had made contact. She'd explicitly told Charlie to steer clear of him should he come to the house. Well, this *wasn't* the house and Charlie *wasn't* a kid. What did her mother know? She'd stopped Charlie from knowing about her dad for all these years and Charlie was determined she wouldn't do the same with her grandad.

A sleek black limo pulled up beside them and the driver got out, circling the car and opening the back door. Charlie's grandad gestured for her to enter. She hesitated. What if she'd got this wrong? She wasn't her mother's daughter for nothing. She couldn't just get into a car with some stranger because she thought he was her grandad. 'I need proof. I need you to show me something that proves who you are.'

The old man's lips twitched as if he was pleased with her. 'You have your father's sense of self-preservation.'

Charlie's eyes narrowed. Was he just a little smarmy? A little condescending? 'Actually, it's just as well I don't, else I'd maybe end up murdered just like him.'

Fuck, Charlie, what are you playing at? She didn't know where the words came from, she just knew that she needed to keep a little distance between herself and this old man. Like her mother, she used words as her weapon of choice ... although she was well aware that her mother wasn't averse to using more than words should the need arise. Well, she too could do that ... no problem. The old man blanched and he cast a hand over his face as if her words had wounded him. Well, maybe they had, Charlie didn't care. Why should *she* be the only one hurting? 'Well, do you have proof?'

He slid into the seat, rubbing his thigh. When he'd settled, he rummaged in the breast pocket of his jacket and extracted a photograph that was folded in two. He handed it to Charlie, who grabbed it and opened it eagerly. There were four people in the photograph. She recognised the man before her and an older woman – his wife? Her focus turned to the younger man who stood at the end of the quartet gazing into the middle distance as if daydreaming.

Although he wasn't smiling, she recognised him from the picture she'd coveted so often in her mum's drawer. That was her dad. His lips were finely sculpted, the defined cheekbones and the short hair. He was a little younger than in the photo her mum had, but it was definitely the same man. Her eyes slid along to the other young woman – his sister? Her aunt? She raised her eyes to meet her grandad's and found he was studying her intently. She didn't flinch. 'Who are the women?'

He exhaled and then reached out to take the photo from her. With a gnarled finger he pointed first to the older woman. 'That is my wife, your grandmother – your *Jida*.'

Charlie studied the woman. She was slight, but her eyes smiled. Charlie decided that she looked nice. 'Jida?'

'Yes, that's the Arabic for grandmother. Grandfather is *Naqil*, perhaps you will call me that?'

This was all a bit too much for Charlie to take in at once, so she pursed her lips and didn't answer, instead pointing to the second woman. 'Who's that?'

Her grandad paused. His finger swept over the young woman's face and it took so long for him to reply that Charlie thought perhaps he was going to ignore her question. At last, he raised his eyes and with a tense smile, he spoke. 'Ah, that, Charlie, is your father's wife Tabana.'

200

For a second Charlie thought she'd misheard. She thought he'd said that the woman in the picture with the extra-long black hair and perfect eyebrows was her dad's wife. She shook her head and, frowning, took a step back. The tension that had lifted just minutes earlier barrelled back over her like wicked waves in a storm – a tsunami drenching her, pushing her underneath, making her think she couldn't swim, that she could only drown.

And that thing happened, the thing she dreaded, but this time it was hitting her with no warning, slamming into her chest, making her heart pound right up to her ears. She raised her arms and folded her head into her chest, careless of her dropped purchases. She couldn't catch her breath, it was hurting. This time she *was* going to die. She knew it. She was going to die, all alone without her mum, her brother or her sister. Without Marcus. All alone, with her mum thinking she hated her. All alone with this liar – this liar that was saying things about her dad that just couldn't be true.

Arms were round her shoulders – the driver, helping her into the back seat beside the old man, her grandad. The old man was mumbling words that made no sense as he slouched in the back seat, face ashen. Then … 'Is she all right?'

At last the lights going off around Charlie's head stopped moving, stopped flashing. Their intensity calmed. The pressure in her chest eased, the pounding slowed and air, sweet and pure flooded her lungs as she slowed her breathing.

'Are you all right?'

It was her grandad's voice, worried, rasping as if he too was about to have a panic attack. She managed a nod. Then realising the car was now moving, she pulled herself forward using the front passenger seat. 'Stop, let me out. Where do you think you're taking me?'

The driver ignored her and the old man leaned over and patted her knee. 'It's okay, Charlie. You are safe. Don't worry. We are going to my hotel where we can have tea and talk about you

201

coming home with me … to Palestine, so you can meet your grandmother.'

Charlie glared at him. 'You've no right to take me away from the car park. None at all. I don't want to talk to you. You are a liar.'

He closed his eyes for a second, inhaled through his mouth and exhaled through his nose. 'I have not lied to you, Charlie. I have no need to lie. This must all be very shocking for you, but you must understand that it is also shocking for me. Until recently, I thought my son was living his life happily here with your mother. I thought he had abdicated his responsibilities in Ramallah and left his wife. Now, I discover he had not. Now, I discover I have a granddaughter. Now, I discover that because he was going to leave your mother, she killed him.'

Charlie started. Was this man for real? Did he really think her mum would kill her dad? One look at his face told Charlie that he was perfectly serious. God! She was stuck in a moving vehicle with a deluded old man. What sort of mess had she got herself into this time? And *she* called Haqib stupid? How messed up was this?

'Don't be ridiculous. My mum's a police officer. She's not a murderer. You're deluded. She leaned forward again and began banging on the partition that had just seconds before swished up to a closed position. 'Let me out!'

'He can't hear you. He doesn't want to hear you. He will do exactly what I want him to do.'

Charlie's cheeks flushed hot. Electric jolts were trammelling up and down her spine. Her security was threatened. She was vulnerable and her mum had always taught her that if she felt vulnerable then she needed to extricate herself from the situation by whatever means available to her. Charlie racked her brains. Come on, come on! Could she do something? What? She had it … the only weapon at her disposal. 'If you *ever* want me to call you Naqil, then you will let me go … *now!*'

Her words floated in the air-conditioned car. At first, she thought she'd failed. Seconds passed, each one seemed to last an hour. By her sides, her fingers clenched into her palms, cutting them. She welcomed the pain, it gave her some relief. When his shoulders slumped, she released a silent breath and kept her eyes trained on him. He tapped the partition with his walking stick and the driver sent it whirring downwards. 'Stop the car and unlock the doors.'

He'd locked the doors? She heard the click as the locks disengaged and before the car rolled to a complete standstill, Charlie yanked the door open and scrambled out onto the pavement. Legs shaking, she held the door in one hand for support and leaned in. 'You are a miserable old man. You frightened me and I won't forget that. But, more importantly, I hope you are a liar, for if you're not, then your precious son is a bigamist and I'm a *bastard*. Sure you still want to have contact with your *bastard* grandchild?'

She slammed the door shut, spun on her heel and walked away without turning back. She had a lot to think about and the only person she could think of to talk to was Haqib.

Chapter 38

Nikki dragged on her jacket and then, looking at her fingers, rushed to the sink and let the cold water wash away the blood. 'I'll check the app on my phone, but let's go. After we find her, we might have time for the tunnels.'

Rushing out of Sajid's flat, they headed for the lifts as Nikki fiddled to bring up the app on her phone. 'Charlie's at home – or at least her phone is.' She dialled the home phone number and heard it go to answer phone before dialling Charlie's mobile. And when at last it was answered with an impatient, 'What?' Nikki nearly sank to her knees, the relief making her joints shake. 'You okay, Charl?'

'Why wouldn't I be?'

Nikki didn't care that there was an edge to her daughter's tone or that her words were snippy or that she'd skipped school. All she cared about was that she was safe. 'I want you to lock all the doors and put the chains on, okay. Don't open them for anybody but me or Marcus. You're gonna phone Marcus and tell him Franco's back. Get him to pick up Ruby and Sunni. You gonna do that, Charlie?'

The exaggerated sigh that drifted down the line was so typical of Charlie, but Nikki recognised it as her 'Okay, if I must' tone and was instantly reassured. Marcus would look after her family – he always did.

She was just about to hang up when Charlie spoke again. 'Don't know what all the fuss is about anyway. I'm not scared of Franco and as for *him* – well, he's just an old man. No way would he get the better of me, grandad or not. I don't get why you're worried about Ruby and Sunni though. It's me he wants to take back to Palestine, not them.'

A sheet of ice slid through Nikki's heart. 'What?' The single word jettisoned from her mouth like a projectile. Perhaps it was her tone that made Charlie answer her immediately without her usual prevarication. 'Aw, chill, Mum. I told him to get lost and then he opened the car doors and I got out.'

Nikki gasped. Attempting not to let her distress translate into her tone, she lowered her voice. 'You were in his car? And what do you mean "he opened the car doors", were the car doors locked?'

'Yeah, his driver locked them after I had my panic attack. And they were driving me to his hotel. He says he wants to take me to Ramallah. Says that's in Palestine. Wants me to meet my … aw shit, can't remember what he called her, but he meant my granny.'

There was silence for a moment as Nikki tried to dislodge the block of ice that was rapidly freezing her entire body.

'You okay, Mum?'

'Yes, yes 'course I am. S'pose you had to meet him sometime.' Despite her words, Nikki's tone said the exact opposite and Charlie wasn't slow to pick up on that as she gave one of her snorts. 'Yeah right. Well, I'm not sure I want to go.' She paused. '… And I sure as hell don't want to meet his *other* wife.'

'Other wife?' Nikki was puzzled now. Khal had never said his dad had two wives. 'Your grandad has two wives?'

'Duh, no! Dad's other wife. The one he married before you.'

Had she misheard? No, of course not. Charlie had been clear … crystal clear.

Chapter 39

'What we need is more information on the victimology. The more we find out about *them* the better chance we have of catching this sicko.'

Saj was trying to distract her, but it wasn't working. Nikki nodded absent-mindedly, her fingers twanging the elastic band on her wrist, the pain a distraction from her desire to scrabble through Saj's kitchen drawers till she found a blade, sharp enough to lance her pain. The repeated action had formed a red welt around her arm and with each ping, instead of decreasing the desire to self-harm, it increased. Her mind was still on the bomb that Charlie had dropped. Sajid was trying to lighten the atmosphere, trying desperately to distract her, but Charlie's words kept advancing on her like huge trolls dominating her vision. KHAL'S OTHER WIFE – HIS FIRST WIFE. It was like the words were determined to engulf her, to dwarf her. They seemed to stand ten feet high – angry and volatile – like they could explode and consume her only to spit out the bones, just like the killer had done to Khal's bones. Had he betrayed her? No, surely not Khal. She tried to remember the love light up his eyes – that sparkle that told her that she was the only one in the entire world for him. But she couldn't. It was gone! Another layer of ice joined the layer of permafrost that already covered her heart. That was the only way to protect it – the only way to protect herself.

When she'd heard that Khal hadn't left her by choice but instead had been killed, a momentary flicker had lit up. He *hadn't* left her. He'd been taken. He hadn't betrayed her. He'd loved her. *Now*, only twenty-four hours later, her gut had been ripped out again and she was as bereft and deceived as she'd been fifteen years ago. She should have known better than to nurture even a glimmer of hope.

Fuelled by the urge to do something, anything, Nikki raised her hand to Sajid to tell him to stop and left the flat. Once in the hallway, she took a deep breath. There was *one* person who would know the truth. One other person who Khal would have confided in. She dialled a number on her mobile and waited until it was answered. 'Jacko, you need to come clean with me right now.'

The silence at the other end of the phone told her more than words could that Jacko had indeed been keeping secrets from her. At once her copper's instincts engaged and she decided to be cagey about what she knew. She'd always thought, despite her fraught relationship with his sister, that she could trust Jacko. Now she wasn't so sure. That hesitation, that momentary silence spoke volumes. He knew stuff about Khal that she didn't, and she was determined to get to the truth.

'Well?' She made her tone coarse, demanding. Let him sweat.

'Hi, Nikki. Was just about to call – see how you were getting on.'

Massaging her forehead, Nikki closed her eyes. Jacko's voice was overly effusive. He was definitely hiding something. If she'd had the time she would have turned up at his door, but she didn't, so she'd have to rely on her knowledge of him. He hated being forced into a corner, hated not having time to mull things over. Well, he'd had fifteen fucking years – that was long enough. Nikki was about to exert every ounce of pressure she could. 'Cut the crap, Jacko. I know everything. Now before I hang up and head to your house, you'd better start talking. Tess at home, is she?'

In her mind's eye she could see Jacko, raking his hand through his hair, biting his lip. Her mention of Tess had been a low blow, but she was at war and she meant business. She'd never quite got to the bottom of the animosity between her and Tess. The other woman had always seemed a bit unbalanced, a bit on the edge, to Nikki. Jacko always protected her. Hell, he still lived with her. Nikki wondered if Tess had anything to do with the secrets Jacko was keeping.

'Fuck, Nik. What do you want me to say? Tess didn't mean owt by it. She's just always been affected by having to look after mum, when she was ill. Made her a bit … off-centre … a bit …'

As Jacko's voice trailed off, Nikki tried to make sense of his words. She'd wanted to find out about Khal's first wife – his only wife, in fact, as that marriage nullified her own one to Khal. As the realisation of that sunk in, her stomach lurched. When was this nightmare going to end? Kicking the wall next to Saj's front door, she gathered her thoughts. Jacko was covering for Tess and she wanted to get to the bottom of that. What could the other woman have done that was so bad … tried to poison Khal against her? No, that didn't seem right. Khal would have laughed at her and told Nikki. Little bitch probably knew about Khal's first marriage.

'I know the basics, Jacko. But I need to know everything Tess has done. That's the only way to protect her and I know that's what you want. To protect your sister. You need to come clean. Get it off your chest and then we'll talk about all the other stuff.'

Apart from Jacko's breathing, the silence was interminable, yet Nikki held fast. Jacko hadn't hung up, which meant he was ordering his thoughts. He'd tell her, she was sure of it. In the end, his voice was barely audible when he spoke.

'She's fragile, is Tess.'

Having been at the end of Tess's scathing comments on numerous occasions, fragile was the last word Nikki would have used to describe her … toxic would have been her first choice.

'She was jealous, like – jealous of you and Khal. She liked him, you see.'

Tess hadn't been the only woman who fancied Khal, Nikki knew that, but none of the others had poured venom on her like Tess had done.

'She only wanted to get his attention – that's all. She wanted him to *see* her, spend time with her. That's why she did it.'

Nikki's heart was hammering. She wasn't sure where this was going but it scared the hell out of her. 'What did she do?'

Jacko swallowed so loudly Nikki could hear it down the line. 'She blackmailed him.'

'Blackmailed him?'

'Aw, Nik. I'm sorry about all of this – really sorry. Tess heard me and Khal talking. He told me about … well, about that missus of his back in Palestine …'

Although she'd been expecting it, the words were like a sledge-hammer to the gut.

'It were after you were married and he were a bit pissed. I wanted to tell you, but, well, he was my mate. Nikki? Nikki, you okay?'

Deep breaths, that's all she needed to do. No way would she let him sense how gutted she was. 'And your bitch of a sister blackmailed him how?'

She suspected she knew the answer, but she needed to be sure … needed to hear Jacko say the words.

'She told him, unless he paid her five hundred quid every month then she'd tell you about his other wife.'

That was why Khal had less money. Why he'd taken on a job as well as studying. That little cow was blackmailing him. But Jacko was still talking.

'Just before he went missing, Khal told her he was done paying her the money. Said he was going to tell you everything ... shit, Nik, I'm sorry ... I ... I should have told you.'

Resting her forehead on the wall, Nikki barely stopped herself from crashing it onto the sandstone. Everything she'd believed was warped. The strength she'd taken from her friendship with Jacko was a lie. It was as if the last remnants of Khal had been stripped away from her and replaced by a series of sordid lies and betrayal.

'She needs help, Jacko. Your sister needs help and if you won't get it for her, then I bloody well will. Got it?'

Chapter 40

Nikki fidgeted in the seat and tried to focus on the passing view and the radio as she and Sajid drove along Manningham Lane into town. Huge mill buildings contrasting with Eighties' dull. The rain splattered against the window, matching her mood. Bradford had never looked darker to her, yet no matter how dark her soul was, how empty *she* was, she would still work to find out who'd covered Bradford's cobbled streets with pain. Who'd denied her and Charlie the truth, who had snuffed out an, as yet unknown, number of lives? And, in doing so, she would be ruthless. After all, the one thing she'd inherited from him was his ability to be tough. Her fingers worked their way over the raised scar across her neck. She wasn't her father's daughter for nothing.

'... *Remains found in the Odeon car park have been identified and concerns mount over the possibility that Bradford is once more in the grip of a serial killer – one that appears to have been active for as long as the Yorkshire Ripper. Here we have Detective Springer from the district's Cold Case Unit dispelling these worries ... "the proximity of the remains in the car park indicate a spree murder that has long since run its course. All possible steps will be taken to identify the perpetrator and moves are underway to contact family members" ...*'

Tutting, Sajid banged the heel of his hand on the steering

wheel. 'Can't believe she's completely discounting the idea of a multiple killer. She is either very naive or she's incompetent.'

Nikki snorted, the mere sound of Springer's supercilious tones enough to make her focus. 'Her refusal to even consider a link between the homeless victim and Khal and these other remains is out of order.'

Sajid turned into the alleyway in front of Sunbridge Wells where Bradford's recently refurbished tunnel area, originally the site of a women's prison, played home to a range of eateries, pubs and quaint shops. He pulled to a stop. Getting out, he placed a note on the dashboard of his Jag, declaring they were there on official business. Nikki got out, her legs stiff, her shoulders aching. Thrusting her hands into the pocket of her leather jacket, she looked around the area. If the map was accurate, the access point to the tunnels heading in a maze underneath the city, was over by the steps leading from Sunbridge Road down to here. She and Sajid marched over and, after ascertaining that the place they were looking for was where the beer barrels were piled up in a small fenced-off area, they stopped.

'Looks like we'll have to move these.' Sajid pouted, like a small child being asked to tidy up someone else's junk modelling mess at school.

Nikki managed a grin; she had to concentrate on the job in hand. Charlie sure as hell hadn't misinterpreted her grandad's interest in her. She'd need to deal with that … and soon, before it got out of hand. For now though, she needed to put that thought to the back of her mind. As they contemplated what to do, a man in a high-vis jacket approached from the Sunbridge Wells entrance. His bare arms and stocky build told Nikki that he was probably employed by one of the breweries and sure enough, as he headed towards a large beer van, she realised she was right. Jogging over, she smiled and flashed her warrant card, 'Any chance you can help us, mate? We need access to the tunnels that run underneath this area.'

'Right, you'll be needing to talk to Tim inside. I've just given him back the keys, like. Just dropped off a whole load of barrels.' He looked at Nikka, his gaze moving up and down her body. Glaring, Nikki was about to comment when he spoke. 'I've got a couple of disposable overalls in the back if you like. Drown you like – you're just a bit of a lass and all – but you can roll them up. It's filthy down there – full of rat piss and such. Your big buddy over there might just about squeeze into the XXL ones.'

The smile fell from Nikki's lips. Rats! Fucking rats. Of course, there were rats. She shuddered and followed the helpful man to the back of his lorry as Sajid headed off to get the keys. He was right. The overalls dwarfed Nikki and they smelled vaguely of hops and foist. Mind you, any added protection against scratchy critters and slithering tails was well worthwhile. Bending over, Nikki rolled up the legs till they reached her ankles and then as an afterthought, rummaged in her pockets and took out two large elastic bands. She often collected them from where the postman dropped them on the road outside her house and used them when the urge to cut was strong. Leaning against the lorry, she pulled them, one at a time, over her trainers and allowed them to snap into place around her ankles. Take that you little fuckers – no way you can get up my legs now, eh? She was just repeating the process when Sajid returned, holding a large rusty looking key on a circular key holder. It looked like it came from a dungeon or something and that thought again made Nikki shudder. Dungeons had rats – she was sure of that.

Together, Nikki, Sajid and the beer delivery man clattered the beer crates out of the way until a four-foot-high door became visible with a shiny padlock hinged through a latch. The padlock's obvious newness and size seemed in direct contrast to the rusty old key that Sajid held. Nikita's eyes drifted downwards and she saw an equally rustic-looking keyhole in the door itself beneath the padlock. Sajid stepped forward and inserted the small silver key that was also attached to the keyring and the padlock sprung open. Visions of every horror film she'd ever had the misfortune to watch flooded Nikki's mind. Rats featured heavily in almost all of them and a familiar tension spread across her chest. Sajid, seemingly completely at ease, took the larger key and inserted it in the lock.

The beer man peered over Nikki's head, his body eliciting a not altogether unpleasant aroma of male sweat combined with beer. His broad stature was vaguely comforting. For sure he'd be able to see off any rats that dared to show their twitching little snouts. 'You need to wiggle it a bit to the side. You know, jiggle it. It's a bit temper mental like.'

His mispronunciation of the word temperamental made her smile. Khal used to say that. That and escape goat were his linguistic idiosyncrasies. Thinking of Khal made her think of rats again and as Sajid opened the door, she let out an involuntary yelp and jumped backwards. The two men rolled their eyes and if Nikki hadn't been so embarrassed, she might have taken great delight in boxing their ears. Besides, she was well aware that Sajid might be all brave when it came to rodents, but arachnids were in another league for him and Nikki reckoned there'd be a fair few cobwebs to contend with when they got down into the cellar and tunnels.

Relieved that the door opening hadn't released a barrage of skittering feet, and disgusting rat-pissy odours, Nikki straightened her spine and stepped forward. It was dark and for a moment her eyes couldn't adjust to the shades of grey and black that moved like silk before her. Aware of Sajid stepping forward, she stuck her head through the opening. Relief flooded her when a swaying light bulb sparked to life, sending dull, yellowy light around the immediate vicinity. Sajid rubbed his head and muttered something about 'fucking light' under his breath.

Nikki stepped through onto a platform with steps that would take her further into the cellar – into deeper gloom, away from the frail light. Sajid went down the stairs, while Nikki scanned the area, her ears tuned for scratching sounds. She moved deeper inside.

From the entrance, the beer man coughed and as Nikki turned around, he threw something at her. 'Here, you better take this with you.'

Nikki caught the heavy item. 'Last thing you need is someone seeing the door open and locking the padlock, eh?' He laughed, as if it would be the funniest thing imaginable if that happened and Nikki realised that she didn't really like the man after all – despite him supplying overalls.

As he departed, he pulled the door closed behind him and a sense of impending doom slipped over Nikki like a cloak. Now, it was only her and Saj against the rats … oh, and possibly a serial killer too. She turned and began her descent into the bowels of hell, thankful that yet again, Sajid had found a light switch.

In the cobbled, damp-smelling cellar, Nikki glanced round. In one corner there was a substantial pulley which she presumed was to transport the beer barrels up to whichever establishment needed them. She wasn't entirely sure where each of the pubs and wine bars stored their beer and she didn't actually care. She had other things to think about. Sajid took out the folded map and glanced into the gloom to their left. 'This way.'

They walked in single file past a wall of piled barrels that created a narrow corridor directing them into further darkness. If she didn't feel that her credibility had already been damaged by her earlier yelp, Nikki would have grabbed on to the bottom of Sajid's jacket. Instead she stayed as close behind him as she could and tried to focus on his back and the light from his phone torch that was their only illumination going forward, rather than the slightly damp cold stone walls that arched over her from either side making her realise that she was verging on claustrophobia too. Bad enough the damn rats, but now this.

Breathing through her mouth made it easier to avoid the mildewy smell – however, it tasted worse than it smelled, so Nikki slowed her breathing right down and tried to avoid deep inhalations. They walked in silence, Sajid crouching to accommodate the low roof.

After a few minutes, Nikki got the sense that they were heading uphill again. A couple of times Sajid had stopped as they neared an arched exit that would have taken them into another tunnel. He consulted the map and then continued. Now they'd reached one from which a trickle of water was flowing. He guided his torch to the floor illuminating a drainage system that drained the water further underground. Sajid's voice echoed through the dim light, eerie and ghost-like. 'Bradford Beck – coming down from Listerhills. You know the beck at Theatre in the Mill. Well, I reckon, this is water draining from it. It probably flows fully underneath here into the sewers.'

Nikki groaned in silence. Sewers meant filth and filth meant rats. She wished he'd give up on the geography lessons. 'You following the tunnel that takes us to the ice rink? We need to see how that pans out, if it exits near where Stephanie Fields was found.'

'Just a bit further on, I think then to the left a little. Maybe this tunnel will swerve left anyway.'

The cobbles were slippery with the water and twice Nikki had to grab onto Sajid to stop herself losing her footing completely. The last thing she wanted was to be at eye level with her four-legged adversaries on the ground. Sure enough, after a few hundred yards, the tunnel seemed to swerve left and took a sharper incline. Keeping up with Sajid's larger strides had Nikki breathing heavily. On the plus side, their pace gave her little time to focus on her surroundings and the prospect of scratchy compatriots.

When Sajid stopped and pointed his torch beam towards the wall, Nikki saw a heavy wooden-slatted door, weathered through time. It was then that a scurrying sound behind her and the scamper of something heavy skittering across her foot, made her rear back, onto one leg, lifting the other and propelling the creature into the air where it plummeted towards Sajid, hitting him on his hand on its way to the floor and sending his phone clattering to the ground. The darkness was immediate and absolute. Over the hiccupping sounds of her own breathing and Sajid's curses she heard what sounded like a trillion clay paws scraping and scampering over the floor. The stench the tiny claws threw up from the floor was like centuries worth of ammonia invading her nostrils in one fell swoop. Not even in Jorvik Museum in York had she been faced with such an assault. Her legs started to shake and she turned in a circle, again and again in a desperate attempt to escape them, her skin crawling at the thought that she'd be engulfed by the creatures.

'Fuck, oh fuck, fuck.' She couldn't say anything else. She couldn't stop moving and she couldn't think straight so abject was her fear.

'Nikita!' Sajid's tone was sharp.

When he touched her arm, she jumped and her arm flailed out to her sides. Sajid's muffled oath told her she'd caught him with her arm. 'Fuck, fuck. Can't breathe, Sajid.'

'For Christ's sake, Nikki, use your damn phone. Don't be such a bloody wuss.'

As his words penetrated the fuzz of her brain, Nikki stopped, stock-still. Her breathing filled the air and as her eyes tried to focus on something, anything, her fingers played over the surface of her phone. Thank God her phone threw off a glimmer of light. *Where's the damn torch app? Shit, where is it?*

At last, a narrow ray hit the dank floor. Nikki, desperate to check out the rodent situation, played her beam over the walls and ceiling, her heart thudding as she did so. Landing the light on Sajid's face, her heartrate slowed when she saw his grin. 'Don't be a tosser, Saj. There's a cobweb with a spider just to the right of your ear.'

It was gratifying to see the huge man shriek and duck, his

arms paddling above his head, his mouth screwed up like he thought he'd ingest a spider if he spoke. Her only regret was that the beer man wasn't there to witness her colleague's fall from macho man grace. 'Gotcha!'

Sajid huffed a sigh and with a fearful glance at the ceiling, he lowered his arms. 'Direct the light to the floor, Nik. I need to find my phone.'

Unfortunately, his phone had landed in a puddle. Nikki, reluctant to consider what liquid the puddle consisted of, offered him an old duster she'd found in the pocket of her borrowed overall. 'Maybe just use that to pick it up, eh? We don't want you bringing the plague to Trafalgar House now, do we?'

Accepting her offering, Sajid picked up his phone, shook droplets of foul-smelling liquid off it and tentatively tried to open it. It was dead. 'Looks like we're relying on yours, boss.'

As he uttered the words, Nikki's torch beam faltered and faded a little. She glanced at the battery sign. 'Ten per cent. Get us out of this fucking nightmare, right now.'

She stepped closer to the door, turned the handle and yanked. It wouldn't budge. Again, panic rose in her chest. If they didn't get out right now, her phone didn't have enough power to get them back to the Sunbridge Wells exit. Why the hell had they come here on their own? They hadn't even told Archie where they were exactly. Shit, shit double shit crap!

Chapter 41

Springer glared at the pictures that hung on the wall of the spare incident room at Trafalgar House. She was pissed off that she and Bashir had been relegated to this crappy little cubicle in the bowels of the building, with no windows and every piece of furniture being a discarded piece of shoddy old furniture from the renovations. It didn't help that three incident rooms were out of use because of said renovations and that some of the excess furniture was now piled up high in the corner of this room and covered with sheets that smelled of turpentine and fags.

Parekh's words kept going round and round in her mind. The identification of the other remains found at the same site as Khalid Abadi was disturbing and had added both pressure *and* a new dimension to her investigation. Parekh had been insistent that the remains found some years ago at Sunbridge Wells were linked, and now a prickle of unease kept niggling at the small of her back. She stood up and stretched, placing her hand in the hollow just above her coccyx and pressed hard. Was her dislike of Parekh clouding her judgement? She'd never had time for cocky shits like her. She was sure that Bradford police's diversity policy was responsible for her quick shimmy up the ladder. What was it folk like her were called nowadays – it wasn't half-caste anymore, dual heritage or some such crap? Like the fact that her mother was slapper enough to get caught with someone from outside her culture was grounds for Parekh making DS. Talking of slappers, Nikki may well have wiggled her way up the ladder via a jiggle under the bedsheets. How many fathers did her kids have? *Huh? And here I am relegated to cold cases no one gives a toss about.*

She exhaled as Bashir pushed the door open and entered with a pile of box files tucked under his chin. As well as balancing the boxes, he was carrying two disposable cups of coffee. At least for a Paki, Bashir was all right. He did whatever she said and, more importantly, he was the source of a constant supply of coffee.

'Any word on the ID of the final remains yet?' She wished her tone didn't sound so accusatory, but she couldn't help it. It was a dead giveaway that she was stressed. Mind you, Bashir probably didn't even pick up on it. He was a man of little perception, few words and even fewer ideas – the ideal gopher – go fer this, go fer that. That's what his epitaph should be.

'Not yet. Campbell says he'll send them through as soon as they got anything. All depends if there's anything in the system.'

That was another thing that annoyed her about Bashir. His Yorkshire-isms didn't ring true. Didn't seem right – not when mixed with his thick Pakistani accent. *Born in England and still sounds like he arrived in the country only a year ago.* She indicated that he should plonk the boxes on a table at the side and continued her perusal of the victims' photos. Khalid Abadi went missing fifteen years ago. Victim two, Leo Gayle, went missing in 2005. Victim three, Lorna Mooney, reported missing in 2008. Their fourth victim was as yet unidentified, but the pathologist thought those remains may have been buried more recently.

What did it all mean? Were they linked? She supposed they must be. So far it seemed that they had suffered a similar fate, yet Springer could not for the life of her work out what linked them and how they could have missed a murderer who'd killed at least four times over a course of fifteen years.

The door was thrust open and DCI Archie Hegley marched through. His face was stern and despite the huge wobbling belly that preceded him into the room, Springer had the sense to realise he meant business.

Archie strode over to the board she'd created and yanked one of the pictures off. 'What the hell is this doing here?' He waved the picture at Springer and speckles of spit dappled her nose.

She screwed up her face and side-stepped Archie, moving behind him, forcing him to manoeuvre his bulk in the limited confines available in between the two tables where Bashir had moments before deposited his boxes. She snatched a tissue from a holder and using exaggerated movements, wiped her face. 'I'd have thought that would be perfectly clear, Archie.'

'Don't you use the proverbials with me, Springer. Nikita Parekh is no longer a suspect in this investigation and you damn well know it. Unless of course you're still trying to investigate these deaths separately? And mark my proverbials, if you are, you won't be SIO for long, I'll see to that.'

Springer shrugged. 'As SIO I think it's my prerogative to explore each and every investigative avenue open to me. I can't ignore a clear and obvious link just because DS Parekh is one of your cronies now, can I? You wouldn't expect me to, surely?'

As Archie rolled on the balls of his feet, hands clenched by his sides, Springer forced her lips into a slight patronising smile. 'I know she's a *particular* favourite of yours, but I can't exclude her from our investigations just yet.'

Intrigued by the peculiar puce colour that Archie turned, Springer stepped forward and gripped the photo that hung limply from Archie's hand and pulled. At the last-minute Archie's grip intensified. He yanked it back, the force of his actions pulling Springer off balance a little. When she released it, he lifted it in front of her face and ripped it in two … then in four and then in eight, before tossing it in a nearby bin. 'She's not a suspect.

I've got my eye on you. You don't make progress on this and I'll have you. Got it?'

Springer deliberately widened her smile as he marched out. Inside, her heart was racing and the fire at the base of her spine now licked up towards her shoulder blades. She really needed to get a damn handle on this and pronto. She turned to Bashir. 'Well, what are you waiting for. Get those boxes open and get me something.'

Yep, that backache was rapidly becoming a ball ache. She pressed two fingers tightly over the bridge of her nose before returning to her previous position perusing the crime board. The space under the heading *Suspects* glared out at her like a Belisha beacon. The absence of Nikki Parekh from the board reduced their suspect pool to a grand old total of zilch.

Chapter 42

Deano walked back towards his house. His gut ached and the whole business with Franco had unsettled him big time. How much did Franco know? Was it just about Parekh or was it more than that? He couldn't shake off the feeling that it was more than just about the police officer. He hadn't heard from Franco's missus for days. Okay, she might have decided that Franco was a better bet than Deano. Hell, he couldn't blame her for that – she'd be right to think it – but surely, she'd tell him. Break it off properly. Not just complete silence. What the hell could *he* offer her other than a life on the run escaping her psychopathic ex? Still, she could at least tell him to his face, not just cut him off. Which brought him right back to his biggest worry. Had *she* cut *him* off or had she been *made* to cut him off? Apart from the dull ache in his belly, his gut told him that he *and* Kayleigh were in trouble … big trouble. What the fuck had he been thinking when he hit it off with Franco's skirt? Fucking idiot, that's what he was. Now he'd have to extricate himself and God knew that wouldn't be easy.

The rain had eased off a bit for now, but he still kept his hood up over his head. It gave him the chance to look around, see who was keeping an eye on him without them eyeballing him doing it. If he knew Franco, he could be sure that his network was keeping tabs on him. That's what made it so hard to get one over on the boss. He grinned. The thing was, Franco might be able to put the fear of God into the little turds, but he couldn't give them back the brain cells they'd already obliterated through drug use. The lads by the alleyway were still there, the bitter smell of their spliffs drifting across the road, sharp and strong. At least it eliminated the stench of urine and dog shit that was normally there. They might think they were on the ball, but Deano was aware that their reflexes and observational skills were severely diminished. Perhaps he'd be able to pull something over on those two.

Deano thought about going over and asking them for a bag of weed but reconsidered. Didn't want to end up wasted, like them. Not till he'd sorted his shit out. Plenty of time for a joint later on, after he'd come up with a plan. He gave them a wave and yelled, 'Y'all right, lads?' across the road. *Not exactly* Line of Duty *calibre, them two – more like bloody* Keystone Cops.

The car further up the lane was still there too. Wankers had parked under one of the few streetlights that were still working. As he turned to go up the path to his house, he saw two slumped figures in the vehicle's front seats and the telltale flicker of moving light. Idiots were probably watching Netflix on their phones … or porn. The fact that Franco had utilised such numbers to keep an eye on him sent a spike of fear through him. This was bad news. This couldn't just be about Parekh. This was something more. This was Franco keeping proper tabs on an enemy. Hadn't Deano, on occasion, been called in to be part of the same sort of surveillance operation? All too often these sorts of stakeouts ended up in a trip to the pig farm.

He unlocked the door and entered the house and it was only then, when his shoulders relaxed and his heartbeat slowed, that he realised how on edge he'd been. If Franco had lifted him from the streets tonight instead of toying with him like a Rottweiler with a rag doll, he'd be well and truly fucked. At least now he had a fighting chance. Now he could put his plan into action.

After Big Zee had chucked him out of their car at the end of the road, he'd gone into the shop. The beginnings of an idea forming in his mind, he'd wandered round for ten minutes, playing out the scenarios in his mind until he was sure he was on the right track. He'd lifted a few items from the shelves and paid for them. Back home, he tucked the bag of stuff he'd bought at the corner shop behind the table where the house phone stood surrounded by takeaway leaflets, rizla papers and a half-full ashtray. Leaning back on the cold UPVC door, he allowed his breathing to slow and his muscles to relax. Acrid sweat hung in the air and as he pulled his hoodie over his head, he realised it was coming from him. He raised his head and yelled upstairs. 'Ma, gonna put a wash on for me?'

His mum appeared at the top of the stairs, bundled in a shapeless jumper that leached the colour from her face, her hands each tucked into the opposite sleeve. 'What's that, Dean?'

'Put a wash on for me, Ma. Need it done pronto. There's a bag of dirty clothes in my room and these an' all.'

He dropped the hoodie on the hallway floor, stripped off his T-shirt, kicked off his Reeboks and added his jeans to the pile.

Margo sighed, but disappeared off the landing and by the time Deano, wearing only his Calvin Klein knock-offs, had run up the stairs, she was leaving his room both hands wrapped round the bag of clothes. Deano brushed past her, grabbed a towel and said, 'Hold on I'll give you these too.' As his mum averted her eyes, Deano whipped off his boxers, tossed them on top of the bag and strutted into the bathroom, towel draped over his shoulder.

'You won't mess up the bathroom, will you, Dean love? I've just cleaned it and you know what Roddy's like.'

Deano ignored her as he flicked on the shower and stepped in. As the warm water pounded his body, he ran through his plan for the umpteenth time. He was sure it would work. Sure, he'd thought it through. There were two main objectives and he thought he'd covered both angles: his stepdad would get what was owed him and *he'd* get access to Nikki Parekh. Job done. Well, it would be, if Parekh went along with it anyway. *She* was the single uncertainty in the plan. *She* was the only possible spanner he had come up with. On the other hand, she was his only chance too. Things had gone too far and he was compromised. He saw it clearly now. Franco didn't trust him – maybe he suspected something. Could be he was just narrowing his circle. Whatever, Deano's usefulness to him seemed to have expired and he'd seen what Franco did to people he no longer had use for. Last thing Deano wanted was to land up as pig feed at Sowerby's Pig Farm on the A659.

Stepping from the shower, he got dried, tied the towel round his waist and headed back into his bedroom. A cursory glance round his room told him it was untouched. The only thing missing was the laundry bag his mother had taken and, judging by the racket coming up through the floorboards, was now in the washing machine. He got dressed, all the while going through his plan. With Franco, it paid to be meticulous.

Sticking a smile on his face, he went downstairs. His mum was looking into the fridge when he entered the kitchen, her haggard face carrying the worried expression of someone so cowed they didn't have any self-worth left at all. 'Sausages. It'll have to be sausages again. Roddy won't like it, but I got nowt else in and no money to buy owt. He took my last tenner this morning.' She shrugged her skinny shoulders and shut the door.

Deano walked over and popped the kettle on. 'Look, Ma. Don't worry. I came into a bit of money today. I'll buy us all a take-out for tea. Chinese. We'll do a Just Eat – the three of us – and watch a bit of telly. I got some beers in, we'll have a grand night.'

Margo slumped into a chair and ran shaking fingers through her greasy hair. 'You sure, Dean? You'd do that for your old ma? You're a good lad, you are. Right proud of you. The way you take care of me and all.'

Deano walked over and leaning down dropped a kiss on the

top of her head, hiding his grimace as the stale smell of yesterday's fr-up and sweat filtered up from her greasy hair. ''Course I would, Ma. Now, just you have a cup of tea and relax. You work too hard, you know. Have a couple of hours off. Go on, drink your tea, put your feet up and relax. Roddy won't be back for a while yet.'

He pulled her to her feet and guided her through to the tiny living room – a compliant puppet, too worn down by life to resist, too thankful for any morsel that was thrown her way. It made him sick. He despised her ... her weakness, her neediness. Now, once and for all, she'd pay for all the times she'd stood by and let whichever 'dad' was currently occupying her bed to knock seven bells out of him. This was payback and Deano had no regrets.

Once she was deposited in the oversized couch with the TV controls right next to her, he went back into the kitchen and made her tea adding just enough Lorazepam to knock her out for an hour or so ... just till everything else was set in motion.

His mum snored softly, her lower lip trembling every time she did so. Sprawled on the couch, she looked so little. She looked as if her bones would disintegrate if she was hugged too tightly, but she was stronger than that. Deano had seen her withstand beating after beating, cut after cut, fracture after fracture. Her sunken eyes with huge dark swollen bags sagging beneath them, made her face seem skinnier. Her shoulders and hips had the appearance of coat hangers holding up her misshapen jumper and baggy leggings. Had she always looked like this? Deano frowned. He couldn't remember her ever looking any different. She'd always been a useless pile of bones. Satisfied that she was sound asleep, Deano removed the empty tea mug and gave it a cursory rinse under the kitchen tap before retrieving his stash from the hallway.

He plonked the litre bottle of cheap whisky on the kitchen table. Everything had been easy so far. Now all he had to do was wait for Roddy to come home – a bit of fuel to the fire and then it would be all systems go. Sorted.

Chapter 43

By the rapidly diminishing light of her phone, Nikki met Sajid's gaze, her heart stuttering in her chest. Should they make a mad dash through the tunnels to the other exit? Could they take a risk that one of the closer doors were open? 'Well?'

Aware that her voice had taken on a vaguely panicked tone, she cleared her throat and repeated the word in a more normal tone. 'Well?'

Sajid grinned, extracted the rusty keyring from his pocket with a flourish and edged his way past her. 'Oh, didn't I mention? This is a master key. Supposed to open all the tunnel exit doors. The only one with a padlock on the outside is the Sunbridge Wells one because it serves as a stockroom for the pubs.'

Nikki wanted to punch him hard on the arm, but retrained herself, instead aiming the beam of light at the lock. 'Get a move on then.'

Sajid inserted the key in the lock, jiggled it about a bit and then kicked the door, 'Bloody thing!'

Nikki's heartbeat increased to staccato rates. 'Try the other way.'

Sajid rattled the key a bit and then glanced at Nikki, his mouth split in a huge grin. Nikki punched his arm and pushed past him to open the door for herself. 'Idiot!'

The door had barely scraped open when Nikki all but fell out of the tunnel, drinking up great gulps of air, ignoring the chill bite that hit the back of her throat as she did so. She bent over, hands resting on her knees. Her body juddered with a final shudder as she absorbed her freedom from the rat-infested tunnel behind her. Aware of Sajid behind her, his overalls rustling as he moved to join her, she straightened. One after the other, with Nikki in the lead, they climbed up the handful of steps that led to level ground.

She glanced up and tried out a smile as she observed her partner. With the overalls hood pulled tight round his face and smears of dirt on his cheeks he looked like a mucky kid. The bottoms of his overalls legs were damp with a strange coloured liquid and a quick glance down told her that hers were the same. She noticed a couple of stray cobwebs on his shoulder, yet refrained from mentioning it. Her earlier pissed-off mood had evaporated and she was content to strip off her overalls with a shudder and try to put the entire episode to the back of her mind. If they needed to further examine the tunnels at a later date, she decided that she would absent herself from the proceedings.

Overalls off, she regarded the area around the tunnel exit. They were behind the ice rink and the newish student accommodation, in a private car park that was nearly devoid of cars. Seeing a nearby skip, Nikki grabbed Sajid's overalls up from the floor where he'd dropped them and deposited them, with her own, in the bottom of the skip, hoping that no one had seen their exit from the dungeons, as she was now beginning to refer to the tunnels in her mind. 'Lock up before we forget – don't want anyone else getting access. I'll phone the Alibi bar manager and tell her to use her key to lock that entrance.'

The entrance to the tunnel was tucked into a corner and down some stairs, so not visible to most. As she perused the area, Sajid got out the map and pored over it before prodding an area on the map with his finger. 'Here! That's where Stephanie Fields was found.'

He looked at the map and then lifted it and turned around, surveying the area. 'Over here, near the delivery door to the ice rink.'

They walked over and looked down at a frost ruptured area of about twenty feet by fifteen that sprawled in an elongated oblong along the length of the building. The tarmac was a different colour to the surrounding surface with a ribbon of darker cement joining it to the surrounding ground.

'Burst mains, wasn't it?' Nikki looked at the area and then glanced back to the tunnel exit. 'Easy for someone to move a body from the tunnel to here. Would maybe need to be strongish, but the victim wasn't exactly a big person.'

As the wind picked up, sending a crisp packet swirling round the car park, Nikki looked around. 'There's no lighting here. We need to check that out and whatever security measures were in place in 2003. Also, we need a list of the establishments that have access to these keys and which of their users or employees had access too.'

She shoved her hands in her pockets. 'Can't be sure any list would be conclusive, but it would be a start. Also, the victimology needs really looking at. For now, I can't see a link, but once Archie sends us details of the cadavers found with Khalid, we might be able to formulate some hypotheses.'

She sighed and glanced at Sajid, who, dutifully as ever, was just finishing off noting down her comments in his ever-ready notepad. She should get straight back to Charlie, but the thought of seeing Marcus so soon after the other night, combined with the fact that her skin still crawled with the memory of the rats, and the knowledge that Charlie would only offer her another dose of cold shoulder, made her hesitate. 'Drink? Mannville Arms?'

'Thought you'd never ask. I'm bloody gasping.'

As he started to retrace his steps, Nikki cleared her throat. 'Eh, where do you think you're going?'

Laughing, he winked at her. 'Not up for a short cut then?' He jerked his head towards the tunnels.

Nikki shuddered. 'Yeah right. Think we'll take the long way this time.' Bracing herself against the wind that whipped her ponytail into her face, she marched ahead of Sajid to the front of the ice rink building and ignored his snigger. They both knew that he was as scared of spiders as she was of rats.

Chapter 44

Roddy came home already four sheets to the wind and with an attitude that made even Deano blanch. Deano's stepdad worked with Bradford Landscaping and spent most of his days outdoors tarting up the greenery around the city centre and Bradford's many museums and art gallery sites. He barged into the house. Boots, caked in mud, were kicked into the corner, leaving a wet muddy stain on the paintwork. Wobbling, he leaned on the wall knocking the phone table over and depositing an equally filthy handprint halfway up the peeling wallpaper. He brushed past Deano, elbowing him in the ribs and mumbling under his breath about half-breeds and scroungers and rolled through into the kitchen where he stopped, abruptly. Swivelling round, he glared at his stepson with glazed eyes and opened his mouth releasing a combination of garlic and beer into the atmosphere before shouting, 'Margo. Where the fuck are you?'

Things were going to plan so far, so Deano shrugged and motioned into the living room. 'She's been lying about in there all day watching *Loose Women* and shit. Told her to get to the shops. Even gave her a twenty, but she wouldn't budge. Lazy cow.'

Deano could almost see the Neanderthal cogs turning as Roddy, swaying a little, thought about this. He blinked, and then propelled himself unsteadily through to the living room. As Deano expected, he took one look at Margo sprawled on the couch, saliva drooling from her mouth, snoring gently, and flipped. Raising one foot he aimed a kick towards her belly, missed and only just managed to regain his balance. 'Fucking bitch! Get up! Where's me tea?'

Margo didn't move, her snoring puffing out between semi-open lips. Roddy was only beer-pissed, so Deano stepped in. If left to his own devices, Roddy would crack open another can of lager, slouch in the armchair with the telly blaring and drift into a less elegant sleep than his wife. That wasn't in Deano's plans. No, he needed Roddy whisky-pissed, for then he'd cross the barrier from nasty to downright vicious and enraged.

'Never mind that lazy cow. Let's you and me have a drink in the kitchen.'

Roddy looked at him, his expression saying that was the last thing he'd do even in his semi-inebriated state. So Deano whipped the whisky bottle from behind his back and waved it in front of Roddy. It was as if Christmas had come early. The big man's eyes lit up like a tree. All it needed was for his huge bloody nose to start flashing and he'd look like Rudolph.

His hand whipped forward and he snatched the bottle from Deano. 'Sod off, you little shit. This is a man's drink, not for little poofs like you.'

He barged past Deano into the kitchen unscrewing the lid as he did so.

Deano stood in the doorway, hands in his pockets with his fingers crossed. He needed his plan to work. It just *had* to work. This was his last chance.

After opening a few cupboard doors in turn, Roddy slammed each shut with a ferocity that rattled the units, until he found what he was looking for. Humming, he grabbed the tumbler, slammed it on the table and sloshed a triple measure of the amber liquid into the glass. He raised the glass in a toast to an imaginary audience and took a huge glug before falling into the chair, sending it screeching a few inches across the floor with his weight. Noticing that Deano was still there, he scowled and words slurring, said, 'Thought I told you to sod off,' before refilling his near empty glass.

Deano, pleased that his plan seemed to be working, slouched off upstairs. He'd give it an hour to let the whisky kick in and then hopefully Roddy's response to every injustice ever suffered (of those there were many), every slight endured (and these were frequent), every put-down perpetrated against Roddy McGonagall (and those were constant) ... would erupt.

Sweet!

Chapter 45

Over the years, I've learned that they go through a cycle of responses. Initially they are compliant – too drugged to be otherwise. But, when they start to come around, their brains fuzzy, bodies sore, the adrenaline soon kicks in and that's when things get interesting. The experts call it 'fight or flight' – 'the instinctive physiological response to a threatening situation, which readies one either to resist forcibly or to run away.' It makes me laugh – stupid thing to call it, for, in this particular instance, neither option is a possibility. Still, it makes for interesting footage. You would expect my first instinct, bearing in mind my history as a caregiver, would be to mollycoddle them a bit. That's not how things work. They've been mollycoddled enough. Now it's time for them to prove themselves.

I have to say though, it's good to have a fresh victim. A live one, so to speak. There's a limit to the satisfaction a video provides, but a live one ... well, that's altogether more appealing. Mind you, this bit is not my absolute favourite part of the entire proceedings, but it's pretty much up there with the best bits ... that sluggish awakening, pulse rate fluttering, eyes blinking like a newborn's the first tentative motions followed almost immediately by quicker, more frantic ones, as they realise they are tethered. I've done my first edit; an initial cut, with some prepared dialogue. Granted, I'm a little rusty, still, for a first cut, it's quite good ... quite professional, even if I say so myself.

18th October 2018. Time 19.45. Day One

Our captive is just beginning to rail against his ties. See how weak his movements are as he tries to focus. His memory will be unclear, his attempts to free himself uncoordinated. If he's not careful, he'll cause more damage as the ropes dig into his flesh. The chair arms are hard and the bindings are tied tight. Note the deep red ridge around his wrists and ankles. Every movement sends pins and needles jolting up the arm, inflaming the joints, making each vein ready to burst. Watch, for shortly the pain will awaken him, start the adrenaline surging through his bloodstream, make him realise that his options are limited.

Focus on the face. Can you see the eyes fluttering beneath his lids? He's trying to pull himself out of the fuzz. Trying to force himself to react. Everything will be dull and heavy – his limbs leaden, his head throbbing as dehydration makes him crave liquids. Ah, here it comes – the slow lapping at his lips, trying to suck saliva long dried up into an arid mouth. Lips are cracked and bleeding. His tongue sticks to the roof of his mouth – swallowing is hard, yet he forces himself. Once, twice, he does it. Hear that sound? Like gravel at the back of his throat. That's how dry it is. Now the croak – wait for it ... wait ... ah ... here it comes, listen, now. You don't want to miss it ...

'... 'llo.'

Now the pause. Throat like slithers of glass, and here we go—

'... 'ybody there?'

Head lifts, eyes blinking like an owl in a tree disturbed by a police helicopter spotlight. How apt – for he is a felon, a miserable little thief who has had every opportunity and yet thinks he can play with the big boys. Steals other people's opportunities – damages their lives, condemns the normal people to servitude. Wonder how he will respond to my questions. Will he be the one to break the mould and prove me wrong?

236

I think not. However, his last request might be interesting. Will he want a last hit of cocaine? Send a message to his mum or maybe his partner – that big oaf he often hangs around with, pretending they're just friends when everyone knows they're homosexuals. Well, maybe not everybody. You need to be intuitive to pick up on that – tuned in to the vibes. Maybe most folk have missed it.

Aw look, he's looking right at me. Knows he's in trouble now, doesn't he? Knows he can't fight or buy his way out of this mess. Not this time.

'What do you want?'

Oh dear, as predictable as ever – just what I expected. It confirms my belief that what is about to unfold is no more than his just desserts. Mind you, don't say I'm not fair. Over the next few days he will be given every opportunity to prove his worth. All he has to do is answer the question to my satisfaction. Not hard, is it? Only a question and the answer's right there in front of him, if he'd only engage his brain. They never do though – not so far anyway.

I'm looking forward to this. It's been a long time. Too long? Perhaps. On the other hand, it might just make it all the more satisfying to confirm what I've always believed – to confirm that some of the chosen ones are missing that integral ingredient. The egg that binds the mixture – the yeast that makes it rise. Oh yes, there will be few surprises over the next few days.

Chapter 46

The warmth hit Nikki as soon as she entered The Mannville Arms. The open fire was roaring in the corner and after the smart walk through the increasingly whirling wind, her cheeks were raw and cold to the touch. Sajid's looked similar. She made her way over to the bar, leaving her colleague to head to the toilets to wash his hands and wipe the last of the tunnel dirt off his face. She'd do the same in a moment, but for now all she wanted to do was get a pint. Gordon was his usual taciturn self, grunting at her as she ordered two pints of Sheep Dip ale. She didn't let that put her off. She had a lot of time for Gordon. Unlike some of the customers, Nikki valued a barman who could hold his tongue. She wasn't one of life's small talkers herself. 'Nancy not in today?'

Gordon's grunt was all the reply she got, so she grabbed the two pints in her just-beginning-to-warm-up hands and headed to the table nearest the fire. She didn't normally choose to sit in the open like this, but the draw of the flames after the chill wind was too much to resist. She much preferred ensconcing herself in one of the booths, ignoring the stickiness of both the carpet and the upholstery. She placed the glasses on the table and snagged the chair nearest to the fire for herself. This offered her an uninterrupted view of the booths along the back wall. Waiting for Sajid's return, she did a quick headcount. The Mannville was rarely heaving at teatime. Students didn't tend to hit the pubs till nearer nine, but tonight there was a low buzz of chatter indicating that it was busier than normal.

As her eyes drifted over the room, she saw a big lad she vaguely recognised facing in her direction, stripping a beer mat between his fingers and talking animatedly to someone with their back to her. The lad's expression was earnest, his head nodding as he spoke. Angling to the right a little, Nikki tried to see who he was talking to. Perhaps that would allow her to put a name to the lad's face.

As she peered into the dully lit booth, the other lad turned his head as if, like her, casing out who was in the pub. Nikki froze. Her eyes narrowed and before she could stop herself, she was on her feet and striding towards him. 'What the hell do you think you're doing in here?'

Franco barely lifted his head. Sprawled in the booth, a half-drunk pint before him, he smirked. With dope-glazed eyes, he commenced a slow nodding motion that made Nikki itch to slap him. 'Yoll, it's the oinks. Hope you're off duty, pig. If not, I'll have to report you for breaking the law.' He giggled, a high-pitched pot-fuelled sound that returned that itch to Nikki's hand. 'It'd be my civic duty.'

Nikki leaned right over him, and banged her hand on the table, loud enough to silence the rest of the room as everyone turned their eyes on the scene that was unfolding. From his position behind the bar, Gordon picked up a beer glass and began drying it, his gaze never leaving the table in the corner. Nikki waved a hand at him to let him know she'd no intention of this escalating too much and got a taciturn nod in response.

Pushing her face tight up to Franco's, she could smell the weed coming off him in waves combined with the sickly-sweet smell of some high-end aftershave, no doubt advertised by some muscly actor or footballer. She almost preferred the ammonia smell from the tunnels.

'You!' She prodded her finger as hard as she could into his shoulder, making him wince and rub it. His lower lip jutted out like a petulant child as she continued. 'Ever.' She repeated the jab with equal force. 'Go near my sister's home again and I will.' She administered the third prod of the evening. 'Chop your balls off, put them through a mincer and force feed them to you and your vile little goons. Got it?'

Franco tried to jump to his feet but, hindered by his own lack of coordination, the table and Nikki's close proximity, he fell back onto his arse. He glared across the table at his friend. 'You gonna do something about that?'

Big Zee, that was his name. She remembered now. Nikki usually saw him with a smug little scrote that rented a student house near her.

Franco's mate jumped to his feet and towered over her. He looked less wasted than his boss and that worried Nikki. He looked ready to challenge her, when a larger figure appeared behind her, casting a shadow over the none-too-clean tabletop. Sensing his comforting presence, Nikki smiled. *Sajid to the rescue.*

'Maybe we'll just sit down again, eh?' Sajid's tone was firm. He placed a hand on Nikki's arm and tugged. 'These two tossers are leaving. They won't be back. This pub is now off limits to them, so let's you and me go and enjoy our drinks in peace.'

He raised an eyebrow in Gordon's direction and was awarded one of the barman's signature nods.

Nikki glared from Franco to Big Zee, her eyes still narrowed. It went against the grain to let Franco walk out of there in one piece. He'd threatened Anika and Charlie – but now they had him in their sights they could at least keep an eye on him and his arse-wipe mates. She nodded once, abrupt and fast, and strode back to her seat. Sajid lumbered over behind her, scraped his seat round to Nikki's side of the table and sat down. From here he could keep a proper eye on these two. Picking up Nikki's phone, moaning about his broken one under his breath, he took a quick photo of the two lads and sent it to Archie with a request to get the uniforms to keep an eye on both of them.

In a final show of defiance, Franco stood, peered round the room before taking a last draught of his drink and then swaggered towards the door. Big Zee hesitated and kept glancing at Nikki until Franco's sharp demand spluttered across the room, 'Now, Big Zee – no pigs on this one, okay?'

Nikki wondered what that was all about, then turned her attention to Sajid. Within seconds, he had her laughing as he relived her earlier antics in the tunnels. Happy to return the banter in spades, Nikki sipped her pint and joined in. Her earlier tension had evaporated a little now she'd challenged Franco, although she was still concerned about Khalid's dad's insistence on contacting Charlie. *That* she'd have to deal with before too long, but for now she'd have a drink with her mate, before going home to sort things out with her truculent teenage daughter.

A good plan … until her phone rang. After that it was one mad dash back down the hill to where they'd parked the car earlier at Sunbridge Wells. For once, Nikki was in the lead, with Sajid trailing behind. Amazing how a threat to someone vulnerable … someone you considered to be under your care, could jump start a super dose of adrenaline that could turn a dog-tired, wrung-out woman into a sleek, snappy greyhound with a rabbit in its sights.

Chapter 47

As she turned into Lister's Avenue, Nikki saw the blue of the ambulance light revolving in the darkness. Saj had dropped her at her own car in case they needed to split up and he'd beaten her to the scene. She screeched to a halt and barely stopping to slam the car door shut behind her, she ran over to the ambulance. It was double parked next to a car with no tyres, chassis held up by a pile of bricks. The ambulance's rear door was open and the paramedics were positioning a trolley on the back lift, ready to raise it into the ambulance. The small frame on top barely made a dent in the blanket that covered her. Her eyes were shut, whether because of the swelling around them or because she was unconscious wasn't clear. A drip had been inserted and one of the paramedics held it aloft as they sidled past her with a gentleness born of frequent practice, into the vehicle.

Looking to the right, Nikki saw Deano sitting on one of the fold-down passenger seats already belted up ready for the off. His head was down, and Nikki couldn't see his face. She couldn't tell if he was hurt too. 'Deano?' Despite her previous anger with the boy, her voice was tender. 'Deano, you okay?' He raised his head and Nikki saw that apart from a slight weed glaze, he seemed unhurt. *That was something!* She leaned into the vehicle as the paramedics administered to Margo. 'You need to look after her now, okay?'

Something flickered in his eyes as he nodded and his mouth twitched. Nikki frowned. Was he laughing? Surely not? No – of course not. It'd be the weed making him stupid. She'd seen it before … arresting young lads who could do nowt but laugh as she read them their rights. By the next morning when the effects of the weed had worn off, it was a different story. Reaching over she grabbed his arm and squeezed, her fingers pressing hard.

'Look after her,' she repeated, and waited till he'd nodded, before releasing her hold on him and stepping back.

As the paramedic slammed the door shut, Nikki cast her eyes round the scene. 'She gonna be okay?'

The paramedic shrugged. 'Hard to tell – she's in a bad way. We need to get a move on.'

The medic's words were like a mallet to Nikki's stomach. She'd tried to look after Margo for so long and now the worst had finally happened. Her eyes narrowed as they homed in on the police car parked along the street. Sajid was standing by the rear passenger door and Nikki could tell from his posture that he was barely controlling his anger. His large body blocked the figure that stood next to a waiting uniformed officer, but Nikki had no doubt who it was. Without stopping to consider what she would do when she got there, she ran over to it, pushing Sajid out of the way. Roddy McGonagall was handcuffed and as she reached him, the uniformed officer placed her hand on his head ready to guide him into the back of the car. Nikki flexed her fingers, trying to release the anger that threatened to explode from her. How many times had this brute done this? How many times had he got away with it? She only hoped that *this* time he hadn't succeeded in killing Margo.

Roddy glanced up, stopped, one foot in the vehicle. He jerked his head to remove the hand that was pushing him into the back and a smirk contorted his mouth. When he spoke, his words slurred. 'Aw, if it in't the half-breed come to slap my wrists for me. That's nice.'

He cleared his throat and Nikki, sensing what was coming, moved to the side so that the glob of phlegm landed somewhere to her right. Waves of whisky engulfed her. Roddy was on the harder stuff tonight. The officer yanked his handcuffs with one hand and replaced her hand on his head. 'Get in, now.'

McGonagall threw back his head and laughed.

Nikki wanted to punch him, wanted to rant and tear at him, call him all the vile names she knew, but she refrained. Instead, her voice low, her gaze steady, she said, 'I'll have you for this McGonagall. Make no mistake. This is the last time you'll do this.'

Just before the door slammed on him, he spoke with the precision of a lifelong drunk. Despite being slurred, each word was clear and venomous. 'Not been on the whisky for months, I ain't. That other little half-breed set me up for this. Wants me gone. Wants the house for himself, that one.'

He stuck his middle finger up at Nikki. 'So, porky pig, looks like I'm not culpable. Not if I've been knowingly supplied with whisky.' He started to laugh and tried to slap his thigh, missing by a good two inches.

There was nothing more compelling than the lucidity of a drunk talking sense. Nikki, her mind whirling, watched the car drive off. Was Roddy just talking through drink or had Deano really set this up? If anyone was aware of the effect spirits had on his stepdad, it was Deano and she'd certainly smelled cheap whisky coming off him in rafts. Last time she spoke to Margo, the other woman had assured her that Roddy was sticking to beer only and true enough, although she'd no life to speak of, Margo hadn't sported any visible injuries for a while now. Nikki screwed up her mouth. Roddy McGonagall was too vicious when under the influence of spirits to care what visible trace he left on his partner. On beer, he was cruel right enough, but he stopped at doing much more than pushing her around – not that pushing

Margo around was acceptable either, but it was preferable to the sort of injuries that could leave her friend comatose.

Nikki turned on her heel and glanced round at the crowds who had gathered. Most were neighbours, who hung about the pavement or in their gardens, but she detected movement in the cobbled alley to the left. She peered through the dimness, pleased that the streetlamps cast some light onto the street. Was that Franco? Was he following her? She took a step towards the alley, but before she could get there, someone called her name. She glanced round and saw a uniformed officer waving at her.

'Give me a minute, yeah?' When she turned back to the alleyway it was empty. She could have sworn she had seen two figures loitering there and she was almost sure one of them was Franco. If it was, this put a whole new complexion on things. She turned back to the officer who'd greeted her and listened as he explained that Deano had called the incident in and that they arrived shortly after the first responders. Leaving them to finish off getting statements and getting the scene processed, Nikki gave a wave to the remaining officers who were trying to take statements from the neighbours congregating outside and walked over to Sajid.

'You go to her, Nik. I'll stay here and then head back to the station later to see if that bastard has sobered up enough to interview.'

Nikki could have kissed him. That was the main reason she loved working with Sajid. He was intuitive. They made a good team. She nodded and got back into her car. Now she had two things to worry about. First, if Roddy McGonagall had been speaking the truth, she'd make it her business to find out if the little toad Deano was responsible in any way for what had happened to his mum. Secondly, if Franco was monitoring what happened in Listerhills so closely even after what he'd done to Haqib, and after her earlier brush with him, then he clearly had a bigger investment in the area than she'd thought.

She got into her car, turned the key in the ignition and glanced in her rear-view mirror. A car a couple of spaces behind started up too. Coincidence? Maybe. Usually, Nikki would have driven straight down the street and turned onto the main road, but something, possibly that fleeting glance of Franco and his thug, made her hesitate. Instead, she accelerated quickly, did a U-turn at a speed Lewis Hamilton would have been proud of and headed back the way she'd come. As she neared the other car, she slowed and keeping her head pointed straight ahead, strained her eyes to the side. There were two shapes in the vehicle – both in the front. By the interior light of the car, she saw the driver, head bowed as if he was fiddling with the radio. She couldn't be sure it was Franco, however, Big Zee's distinctive frame was instantly recognisable in the passenger seat.

Driving on, she looked in her rear-view trying to catch a glimpse of the number plate, but it was covered with muck. A trick often used to save having to steal a legitimate number plate from another car. Pissed off, she continued on her way. Her final glimpse of the car before she turned off, was it driving towards the opposite end of the street. Perhaps it *was* just coincidence. Possibly Franco had turned up to see Deano and decided to stay for the fireworks, watching from a safe distance to keep out of the way of the uniforms.

Chapter 48

Resigned to spending yet more time at Bradford Royal, Nikki headed down Ingleby Road, keeping an eye on her rear-view mirror. Franco sticking around after what he and his goons had done to Haqib seemed a bit reckless to her. Mind you, his attack on Haqib hadn't made him keep his head down, had it? He'd still rolled up to terrorise Anika and then later on turned up at her watering hole. Little tosser's arrogance knew no bounds! Unless, of course there was some other agenda going on that she knew nothing about. Her stomach rumbled – she hadn't eaten at all today and she was starving, but she couldn't just leave Margo with Deano. She had to at least show face, find out what had happened and, of course prod the little scrote until he told her the truth about what had gone on tonight.

She thought she saw Franco's car behind her in the rear-view mirror. Keeping her driving steady, instead of taking the left that she would normally take to get to BRI, she drove straight at the Morrisons traffic lights. The car behind her also accelerated to follow her through the lights. Was he following her? She wasn't sure, but she didn't like it. Seeing Franco near her home had put her on edge. He was usually hard to find, like a nasty smell under the floorboards, difficult to find but persistent as hell. Yet, today he'd been visible not one, not two, but three times. The fact that he was there with his trolls meant that something was afoot and she'd bet money on it being something to do with Deano. She'd got the impression that they were keeping an eye on her too. What other reason could they have for turning up at the Mannville? What was it Deano had said about Franco when she'd spoken to him last time? 'He'll kill me. Franco will kill me.' Maybe he hadn't been visiting Deano. Maybe he'd been keeping an eye on the little turd. *Seems I've something in common with Franco after all.*

Keen to get to Deano to find out why Franco was in Listerhills, yet reluctant to let Franco know she had contact with the lad, she decided to enlist Ali Khan's help. If she turned up at his taxi rank, they'd be able to work out some sort of tactic to get her to Bradford Royal Infirmary without Franco knowing she'd spoken to Deano. Better make it quick though. Margo looked bad and Nikki wanted to get there before it was too late. Margo had been a good friend to her in the past.

Tiredness weighed heavy on Nikki and she longed to get home and to bed, but she needed to be with her friend. She felt a momentary pang as she remembered Charlie. She owed Charlie some time … and Marcus. Shit, when would this all end? When would she have the chance to repair the damage with Charlie, sort out Khal's old man and deal with her own grief? Exhaling, she straightened up in her seat, rolling her shoulders to ease the tension. She'd no time to be a wuss. Just needed to get on with it – as always.

Ali's taxi firm was on Toller Lane, set back off the road between an Asian sweet shop and a knackered old newsagent. Ali had been in business for as long as Nikki could remember. When she and Khalid had been students it was Ali's dad who ran the business. Now that his dad had Alzheimer's, Ali ran it on his own. Nikki pulled into the large car park reserved for taxis and got out. Light spilled from the office window as she approached, and the constant ringing of phones told her business was good. She was pleased. He'd recently won the BRI accessibility contract from a rival and was employing more drivers than ever. If there was one thing Nikki was sure of, it was that this was one of the taxi businesses in Bradford that *didn't* launder money.

Waving at a couple of the drivers who were smoking outside whilst waiting for rides, she pushed open the door and stepped through, aware that the ring from the small bell wouldn't be heard above the phones and the loud chatter of the operators as they directed drivers. The first thing that hit you when you went into Ali's front office was the heat. Jenny, his manager, was always cold and now that the clocks were about to change and the autumn winds had been picking up, she'd upped the heating accordingly. The second thing was how organised it looked. A row of computers and phones faced the door and behind each sat a microphoned operator. The walls were painted a clean Magnolia and the wooden floor sparkled.

Nikki approached Jenny who was talking to a client and, catching her eye, Nikki gestured towards the inner office. Ali would be in his sanctum, no doubt praying, reading the Quran or doing his books. Jenny nodded and waved her away, leaving Nikki to walk down the short corridor to Ali's office. Jenny and Nikki would catch up another time. Over the years, the two women had become close. Jenny had also lost her husband young and now the business was her life. Ali paid her handsomely for her dedication. Often Nikki wondered if something was going on between the two, but if it was, they kept it a fiercely guarded secret. Knocking on the door, Nikki waited for a mere second before his rumbling voice bid her enter.

The office was large and as messy as the outer office was orderly. Ali jumped up from behind his old wooden, rather wobbly desk and, forehead wrinkled with concern, said, 'Thank Allah, you are okay, Nikki. Your friend Sajid wouldn't take no for an answer the other day.'

He shrugged his large shoulders, straining against his shalwar. 'I was in an awkward position – police and all.'

'Don't worry. It's all sorted. What I'm here for is a different matter. I think I'm being followed by a Ferrari and I need to get to BRI without them knowing I've left the premises.'

Ali's frown deepened. 'Are you in trouble? You seem to be spending a hell of a lot of time at BRI recently.'

Tell me about it. 'No, this is one of my neighbours, but the lads outside don't need to know I'm there. I need to talk to her son without them sussing it out.'

Lifting his phone, Ali spoke a few words in Urdu, then nodded his head. 'Haris is going to drive round the back as if he needs his car hoovering. We'll give him five minutes to hoover it and then you can slip in the back seat. I asked him if there was a Ferrari anywhere in the street and he sent one of the lads up to the shop to check. Now, how are you, Nikki? How's the kids? I heard about Khalid – I knew he wouldn't have left you. Not Khalid.'

After catching up on family for a few minutes, the desk phone rang and when the conversation was over, Ali said, 'There's a Ferrari with two idiots parked up along the pavement near the shop. There's also another car – a Rover, with three guys in – all white. My lad wasn't sure if both cars have eyes on you or if they're staking out us or each other. We'll be keeping an eye on them, that's for sure.'

Nikki wasn't sure how to feel now her suspicions were confirmed – the Ferrari would be Franco, but the other vehicle was worrying, whoever it was there for. She doubted that Franco would risk owt in public. Even he wouldn't attack a police officer in the middle of Bradford with witnesses around. So, what was his game? The fact he'd been hanging out near Deano's house made her more convinced something was going on. Ali's phone buzzed again and he stood up. 'Car's ready round the back. You hide in the back seat and Haris will drop you off at the back BRI entrance where the tunnel is. We have a card for the barrier so we can pick up nurses who are off duty. That way no one will see you going in.'

Nikki shook her friend's hand. 'Yet again, I owe you one.'

But Ali shook his head. 'No, these small favours do not yet make up for what you did for my family. I still owe you – besides, we're friends now. Who's counting?'

Such sincerity made a small smile cross her tired face. He was a good friend and his faith in her was irreplaceable. But what really made him worth his weight in gold was his ability to make her laugh. To raise her spirits.

Ali hugged her as she climbed onto the back seat of the taxi and lay down. Haris, in direct contrast to Ali, was a big taciturn man who smelled strongly of smoke. He was Ali's right-hand man – his cousin – and, despite his lack of conversation, Nikki was glad he was the one to escort her to BRI. When they arrived at the barrier, the chatter from the microphones and the Asian radio station on low the only noise, Haris spoke for the first time. 'Both vehicles are still at the taxi rank. Give me a call when you want to go back and pick up your car. I'll follow you home – make sure those idiots don't try anything.'

Nikki thanked him and crawled out of the car. As she approached the yawning dark hole that signalled the start of the tunnel that led to the back entrance to the hospital, Nikki's heart sped up. The first few lights were out – again! The brick walls with their insidious cold gave her the heebie-jeebies and her thoughts automatically went back to the city centre tunnels and rodents – big dark rodents with sharp claws and toothy teeth. Shit! She'd had enough of tunnels to last her a damn lifetime. She shuddered and swore, again. *Come on, Nikki, get a bloody grip on yourself. These tunnels are well used. No rats, no wormy tails, no scurrying feet.* She flicked her phone light on and holding her breath took her first step in, trying not to jump when two Filipino nurses appeared from the flickering light she could now see just ahead. They smiled at her as they passed – not a care in the world. Feeling a little silly, Nikki switched her torch off, pocketed her phone and straightening her back, headed for the flickering lights, managing to keep her pace to just this side of a frantic run. Her breathing eased when she reached the lit area of the tunnel which took her into the bowels of the hospital. From here she took a circuitous route up to the Intensive Care Unit where she'd been told Margo had been taken.

Chapter 49

It had done him good to see Khalid's daughter, his granddaughter, up close today. She looked very much like her father and although that made him sad, it also gave him hope. In temperament, though, she was too much like her mother and that would have to be sorted out before long. He'd allowed her to leave when she'd got upset, but he would bide his time – persevere. How could she possibly want to remain with that mongrel mother of hers with her bastard children in that dingy estate? He could offer her so much more. True, Tabana would perhaps find it hard to accept her husband's daughter into the home, but if he and Enaya planned things carefully, that could work out. A suitable match and Tabana would no longer be *his* responsibility. Khalid's defection to stay in the UK had been an embarrassment, but now they knew he hadn't voluntarily remained, they need be embarrassed no more.

He looked out the window. This relentless rain made his limbs ache, his bones throb and he yearned for the warmth of the Ramallah sunshine. The time difference was sapping all his energy too and if it wasn't for the phone call that he awaited, he would have succumbed to the too-soft bed. A light tap at the door told him his light snack had arrived. Bradford had a reputation for selling only halal chicken, yet Burhan couldn't trust that. Pakistanis, he'd learned over the years, were not to be trusted and he was certain that the Bradford ones would be no different. So, he'd selected a vegetarian meal – tasteless and insipid.

He let the round-faced waiter in, tipping him grandly for setting up his food on the table near the window. Driving rain hammered against the panes making Burhan wonder if perhaps the glass would break. He lifted an imperious finger and indicated the sheer black pane. 'Close the curtains.'

Rushing round, his eagerness accelerated by the hope of another substantial tip, the boy whipped the curtains shut, immediately muffling the pebble drops of rain. That one single action made the room feel warmer, made Burhan's bones less achy, his head less heavy. He smiled and tossed another ten-pound note towards the beaming boy, laughing aloud as the lad failed to catch it and scrabbled about near the carpet to retrieve it as it fluttered down.

Burhan nibbled at the food in front of him, spearing over-cooked veg with a fork and forcing himself to eat it. He'd be no good to anyone if he got any more ill. The solicitor should have called by now. This was important. He'd made a substantial payment up front and expected preferential treatment. He glanced at his watch. He'd give him another ten minutes and then he'd make the call. *They* should be dancing to *his* tune. He was the one paying after all. As he pushed his plate of half-eaten food aside, his phone rang. Snatching it up, he dabbed the cloth napkin against his lips, before answering, his tone abrupt. 'Yes.'

'Good evening, Mr Abadi. As agreed, I am phoning you with the progress I have made. Firstly, I have secured a reputable private investigator who now has a team of his employees monitoring Nikita Parekh and her daughter at all times. It will be expensive, but, as you said, money is no object.'

Burhan scowled. From the investigator's obsequious tone, he deducted that his earlier impatience had not gone unnoticed and the mention of money came as no surprise. He'd summed up, correctly it seemed, that Abubakhar Husayni was, most definitely a money-grabbing little sleazeball. It made no difference to him. As long as he got results, the man would be paid, as would the investigators he had employed. 'Of course, I'll transfer the money – but only after each *satisfactory* daily report into the comings and goings of *both* my granddaughter and Nikita Parekh, understood?'

The solicitor grumbled, but Burhan brushed his mumblings aside. 'What else do you have for me?'

Even through the phone line, he could sense the solicitor's excitement and it gave him hope that perhaps, after all, everything would go to plan.

'It seems that Nikita Parekh's sister is our way in. She is in a relationship with a prominent Bradford councillor – a married councillor with an interest in policing in Bradford.'

'And that helps me how?'

'Well, the councillor Yousaf Mirza has fathered a child with Parekh's sister, yet still lives with his wife, with whom he has a further two children. He does not publicly recognise his illegitimate offspring and when I, shall we say, quizzed him about his mistress' sister, he was keen to assist us in our endeavours.'

Burhan nodded. This was good news. He needed to pressure Nikita Parekh from all directions. 'Be specific. I want to know exactly how this helps me.'

'Well, Councillor Mirza has served on many committees with DS Springer who worked with Missing Persons and now heads up the Cold Case Unit in Bradford. He informs me that she is insistent that Parekh is still a person of interest in your son's death. He has expressed his desire for a swift and satisfactory conclusion to the investigation.'

Tapping his fingers on the table, the waft of stale food curdled Burhan's stomach. He'd listened to the news earlier and he was well aware that other remains had been discovered. The likelihood that Parekh, slut though she may be, had murdered his son, was diminishing rapidly. He sighed. The decision he had to take now was, did he continue to muddy the waters by exerting pressure on the officers investigating Khalid's death to pursue Nikita Parekh *or* did he call them off and insist on a more expansive investigation? He bit his lip. Khalid was long dead and the important thing now was the endgame and the endgame was bringing Khalid's daughter back to her grandmother … back to her family. If that meant that Khalid's real killer remained at large until they could remove Charlie to safety, then it was a small price to pay.

'Do whatever it takes. Get your investigators to dig up the dirt, force your councillor to exert pressure and make that woman pay. I want my granddaughter at home with her family … no matter the cost.'

Chapter 50

Not for the first time that day, Nikki wished she was at home. Much as she'd nothing against hospitals and, as far as her limited experience would allow, Bradford Royal Infirmary was no worse than most NHS hospitals across the country, she could cheerfully never visit it again. Unfortunately, in her line of work, that was very unlikely. She buzzed for entry to the Intesive Care Unit and, after showing her ID, was allowed in. Heading straight for the nurses' desk for an update on Margo's condition, she discovered that her friend had just been taken up to surgery to investigate a suspected brain haemorrhage. In addition to that, she had extensive bruising all over her body. Her head had been subjected to a series of traumas and the prognosis was undetermined.

A familiar coil of anger wrapped itself round Nikki. Every bone squeezed against her internal organs and dizziness made her grab hold of the desk. Waving away the nurse's solicitous attention, she made her way to the waiting room, each step measured, her hands clenched by her sides. She needed to sit down. She needed to think. If she'd managed to convince Margo to dob Roddy in before now, then this would never have happened. Her friend wouldn't be lying in an operating theatre at BRI with little chance of surviving. She *should* have insisted that Margo leave Roddy. She should have put more pressure on *him*. Forced *him* to leave. Instead, she'd taken a back seat, and look what had happened.

She opened the waiting-room door and walked in. Deano was sprawled over three seats, his hoodie up over his head and the jacket he'd been wearing earlier draped over his prone frame and pulled up under his chin. The anger constricting her body broke free and a flash of blinding light scorched her eyes. Before she could stop herself, she was beside him, kicking one of the chairs away, forcing his feet to clatter to the floor. Within seconds, her hands gripped the material under Deano's throat and yanked his slight frame upwards. Amid the faint aroma of Lynx and fags, his eyes sprung open, startled. She yanked him closer to her and allowing every venomous thought to show in her face, she shook him. 'You fucking little toad. You *could've* stopped him. You *should've* kept an eye on him.'

The door opened behind her and hearing the gasp of air, Nikki released him, flinging him back onto his makeshift bed. As he rattled back onto the plastic chair, Deano's mouth lifted in a taunting grin and the urge to slam her fist into his face had never been stronger. Instead, hot-faced, Nikki turned and forced herself to smile at the nurse who stood wide eyed, her gaze moving between Nikki and Deano. The mug of tea in her hand trembled enough to slop muddy liquid onto the floor. 'I brought you some tea with sugar – extra sugar.'

Nikki exhaled and rolled her shoulders, trying to release the knots that throbbed there. From somewhere, she dredged what she hoped was a reassuring smile and stepped forward, hands outstretched to accept the drink. 'Just what I need right now.'

With alacrity, the nurse nodded, an uncertain smile flicking over her lips and with a quick glance at Deano, who had once more raised his feet onto the chair opposite, she turned to leave. Pulling the door open, she turned back. 'Get your feet off the chair or …'

'Yeah, or what, *darling*?'

The nurse straightened, pulled her tunic more firmly over her hips and held his gaze. 'I'll get the security guards to remove you. We don't usually let stoners hang around in here. I were just being respectful on account of your mum, but that works both ways.' She indicated his feet, 'Got it?'

In exaggerated slow motion, Deano pushed himself out of his slouch and swung his legs round till both feet touched the floor, his elbows resting on his knees. 'Happy?'

'Perfectly.' The nurse smiled at Nikki and exited the room, leaving a heavy silence behind.

The smell of the sweet tea teased Nikki's nostrils, eliciting a strange reaction – a combination of nausea and craving. Her stomach rumbled, telling her to drink the damn tea before she fainted. She was aware the sugar rush would give her a short-lived spike. Maybe enough to let her deal with this little scrote. She sat opposite Deano, glowering at him as she blew on her tea. 'You better start talking to me, you little shit. Roddy's blaming you for this, saying you set him up.'

Deano shrugged and leaned forward resting an elbow on either thigh, an 'I'm tough so don't fuck with me' look on his face. 'You believe that? Wouldn't want my own mam hurt now, would I? He's a lying dick.'

Nikki could well believe that Roddy McGonagall *was* a lying dick; however, there was something in Deano's eyes that made her pause. That look combined with Franco's presence made her wonder. Her gut told her she'd been wise to cover her tracks on the way here. Now was her chance to find out if Deano thought the same. 'Saw Franco outside your house. Think he's got a thing for me, cos he followed me here. Set up shop outside with those goons of his.'

Deano pulled an arrogant smirk across his face, but not before it had paled slightly. His leg began to jiggle up and down as he patted around his trousers, presumably looking for smokes. 'Followed you?'

Nikki grinned. 'Yeah, that's right. He followed me *all* the way from your house to here. Thing is, I can't work out why. Any ideas?'

Jumping to his feet, Deano moved to the window, peering this way and that through the rain as if, from the third floor, he'd be able to identify the thugs below. He spun round. 'They didn't see you, did they? Shit!'

He thrust his hands in the pouch at the front of his hoodie and began pacing the room, his feet dragging across the linoleum as he moved.

For a full minute, Nikki watched, happy to let him suffer. 'That cause problems for you, does it? Franco knowing I'm here?'

Deano scraped his fingers across his shaven skull, knocking his hood from his head. The swastika on his temple looked alive as it beat a tattoo against his skin. *Well, well, poor Deano's not feeling so good.* He began to pace the room whilst Nikki sipped her tea, allowing its overly sweet warmth to trickle down her throat, warming her as it went. As it landed in her belly, her stomach gurgled again – more in welcome this time. 'Maybe it's time for you to tell me everything.'

Hiding her distaste for the piece of vermin in front of her, she kept her voice low, reassuring. 'Come on, sit down and just get it *all* off your chest.'

'Nobody's allowed in here, are they? Only relatives like, yeah? Relatives and the pigs – that's it, innit?' He breathed out in short sharp pants, like a boxer gearing up to start the knockout round. He looked like one of those rodents she was so afraid of – maybe a bigger one, like a weasel or a ferret. Whatever, the irony of her lack of fear for this big one in comparison to the smaller ones, was not lost on her.

Dragging a chair over, he sat opposite her, his scraggly shaved head bobbing, his breath rancid with fear. 'You gotta help me. I'm in deep with Franco and he's gonna kill me.'

Nikki thought for a second and then brought her phone out. 'If you're giving me juice on Franco, I need to record it.'

'Fuck's sake.'

'Your call, Deano, your call.'

Exhaling, Deano thought for a moment before nodding. Nikki, not giving him the chance to reconsider, set her phone to record before reading him his rights.

'Shit, you're arresting me?'

'I'm not – not yet anyway. Just keeping everything on the straight and narrow, for both our sakes. Need to keep it legit, don't we?'

Leg bouncing up and down and as if he thought it would offer some protection from whatever was going to happen next, Deano dragged his hood up over his head, casting a shadow over his face.

Nikki frowned. Was that a tear in his eyes …? Tough. If it was, he deserved it. 'I need you to specify that you're not speaking under duress and then repeat what you've just said. Deano nodded and then, after clearing his throat, did as Nikki asked.

'So why exactly is Franco after you?'

'He's found out about me and Kayleigh. I know he has. She's not picking up my calls on the burner we have and I don't know what to do. Me and her were in love, get it?'

Maintaining a neutral expression, Nikki continued. 'And Kayleigh is …?'

'Franco's baby mama, innit.'

For fuck's sake … Like an American hood movie from the South Side of Chicago to bloody Listerhills in Bradford … Baby mama indeed. Stupid little idiot. Of all the lasses he could have got mixed up with, Deano had to choose the girlfriend of the biggest psycho in Bradford. For a nanosecond, his apparent concern over Kayleigh made Nikita's estimation of Deano go up a notch. But his next words showed him to be the selfish little shit she'd always believed him to be.

'Stupid bint recorded us, din't' she? Got herself up the spout too. Says it's mine, not Franco's. Can't believe her though. Fucking whore – spreading her legs for Franco's right-hand man and then threatening to show the video to Franco. Bet she's screwed that fucking Big Zee too. Shit – she must've known he'd kill us. He's bloody mental, Franco is. *You* saw what he did to your Haqib.'

Nikki *had* seen what Franco had done to Haqib, but she deliberately pushed all thoughts of her nephew to the back of her mind for now and focused on the sexist little turd before her. She wanted to slap him. Clearly the whole idea of 'taking two to do the shadoobie doobies' had escaped Deano, as had the concept of mutual responsibility. Mind you, Nikki would admit that her own idea of mutual responsibility was to keep the father of her kids at a distance. Kayleigh would have been well advised to have taken a leaf out of her book, if Franco and Deano were anything to go by. At least Marcus was a decent bloke.

Nikki couldn't quite get her head around why Kayleigh would risk everything she had with Franco for Deano – all the money, the nights out, the drugs, the high life, the posh house out Ilkley way. Didn't add up. Unless, of course, Deano had hidden depths that had escaped Nikki's notice. *Yeah right!* 'So, Deano, you fear for Kayleigh's safety?'

'Aw fuck off, pig! It's not *her* damn safety I'm bothered about, it's me own. I've seen what Franco does to folk he takes a dislike to and I don't want to end up on one of his pig farms.'

'Franco make a habit of disposing of people on pig farms, does he?' This was it, the big one. She could see the calculation in Deano's eyes. Either he went all in right now with Nikki and blew the lid off Franco's enterprise in order to get him locked up for the long haul *or* he went it alone against Franco. Nikki counted down from ten in her head. Her bet was on reaching no more than five before the little turd caved. She reached seven.

'I've got it all written down.' He scrabbled in his pockets and took a lined A4 sheet of paper out. It was scruffy and covered in big loopy writing.

Proof definite it was not, but it was a start.

Holding it out to her, Deano continued, 'That's every dealer he offed for not paying up on time. You think that manky little nephew of yours got it hard … well, he's one of the lucky ones. Franco's a fucking psycho. I can name at least ten that he's fed to the pigs and I don't want to be number eleven, you get me?'

Nikki did indeed get him, but she had to be sure that she also got Franco … trussed up like a turkey preferably. 'Did you see him killing them … feeding them to the pigs?'

Deano avoided meeting her gaze and shuffled a bit on his seat. He could probably tell that less than concrete evidence wasn't going to cut it. Finally, he shrugged. 'We all know he does it. Him and Big Zee and Tyke.'

Nikki let it go for now. Saj would press harder during the follow-up interview. For now, she wanted a sense of what he could give them. 'We'll need everything you got, Deano. Every little thing. We'll need all the drug shit, all the underage prostitution and grooming racket, all the murders, all his associates – the lot. Dates, times, photographs … concrete evidence. That's the *only* way out of this for you. You got that – concrete evidence?'

Although, he tried to hide the cloud that flitted across his face at Nikki's words, she caught it. Little turd didn't have anything concrete despite his big talk. He was playing for time. Still, maybe he'd have something they could build on.

Deano, head bowed, appeared to think about that for a moment. 'I think he's done summat to Tyke too. Earlier on it was just Big Zee. Tyke weren't anywhere to be seen.'

When Nikki had seen Franco earlier on, he'd been with Big Zee at The Mannville Arms – Tyke hadn't been there.

'Why would Franco want to do summat to Tyke – he screwing his *baby mama* too?'

Deano sniffed and wiped his sleeve across his nose, leaving a trail of slime along the cuff. Noticing it, he used the other sleeve to rub it away.

Nikki's stomach contracted and she wished she'd not bothered with the tea.

'Him and Big Zee are poofs, right? They think nobody knows, but we all do. Franco don't like it. Dun't want anybody thinking he's one of them, does he? That's why I reckon he's fed Tyke to the pigs.' He looked at Nikita, his eyes sharp and calculating. 'I'll get Witness Protection, yeah?'

Nikki shrugged. He'd given her a shedload of information to process, but none of it was corroborated yet. It was all hearsay. She'd need to get Archie on the case to dig up the evidence. However, there was one way more important issue to deal with. 'Not my pay scale, that one, Deano. Let's talk about what happened tonight, eh? With your mum.'

Bottom lip pouting, Deano shrugged and his voice took on a whingeing tone. 'Couldn't just walk up to you in the street now, could I? Franco and his boys have been following me everywhere. Had to box clever with this one.'

Nikki's chest tightened. This was the bit she really needed to hear. 'You lost me, Deano.'

'Well, I knew I could cut a deal with you. Get Franco locked up and off me back, like. But Franco had already warned me off after one of his boys reported me talking to you the other week. Needed to find a way of speaking to you without him finding out.'

He glared at Nikki, his bottom lip turned down and an ugly spark of anger in his eyes as his fists clenched in his lap. 'But you fucked that one up, didn't you? Fucking Franco tailed you here. Now you gotta get me out of this mess. Arrest him – get him and Big Zee off the streets. Won't be safe for me otherwise.'

And he was on his feet again, pacing the floor between where Nikki was sitting and the window where the rain still lashed.

But Nikki wasn't satisfied, she kept her tone neutral, interested, like she thought he was the best thing since wholemeal chapattis. 'What did you do?'

Too busy pacing to look at her, he snorted. 'Was fucking easy.

She's so needy, is me mam. All I had to do was offer to buy a Chinkies and make her a cup of tea and she were happy. Drugged her tea, so when the old bastard came back, he lost it with her. Started goin' off on one.'

Deano slammed his skinny arse onto the chair next to Nikki's, sending it crashing against the wall. 'But he's been off the hard stuff for months – he'd only had beer, so he crashed next to her, moaning on.'

Bending one leg over his opposite knee, Deano cradled it with both arms, his foot drumming a silent beat mid-air. His voice took on a lighter, self-satisfied, almost gloating tone. 'I'd planned for that though. Gave him a bottle of whisky and waited. Didn't take long for it to have an effect. Never seen him so pissed off. He were raving and raging and she were lying there drugged up, not getting what were happening to her.'

He ran his sleeve over his nose again and Nikki averted her eyes. She was disgusted enough by his words without being subjected to his grotesque personal habits too. She'd suspected he was culpable in what had happened to Margo, but hearing all the venom, the complete disregard for his own mum spout from his lips, made it hard for her to hold it together. She had to though ... had to get the admission from him. Not because it would make one whit of difference to his ultimate prison time – she doubted he'd participated in his mum's beating – but because *she* needed to hear it. Needed it etched in her heart so that she'd focus on making sure he got what was coming to him.

'When I were sure he'd done enough for the oink oinks to call *you* in, I phoned 999.'

Taking a moment, Nikki tensed and then released her shoulder muscles trying to get her head round what he'd revealed, and then he was holding out his phone to her, smiling, like he expected a pat on the head.

'Here, I recorded what Roddy boy did to her. It's all there. Got it all on record.'

Swallowing, Nikki wished she had water as her mouth was dry – milk from the tea clagging her throat, making it tight. The little bloody toad had *recorded* his mum being beaten to a pulp? He *hadn't* called for help straightaway – he'd *recorded* it. Surprised he didn't upload it to bloody Facebook as well. Something else he'd said struck her. 'What do you mean "done enough to call me in"?'

He snorted. 'She told me you had a deal with the uniforms – any time there's shit going down at ours, you get called in pronto.'

A red haze descended over Nikki. She'd suspected something like this, 'course she had. But hearing it leave his lips like he didn't care – like Margo was just a piece of trash to be manipulated for his gains, like she wasn't worth owt? It was like machine-gun fire to the gut. His mum was in an operating theatre fighting for her life because her piece of crap for a son had set it up so her piece of crap for a husband would knock her senseless. This was too much … too fucking much. She snatched his phone from him, ignoring his objections, and thrust it in her back pocket, commenting for the recording that she had confiscated evidence pertaining to a crime.

She stood up and, lips tight, left the room without saying another word. The uniformed officer who was there for Margo happily promised to stand guard over Deano whilst Nikki called it in. As she hung up, the ward door swung open and a tall surgeon, still in scrubs and a theatre cap walked up, his face serious. The nurse Nikki had spoken to earlier rushed to meet him and they exchanged a few words before he continued towards the waiting room. Nikki took out her warrant card and flipped it to him before he entered. 'How is she, Margo McGonagall, how is she?'

The surgeon paused and with a small sigh shook his head. 'She arrested on the table and we couldn't bring her back. I'm sorry.' And he pushed open the door and went to tell Deano.

In a haze, Nikki walked over and looked through the small glass panel in the door as the surgeon told Margo's eldest son that his mother was dead. A concrete slab had taken up residence in her chest displacing the anger. Nikki was numb. The surgeon extended a hand and squeezed Deano's shoulders.

Surely, he'd show some remorse, some guilt, some emotion, anything – but Deano shook the surgeon's hand off and continued his pacing, his face contorted, his mouth going like the clappers. Nikki heard the soothing tones of the surgeon followed by Deano's harsher ones. The surgeon spun on his heel and moved to the door. As he opened it, Nikki heard the words, 'She was a useless old slag anyway,' drift through.

The surgeon caught her eye and mumbled something that sounded remarkably like, 'Little fucking bastard – doesn't deserve a mum.'

It had been a bad night for everyone.

Chapter 51

'I'm getting really worried now, Franco. It's not like Tyke – you know it in't.'

Franco was getting more and more fed up with Big Zee's moaning. They'd been here for hours and even with the heat on, it was nippy. Added to that was the stink of Big Zee's garlic breath. When he'd sent him up the road for food, he'd meant a Chicken Cottage burger meal not a fucking kebab with red onions and garlic mayo. Parekh had disappeared into the taxi rank ages ago – nearly an hour. What was she doing – issuing blow jobs to the Paki drivers? Wouldn't surprise him – if she was owt like her sister then she'd be a dirty little scrubber. Fuck, had Big Zee farted now? He buzzed a switch and the window rolled down with an effortless hum, letting in a welcome waft of fresh air and a sheet of rain. He pressed the button again and the window went back up.

'Give it a rest, eh? Tyke's probably pissed off somewhere getting his leg over some cool blonde with long legs and a Brazilian.'

He cast a sideways glance at Big Zee. Everyone knew the two of them were at it – Big Zee and Tyke – he just wanted to get back at the other man for the noxious fumes he was creating. 'Yeah, a snatch, smooth as a baby's and smelling of roses. Mm-mm– that'll be where he is. No need to worry, big man.'

Big Zee balled up the last of his kebab in the paper, squishing the polystyrene container and leaking mayo onto his trousers. With his lips all pursed up and angry, he looked like he wanted to throw it with force out the window. Franco grinned – *too damn easy to wind the fucker up!* He glanced in the rear-view mirror and frowned. That was another thing that was bothering him. That car parked up behind him with three blokes inside. What did they want? Was it another takeover bid or something? With Tyke gone walkabouts they were a man down – mind you, Big Zee was well able to handle himself. Still, it was a worry. So far, the men had maintained their distance. He'd just keep an eye on them for now.

He leaned over and cuffed his mate on the arm – just hard enough to make him wince. 'Lighten up, BZ, Tyke'll turn up again like the proverbial bad penny. You know he will, then you can get all smooochy moochy again.'

'Fuck off.'

Big Zee shrugged off Franco's hand and leaned against the passenger door, his face averted. Sulking, no doubt. If there was one thing Franco couldn't stand it was sulking. He hated it, especially on a stake out. He wanted a bit of banter, a bit of chat, some toons. He flicked the CD on and started bopping his head in time to some heavy grime, hoping that would lighten Big Zee's mood.

'Aw, for fuck's sake, I don't care if you're shirt-lifters, the pair of you – after that little tosser, I'd prefer it. Least I don't need to worry about you two dipping in my baby mama's honey pot.'

Big Zee made a sound in the back of his throat, but his shoulders seemed to relax. Maybe he'd lighten up in a bit. Now what the hell was Parekh doing? He'd been sure she'd hotfoot it to see Margo at BRI. Maybe he'd miscalculated? Maybe he should have gone straight to BRI and left Parekh to her own devices. Maybe she'd more on her plate to worry about than Deano and his scrawny ma. Word on the street was that she'd offed her old man and buried him in the Odeon car park years ago.

He nudged Big Zee. 'Come on – let's go.'

Straightening up, Big Zee tucked his food wrapper down the side of the car seat and gripped the steering wheel. 'Where to now? Thought we were keeping an eye on the skanky cow.'

'BRI – think we'd be better keeping an eye on Deano. I want him to pay for what he's done and just cause his mum's laid up in hospital, dun't mean we can't sort him out.'

As Big Zee drove off, Franco looked in the rear-view mirror. Seems the other car wasn't interested in him. Must be Parekh then. Wonder who else she's pissed off.

Chapter 52

Margo's death sat heavy with Nikki. She should have made more of an effort to convince her friend to kick Roddy into touch. Should have got rid of Deano when she had the damn chance. Should've run the little scrote off the estate – left him to his fate with Franco. Instead she'd been preoccupied with a man who'd been dead for fifteen years. What did that say about her? She'd allowed herself to be distracted and she'd ended up doing nothing very well. Her ex-father-in-law was hounding her daughter. She hadn't spent the time she should have with Charlie, talking to her about her dad – about how Khal had made her feel, about his warmth and about how much he would have loved to have a daughter, about how like him Charlie was.

They'd taken Deano to Trafalgar House a couple of hours ago and Nikki was itching to find out what he was saying, what else he'd added to corroborate his earlier statement. Sajid was in charge of pinning things down and she had every faith in her partner's ability. Still, she wanted to be the one to tie things up.

Sitting in the back of Haris' taxi, exhaustion swept over her and she had a sudden urge to phone Marcus. She wanted to hear his voice, allow him to tell her everything would be all right, to tell *him* she didn't want him to leave her. She frowned. When the hell had she come to that conclusion? She hadn't been thinking about it. She'd barely had time to draw breath today, never mind think about her relationship with Marcus, so what had prompted that realisation? Finding Khalid? Whatever it was, she needed to park it for another day. Right now, she needed to get Franco locked up – *that* was her number one priority.

As her taxi made to turn right in adherence to the hospital's one-way system, Nikki saw Franco's car, with Biz Zee's looming figure distinct in the driver's seat, pull in to the bottom entrance. Remembering Deano's claims, she strained to see if she could catch sight of Tyke, but to no avail. Maybe there was something to Deano's claims after all. However, if Franco and Big Zee had come for Deano, they were too late … too late for Deano and much too late for Margo.

She peered beyond Franco's car, looking for the other car that had been following her earlier, but couldn't see it. 'That other car still hanging around outside the taxi rank, Haris?'

'Yep – three men – not from round here. Still there. Ali just texted to say that Franco's gone now though. That him I saw just pulling in?'

Nikki grinned and nodded. There were no flies on Haris. He saw everything, but said little … her kind of man.

'Where to?'

She'd nowhere else to go to, so she gave him Sajid's address. She couldn't face the scrutiny at home, besides they still had work to do. Pulling out her phone, she dialled Archie's number. 'What's going on? Deano still spilling? Can't I come down, just to apply a bit more pressure?'

'You can't show your face here, Nikki.'

'But …'

'I'm having none of your proverbials, lass. No means no, okay? We'll deal wi' Deano, but you can't come in. If we take it further wi' Franco, I want tae be sure we have enough to put him away for a long time, but the lad's already beginning to backtrack …

272

Can't remember the location of the pig farm. Thinks it was more Manchester way and that there might not have been any bodies efter all. Now he thinks about it, he reckons half the guys he accused Franco of offing have just gone on holiday.'

Nikki wanted to drive straight there and drag the truth from the lying little bastard's mouth, but her hands were tied. She'd been aware that Deano could backtrack. Franco was terrifying and they'd never managed to get any of his lads to turn on him so far – probably because they all ended up as pig swill before they got the chance. However, some of what Deano said might help them piece evidence together. Looked like, with regards to Franco, they would have to play a long game. It was more than frustrating, but that was life.

'Anyway, moving on to Khalid's investigation, Sajid's on his way home soon. I suggest you both have a good night's sleep and be ready to crack on tomorrow. I've arranged for a more detailed investigation of those tunnels. Don't know if you're on to anything, but ma proverbials say you might be. Go haim. Spend some time wi' yer lass and yer family and hae a good night's sleep.'

Mumbling noncommittally, Nikki hung up just as they pulled into the underground car park at Sajid's flats.

She rummaged in her pocket for some money but Haris shook his head, 'No charge … the boss said so.'

Thursday 25th October

Chapter 53

Her mum as usual had told her that she and Marcus had the kids and that Charlie was fine. Sometimes, Nikki wondered how she'd cope without her mum and Marcus to help out. The floor outside Sajid's flat was cold and hard, yet still Nikki found herself dozing off as she waited for him to get home. Her backside might have been cold but the ambient temperature in the corridors of Listers Mansions kept the rest of her warm. Huddled into her leather jacket, back resting against the wall next to his door, she stretched out her legs and crossed them at the ankles. Nikki dipped her neck forward and with her chin almost resting on her chest, she closed her eyes. Her intention had been to think things through – to get her thoughts in order.

Thoughts about what she'd like to do to Deano and his bullying had given way to grief about the loss of her friend. She'd allowed herself no tears; instead she channelled her emotions into the bigger picture. For one, she had the Franco–Deano drugs triangle to consider. Deano's statement, when followed through, might prove fruitful. Mind you, there was always another drug lord waiting in the wings to take over and Bradford seemed to attract more than its fair share of them from Manchester, Sheffield, Leeds and the like. Big Zee's attitude in The Mannville Arms puzzled her too. Combined with what Deano had said about Tyke, she wondered if she should try to speak to Big Zee on his own. Tomorrow, she promised herself.

Her mind moved on to Khal and the tunnels and the other missing persons. She shuddered; the mere thought of those tunnels and their rodent inhabitants sent a shiver down her spine. Could she and Sajid be seeing links that weren't there? Could there really be a serial killer in Bradford who had gone undetected for years? Was that all just a coincidence? It didn't seem likely. Didn't most serial killers crave recognition, crave the notoriety? In all her years of policing, she'd learned to believe that what some called a gut feeling was actually the result of years of honing their detecting skills – sharpening their instincts, following logical patterns to reach the end goal. If Sajid hadn't been behind her on this one, she might have doubted herself. She was grieving, she was in shock, she hadn't slept in two days and she was personally involved. However, Sajid was her barometer. He balanced her out, made her question, analyse and justify her observations and he'd backed her on this. It was with this thought running through her mind that she drifted into a fitful doze where giant rats with elongated claws and tails that swished and twitched like cowboys' lassoes chased her through the corridors of Trafalgar House, each morphing into DS Springer every time she tried to wake herself up.

When her shoulder was gripped with sharp talons, she started and began to scramble to her feet, before she realised it was Sajid bending over her, not so much as the whiff of a swishing tail or scrape of feet in sight or sound. She exhaled and accepted his hand as he helped her to her feet. 'You could've been a bit less rodent-like in your approach.'

Sajid smirked, getting the reference as he hitched his heavy man bag onto his shoulder and opened the door with his other hand. 'Been waiting long?'

Nikki was about to shake her head when she glanced at her

watch and realised it was nearly four in the morning. 'A couple of hours. Didn't want to wake Langley up, so I camped out here.'

Sajid flicked light switches on and ushered her in. 'I'm going to bed. You know where everything is. We'll talk tomorrow.'

And leaving her alone in the dimly lit hallway, Sajid disappeared into his bedroom and within seconds there was silence in the flat. Nikki strained her ears, wishing for the incessant noise of her own home. For a moment she wished she'd gone back there, then realised that she'd have been engulfed with questions she couldn't answer or wasn't yet ready to answer. For tonight Sajid's home might be as silent as a crypt, yet it was probably exactly what she needed. She took herself through to the small single room that she'd used on previous occasions and settled down into a fitful sleep full of disturbing dreams that had nothing to do with tunnels or rats …

'Caaaatheee, it's meeeeee …' Khal's singing voice was a deep baritone that got whipped away on the wind as we gambolled over the Haworth Moors.

Was that Cathy, was it me? Hair tangling in the wind, giggling … tripping, escaping Heathcliff, laughing out loud.

… Khalid's caresses, cheap wine and cornflakes for dinner …

… tartan pattern across thighs, warmed by love and single bar of electric heater …

Nikki started awake, the sheets tangled round her legs, memories of that day sharp in her mind. A glance at her watch told her she'd only been asleep for a half an hour. Her head pounded as she tried to push the image of her and Khal together from her mind. Wide awake again, her thoughts drifted to another conversation. One they'd had days before he disappeared. It had a completely different meaning now.

'It's hard, Nikki. I'm their only son. I don't want to disappoint them any more than I already have.'

I wrapped my arms round him, squeezing so tight. 'How could

you disappoint them? You got married to the woman you love. If they can't understand that, then that's their problem.'

His face had clouded over, just for a moment, then he'd smiled that sad smile that was becoming more frequent in the weeks after their marriage. His words shook as he'd said, 'You don't understand, Nik. It's more complicated than that.'

'Then tell me – explain. Make me understand.'

But it was too late by then. He'd already moved away from her, leaving her on her own by the fire wishing she could reach him.

She realised now that the truth was, it had always been too late for her and Khal. They should never have been. He had betrayed her – he'd never been hers. She swung her legs off the bed and reached for her jeans. But he was Charlie's ... he was her daughter's dad.

Chapter 54

'I just don't get why she always has to be like this, Marcus.' Charlie flung her books into her schoolbag. 'The absent mother. The damn saviour – everybody more important that the rest of us. It's crap. Fucking crap and I hate her.'

She flounced over to the fridge, jerked the door open, grabbed the milk and poured a large glassful, slopping dribbles all over the work surface in the process.

Marcus cradled his tepid coffee cup in both hands and waited for Charlie's outrage to die down. He got that she was angry. Poor kid had just found out the dad she'd thought had deserted her, had actually died at the hands of a possible serial killer before she was even born. As if that wasn't bad enough, she'd sort of been abducted by a grandad she didn't know existed until recently and where was her mum? Off fighting the demons instead of facing up to the ones at home … that's where.

He winked at Nikki's mum, Lalita, who was busying herself washing up the breakfast dishes and making a good impression of the 'hear no evil' monkey. He wished Charlie would adopt the policy of the 'speak no evil' one, but on the other hand, he had every sympathy with her. He leaned over and ruffled Sunni's dark hair. 'Come on, shoes on and off to school. Aji-ma's taking you today.'

Sunni jumped down and ran past his sister, flicking her with his hand as he went. 'Glad it's not you Charlie Barlie, moaning Marlie. You's being a dick again.'

Lalita Parekh and Marcus yelled, 'Sunni!' in unison and he increased his pace to escape into the hallway from where sounds of him scrabbling to find his school shoes drifted through to the kitchen.

Ruby got up, took her mug to the sink and hugged her Aji-ma before dropping a kiss on Marcus's cheek. 'Bye, Dad.' As she left the room, she added, 'Good luck with Charlie, she's being a real draaama queen.'

Marcus stifled a grin and shouted, 'Have a good day, Sunni, Rubes.'

He waited till Charlie's grandma and the two younger kids left the house before speaking. 'You need to cut your mum some slack. She's had a hellish couple of days.'

Charlie's expression told him she believed *she'd* also had a hellish couple of days … and it was true. He tried again. 'She loves you.'

Charlie snorted, 'If she loved me, she'd be here giving me a good reason *not* to go to Ramallah with my grandad.'

Marcus's lips tightened. He'd have a few choice words to say to Burhan Abadi when he finally met him. There was no way Khalid's dad was taking Charlie away from them. Nikki and he might have their problems, but Charlie was as much his kid as the other two and he wouldn't let her go without a fight.

Charlie slouched over and scraped out the chair next to Marcus. 'Why do you let her get away with so much, Marcy?'

'Your mum has a lot of responsibility. You know that. Your Auntie Anika is a disaster area, Haqib's always in trouble, Aji-ma needs her and she works hard at her job.'

Charlie dunked a biscuit in her mug, trailing droplets of milk as she raised it to her mouth. With her milk moustache, she looked like the 14-year-old she was. Her usual teenage attitude hidden beneath worried eyes.

Marcus tried again. 'Margo died last night.'

Charlie blinked, holding a sodden biscuit centimetres above her mug, until it fell in with a splash, depositing more milk over the table. 'Margo? How?'

She dipped two fingers into her mug, her head bowed over it, as if the retrieval of a soggy Rich Tea required all her attention, 'Don't bother, I know. Bloody Roddy, weren't it?'

'Yep.'

'Inevitable really. She all right? Mum, I mean.'

Marcus had spoken briefly to Nikki that morning on the phone and it didn't take her presence in the room to tell him how badly she was affected. Her monotone and clipped words told him how rigidly she was holding herself under control. Her forehead would be knotted together, her small body stiff and non-pliant. He worried that she'd break – splinter into fragments of dust and just be blown away on the wind like she'd never been here. He wasn't sure what he'd do, how he'd feel if that ever happened. Nikki came with baggage. He'd always known that. Brittle, distant, honest, solid. Those were the things he loved about her. He just wished that she could be a little more like a willow and bend with the breeze rather than balk against it. 'She blames herself. You know your mum.'

Giving up on the biscuit, Charlie wiped her fingers down her leggings. 'She needs to loosen up. Needs to let us – you and me – in sometimes – share the load. She can't do everything on her own forever. As for Auntie Anika. Well, she just needs to wise up and kick Yousaf into touch. Haqib and her'll be better off without him – we all would.'

Marcus hid his smile. Charlie had an old head on her shoulders. She carried a lot of baggage with her too. Sometimes he worried that Nikki expected too much from her.

Standing up, Charlie grabbed her bag and dropped a kiss on

Marcus's head. 'Love you, Marcy. Together we'll get her through this.'

As his stepdaughter walked through the door, the smile faded from Marcus's lips. For once he wasn't sure if Charlie's words rang true. This time he wondered if *he* wouldn't be enough for Nikki and the thought chilled him.

Chapter 55

When she'd hung up on Marcus earlier, an overpowering urge to throw herself back into the bed and pull the covers over her head had hit her. Marcus had been monosyllabic – distant. She'd hurt him badly and yet still, there he was, looking after *her* kids, sorting out *her* mess, keeping *her* life under control. She wished she had the words to tell him how much she appreciated him – loved him. Was it love, though? Or was she just using him because he was so reliable. He slotted into her life, demanded little and expected nothing in return. Maybe she'd pushed him one step too far this time. Maybe Khalid's remains being discovered was an omen – a warning sign that they should end things. She lifted her hand and touched her cheek. It was wet. Using the bedsheet, she wiped the tears away, wondering when they'd started. She didn't cry – it wasn't her thing. And yet here she was doing it again.

She wiggled her nose to stop any more coming out and as she did so, one of Marcus's stock phrases came to her. 'You can't change the past, Nikki, but you can design your future.' Maybe Khal turning up was a sign for her to design her future – the thing was, did her future have room for Marcus?

Low and tuneless singing from beyond the spare-bedroom

door told her that Sajid or Langley had surfaced. Rather than risk an eyeful of either in their Calvin Klein's, she shuffled over to the en-suite, had a quick shower and feeling like a right minger got dressed in the previous day's clothes. Maybe she should consider packing a suitcase to leave at Sajid's for these sorts of occurrences. She grinned … yeah, he would just love her playing gooseberry!

When the smell of coffee and the sound of Capital Radio drifted through, she sidled to the kitchen, and saw that whilst Langley was busy buttering toast, Sajid was already looking at the maps they'd pinned to the wall. With a brief 'hi' to Langley, she grabbed a coffee and joined Sajid.

He looked at her, his eyes grazing over her face and she wished that she'd been able to apply a little foundation to cover the blue bruises beneath her eyes. She looked like she'd done a round with Tyson Fury and dimming the bathroom lights hadn't made her reflection any more attractive.

'Well? I see someone didn't sleep well.'

Sipping her coffee and ignoring his words, she leaned against the table and injected some certainty into her voice. 'Victimology. *That's* the best place to start. If we're right and these are the victims of a serial killer, then we need to work out what links them.'

Sajid's snort was explosive. 'I've been trying to work something out but keep coming up with blanks. There's nothing to link them at first glance – different racial groups, different ages, different sexes. If this is the works of a serial killer, then he's not following the usual patterns – he doesn't seem to have a "type".'

'Give me the rundown.'

Sajid stood and pointed to the first picture. This is Mark Hodgson, discovered when they were doing building work at Sunbridge Wells in 2012. Aged 21. Homeless for a couple of years after dropping out of university. In and out of Lynfield Mount, after two psychotic episodes. Wasn't reported missing initially.

Originally from Leeds, the lad had fallen off his parents' radar as his mental health deteriorated and it wasn't till he was found that his parents realised he'd not just severed ties with them. Only had a few friends – all of whom had given up on him as his behaviour became more erratic and he stopped taking his meds. In effect nobody noticed the poor sod had disappeared.'

About to wonder at how nobody had noticed his disappearance, Nikki bit her lip. Shit. It seemed like it was easy to convince yourself that a missing person wasn't actually missing. *Is that how their killer did it?* Did he target people that wouldn't be reported missing on purpose?

That didn't ring true really. Nobody would imagine that Khal wouldn't be reported missing. It was only because she was privy to the extent of the pressure from his dad that she assumed he'd gone back to Ramallah. Otherwise she'd have reported his disappearance like a shot. She paused, allowing the flicker of guilt to palpate her heart. She should have realised anyway. She should have reported him missing … call herself a police officer?

Sajid had moved on to the next set of remains. 'This is Stephanie Fields, 19, discovered behind Bradford Ice Rink in 2003. As you can see, Stephanie is black. The initial investigation stalled when all reported sightings of her led to dead ends. Unfortunately, her remains were cremated, a sloppy decision or an oversight …? Working from the post-mortem photographs, Langley inferred that the striations on the bones could be from a similar tool that was used on both Khalid and Mark – the cremation makes that impossible to prove conclusively.'

'What the hell is linking the victims, Saj? Different races, different genders.' Nikki flicked through the report on Stephanie Fields. 'Fields was pregnant when she disappeared. Her boyfriend thought she'd decided to abort the baby and because he was so against it, figured that she'd disappeared off to do the deed whilst he was working abroad. She'd been gone for days – nearly three weeks before he decided to report her missing. Her work – she was a trainee midwife – had phoned him repeatedly when she didn't turn up for work and he'd said she was ill. He told officers that he expected her to come back after she'd got rid of the baby. Charmer! Reading between the lines, it looks like the investigating team thought he was good for it, but unfortunately various people alibied him and it was a no-go.'

'He sounds like a bit of a tosser.'

'So what links a Palestinian engineer in his early twenties, a homeless white male in his early twenties, a pregnant black nurse in her late teens and …' She tapped the reports that had come in from the boss first thing, 'A white female prostitute visiting friends from London, a white teenage lad and an as yet unidentified male victim?'

'What makes it harder is that they all disappeared at different times – different years and were discovered in different places. Maybe it's just a random thing?'

Nikki shrugged and pointed to the map. 'Not so random. We've identified a possible hunting area. These tunnels play a huge part in this. Archie's got two IT detectives inputting every little bit of information we have on the victims – hopefully one of their programs will turn up trumps, for I can't see a link other than the dump sites being in such close proximity to those damn tunnels.'

She reached over to the sofa where she'd thrown her jacket the previous night and started to put it on. 'Come on, Archie's got a team of uniforms going through the tunnels.'

Sajid grinned. 'And you're keen to get down there with them?'

'Yeah right. No, you and I are going to check out things above ground. Archie's just emailed me a list of possible building sites over the past fifteen years, in the vicinity of a tunnel exit point.'

Sajid groaned and, mumbling to himself, went to put his shoes on whilst Nikki waited by the door.

'There's only nine likely sites. That's not too bad. Archie's managed to get the building site managers for some of them to meet us there and he's sent two uniforms to meet us at any site we think might be worthy of a more detailed inspection. If they look likely after we've discussed it with the site manager, the uniforms can explore the tunnels – try to come up with a likely route. First one's in a car park near the Black Swan off Thornton Road. Major waterworks issue in 2009 and the Black Swan being a pub has access to the tunnels via their cellar. That's our first port of call.'

Sajid brightened up. 'Serve real ale there, do they?'

Nikki laughed. 'Not sure it's that sort of venue. Besides I've not even had breakfast yet.'

Chapter 56

Arriving at the Black Swan, Nikki and Sajid were met by a wiry man in a hard hat, well-used steel-capped boots caked in mud and a high-vis vest over a short-sleeved T-shirt. Nikki shivered looking at him as the wind thrashing along Thornton Road whipped at her already drenched ponytail. The pub was closed but a couple of glasses had been blown off the windowsills and shards of glass were now scattered over the pavement amid a spread of cigarette ends.

'Gurpreet Kohli. Got sent over here by't council. I was the site manager in 2009.' He extended a large hand and gripped Nikki's in a solid handshake before repeating the process on Sajid.

Nikki smothered a smile when Sajid winced and started to move towards the back of the building where a small concrete covered car park nestled between a terrace of houses with boarded-up windows, the back of the Black Swan and a small garage from which the strains of Britney Spiers drifted. The concrete was crumbling and looked like it hadn't been touched since 2009. Weeds had erupted, skinny and sad, from splits over the tarmac and potholes filed with brown sludge polka dotted the surface. The periphery was a combination of grass growing up the green graffiti covered wire fencing and crisp packets and other detritus caught between the holes.

Rain peppered Nikki's face with stinging sleet and she hunched her shoulders wishing she'd swapped her leather jacket for her parka. This was a secluded enough area and would offer enough privacy for their serial killer to go about his business, especially at night-time. She wandered over to where old railings with flaking black paint bordered three crumbling narrow steps which led down to a door that was worse the wear than the one at Sunbridge Wells and the ice rink. Peering over the railings, she saw movement beneath her. Startled, she jumped back. *Bloody rats!* Her entire body went on high alert, each hair follicle doing a Mexican wave right up her arms to her shoulders and back again.

As she tried to control her reactions, not wanting to lose face in front of the builder, she peered over again and saw a body crawling from a flattened cardboard box and unfurling their limbs from what looked like a pile of clothes bundled at the bottom of the steps. Her heartbeat slowed as she looked at the emaciated young lad with huge staring eyes blinking up at her. He looked about the same age as her Charlie. She looked at Sajid and jerked her head in the lad's direction. Understanding her meaning, Sajid approached the lad whilst Nikki turned her attention back to Gurpreet. 'You remember working here then, do you, Gurpreet?'

Gurpreet tutted under his breath as the homeless lad's voice rose when Sajid spoke to him. The curl of his lips spoke volumes as he scowled in their direction. Seeing that he was about to join Sajid and insert his tuppence worth, Nikki moved away from the tunnel entrance. 'Where exactly was the building work?'

Still glancing behind him, Gurpreet followed her and pointed to his right to a squarish area that was distinctly different in colour to the surrounding ground. It looked to be about four metres square and Nikki doubted that a body could have been dumped there without being noticed by the crew. 'Was it a particularly deep dig? You know, deep enough to conceal something during the night that the workers wouldn't notice the next day?'

'You mean like … like a body or summat?' Gurpreet glanced back at the lad that Sajid had calmed down. He was now sitting on the top step whilst her colleague was on the phone, presumably to social services. Nikki could almost see Gurpreet forming thoughts of a rough sleeper buried on his watch.

He swallowed and tipped his hard hat back on his head revealing a red welt where it had dug in across his forehead. 'Shit!'

He frowned and began pacing the periphery of the area that had been dug up all those years ago. Nikki, realising that he was thinking back, weighing things up in his mind, waited patiently. Finally, he turned to her and shook his head, his chin lifted as if to assert his next words more strongly. 'Nah.'

He continued with the head shake as he spoke. 'Nah. Not a big enough area. We'd have had to be blind not to notice if summat' – again, he glanced at the lad who was now getting to his feet and gathering his assortment of belongings together into a tattered and damp looking rucksack – 'or some poor sod for that matter, was dumped in there. Besides, we dug this area up and refilled it on the same day. We left it for lunch probably, but we'd have noticed owt out of the ordinary. It wasn't a wet dig – just a little slurry at the bottom. No room for a body, if that's what you're after?'

Nikki ignored the question in his words and had just held out her hand to thank him for his help, when a yelp from behind had her spinning round. The young lad whom Sajid had been talking to, was haring out of the car park and onto Thornton Road. She was just in time to see Sajid's arms spinning in the air as he tried to keep his balance, before tipping backwards and landing down at the bottom of the crumbling stairs.

Nikki darted towards Sajid, whilst Gurpreet headed after the young lad.

'Leave him, Gurpreet. He's gone.' Nikki knew better than to try to find the lad. Sometimes you couldn't help them. Sometimes they had to make the decision for themselves and not have it forced on them. Peering down at her colleague over the railings, Nikki tried to smother her smile. Sajid was sprawled on the small landing at the bottom, his long legs stretching up the steps, nearly reaching the top one, his back squashed against the back wall of the staircase. His normally pristine clothes were now covered in mud and, judging by the ammonia scent drifting towards her, something a lot more distasteful. She skirted the railings to the top of the stairs as he pulled himself up, brushing off wet leaves and muck. Face set in a scowl, he cursed under his breath. 'Next time, *you* fucking deal with the waifs and strays, okay?'

Glad that he was seemingly unhurt, Nikki, deadpan, said, 'This isn't one of our sites. The tunnel entrance is too restricted, the stairs leading down alone would make it too hard to transport a body up, besides which, Gurpreet says the excavation area wasn't left for long and it's too small to be able to cover a body. Come on.'

Anticipating Sajid's reaction to her next words, she grinned. 'We'll nip into Primark for you to get a change of clothes before heading on to the next site.'

The look Sajid sent her made her laugh out loud as he said, 'Yeah right. Surely, we can do a detour to my flat. Where's our next port of call?'

Behind her, Gurpreet cleared his throat. 'Eh, well, Thinking about that. It was around that same time that we were called up to the cathedral. That were a right big dig. We had to go deep and the area was open for at least a week, by my reckoning. That would be more like what you're looking for, I reckon.'

Looking at the email attachment Archie had sent, Nikki nodded. 'Yep that's one of the sites we're looking at.' Ignoring Sajid's mumbled moaning, she held her phone out to Gurpreet, with the site list visible. 'You on site for any of these digs?'

'You're looking over quite a timespan, aren't you?' Gurpreet chewed his lip, 'This is making me uneasy. You saying someone's been going about dumping dead bodies all over't place for years?'

Hands thrust into her pockets, fingers crossed, Nikki forced a smile to her lips and met his gaze. 'No, 'course I'm not saying that.'

'It's just, like, I heard about them bodies found near the Odeon an' all.'

Nikki laughed, her laugh tinkling falsely even to her ears. Ignoring Sajid's eye roll, she lied, 'Different case altogether, Gurpreet. Nothing so scary as buried bodies – that's well above my pay grade.'

Glancing between the two officers, Gurpreet frowned, his eyes clouded, his brows meeting in the middle. 'Well, like I say, I was at this cathedral one and this one on Tumbling Hill Street. Used to be a pub there years ago, I'm told. Tumblers or summat. Seem to remember both of these were sizable operations over at least a few days, if not more. That what you're looking for?'

Chapter 57

By the time they'd visited the Bradford Cathedral site, which in actual fact was down from the cathedral itself, Nikki and Sajid were sure that that could indeed be a site that might house one of the missing persons who had never been found over the years. The main problem would be convincing anyone to excavate the sites without real proof that someone was buried there and in fact without evidence that any of the missing persons were indeed dead. However, Nikki was pleased that they'd managed to narrow prospective sites down to only a handful. The cathedral site, as suggested by Gurpreet, was a good contender, as was the Tumbling Hill site which now was host to a number of university buildings.

Sajid, rather than 'lower himself' – his words, not Nikki's – to buying from Primark, had struggled on with his soiled clothing till they'd visited the sites designated to them. Nikki, despite Sajid's scoffing, had insisted they cover up her car seats with newspaper before he sat down. And he'd spent the rest of the afternoon moaning and pointing out the number of times his clothes had been stained previously with remnants of chocolate or pop in Nikki's car. 'Your car's a health hazard anyway. No need to be so bloody protective of it now!'

Not entirely jokingly, Nikki had driven back to Sajid's flat with the windows down to 'rid the car of the piss smell' that seemed to get stronger as the hours passed. Now, he'd bagged his clothes up and left them by the door ready to go out into the bin.

'You not even going to just get them dry cleaned?'

But Sajid had been insistent that after being treated like a leper and smelling of human piss for most of the day, he'd be unable to ever wear them again without imagining the smell still there.

Nikki looked down at her own jeans and misshapen jumper and tried to work out how old they were. All right for Mr La Di Dah Sajid with a bit of money in his back pocket to discard clothes like they were potato peelings, but for Nikki, every penny seemed spent before it had even gone into her bank account. Taking advantage of his posh coffee machine, Nikki helped herself to a vanilla latte, whilst Sajid showered and changed. Truth was, she too would be glad not to have the smell of piss in her nostrils anymore and as an added indulgence she lit his mandarin Yankee candle and settled down to study the reports from the IT team that had just come through.

They'd tried to work out some sort of link in the victimology using the limited information they had from the time when the victims had first been reported missing. As the victims' relatives and friends had been re-interviewed, they'd added that information to the mix too, yet still there was nothing concrete to show a link or a common thread between them. Placing her cup on the coffee table, Nikki began sticking the printouts from each victim onto the screen Sajid had purloined from Trafalgar House earlier in the week. Six victims to date and nothing concrete to link them. What were they missing? The warmth of her latte comforted her as she studied them.

Turning her head a little, she looked at the map Sajid had been drawing on earlier. Shuddering at the mere thought of the tunnels, Nikki put her mug down on the table and began tracing the lines from where each of the remains had been found. The Odeon car park, Sunbridge Wells, the ice rink. Simmering away in the back of her mind was the thought that they needed more dump sites, and that irked her. It was as if she was demanding more bodies, more death. What they actually needed was for there to be *no* more bodies, no more victims, *no* more dump sites. What they needed was to catch this fucker – that's if he was still around. What if he'd left the area and moved on to another city? Nikki frowned and dismissed that thought. If he'd moved on and was still active, HOLMES would have caught it and so, she reckoned, he wasn't active anymore. Besides, it would be near impossible to replicate this scenario in another city – what with the tunnels and building works and so on.

Nikki reckoned that whoever their killer was, he was a local man. One all too familiar with the underground tunnels and with access to them. Where the hell was the information on that? She'd get on to uniform, see what was going on there. Maybe he was dead, or in prison for another crime? She made a mental note to get the techies to get information on any violent convicts in the area who had either gone to prison or died during their time period. Her thoughts fleetingly landed on the Yorkshire Ripper. If they were right, then this killer had outdone Bradford's worst. Not only did it seem likely that he'd claimed more victims than Peter Sutcliffe had, but he'd flown under the radar for a long time. He'd had free rein to exploit, torture and kill for too long and it made Nikki's piss boil. Someone somewhere had given this monster a key to her city, but now he'd fucked with the wrong officer. He'd killed Khalid and that made it personal.

She sat down, one calf balanced on the knee of the other leg, jiggling up and down as she looked at the map. If she was to transport a body through those tunnels she'd want to travel downhill. It wouldn't make sense to try to manoeuvre a dead weight uphill, over the slippy cobbles. So, that being a starting point, the likelihood was that the torture site was either higher than or level with the ice rink which, to date was their highest known site. Hearing movement behind her, Nikki sipped her coffee and spoke her thoughts aloud. 'I reckon the torture site must be uphill to the highest dumpsite, which was the ice rink. What do you think?'

Langley draped his arms around Nikki's neck from behind and kissed the top of her head, 'Lovely to see you too, my sweet.'

Nikki jumped, spilling her coffee over the sofa.

Langley just shook his head and headed to the kitchen for a wipe to clean up the mess. 'You're lucky Sajid didn't see that. Where is he, by the way? And please don't tell me that the pissy smell coming from that bag in the hallway has anything to do with him. Talk about passion killer, having a boyfriend who pisses himself.'

Nikki, mid gulp of coffee, snorted, sending liquid spurting from her nose and onto the sofa once more.

With an exaggerated sigh, Langley handed her the packet of wipes. 'Get it cleaned before he comes back.'

As she soaked up the liquid, Nikki told Langley about their day, including Saj's fall. Slapping his thigh, Langley laughed. 'I bet he loved that.'

'Yeah, that's why he's been in the shower for the past half-hour.'

Langley wandered over to the map that hung on the wall and studied it. 'Back to what you said before, Nik. I think you're right. Nobody in their right mind would willingly traipse a dead body uphill – especially not the steep hills we have in Bradford.'

As Nikki joined him, he picked up a pin and attached one of Sajid's multicoloured strings to it and pinned it to the wall at the Sunbridge Wells site, then he stretched the string and repeated it with the ice rink and Odeon sites.

Nikki, seeing what he was doing said, 'We suspect the tunnel at the bottom of the cathedral might be a site too – we're waiting for it to be excavated – and possibly Tumbling Hill Street, where Tumblers Bar used to be.'

'Hmph. It's a bit of a longer trek but it's all downhill and then flat with only a slight incline to the tunnel exit.' Langley placed another stringed pin there. 'So, let's consider this … if the cathedral exit is where the killer is based then …'

'No. It can't be that one. We explored there today. It's filled with old pews and suchlike and used by the cathedral regularly for storage. There's no space. The deacon says it's been like that for as long as he's been there and that's upward of twenty-five years. Besides, it's too much of an uphill hike to the other sites. The ice rink merits more investigation, I reckon.'

'Sunbridge Wells?'

Nikki shook her head, 'Again, quite a sharp uphill to the ice rink. It's doable at a push, but bearing in mind the recent overhaul the Sunbridge tunnels have had, it's unlikely to house a torture site.'

'Okay, so what other entrances do we have?'

'There's one at the Theatre in the Mill.'

Langley took the string from each of the sites in turn. 'Okay, the tunnels from the theatre to the ice rink, meander in a roundabout way and would involve a hell of a twisted route.'

'Forget that one then. Do Tumbling Hill now.'

Langley repeated his trick with the string with each of the other tunnel entrances stopping only to kiss Sajid when he finally emerged from the shower smelling of Invictus with his hair still damp. By the end of the process, they had identified five entrances of interest: Tumbling Hill Street, The Mannville Arms, The Black Swan, Bradford Royal Infirmary and one snuggled in behind the Telegraph and Argus offices.

Sajid high-fived Langley. 'We owe you a meal at the very least for that.'

Nikki snorted. 'Okay, McDonald's it is. Where's my phone? I'll Just Eat it.'

Langley collapsed onto the sofa holding his stomach and groaning, 'Don't make me eat it, please don't make me eat it.'

'Chinese?' Nikki's tone was wistful. Her kids didn't like Chinese food much so it was a rare treat for her to eat it and, she realised, she hadn't eaten since the slice of toast she'd snaffled from Langley as she left the flat that morning. Langley rolled his eyes, grabbed his phone and dialled. 'Sajid will pay for this. Of course, that will be after he's removed his disgusting pissy clothes from the front door.'

A little huffily, Sajid glared at Nikki but went to do as Langley had asked.

'How come he never does what I ask so meekly?' asked Nikki.

Langley grinned. 'You're in the spare room at the minute and he doesn't like the couch.'

Still laughing, Nikki grabbed her phone as it started to ring. She hoped it was Charlie, but it was an unknown number. 'Yes?' She instantly recognised the voice on the other end of the phone.

'I need your help.'

Sighing, Nikki listened for a moment and then was off, grabbing her leather jacket and yelling. 'Save me some Chinese for me, will you? I'll be back.'

Chapter 58

Nikki had never been asked to meet up with someone in a gym before. Well, not someone who had been hysterical on the phone and was begging her for help anyway. So, against her better judgement she'd decided to meet him. The drive along Manningham Lane, round to Jacob's Well roundabout and up Leeds Old Road, took her past the cathedral and her thoughts were drawn to what they might find on excavating – that's if Archie could pull enough strings to make it happen. On the one hand she wanted her hunch to be wrong, on the other, she was aware that some good might come out of it being right. Offering closure to families was a good thing, but Nikki always felt that she'd extinguished a tiny flicker of hope. For her, finding Khal's body had been bittersweet. The knowledge that he hadn't deserted her only slightly assuaged the gaping loss that seared her soul. Donning her detective's hat, Nikki knew that new forensic evidence may well provide greater insight into the case. It might be just what they needed to break the case apart.

Halfway up the long road, Nikki became aware of a vehicle about two car lengths behind her. Was it the same car that had followed her the other night? The one that she had initially thought had been following Franco? The one Ali's taxi drivers had noticed. She wasn't sure of that, so she used voice recognition to dial a number on her mobile. When Ali answered, she quickly explained the situation and outlined what she wanted. By the end of the evening, Nikki was sure she'd know exactly who was following her and why.

Hating the stale stink of sweat combined with Lynx that accompanied the very male huffs and puffs, Nikki hoped she hadn't been set up. But the gym on this side of town in the new Odeon complex off the Thornbury roundabout was well away from Franco's pissing ground. Having shown her ID to a blonde woman with biceps the size of Nikki's waist, she'd been grudgingly admitted. The weights area at the back was dominated by young men in sagging trackie bottoms and body forming T-shirts, some of whom raised an appreciative eyebrow whereas some just stared blatantly as she weaved her way past them. Despite her size, one look from her was enough to quell any comments that might have been coming her way.

She reached the back of the gym and was rewarded when Big Zee popped his head from behind a battered leather punch bag. If she'd been expecting him to be wearing workout gear, she'd have been disappointed for he was in his usual scruffy skinny jeans and hoodie. Rather than his usual arrogant sneer, his face carried a worried expression. Before coming completely out from behind the punch bag, Big Zee cast a furtive glance around the room and then motioned for Nikki to follow him.

Intrigued, Nikki trailed after him beyond the exercise bikes, treadmills and rowing machines right to the back of the room. This was an area where less testosterone was required, Nikki thought, as she took in a couple of older men on the rowing machines and a woman who was trying to work off some bulk on a treadmill. All three were numbly watching blaring music videos on a screen near the ceiling. What did Big Zee want with her and why was it so imperative that Franco knew nothing about it?

Once there, he held a master card to an electronic key that allowed him access to a room further beyond. 'My sister's the manager here. She's letting me use the staff room for a bit.'

Nikki pointed back towards the reception. 'You mean the ...'

Big Zee sniffed. 'Yeah, Holly. She's my sister. There's a family likeness.'

For a moment, Nikki thought he was joking. Not even if provided with a DNA analysis would she be convinced the two were even remotely related. Part of that assessment, she conceded, was because the blonde at the reception desk had looked completely with it, whilst the specimen in front of her looked more Neanderthal than 'thinking man'. Scruffy, out of shape and stinking of fags, Big Zee bore no resemblance to the neat-freak fitness geek who'd allowed her access to the gym. Perhaps it was the sharpness of the contrast between the men pumping weights in the gym and Big Zee. Choosing not to respond, Nikki lifted her shoulders noncommittally. 'Well? What was so urgent you had to contact me without Franco knowing?'

A faint blush appeared on Big Zee's face. 'It's Tyke. He's missing. Been a couple of days now.'

And immediately Nikki got it. Shit, her gaydar had been well skewwhiff till now. Deano had hinted at it, but she'd thought he was being his usual spiteful little self. She didn't think Sajid had even picked up on it. Seeing his distress, she guided him over to one of the comfy chairs that skirted the room and sat down beside him. 'When you say gone, you mean he hasn't told you where he is? You two had a tiff?'

Kneading his arms together, Big Zee sprawled back in his chair. 'Knew you wouldn't take me seriously. Knew you'd take the piss.'

Nikki kept her voice matter of fact. 'I'm not taking the piss. Just trying to get the facts. How long's he been gone? Has Franco seen him?'

'Says he's not.' Big Zee's eyes were all over the place.

'Look, you want my help, then you better just spit it out. All this sneaking about tells me either Franco warned you off asking me for help, or you think Franco's got summat to do with Tyke's disappearance …?'

Seeing the flush across the lad's cheeks increase, Nikki sighed. 'Or both. That's it. Franco's warned you off speaking to me and you think that's because he's hiding summat to do wi' Tykes disappearance?'

Big Zee glanced at the door, then, seemingly reassured that it was still shut and they were alone, he gave a single abrupt nod.

'Oh, Big Zee, you'll have to do better than that, my man. You want my help against Franco, you need to start talking. Right now.'

She waited, allowing him time to consider things for one last time.

'Okay, okay. I think he found out that's all. Now he's making us pay.'

'Found out what exactly?'

'Fuck's sake, 'bout us – 'bout me and Tyke, like.' Big Zee's words sputtered from his lips like rapid gunfire. Now he'd started, it was as if he couldn't stop – had to get it all out.

'He hates folk like us … poofs – that's what he calls us. So, me and Tyke, we kept quiet, like. Now I think he's found out and I think him and Deano's taken Tyke to the pig farm.' Tears had formed in his eyes, but he hastily brushed them away.

Deano was still in prison, but it was good to know that Franco didn't know that. This was the second time she'd heard the words pig farm in relation to Franco and now it seemed even more essential to get someone out there.

She took out her phone and pressed record. 'You want help, then you better start speaking. I want to know everything you know about Franco's connections to pig farms and all about when you last saw Tyke.'

Big Zee looked at her for a moment, uncertainty written all over his face. This was make or break time. He could choose to clam up and Nikki would walk out the door. Or he could man up and perhaps save his boyfriend's life, or at the very least, find out what had happened to him. It all depended on whether, like Deano, his self-preservation was stronger than his love for his partner.

He opened his mouth and began …

'We had a fight, me and Tyke. Tuesday night. Wun't even 'bout owt important – just stuff, like.' He looked at Nikki, waiting for her affirmation.

Despite everything he'd done, a dart of pity pierced Nikki's heart, but then she pulled herself together. God knows how many people this little scrote was responsible for terrorising and killing. A show of grief for his partner didn't obliterate the heartache he'd caused.

'He stormed out. Said he were off to The Mannville Arms for a pint till I'd calmed down.' Threading his fingers together, Big Zee shrugged, his lips turned down like a sulky school kid. 'It wun't me going off on one …'

'And did he go to the pub? Did you check?'

''Course I did. When he didn't come home that night and didn't turn up to do the rounds for Franco on Wednesday, I went and asked. They said they hadn't seen him, although the old man that sits at the end of the bar said he had been in – he's bloody mental though. Nancy says you can't believe owt he says cause his mind's wandered.'

'And you've phoned him?'

'Fuck's sake, 'course I have. He's not picking up.'

'So, what makes you think Franco's done something to him?'

'Tyke was pulling away, getting fed up dealing and being Franco's bitch. Wanted to branch out on his own, with me. I reckon Franco got wind of that and did summat to him. Franco's a psycho. He's not even bothered Tyke's missing. That's what tells me he's done summat to him.'

'But a pig farm? Really?'

Big Zee took out his phone and sifted through his photos. He turned the screen to Nikki. 'Look, that were him a year ago. That's Scotty Dawg. You haven't seen him around recently, have you?'

Big Zee had a point. They'd not seen or heard anything from Scotty Dawg in months. Didn't mean this was him. The photo was dark and showed three figures holding something that could have been a man over a fence. Nikki could just about make out some shapes that may have been pigs. Maybe they could get it enhanced, but as it stood, it was too blurry to be viable evidence. 'Where's the farm? We need its exact location.'

*

After contacting Saj and Archie and explaining everything Big Zee had told her, Nikki waited until two uniforms had collected him, before heading out to her own car. Archie was arranging everything from his end and Nikki was to meet Sajid here, so they could travel together to meet everyone else at the pig farm on the A659.

Walking across the Gallagher Leisure Centre car park towards her car, Nikki was aware of the two silhouettes in a car parked in the row behind her car and the figure in another vehicle a few spaces down. Nikki smiled to herself. A single nod had the single figure exiting his vehicle and moving over to the one that was occupied. In unison, Nikki yanked the passenger's door open, whilst Ali repeated the manoeuvre on the driver's side. Two surprised faces swivelled round and before Nikki had a chance to stop him, Ali landed a punch on the driver's face and then dragged him out of the car allowing him to flop in a pile on the wet ground.

Nikki hadn't needed to resort to physical pressure, for the passenger exited the vehicle, hands out in front of him in a placating gesture. Ali dragged the driver round the vehicle to stand beside the other man. 'What you following her for, eh?'

The two men exchanged glances and then the passenger, who appeared to be the more savvy of the two said, 'May I?' and gestured to his jacket pocket.

With a curt nod, Nikki watched as he pulled ID from his pocket. 'We've been employed to monitor your activities.'

Nikki frowned. Who the hell needed to know her activities? Was it Springer, trying to make sure she wasn't interfering in her rather quiet and, to date, unproductive investigation? A thought came to her. 'My ex-father-in-law, isn't it? The old bastard wants to gather dirt so he can take my daughter.'

Mr Suave shrugged and began to get back into his car, gesturing to his colleague, who was holding a rapidly reddening tissue to his face. 'I'm not at liberty to divulge the identity of my employer.'

Nikki stepped forward and before he had a chance to close his door, she grabbed his collar and squeezed it tight around his throat. 'Well, here's something you can divulge … tell Abadi to get the fuck back to Ramallah and to leave my family alone. We've managed for fifteen years without him, we don't need him now.' Releasing the collar abruptly, she pushed his head down and side-stepping the door, slammed it shut.

Chapter 59

He'd been so easy to take. Drunk and slavering on about love and what could have been. On the surface he'd been the perfect candidate ... an advantaged, middle-class lad with no need to worry about the weight of a ninety-thousand-pound loan around his neck. Father owns a car dealership franchise with umpteen branches throughout Yorkshire. He is the new breed of privileged, entitled slobs who abuse their advantage. A breed of thoughtless millennials who expect everything on a plate, with no thought for those without access to their wealth, their familial support, their financial safety nets, their class. Before the loans it was bad enough. So many barriers to sidestep, so many hurdles to vault, obstacles to avoid ... for the normal folk that is. Not for the likes of him. Now it's even harder. How do you justify racking up such a debt? Well, plenty do. Plenty frivolously take it on, knowing they'll get bailed out if things go to shit. They have no idea what commitment means. No concept of hard work, but most of all, no respect for the huge honour they have ... the chance to better themselves through education. The chance to sidestep the old school tie, the chance to access lives previously only imagined.

Many use their advantage wisely ... but alas, many, like this fine specimen, choose to fritter it away at the cost of someone else's opportunity. How can they be so crass? Giving up on something so valuable because of a pregnancy, or to appease a misguided instruction from your father, or because your mental health diminishes or perhaps, because, like this one, you see the grass is greener if you sell drugs ... less effort ...

His head lolls to one side, a thick sliver dribbles in an elongated string from his swollen mouth, drips, then more drops follow. This one had been almost too keen. That should have been the first warning that he would not be a worthy captive. The first one for years and he is less than substandard. So frustrating ... so very frustrating. Any intelligence he possessed in the first place appears to have dissipated. I know the objective is to prove their lack of worth – but come on, this is beyond ridiculous. Even the simplest questions are beyond him. This will be a difficult recording to edit. I'll have to employ all my skills. Imaginative dexterity will be necessary, but I think I'm up to the challenge. Age is no object. In some ways the passing of years has tempered me.

Looking at him now though, I despair. I would ordinarily record this, but there's no way I want to add inferior footage. His reactions are sluggish and atypical. His participation in the proceedings is miniscule. It's so very trying to see him slouched in the chair, seemingly oblivious to the cuts ... the blood ... the indignities of it all. How could I ever have deemed him a worthy candidate? All my hopes slashed by his anodyne performance. His lack of response is boring ... dull ... disrespectful!

I slam the palm of my hand down on the table that holds the tools. You'd expect a response, to the bang, the clatter of the knives and scalpels, the echo around the room, but no ... there he lies, a stick insect of a specimen, brain activity limited and reactions zilch.

I might as well end it here and now. I pick up the hammer. And move behind him. My entire body wants to slam it down on his inactive brain, but I am stronger than that.

It isn't time yet. He hasn't answered his final question or made his last request. I look forward to that. I won't have long to wait!

Chapter 60

The last place Nikki wanted to be was on a squalid, freezing cold pig farm off the A659 with slashing rain, the ever-present stench of swine excrement and Big Zee's moans driving her crazy. She stepped out of the car and was promptly up to her ankles in muck. Judging from the sounds from the other side of the vehicle, Sajid had too. Archie had ordered a platoon of uniforms to descend on Sowerby's Pig Farm as well as a CSI team. The place was illuminated by bright lights and the sound of deep voices rumbling through the night was punctuated by protesting swine squeals that rent the night air.

Lentry lights illuminated a series of fields each around thirty metres squared. In each one, white low-level corrugated tunnels lined up at one end of the field with about twenty muddy pink-fleshed blobs of varying sizes milling around outside. The area in front of the shelters was a quagmire of shiny muck. Easily accessible along the fence line by raised mud-slathered decking, were huge feeding troughs. About a hundred metres or so away from the field stood a two-storey house flanked by a dilapidated out-building on one side and an equally dilapidated caravan on the other. The house itself was lit up and in the light spilling from the open front door, Nikki saw that the driveway was potholed and unkempt. A bit like the owner, who, she assumed, was the hunched man in conversation with a neon-vested uniform. He wore wellies and a mucky old raincoat and a peaked hat. Seemingly oblivious to the rain, he gesticulated across his land and although his words were indecipherable, his body language was combative. No surprises there. She hadn't expected the pig farmer to take too kindly to being accused of allowing his animals to dispose of evidence, human bodies no less.

Stomping round to join Sajid, Nikki laughed. 'Didn't you get the memo about wearing your wellies?'

Pulling his jacket tighter around his body, Saj glared at her. 'You could've told me.'

'You're such a city boy. If you'd been more observant then you'd have seen me putting mine on before we left.' She held one foot out as if she was a Victorian belle displaying a bit of ankle for a would-be suitor rather than exposing a black plastic boot with slurry of dubious origins dripping from it. 'Besides, did you really think posh shoes were suitable for a trip to a pig farm? Come on, Saj!'

She gestured to the figure that lurked in the back seat of the neighbouring pool car. 'Get him out.'

Making a glooping sound as he pulled each foot from the mud, Saj approached the vehicle and yanked the door open. 'Get out.'

Big Zee, peering round him, wide eyed and anxious, groaned. 'Aw come on, man. Don't want that pillock Sowerby to see me. He'll tell Franco and I'll be in the shit.'

Nikki shook her head. Hadn't the idiot realised that the minute he snitched on Franco and admitted his complicity to disposing of at least five people, including Franco's girlfriend, by feeding them to the pigs, his anonymity and freedom were no longer an option? Pillock!

Saj dragged him from the vehicle. Big Zee was still wearing the same clothes he'd worn at the gym and as soon as the rain and cold air hit him, he began to shiver. Nikki had no sympathy. If he hadn't suspected Franco of offing Tyke, Big Zee would quite happily continue feeding human remains to the livestock. He was more of an animal than the snorting, snivelling creatures in the field. Trying not to imagine what Franco might do to Haqib or one of the kids in the neighbourhood if he wasn't stopped, Nikki exhaled slowly. One way or another Franco was going down for good tonight.

Big Zee's gaze was trained on the farmer and he tried to back away, but Saj grabbed the cuffs that held his hands fastened before him. 'Is this the farm Franco used to dispose of his enemies?'

Big Zee shrugged and Saj pulled harder on the metal cuffs causing the prisoner to stumble onto his knees into the mire. Ignoring his squeals, Nikki stepped forward, and raised her wellied foot till it rested on his back, exerting slight pressure there. 'Is it?' Her tone was sharp and Big Zee again shook his head.

Pressing a little harder, Nikki spoke in a quiet reasonable tone. 'Look, you want Franco to get away with feeding Tyke to this lot?' Her arm extended to include the fields before them. 'Which fields did he use?'

Before Big Zee had a chance to respond, the farmer stormed over, his raincoat flapping behind him. 'What the fuck you done? Franco will kill you. He'll kill us both.'

Nikki raised an eyebrow to the officer that followed the farmer and nodded. 'Book him! Accessory to murder, disposing of a body – and anything else you can think of.'

The farmer raised his voice and tried to duck the officer who was attempting to grab him and lead him to one of the police cars. 'Franco in't been here for weeks, like. Don't know what you expect to find. I in't seen him for yonks. You're all effing mental, that's what you are.'

Nikki waved a hand at the young officer who had now managed to grab Sowerby's arm. 'You telling me Franco comes to the farm sometimes, Mr Sowerby? What does he do, when he's here?'

Sowerby cleared his throat, rolled the product around on his tongue for a second and then gobbed it in the direction of the officer's shoes. He emitted a high-pitched snort when the lad jumped to dodge the phlegm. Glaring at Nikki, his eyes took on a sly look. 'What's it worth for me to tell you, sweetheart?'

Nikki's answering smile didn't reach her eyes and had the desired effect on Sowerby, for his eyes flitted away from her and the grin slid from his face.

'I'll tell you what it's worth to you, *Mr* Sowerby. It's worth the difference between being an accomplice to Franco's dirty deeds which could get you fifteen years, or being an accessory who aided the police in their enquiries which would get you five years tops. Your choice!' She made to move away from him as if disinterested in his reply and then turned and moved right up to him, her finger prodding him hard in the chest. 'Oh, and you call me sweetheart again and I'll feed your balls to your pigs, okay?'

She waited for his nod before continuing. 'When was Franco last here and who did he bring?'

Swallowing hard, Sowerby caught Big Zee's eye. 'He'd be better telling you about the last time. He were there. It were about ten days ago.' He jerked his head in Big Zee's direction. 'He'll know. Me? Well, I get a call to make myself scarce and I lock myself in my house. Can't trust that Franco, he's a real psycho. Saw that one from the window like. Him and his mate, the smaller one. It were them two that dragged the girl from the car. She were screaming, like. I watched from the upstairs window. Franco got out his machete and she screamed again. Think he must've slashed her, big time. I hate it when they scream. Then they just toppled her into the field and made sure she couldn't get out till the pigs were done. Ask him. He'll tell you.'

'You sure that's the last time he was here?'

'Yeah, yeah, 'course I'm sure. Not gonna lie, not now I got you lot all over me.'

She turned to Big Zee. 'That add up, does it? Did you bring Kayleigh here ten days ago? Is that how things went down?'

Head bowed, Big Zee nodded. 'But that don't mean he didn't come back with Tyke. Where else is he otherwise?'

'Well, I don't know, do I? Maybe Tyke did a runner, got fed up with you. I don't see why Mr Sowerby would lie though, do you?'

'I in't lying.' Sowerby's voice was an irritating whine.

'Get him processed back at Trafalgar House,' Nikki said to the uniform, 'and take another officer with you. He's a lively one.'

She turned back to Big Zee. 'Tyke may or may not be somewhere on this farm. Now, by my reckoning there's at least five fields here. The sooner you narrow it down for us, the quicker the CSIs will be able to process the scene. You know as well as I do it'll be hard enough to get any confirmation, but we want to try. So, if Tyke's here and if you want any little bit of your man back, I suggest you start talking. Where did Franco do his dumping?'

Big Zee, still on his knees in the muck, sniffed and rubbed his hand over his face, smearing pig shit and snot all over it. 'That one. The nearest one. Kept it nice and easy, did Franco.'

Nikki turned to another uniformed officer. 'Take him back to Trafalgar House. I'll deal with him when I get back.'

'No, no. I want to stay here. Let me stay.'

Sighing, Nikki nodded once to the officer and turned away, blanking out Big Zee's escalating pleas as she did so. She turned to Gracie, the head crime scene investigator, who'd approached whilst she'd been talking to Franco and said, 'He says that field's our best bet.'

Gracie surveyed the field. 'I'll get cracking. You know it'll be a long shot if we find anything, but we'll do our best. I've put in a call to have a local vet come and help us deal with the pigs. That boar in the corner's a massive fucker and he doesn't look ready to move any time soon.'

The boar, half submerged in mud, was indeed gargantuan. His snout stuck above the muck, nostrils flaring as he snored, both eyes shut. Nikki was relieved that moving livestock wasn't in her job description. Sensing Sajid at her shoulder, she pointed. 'I've heard boars can be vicious. This could be a long night.'

Chapter 61

The damp cold of Bradford had got to Burhan Abadi. Huddled under a too-thin duvet with the heating on full blast and an untouched meal on his bedside table, he felt fragile. He was well aware that it wasn't just the change in climate that was causing shivers to wrack his body. Nor was the miserable cold responsible for the frequent bouts of nausea which periodically engulfed him. The cancer was taking more of a grip and every movement made him want to groan. Things needed to be sorted, and soon, so he could return home ... before it was too late.

Struggling to pull himself into a sitting position, Abadi pushed the duvet down till it was out of sight of his laptop screen which rested on the over-bed table. No point in making Husayni aware of his illness. He Skyped the solicitor, determined to exert pressure. Time was becoming increasingly of the essence. He needed to be sure the solicitor was pulling every lever he had. The only thing he wanted now was to discredit Parekh so he could take Charlie home. The thing was, it was looking less likely that in the current time frame, he'd be able to do so legally. Perhaps it was time for Husayni to really show his worth. Burhan had promised his wife he would bring her granddaughter home and he was a man of his word. There was no way he would leave Bradford without her.

Husayni flickered into place on the screen and Burhan wasted no time in telling him that what was needed was a two-pronged attack. 'You will ensure that the necessary arrangements to transport my granddaughter back to Palestine within the week are in place. Money is no object. Get what you need – a new passport for the girl, people to abduct her and a reputable Muslim woman to accompany her. Meanwhile, in order to influence the Palestinian authorities from allowing her repatriation to England, you will discredit Parekh as much as possible. The less like a good mother figure she is, the less chance my government will agree to her deportation, no?'

'Well, Mr Abadi, all of your suggestions are of course doable. My people already have testimony from a reputable Muslim Bradford councillor, Yousaf Mirza. He has responsibility for local policing and we have managed to, shall we say, convince him that it is in his best interests to comply. He is prepared to muddy the waters and has already begun to exert pressure on those investigating your son's death to consider Parekh. He is also in a position to produce details of her history. He has knowledge of acts that Parekh carried out against her own father when she was a child. These sealed records may be admissible. However, Mr Abadi, it would be remiss of me not to point out that since 9/11, border controls have been strengthened and international travel is strictly monitored. Movement between countries has become very strict. I am unsure how easy it will be to get a non-compliant girl to submit to leaving the country on a false passport.'

Stifling a cough, Burhan lifted a glass of water from the bedside table and took a small sip. It felt cool against his rough throat – cool and soothing. He savoured the sensation, then lifted the glass to his forehead and allowed it to chill his flushed skin. 'I have met with the girl once already. She is very like her mother. What you need to do is convince her that unless she complies, her mother will spend the rest of her days in prison, leaving her siblings homeless. You see, Abubakhar, it is easy when you have a vice to apply, is it not? Set things in play tonight.'

Chapter 62

It had taken over an hour to tranquilise the boar and get it shifted. Ten strong bodies had hefted it through the mud and into the next field followed by sows and offspring. For the next three quarters of an hour the night air had been rent by squealing pigs as they settled into their new home among their siblings, who seemed less than happy to be sharing their field with migrants. Sajid arranged for some uniformed officers to tip more swill into their troughs and eventually the squeals subsided to be replaced by more traditional grunts.

Meanwhile, Gracie and her team plodded on, trying to sift through gallons and gallons of slurry in the faint hope of finding something that would confirm Sowerby and Big Zee's story. Otherwise Nikki was afraid that lack of physical and forensic evidence might allow Franco to escape, yet again.

As she watched the proceedings from her spot by the edge of the fence, Nikki was aware of Sajid coming and going, but she couldn't take her eyes off the activity in the field. They'd got a warrant to search the farmhouse and surrounding buildings and Sajid was coordinating that. Apart from a burner phone which connected to another burner phone and two bags full of used twenties under the floorboards in the main bedroom, they hadn't found much. At some point over the next week or so, they'd probably be able to access the content of the conversations between the two phones, and plot the movements of the other phone during that time, but that didn't make it imminent.

Franco reminded her too much of her father. Same psychopathic tendencies, same lack of humanity. It worried her that Franco had tried to contact Anika. Her sister was vulnerable. Nikki desperately needed Gracie's team to find something, anything, to corroborate Sowerby and Big Zee's testimony. Franco needed to be behind bars because if she couldn't keep him away from her sister the legal way, then she'd be forced to do it her own way. As she stood, her hands gripping the wire fence between the barbs, her entire body was taut. Oblivious to the rain and the cold, she focused on the repetitive movements of the muck-splattered figures in the field and tried to block out the flashes that kept igniting in her mind.

An excited yell from the group standing in the mud broke into Nikki's thoughts. She pulled herself up against the wire, uncaring that the barbs were now pressing into her hands. A figure broke away from the huddle in the field. Gracie. Trudging through the swamp, she approached Nikki, holding something in her hand. 'We got something, look.'

Nikki thought she was going to faint. Blood swept through her body and she wobbled a little. Her eyes moved from Gracie's smiling, mucky face to what she held. Despite the slurry of mud dripping from it, it was clear they'd found a necklace.

'I'll get it cleaned up and photographed. This could be what you're looking for.'

'Soon as you've got decent images, I want them sent to Trafalgar House – to Archie. He can see if either Deano or Big Zee can identify the necklace. Good job, Gracie.'

As the crime scene investigator went off to process the item, Nikki saw that the rest of Gracie's team were going about their work with renewed vigour. The piece of evidence had spurred them on and Nikki hoped they'd find more. She really didn't want to have to kill Franco.

Chapter 63

How could she have been so stupid? He'd already tried to take her once and now, here she was being followed by three huge knobs in an equally huge car. Why was he so persistent? Hadn't he got the message earlier? She wanted nowt to do with him. She was happy with her mum – well, most of the time she was. She was still pissed off with her for not telling her about her dad and she wished she'd just settle down with Marcus. She loved him, Charlie knew her mum did, but she was just too damn headstrong, too independent. Maybe after everything with her real dad was sorted, she'd settle down with him. Make them all a real family.

This was *not* how she wanted to be spending her evening. All she wanted to do was see a film and chill. Forget about everything – her dad, Haqib, her dysfunctional family – every bloody thing. She'd first noticed them idling at the end of the road when she left to go to Iqrah's. Idiots probably underestimated her because she was just a kid. Well, she'd teach them. She knew this area better than them. She'd soon lose them.

Charlie set off towards her friend's and then dipped down the ginnel by Mrs Brown's, ran down the side of a neighbouring garden, vaulted the fence at the bottom and ended up in the next street. That'd show them to mess with her.

Pleased with herself, she walked down towards town and had nearly got to the Fieldhead roundabout near Iqrah's, when she was grabbed from behind and dragged towards a car that had pulled onto the kerb. Flung into the back seat, a hand at the back of her neck pressing her face onto the leather seat, she yelped and struggled.

'Keep your head down, bitch.' The voice was gravelly and she didn't recognise it.

When she'd landed on the seat, she'd extended her arms in front of her to save herself, now she tried to wriggle to pull them out to the side. At last she managed and, propping herself up, she used all her strength to lunge back. The back of her head connected with something, sending a sharp pain through her skull, and eliciting a yelp from the man who was holding her. Without waiting for him to recover, she pushed herself upright and into a sitting position. The man beside her reached out and grabbed her hair, yanking her head down towards his knees. She looked to the front and saw a grinning face looking back at her.

'*You!*'

The single word faded as the thug holding her hair raised his knee and smashed it into her face. Blood spurted from her nose as she fell unconscious to the seat.

Chapter 64

'You need to go home now, Nikki.'

Sajid's tone brooked no argument and, if Nikki was honest, after Archie had confirmed that both Deano and Big Zee had identified the necklace as belonging to Kayleigh, the cold had seeped into her consciousness and every bone in her body was pulling her deeper into the quagmire in which she stood. Sajid was right. It *was* time to go home, but she just wasn't sure she *could* actually move. She opened her mouth to tell him that, but before she could speak, he'd gripped her elbow and was trying to manoeuvre her towards the pool car they'd come in.

There was nothing Nikki hated more than being manhandled, so she jerked her elbow up landing a hit on Saj's chin. 'Get off me.'

Rubbing his chin, Saj took a step back. 'For fuck's sake, Nik, I'm not messing with you. Marcus phoned … Charlie's missing. You gotta—'

But the rest of his sentence landed in the mud, for Nikki was off racing towards the vehicle, all thoughts of cold or aching limbs gone. Charlie. Her little Charlie was gone. As she yanked open the car door, she wondered if she'd pushed her daughter too hard – pushed her away – forced her to escape. But then a more insidious thought crept into her mind. A moment after Sajid had opened the passenger door and launched himself into the seat beside her, she put her foot on the accelerator, and narrowly missing a stationary vehicle, she took off heading back to Bradford. 'Get Archie to go to the Midland Hotel. That bastard's taken my daughter.'

As she drove, she told Sajid about the two men following her and how, with Ali, she'd confronted them at the Odeon car park. 'Bastards must have decided to teach me a lesson big time.' She paused. 'Either way, they're messing with the wrong mother.'

The drive back to Bradford was hair-raising. Nikki broke every speed limit there was and all the while she was firing orders to Saj. Until finally Marcus came on the line.

'She was only going to the cinema with Iqrah Batti. I thought she'd be okay.'

His tone calmed her. 'Where are you, Marcus?'

'Where the fuck do you think I am? I'm parked outside The Midland Hotel with Archie. If that bastard's got our girl, then he won't be taking her anywhere. Not whilst I'm here.'

In the background, Nikki could hear Archie waffling on about 'no proverbials' or 'violence on my watch'. But it was Marcus's response to her boss that filled her heart. 'Look, Archie. You stay here in the car. I'm going in alone. If he's got my daughter, *I'll* sort it. You'd do the same if she were yours.'

To Nikki he said, 'Get here when you can, but I've got this. I promise you, I'll get her.'

Marcus was just getting out of the car as Nikki drove into the small Midland Hotel car park and screeched to a halt, blocking in Archie's car. Flicking the ignition off, she all but fell out of the vehicle and headed straight to Marcus. Never had she needed his presence so badly. She looked up at him, speechless for once. Marcus shook his head and shrugged. 'Come on then.'

He turned to Sajid and Archie who were now both standing

near their vehicles. 'You two stay here. I think we can go and collect our daughter together, don't you?'

Saj moved round, slapped Marcus on the back and got into the driver's seat of the pool car. 'Good luck, you two.' Starting the engine, he spoke to Archie. 'I'll go park this in Forster Square and meet you back here in five. If they've not contacted us by then we'll follow them in, okay?'

Archie sighed and eased his cumbersome frame back into his vehicle. Rolling down the window he yelled, 'Room three-sixty.'

Nikki paused, turned briefly and waved. Archie as usual had her back.

Once inside the plush hotel, Nikki and Marcus headed for the elevator to the third floor. It seemed to take forever and Nikki was aware of her foot tapping a rhythm on the floor as they glided upwards. 'Let me do the talking, eh?'

Marcus raised an eyebrow. 'When have I ever done anything but let you do the damn talking, Nik?'

Shrugging, she refused to feel guilt. She didn't talk much but when she did, she expected to be listened to. Sometimes she wondered why Marcus put up with it. Then in a blinding flash, right there in that poky little lavender-scented lift, she realised that he didn't put up with her. He just listened and then went ahead and did whatever the hell he wanted to anyway. Why the hell had she never realised that before?

Marcus broke the silence as they entered the elevator and waited to be transported upstairs. 'What do you think the old bloke thinks he can achieve by taking her?'

That was a good question. 'Well, according to Khal, his old man always got what he wanted. That's why it was so easy for me to believe he'd left me and gone back to his parents. They had everything – money, a business. I couldn't compete with that. I was broken.'

She risked a look at Marcus. 'Still am.'

Shaking his head, Marcus grabbed her hand. 'Yeah, but we're fixing you. Me and the kids. Slowly but surely we're fixing you.'

The lift pinged and came to a stop. And as the doors slid open, Nikki pulled her hand from his grasp and was off, looking for room three-sixty. 'Here.'

As Marcus caught up, she hammered on the door with her fist, not caring who she disturbed. If her baby was in there, then she'd break the door down if she needed to. There was no response, so she hammered again. Still no response.

Marcus who'd stood silently whilst she knocked, stepped forward, and took a slim card from his pocket. 'This is a master. It's got a special magnetic strip that affects the hotel key settings. It opens most doors.'

'Since when did a landscape gardener need one of those?'

Marcus shrugged. 'Sometimes when the bastards refuse to pay me for my hard graft, I just nip in and take something they don't want to fall into the wrong hands until they cough up. I call it security.'

'And they don't report you?' Nikki's tone was incredulous. How had she not known that Marcus bent the rules on occasion?

'Not so far.'

He hammered on the door one last time, waited a few seconds and when there was still no response, he inserted the fake card. The green light was activated and Marcus pushed the door open, stepping back to allow Nikki to precede him into the room.

Taking a step into the darkened room, Nikki paused to get her bearings. Head cocked to one side she listened, but could hear nothing. Her heart sank. It didn't look like he had Charlie here, so where was she? She flicked on the light and took another step forward. The bed was crumpled as if someone had left it in a hurry … wait … no! It wasn't crumpled. There was someone in it – well, half in it. She and Marcus reached Burhan Abadi at the same time. The old man was hanging half off the far side of the bed, the duvet tangled round his waist, his laptop toppled onto the floor. Nikki put her fingers to his neck, feeling for a pulse She shook her head. 'Nothing.'

'Maybe he'd been sick for a while. He looks very skinny.' Marcus pulled out his phone and dialled emergency services.

Taking out her phone, Nikki phoned Saj, quickly explaining what they'd found. 'Charlie's not here, so I need you to come up and see what his laptop can tell us. You need to take it away before the uniforms arrive. I think he's dead, and they'll confiscate everything. I need to know who he hired to take my daughter.'

Ignoring Sajid's protests, she hung up, passed her phone to Marcus and said, 'Stay. I need you to find out everything you can. I'm going to get Charlie.'

Whilst she'd been in Khal's dad's hotel room, Nikki had realised that there was someone else who might want to take her daughter. Someone who was a lot more of a threat to Charlie than her paternal grandad. Running down the back stairs, she bumped into a drunk couple having a snog at the bottom of the stairwell.

'Can I borrow your phone? I'll give you twenty quid.'

The man, his hand halfway up the woman's skirt, grunted as the woman, glazed eyes fixed on the wall opposite, thrust her mobile in Nikki's direction. As the man seemingly hit jackpot and began to undo his flies, ready for engagement, Nikki grabbed the woman's hand and used her finger to activate the phone.

Turning her back on the rutting figures, she dialled Ali's number and having arranged to be picked up behind Broadway, she tossed the phone inside the woman's open handbag and headed out into the drizzle, hoping Archie and Saj wouldn't follow her too soon. She wanted to have her shot at Franco first and Ali was more than enough back-up for what she had in mind if he'd touched her daughter.

Ali picked her up himself. 'Jenny said you sounded desperate so here I am.'

Nikki clicked her seatbelt into place and directed Ali to drive her towards Listerhills. Deano had told them that Franco was currently shacked up with some woman on Princeville Street, just off Ingleby Road. That would be her first port of call.

There were two ways into Princeville Street. If you were after a low house number, then your best access point was from Legrams Lane. If, on the other hand, you were after a high number, then your best access was from Ingleby Road. Nikki reckoned the Ingleby Road access would be best for them. Halfway up the street, a series of bollards prohibited through-driving, or rather they did when they hadn't been smashed to smithereens. The streetlights had been smashed creating hazy shadows, the only lighting coming from the occasional kitchen window. As Ali drew near to the decimated bollards, he slowed to allow Nikki to jump out. The house she was after was an odd number so it would be a back terrace. Her feet had just hit the ground, when a huge 4x4 mounted the barrier, bouncing over what was left of the bollards with a grating noise and slewing to a halt at the side of the road.

Ali had turned into the cul-de-sac to the right, ready to turn his car round, and Nikki moved into the shadow on the opposite side of the road. It seemed that she hadn't been noticed and she wanted to keep it that way. Wondering who was in the car, she peered through the dark. Two men got out from the front and, as one of them lit up a cigarette, she saw that it was Franco. Her heart sped up. She wanted to go over there and rip his throat out, but she hesitated, waiting to see what was happening.

Half aware that Ali had dimmed his headlights and had pulled up silently behind her, she strained to see what was going on. They were mumbling to each other. Arguing? Banter? She wasn't sure. A door clicked open and the back of the vehicle was flooded in light. A large figure she recognised from hanging around near Deano's house got out. Before he slammed the door shut again though, he bent down and began dragging something from the back seat.

The interior light was still on, but whatever he was dragging was hidden from view by the car itself. Edging to one side, Nikki relied on the lack of street lighting and the background noise of their conversation to stop them noticing her. She got close enough to the vehicle to see the large man from the backseat hoist something over his shoulder. Straining to see what it was, the area was plunged into darkness again when he slammed the door shut. The trio began to move towards the ginnel that would lead to the back terraced house.

Nikki hesitated, trying to visualise what lay beyond the back terraces. Streets with ex Metro housing, and beyond that Ingleby Road. Would she be better to approach them out here? There could be others in the house. Here there were three. She heard the click as Ali closed the taxi door and knew he was behind her. A quick glance told her he had a baseball bat in his hand. Ali was ferocious, and so was she. But these men could have machetes or guns. Franco was not to be underestimated.

A light was flicked on in the front terraced house, illuminating the three men and their package. Nikki nearly screamed, her fingers clenched into fists and she was roaring over the road, Ali two feet behind her. The package was Charlie and she was covered in blood. Nikki landed a drop kick to Franco before he had a chance to even turn around. Always cut off the head of the snake first was her motto. Franco lunged away from her and fell to his knees and Ali was onto the other guy whacking him twice with the bat, once to the knees to drop him and once to the head to put him out of action.

He spun and repeated the knee action to the man that had Charlie. Still gripping Charlie, the big man fell to the ground and when he released Charlie, she landed in a heap, her head hitting the pavement. A roar escaped Nikki's lips and she dived towards her daughter whilst Ali took care of Franco. As she tried to waken Charlie, Nikki became aware of sirens getting closer. Thank God someone had called it in. Within seconds an ambulance, two police cars and Marcus, Archie and Sajid were there.

As the paramedics dealt with Charlie, who had regained consciousness and was complaining of a thumping headache, Sajid told Nikki that whilst she and Marcus had been in Abadi's room, Gracie had rung her phone to inform Nikki that they'd discovered part of a woman's pelvis and three teeth.

'How the hell did you get here so quickly?' asked Nikki, her hand gripping Charlie's tight.

'Ali!'

As soon as Ali had seen the three men in the Land Rover, he'd phoned Sajid. Nikki glared at him when she heard that, but he just shrugged. 'Thought we'd need back-up ... and we did. Fucking sue me, Nikki.'

'We were already on our way though, Nik. We were bringing Franco in anyway – one way or another, Franco was being taken off the streets tonight.'

Friday 26th October

Chapter 65

For the first time in what seemed like weeks, but was in fact only a couple of days, Nikki returned to her own home where she, Charlie and Marcus were greeted by jostling bodies and smiling faces. Haqib had returned home and despite having his arm bandaged, looked as irrepressible as ever. Anika hugged her extra tightly and Nikki knew she'd been told about Franco. 'He'll not come near you again, Ani.'

Anika gripped her tighter and whispered, 'You've helped me get rid of two bad pennies today, Nik. Archie tells me Yousaf has been arrested after attempting to pervert the course of justice by wrongly implicating a police officer and leaking sealed records from said officer's childhood to the *Telegraph and Argus*.'

'Mine?' A familiar tightness bubbled in Nikki's chest. Why hadn't Archie told her this? He'd had plenty of time. They'd been at the hospital with Charlie for a couple of hours and then at Trafalgar House before returning home. The thought of her childhood, her mum's childhood being emblazoned over the front page of the *T&A* was almost too much to bear ... especially after everything else.

Shaking her head, Anika exhaled. 'Oof ... Saj told me Archie nearly eviscerated DS Springer. Apparently, she was the original leak and then he pulled in a favour, don't ask me what, and the story is back under lock and key, where it should be.'

The sisters held each other for a moment, before turning to look at their mother, who was chivvying Ruby upstairs and dragging Sunni behind her. 'You've seen your mum and Charlie, now, it's bedtime. Even with all this excitement you still have school tomorrow.'

In that moment, Nikki realised that, despite her weakness, Anika had their mother's welfare at heart. She squeezed her sister's hand. 'We've always got her back, Ani, you and me.'

'Aw for God's sake, why do you two always get so maudlin – not like *you* lost any body parts or owt, is it? *I'm* the one who's had surgery.' Haqib, pouting like a 2-year-old who'd dropped their ice cream, cradled his poorly hand in the other.

Nikki raised an eyebrow. 'You know what, Haqib? Better head off to your own house before I remember where I've hidden those pills and hand them over to Archie with a detailed report of where they came from. I'm sure Franco and Deano would be happy to grass *you* up if it shaved a bit off *their* sentences.'

Her nephew's face paled and Nikki shook her head. 'Scram, before I *do* dob in a dealer.'

Without waiting for further instruction, Haqib yelled bye to Charlie, and with his mum following at a slower pace, exited Nikki's home.

At once tiredness overtook Nikki. Kicking off her DMs on top of the pile of shoes by the door and slinging her jacket over the banister, she pulled herself up the stairs. When she reached the halfway mark, she stopped. Her gaze found Marcus, who stood, uncertainly by the door. 'You coming then?'

With a tired smile, he followed her upstairs, ignoring Charlie's mock 'being sick' sounds.

*

Two in the morning and Nikki was awake again, Marcus lightly snoring beside her. It wasn't memories of Khal that had wakened her this time. It was thoughts of her dad. The very idea that her and Anika's files were so very nearly exposed to the public had made her toss and turn.

None of that was for public consumption, yet Nikki knew that after the high-profile case where her testimony discredited a previously highly decorated officer, everything about her was deemed public fodder. She didn't care about herself, but she wouldn't put her mother through that degree of scrutiny again. It had taken years for her to be able to hold her head high at family gatherings. Nikki could not be responsible for bringing that shame to the forefront again.

Pulling herself quietly to the edge of the bed, she shrugged Marcus's jumper over her head and pulled on a pair of leggings. By the torch from her phone, she pulled the most recent of her dad's boxes towards her and, as if to reassure herself that he couldn't cause them any more harm, she lifted the lid and began to sift through the photos the private investigator had taken. Older, flabbier and more hunched, he looked like any other middle-aged man. Nikki flung the photos back into the box. She knew better than to underestimate him though. It was time to up the surveillance for a while ... just till she felt less unsettled ... just for peace of mind.

Hearing Marcus mumbling as he slept, Nikki smiled and packed the box away. Marcus had been there for her and Charlie tonight and, for once she hadn't pushed him away. Maybe things were changing. Now all she needed to do was find Khal's killer and put him away once and for all. Climbing back into bed, ignoring Marcus's sleepy moans as she warmed up her cold feet on the back of his legs, she let her mind drift over the case.

Sowerby, the pig farmer, maintained that Franco hadn't been there in weeks and she saw no reason to disbelieve him. Franco too denied it. Mind you, he also denied feeding Kayleigh to the pigs, despite both Big Zee and Sowerby's testimony, so perhaps his denial didn't carry a lot of weight. The fact remained though that Tyke was missing. They couldn't correlate his phone as it was switched off. Big Zee said he was heading to The Mannville Arms for a drink and the last ping on his phone had been in that area … all these thoughts swirled in Nikki's brain as she drifted into a fitful sleep.

When she woke up two hours later, the darkness in the room alleviated only by the streetlights, she was disorientated. Marcus's steady breathing beside her didn't soothe her. Her mind was full of muddled thoughts and memories that she couldn't quite untangle. The idea that she was missing something irked her and the more she tried to grasp it, the further away it seemed to drift … until it hit her, wham, in the centre of her forehead. She knew immediately what had been annoying her since she'd first spoken to Big Zee about Tyke's disappearance.

It was a long shot, but sometimes long shots paid dividends. Pulling on her jeans and Marcus's jumper again, she kissed his forehead and left the room. Running downstairs, she texted Saj, grabbed a pen and left a garbled note for Marcus on the kitchen table, and moments later, regardless of how early it was, she got into her car and drove. There was no way she could wait till morning – not now.

Chapter 66

Nikki was filled with a sense of purpose that wasn't dampened by either the lashing rain or the icy darkness of the early morning. As she drove, wipers on full speed, various scenes from the time Khal disappeared, snippets from the current investigation, Tyke's disappearance and her own instincts all merged together, taking on a greater significance.

Conversations with Jacko and his sister. Tess looking shifty, avoiding answering her directly when she asked if she'd seen Khal the night he disappeared. Jacko following her around like a lost puppy in the days after Khal's disappearance, his story about being ill and in bed that night, backed up by Tess. The information that Khal already had a wife when he married her, proving he wasn't the trustworthy hero she'd always thought him.

How they hung out at various student pubs around town; Tumblers, The Black Swan, The Mannville Arms – all of them together. Nancy and Gordon watching over them, teasing them, interested in their lives. Nancy sympathetic to their problems, Gordon, a reassuring solid figure in the background, keeping them safe. They were all having fun, not taking life too seriously – no responsibilities, their whole lives in front of them. Except for Khal – he hadn't had his whole life in front of him.

Every one of the victims had had some sort of change happening in their lives. Mark Hodgson had mental health issues that caused him to pull away from those who loved him, Khal was being pressured to return to his wife in Ramallah, Stephanie Fields was pregnant. All the victims' lives were in flux – was that the common denominator? No, it was more than that and that's when it hit her. They'd all dropped out of college or were going to and so had Tyke. Big Zee had revealed his boyfriend had been studying anthropology. Was it something to do with that?

Nikki took a right at the mini roundabout and drove past Bombay Stores before turning onto Great Horton Road. Things had become clear and although protocol dictated that she should wait, Nikki had waited too long for this – fifteen years too long.

This early in the morning there was no trouble finding parking. Streetlights illuminated the area, a few bodies straggling their way home after a night on the town, a few restaurants flicking off their lights as they locked up having served the last of their customers. A couple of taxis idled as they waited for their fares, the rain making the streets look sleek and shimmery – like in an old black-and-white movie.

Nikki turned off the ignition and before she could reconsider, she took off at a run straight up to the door. Hammering on it, each bang echoing around the quiet street, and eliciting a chorus of 'Shut the fuck up's or 'Keep it down's.

With no thought to the consequences, Nikki ignored them, and continued to bray on the door, determined to gain access – determined to find out once and for all what had happened to Khal.

The sound of muffled footsteps approaching the closed door made Nikki take a step back. Standing on the balls of her feet, her body on high alert, she listened to the lock turning followed by the sound of bolts being drawn back. There was a moment's hesitation as if the person on the other side had chosen to peer through the peep hole to see who their early morning visitor was.

Nikki straightened her spine and stared straight at the circle, her chin raised, challenging, until the security light sprung to life, making her blink in its ferocity. The door handle depressed and, almost in slow motion, it began to swing open.

Body tense, Nikki held her breath, only now aware that perhaps she should have waited for Saj.

As the smiling figure on the other side of the door was revealed, she relaxed.

Chapter 67

Sajid was wakened by a sharp elbow to his side and an exasperated, 'For God's sake, will you get your damn phone!'

Blinking in the semi-dark room, he groaned and swung his legs over the side of the bed, the persistent buzzing of his phone the only sound other than Langley's exaggerated grumbling in their bedroom. 'Saj, switch that fucking racket off, right now.'

Galvanised by Langley's threatening tone, Saj stretched, rolled his shoulders and picked up the offending item from his bedside table. He'd half expected it to be Nikki or Archie. No one else usually rang at that time of the morning. However, the name that flashed on the screen was 'Marcus' and that brought a chill with it. Why would Marcus be phoning him at a quarter to five in the morning after the night they'd just had? He rarely phoned Sajid. Why would he? His girlfriend was Saj's boss.

Wide awake all of a sudden, Sajid answered, 'Whassup, Marcus?' Straightaway, he was aware of Langley propping himself up on his elbow beside him. Seemed Langley was equally concerned by an early morning call from Marcus.

Despite speaking in a whisper, Marcus sounded anxious. His words blended together as if he was fighting against time. 'She's gone, Saj. Nikki's gone. Left a note. Says she's worked it all out. Says it's all to do with Khal and Tyke's last movements.'

'Where? Where has she gone?' Sajid was already hopping about the bedroom, retrieving socks and boxers from his drawers and dragging clothes from his wardrobe. Langley too had got up and was passing his partner items as Saj spoke to Marcus.

'Says she's texted you, Saj. I just wanted to check you were on your way.'

'What the fuck's she texting for? She should've rung me. I'll be in touch, Marcus.' He rung off, and his fingers flew across his phone till he accessed Nikki's text. One look at it and he was heading out the door, stopping only to put on trainers and a coat.

'Call Archie, Langley. Right now. I think she could be right. It all adds up.'

Chapter 68

Following the landlord into the darkened pub, Nikki could smell the dregs of beer mingled with the floral air freshener Nancy sprayed at the end of every night. Now that she was here, her earlier suspicions seemed ridiculous. She wasn't quite sure how to continue but saw it as a good sign that Gordon hadn't appeared as yet. 'Gordon still in bed?'

Gesturing for Nikki to follow her through to the back room, Nancy laughed. 'That oaf? He's dead to the world. Had a bit of a sesh till an hour or so ago with some of the regulars and now he's crashed out. When he goes on a bender like that, I'm always on my own for the next shift.' She picked up a glass that had been stuffed into one of the plant pots and placed it on the bar as she passed. 'Won't see him till the afternoon now. He's getting too old for late-night drinking. Gone are the days when he could keep up with you young ones.'

Pleased that she'd have a chance to speak to Nancy on her own, maybe take a look down the cellar, prove herself wrong, Nikki settled herself on a stool by the bar. Now, how to bring up her suspicions?

Nancy moved over to the big fancy coffee machine that stood on the back corner of the bar and switched it on. 'What' up,

Nikki? Why you here battering my door at' – she looked at her watch – 'five in the morning? Cappuccino? Latte?'

'Latte would be nice. Thanks, Nancy.' As she watched the older woman fetch milk from the fridge and potter around with coffee and cups, all nice and normal, Nikki began to feel foolish. She'd known Nancy and Gordon for years. How could she imagine that The Mannville Arms, her local for a number of years, was the domain of a vicious, prolific serial killer? She'd spoken with detectives who'd been around during the Yorkshire Ripper case and had learned from them that often the wife was the last to know what their partner was up to. Perhaps they pushed the clues to the back of their minds, perhaps it was their brain's way of tricking them into discarding an idea so appallingly awful that they preferred to dissociate from it than engage with the reality of it.

Or perhaps their partner was just too bloody convincing … or beige … or normal … or shy … or inconsequential.

It had taken them at least fifteen years to realise they had another serial killer in their midst, fifteen years during which time Nikki had seen him, interacted with him on an almost weekly basis. Had she got it wrong? It all added up. The Mannville Arms' proximity to the dump sites, the fact that when she'd checked witness statements, many of the victims had visited The Mannville Arms around the time of their disappearance – something that had been overlooked when they were only considered as missing persons, or as individual deaths. It was only when clumped together that it added up. What had prompted her to check, was the fact that both Khal and Tyke left home to go to the pub, yet apparently neither arrived – suspicious with a capital S. Why hadn't she seen it earlier?

Nancy placed a steaming mug before her. 'You gonna tell me what's up, darling? Gordon needing another little slap on the wrists for not closing up on time? He doesn't do lock-ins as much nowadays though … or did you just fancy a chat? You've had a lot on your plate, girl, what with them finding poor Khal and all.'

A rueful smile crossed Nikki's face. Poor old Nancy hadn't a damn clue. For all these years she'd been the face of the pub, the chatty one, the one the customers became friends with, whilst Gordon had done the donkey work keeping himself to himself. Now Nikki had to blow her bubble. 'No, it's not about lock-ins, Nance.'

She sipped her drink; it was delicious. 'Do you do much of the cellar work, or is it all Gordon?'

Picking up a cloth and wiping the bar down, Nancy grinned. 'That smelly old place – no bloody chance. I don't go down there. That's his domain.'

She jerked her head towards the ceiling 'He can spend hours at a time down there.' She grinned. 'Sometimes think he disappears off there to get some peace and quiet from me.'

A lump had settled in Nikki's stomach. Nancy had always been like a mother hen fluttering around her, asking after Charlie, and the other kids, sympathising about the drugs in the city and, on occasions, dobbing in a dealer. Now Nikki was betraying that friendship. 'Mind if I take a shufty down there, Nance? Nowt official like.'

Nancy shrugged, a confused frown knitting her brows together. 'Well, I suppose so. If you want to. Maybe if you're quick, Gordon won't need to know. He's private that way, like.'

'I'll be quick, promise.'

Biting her lip, Nancy hesitated and then flung the cloth down on the bar and opened the entrance to the bar. 'Come on then. I'll just get the key.'

The two of them, Nancy leading the way, walked through a narrow hallway leading to the back of the pub where a small kitchen and an even smaller office resided. Nancy went into the office, lifted a black-and-white painting of Bradford's trams off the wall, revealing a safe behind it. She fiddled with the lock and then pulled the safe open.

Nikki tried to peer over the woman's head and into the safe, but couldn't see anything other than a cash box. When Nancy turned back round, she was holding a set of keys in her hands. Nikki recognised one of them as being very similar to the one she and Sajid had borrowed from Sunbridge Wells earlier in the week.

Nancy led the way through the kitchen to a door that looked like it led to an old pantry. She inserted a key in the lock, turned it and pushed the door open. Before stepping back to allow Nikki to enter, she flicked a light on, casting an amber light from the single flickering bulb dangling from the ceiling. 'Down you go, sweetie. Think you need to head down and to the right at the bottom of the stairs. There'll be another light at the bottom.'

Hesitating, Nikki peered down the stairs as they tapered off into darkness at the bottom. Memories from her recent experience in the tunnels with Sajid and the rats made her shudder as she approached the first step, telling herself that she wasn't actually going into the tunnels this time. Just doing a bit of reconnoitring round the cellar to see if there was any basis to her suspicions. With a quick smile at Nancy, who stood behind her, arms crossed over her chest, she grabbed the banister, checked her pocket to make sure she had her phone handy and took a tentative step down.

By the time she'd reached the sixth step, cold wafts of air drifted upwards, chilling her cheeks. Behind her, Nancy's breathing echoed and she found the sound oddly reassuring. When she reached the bottom, a definite draft coaxed her to follow its direction to her right. The corridor she found herself in was narrow and before she moved forward into the deeper darkness, she scrabbled around on the wall feeling for the light switch. She didn't realise she was holding her breath until she found the switch and illuminated the area. Although she had misgivings about Nancy's safety following her into unknown territory, she was glad of the other woman's reassuring presence.

Fifteen metres ahead of her, on a slight incline, was a door, similar in size and structure to the ones they'd found at the other tunnels. Staggered along either side of the corridor were two further doors. Relieved that the corridor didn't feel particularly like a cellar, Nikki stepped forward again and stopped when she reached the first door. By her estimation this room was directly under the bar area.

'That's where we keep the kegs. There's a trapdoor from outside down to there; you put the kegs on the rollers. Gordon deals with that.'

Nancy's voice made her jump. Although she'd been aware of the other woman following her, they'd maintained silence since entering the cellar area. 'Can I have a look?'

Nancy thrust the bundle of keys to Nikki. 'It's the long one. Nowt to see in there except cobwebs and the barrels.'

'Any idea why it's locked then?' asked Nikki, her heart beginning to accelerate as she inserted the key in the lock.

'Just Gordon's a bit anal. He brings the kegs down here for storage via the dumbwaiter.'

Taking a deep breath, Nikki thrust the door open and peered inside. The dim light from the hallway barely illuminated the first couple of feet of the room and Nikki had the sense of the darkness before her moving ominously. Conscious of Nancy peering over her shoulder, Nikki remained on the threshold and inserted her hand, feeling around for the light switch. When she found it, she flicked it on, prepared for the same yellowy light that had lit the rest of her exploration of the basement. Instead she was assaulted by a piercingly bright white light that made stars dance before her eyes.

She took a couple of steps inside but before she had a chance to focus, a hefty blow landed between her shoulder blades and she was propelled with force across the room.

Chapter 69

'Sod that.' Marcus spoke the words aloud in response to Sajid telling him to wait at home. How could he just hang on at home waiting to find out if Nikki was all right? Okay, Sajid would rally the troops, but that all took time … phone calls, briefings, orders and then getting there. He, on the other hand, was right there, practically on the doorstep.

He dragged his jacket on, loped upstairs to leave a note by Charlie's bed and then left the house. For a second, he thought about just getting in his car and driving straight there, but something made him head instead next door to Anika's house. Despite the earliness of the hour, the kitchen light was on and as he walked up the steps, her figure was visible, hunched over the kitchen table, a mug in her hand. Anika often suffered from bouts of insomnia and Marcus was glad that tonight was one of her sleepless ones.

So as not to startle her, he rapped gently on the back door. 'Anika, it's me. Marcus. Can you open up for a minute?'

Anika's face was wan when she opened the door, her eyes wide with worry and Marcus felt guilty that he was going to have to alarm her even more. But then again, how many times had Nikki shouldered the worry for her sister? Now it was Anika's turn to be there for Nikki.

Not wanting to waste time going inside, he remained on the doorstep as he explained the situation. He was relieved when, to give her her due, Anika straightened her spine, waved him off and said she'd take care of everything at home.

With barely any traffic, Marcus made it down the hill in no time, all the while hoping Nikki was okay. Turning off Great Horton Road, he saw that Nikki's clapped-out old car was parked in front of the pub. He pulled in beside her vehicle and, switching his headlights off, studied the façade of The Mannville Arms. It was in darkness, the old sign swaying in the breeze. Now he was here, he wasn't entirely sure what to do. Presumably Nikki was inside, yet there were no lights on at the front of the building.

Marcus grabbed a bag from the back seat, slipped out of his van and walked further down the street till he could access the footpath leading to a wide darkened back alley. Switching on his pen torch, he shielded it with a gloved hand and, careful to avoid the numerous potholes, he approached the back of the pub, annoyed when his presence sparked off a barrage of barks from the adjoining property. He extinguished his torch till the barking abated and then proceeded to inspect the area. The pub was fenced off with solid metal gates at the front and metal panelling to either side. The gates had a hefty lock in place. A dim light shone from somewhere in the depths of the building on the ground floor.

Not wanting to attract attention to himself, Marcus, keeping an eye out for company, used his torch to inspect the lock. It was an old-fashioned one, but solid and he presumed there would be bolts for additional security on the other side. In his younger days he'd broken through many similar locks. Glancing up he wondered if he could scale either the gates or the fence, but both were topped by coils of barbed wire. With a sigh, he extracted from his bag a metal handled tool which tapered off and ended in a squiggly coil. His earlier experience as a lock picker would put him in good stead with this one, although it had been a while since he'd done anything like this. With any luck, he wouldn't have forgotten his skills.

Torch held between his teeth, he inserted the tool at an angle and twiddled, conscious of how the metal on metal sound seemed to amplify in the darkness. The lock wouldn't budge, so quelling the temptation to kick the gate he took a deep breath, selected a slightly chubbier tool and repeated the process.

Within seconds, he felt the slight give, and taking his time, he flicked his wrist and heard the satisfying sound of the lock disengage. Releasing a huge breath, Marcus cautiously pushed the gate open, pausing momentarily when it squeaked, setting off a half-hearted yelp from the neighbour's dog. When it fell silent again, he pushed it open just wide enough for him to squeeze through, and entered the yard. Pointing his torch to his feet, Marcus did a quick assessment of the yard, before proceeding, bag slung over his shoulder, to the door. This might have to be his getaway after all.

The light from within the building remained on, but no others joined it, so Marcus trusted he hadn't been heard. Taking a risk, he flicked his torch upwards looking for signs of cameras but there were none. Strange to have such security, yet no cameras. Still that didn't prove anything. To be honest, Marcus wasn't entirely sure how Nikki's instincts or investigation had brought her here. All he knew was that he trusted her and if she thought there was something iffy here, then he'd have her back. He'd never liked Gordon anyway – too taciturn, too intense. It didn't really surprise him that Nikki thought the landlord capable of murder. Although, if asked he'd probably have said that Gordon lacked the brains to remain undetected for so long – just showed you never could tell what might lie beneath someone's exterior.

Three concrete steps led to a solid back door with a heavily curtained window to the right, and Marcus realised that the yellowy light he'd seen from the alleyway was coming from a high-up pantry type window. Standing on tip toes, Marcus looked for chinks in the curtains so he could see inside, but he was unlucky. There was no choice, so he selected another tool from his bag and set to work on the lock. This one proved easier to open than the previous one and as he felt the lock give, he paused, listening for any sign that someone indoors had heard, but all he could hear was the breeze gently rattling a window on the upper storey.

Turning the handle, he hoped there were no deadbolts, or his efforts would have been in vain. When the door slid open, he smiled. He was in!

Chapter 70

Startled, Nikki stumbled before regaining her footing and spinning round. Nancy held a crowbar at waist height and smiled, all pleasantness and jovial camaraderie gone as she took a menacing step forward.

Nancy? Fucking Nancy!

Backing away from her assailant, Nicki tried to gather her thoughts. Sending quick glances around the room she tried to work out an escape plan. The room was huge and seemed to take up the equivalent of three quarters of the pub upstairs. Unlike the external corridor, the cellar was warm, and contrary to Nancy's assertion, it didn't appear to be used as a stock room for beer kegs at all. Rows of bookshelves holding videos or DVDs lined one wall and positioned in front of a mega-sized TV was a reclining couch. It looked like the room had been decked out as a cinema. In the opposite corner were tripods, spotlights and other photographic equipment. Wary of obstacles that could trip her up leaving her vulnerable, Nikki kept retreating as Nancy, crowbar in hand continued to approach.

A strange, not quite human sound came from behind Nikki and she glimpsed a curtained-off area towards the back of the room. Who the hell was behind that curtain and what condition were they in?

Still, Nancy advanced and still, Nikki retreated. How could she have got this so wrong? She'd been sure it was Gordon. Her thighs brushed up against a chair, and glad to have something to use as a weapon, Nikki grabbed it by the back and spun it in front of her. With its wooden legs extended, she made small stabbing movements towards Nancy who flung her head back and laughed.

'You really think that's going to do you any good? You silly girl.'

Nikki blinked. The friendly, effervescent woman she knew had been replaced by a cold, defiant, controlled person. She even looked different … held herself differently. Gone was the slight slouch, the ever-ready smile, and in its place was pure granite. Taking baby steps towards the curtain, Nikki maintained eye contact with her pursuer, all the while making the same small jabbing motions with the chair.

When she spoke, she kept her voice low, so Nancy had to strain to hear her. If she was concentrating on what Nikki was saying she might not be as observant of her actions. 'What's happened to you, Nancy? Has Gordon forced you to do this?'

One thing Nikki was certain of, was that Nancy, with her small frame, could not possibly transport the bodies on her own. 'He make you do this?'

As she spoke, Nikki was making miniscule progress towards the curtain. Whoever was behind there, and she suspected it was Tyke, she was determined they would stay alive. 'Look, put the hammer down and I'll tell them you helped me. Saj will be here soon. You can't escape, Nancy. I *know* you didn't do this on your own … you *wouldn't*. You liked Khal. Why would you kill him?'

Nancy flung back her head, her face contorted, and laughed. 'You stupid little fool. Liked Khal? No, like him was one thing I did not. He was a waster. Just like the rest of them. He was a waste of space. A complete failure. He comes here to this country, takes advantage of our education, *steals* the university place of some hardworking kid who would have achieved great things … and then' – she snorted – 'he thinks it's okay to jack in his course because – and this is all your fault, you stupid little girl – because …' She took a step forward, her hands tightening on the hammer. 'Because Daddy's cutting off the cash flow and good old Khal had to provide for, would you believe it, *his baby*.'

Nikki's heart hammered, her pulse rate through the roof. *What the hell was she on about? Khal didn't know she was pregnant.*

Nancy was still ranting. 'Like all the others before and after him, he was a failure. Your darling Khal was a big failure. Couldn't answer the one question we asked him. *"Why are you here?"* That's all he had to work out.' Her knuckles were white on the handle, her eyes flashing, her entire body shaking. 'Not one of them could answer. Not one of them. Do you believe it? I couldn't have made it any clearer. If he'd owned up to his privilege, admitted that it was his wealth that had taken him so far, showed remorse for using his entitlement … accepted that that's why he was chosen … then maybe your daughter would have had her daddy around.'

As she ranted, Nikki continued to edge her way closer to the curtain, aware that the moaning from behind was becoming more frantic. Whoever was behind there must have heard their voices. What was Nancy raving about though? She'd targeted her victims because she thought they were privileged? It didn't make sense.

Keeping her eye on Nancy, Nikki only hoped that Tyke would be able to move if she managed to talk Nancy down. The other woman's ravings made her doubtful of that, so she pinned her hopes on Sajid having got her text and being on his way.

'Even his last request was pathetic – all about you and the baby. Thought you'd be a good mum, he did. Phew, got that wrong big time, didn't he?'

Nikki could feel the curtain fabric skimming her ankles now, so releasing one hand from the chair she reached back and gripped the fabric. Almost simultaneously she heard a noise coming from the stairs. *Aw shit, Gordon?* Would she be able to rescue whoever was being held behind the curtain *and* deal with Nancy before Gordon came in.

Come on, Saj, get a move on.

Still jabbing at Nancy with the chair, she yanked the curtains creating a gap and froze …

Chapter 71

Pausing just inside the kitchen, stale frying fat sour in his nostrils, Marcus, careful to shield his torch beam, cast it round the small room. There wasn't much in the way of furniture which made it easy for him to stride through the pub kitchen and get to the door. With his ear to the wooden panel, Marcus listened, but not hearing any sounds, he cracked open the door. As he did so, faint light streamed in from the deserted corridor beyond. At the end of a corridor was the bar next to a staircase leading up to what he imagined were the living quarters.

Would Nikki have been taken upstairs? Now that he was inside the house, his earlier confidence that a sneaky entry would be best deserted him. He was effectively breaking and entering the property. The last thing he wanted was to end up with a criminal record. He'd been lucky as a youngster to avoid that. It would be just his luck to end up with one now, as an adult, when he was in a relationship with a police officer ... Not that he was even sure if he was in a relationship with Nikki. They still had loads to sort out, but first he had to find her.

Her earlier note had made it clear that she was going to confront Khal's killer and, as far as Marcus was concerned, that was a risky business. He only hoped he wasn't too late. With that thought hammering in his mind, he stepped into the hallway and considered his options. From the opposite end of the hallway came a dull glow. That decided it – light meant human presence and *that* probably meant Nikki was there.

Switching off his penlight, he crept along, straining his ears for any sounds. The light came from underneath a closed door. Pausing once more at this door, he again listened, but could hear nothing. Glad that he wore gloves, he reached over and depressed the handle. The door swung inwards and Marcus realised he was on the landing at the top of cellar stairs. There was no sign of anyone near the bottom of the stairs and although the light was dim, he decided to risk going down. Glad that he wore trainers, he descended the concrete steps. His body tense, ready to react if necessary, his breathing was shallow, catching in his throat, almost choking him. He remembered this sensation from when he used to burgle as a teenager and was aware that the best way to handle it was to slow it down and focus on one thing at a time. He straightened his back and wished his legs didn't feel quite so jelly-like.

At the bottom of the stairs, he saw another light, brighter this time and then voices. Was that Nikki? There were a few doors, one straight ahead and at least two more. It was Nikki, he was sure of it … and someone else. A voice that was familiar, but he couldn't place it. As he neared, he realised someone was ranting, shouting … as if they were out of control. He slipped his hand into his bag, grabbed a pin hammer and ran the last few metres down the corridor and approached the room.

Chapter 72

As she pulled back the curtain, Nikki couldn't believe her eyes. A hooded figure in black, holding a cattle prod, stood within arm's reach of her, obscuring all but the feet of the inert figure tied to a chair behind him. Her brain instantly recognised that her best means of escape was through Nancy. She spun on her heel, still holding the chair and as she turned, a familiar figure dashed into the room. Nancy, seemingly hearing Marcus's entrance, spun towards him, snarling, whilst Nikki, heart galloping, used the momentary distraction to increase the space between her and the hooded figure. She surged forward, adrenaline lending her speed and jabbed the chair into Nancy's back. Two of the legs broke off and clattered to the floor, leaving Nikki holding an ineffective chair back.

Nancy didn't seem to notice the impact as she continued towards the new arrival, her crowbar raised above her head, a yell of rage spewing from her. Nikki glanced round for something, anything that she could use to stop Nancy attacking Marcus, but she was too late as the metal tool descended with a sickening thud on Marcus's skull less than a second before his smaller hammer grazed Nancy's shoulder. He fell to the ground.

'Marcus!' Nikki cried.

Behind her, the hooded figure moved and, choosing speed over self-defence, Nikki glanced at Marcus who was slumped on the floor with a growing mushroom of blood pooling by his head, and then took to her heels and ran, elbowing Nancy aside.

Looking first one way and then the other, she panted from the room. Upstairs she'd be locked in and Nancy had the keys … but … the tunnels. If she could just open the door and escape before the hooded figure reached her, she'd be able to hide, maybe even find one of the exits.

Slamming the door behind her, she heard Nancy screeching, 'What are you waiting for, Gordon? Go get the bitch.'

Not waiting for Gordon's lumbering figure to catch up, Nikki took off down the corridor to the door at the end, hoping that the key Nancy had given her earlier would work smoothly. A quick glance behind her as she inserted the key in the lock told her that Gordon was in the corridor and thundering towards her. What he lacked in speed, he made up for in scariness. The cloak wafting behind him, his face partially obscured by the hood made Nikki wish she hadn't turned around. Focusing her attention on the lock, her knees almost sagged as it turned and the door sprung open.

With only thoughts of getting help for Marcus, she took time to tug the key free. If she reached another exit, she'd be able to get out and get help. She stepped through and just as Gordon reached the door, she slammed it back, wishing she had time to lock it behind her. She knew, however, that her weight would be no match for her assailant. Instead, she stumbled forward, her hands extended on either side, her fingers skimming the damp walls.

It was pitch black and yet she tried to run. Seconds later, Gordon pulled the door open, and moments before his massive frame blocked the light, she saw a wheeled trolley directly in front of her. But it was too late to stop and she tripped over it, pulling it down on top of her. One of the handles hit her cheekbone.

Scrabbling out from beneath the trolley, uncaring of the smell of rat piss or the dampness, Nikki pushed herself to her feet and ran, splashing through puddles as she went, one hand frantically trying to locate her phone in her pocket.

Gordon's heavy footsteps seemed to be gaining on her. Spurred on by her memory of the cattle prod, Nikki sped up. She needed to see where she was going or else she might fall again. She couldn't afford to miss noticing an exit in the dark. Gordon had the advantage of knowing these tunnels better than her, but she was faster and fitter. Already she could hear him panting and perhaps it was wishful thinking but was he slowing a little?

At last she found her phone and slowing only to use the light from her home screen to locate her torch app, she propelled herself forward, her passage eerily lit as she ran. Bouncing the torch off the walls and to the floor in front, she hoped she was going in the right direction. She wished she'd paid more attention to the maps. Sajid had studied them, tracing his finger over the different routes. She'd give anything to have his company right now. The cold air was beginning to catch in her throat, and dampness surrounded her, closing in on her ... her steps faltered, her muscles ached. At the same time as she became aware of a different texture beneath her feet, they slipped away from her and she landed on her backside. Seconds later a flash of light was followed by an excruciating pain that hit her shoulder. Stunned, she shuddered, struggling to keep her eyes open. Fighting to remain conscious, she felt herself being hefted into the air and positioned on something bony that smelled of beer and man sweat.

Chapter 73

Only half aware of being bounced along on Gordon's shoulder, Nikki tried to see through the cotton wool inside her head. Visions of Marcus taunted her. Immobile on the concrete floor, blood … so much blood, everywhere … He'd come for her and, just like with Khal, she'd let him down. Her shoulder throbbed big time and she suspected her cheekbone might be cracked too. She craved to fight, to pummel Gordon's back, but she bit down on that emotion and focused on keeping her body slack as if she were unconscious. What could she do? From the minute she'd entered the cellar, her phone had had no signal and anyway, she'd dropped it in the tunnels when Gordon attacked her with the cattle prod. She was out of options.

As they re-entered the cellar room, Nikki, through half-shut lids, tried to get the lie of the land. Marcus appeared to still be unconscious. His forehead was swollen and covered in blood and his pallor made him look ghost-like. *Come on, Marcus, hang on in there!* Gordon walked past Marcus and dropped her like a sack of potatoes onto a wooden chair similar to the one she'd broken over Nancy's back, except this one had arms. Nikki allowed her head to loll forward as if she was still unconscious and remained motionless as he tied her arms and legs to the chair.

360

'Little bitch's boyfriend bruised my shoulder. She'll pay for that.'

It was Nancy's voice and when Nikki squinted, she could see the woman's feet just in front of her, incongruously clad in fluffy pink slippers.

A deeper voice responded. 'We need to get rid of this one too, Nancy. Never got the chance before she interrupted us. Can I finish it off now? Do the last request bit? I checked, there's a great dump site behind the Interchange. I can get it there tonight.'

Nikki risked a peep at the person occupying the other chair and nearly gasped aloud, for the chair was occupied, not by Tyke, but by a woman. Despite the bruising distorting her face, she recognised her. It was Tess and she looked to be in a very bad way. Which begged the question, where the hell was Tyke? Probably at the pig farm. Was it by pure chance that linking Khal and Tyke's visit to The Mannville Arms, she'd stumbled on this? Pure fluke?

Nikki could hear the annoyance in Nancy's voice as she replied. 'Don't be daft. We don't have time right now. We'll deal with Tess later. Truth is we should have dealt with her fifteen years ago when she worked out what we were doing. Her and that stupid brother of hers. We were too soft then – taken in by the fact that she could be helpful on occasion. Still, she's paying for it now. We need to clear up Parekh and her boyfriend first. Need to dump them outside … maybe in the back alley. But we need to be quick. Need to make it look like someone outside did it. You leave the talking to me when the police come, right? They're too stupid to work it out.'

With what Nikki thought was a surprising show of perceptiveness, Gordon said, 'What if Parekh's told them already? What if they're on their way now?'

The sound of someone being thumped, followed by an 'ouch' told Nikki that Nancy wasn't impressed by that idea. 'Idiot. If she'd told her police buddies, *they'd* be here now instead of her half-wit boyfriend.'

As the other woman's feet disappeared from Nikki's vision, she allowed herself to take a deeper breath. Saj would be here any minute, she was sure of that. Wishing she knew what the time was, Nikki tried to move her head to see if she could see her watch. If it was after six, Saj would be awake and have got her text. All she needed to do was keep them alive for a bit longer. Someone moaned and Nikki's heart sped up. Was it Marcus? A quick glance told her Marcus hadn't moved. She risked another peek at Tess. Trussed up, half naked on a chair to her right, Nikki could see Tess had been cut numerous times and just beyond her stood a trolley table with a variety of cutting instruments laid out. Despite what she'd just heard about Jacko and Tess's complicity, Nikki didn't want the other woman to die. She had issues that should have been dealt with earlier. Jacko had enabled her increasingly erratic behaviour over the years and Nikki had, for the sake of friendship, gone with it. How many people had died because she had turned a blind eye? If she ever got out of this alive, Nikki would make sure that every one of them got their comeuppance.

Gordon shuffled off, presumably into the corner of the curtained room and began muttering to himself. The thought that she'd heard him speak more in the last half-hour than she had in the last fifteen years almost made her snort. She bit down on the hysterical laughter trying to escape and focused on her breathing. *Come on, Nikki! Get a grip!*

As she tried to work out her plan of action, Nancy and Gordon conversed in muted tones, moving around the room. Various sounds drifted to her; the swish of the curtains, metal on metal, something being rolled on wheels. *What the hell was going on?* Her options were limited. At a push, she might be able to rock her chair backwards and it might break. However, if she did that and it didn't break, she'd have alerted them to the fact she was conscious.

As it happened, she didn't need to make the decision, for her hair was grabbed and her head jolted backwards. Startled, Nikki, eyes wide, looked up into Gordon's face. His gaze was expressionless, his eyes dead and yet pressed against her back was the evidence of his arousal. Refusing to blink, Nikki stared him out, ignoring the sharp blade of a knife at her throat. She'd been in equally bad situations before and the secret was never to show fear, because they fed off it.

Nancy paced in front of Nikki, bouncing the crowbar in the palm of her hand. 'Now we've got your attention and your little "I'm unconscious" charade is over, let's begin. The first thing I need to know is, have you told anyone else where you are?'

At Nancy's words, Nikki shifted her gaze from Gordon. Behind Nancy she could see Marcus, still lying motionless, still looking pale. Despite the blade biting against her throat, Nikki gave a single shake of her head.

'You might want to reconsider your answer, Parekh. If you lie to me, I will make sure your kids suffer. Gordon and I have an escape route planned, you see. We know these tunnels inside out. We'll hear your colleagues coming and get out – killing you three before we leave, of course.'

Nikki bit her lip. Let the other woman sense uncertainty. The truth was, Nikki was pleased to have it confirmed that Marcus was still alive, although she couldn't be sure how much longer he'd last. He had lost a lot of blood. The threat to her children sent a bubble of rage fizzing in her stomach. She wasn't stupid enough to trust Nancy. Hadn't she failed to pass on Khal's last request until now? Still, it went against the grain to play Russian Roulette with her kids' lives – but she had no choice. It was either play for extra time or give in now. She shook her head again and managed a hoarse, 'No, only Marcus.'

Nancy snorted and then a spotlight blinded Nikki. As Nancy began rolling a film camera around the area, Nikki realised that the curtain was actually a backdrop and she was centre stage in Nancy and Gordon's weird fantasy. Gordon wheeled his trolley

363

of tools beside her and picked up the cattle prod. Talking in a David Attenborough sort of voice as if she was doing the voiceover for a wildlife programme, Nancy pointed it at Nikki's face.

'And here we have our final captive. She doesn't quite fit the usual criteria, but she is a worthy speci—'

A thump from above made Nancy pause, her eyes narrowing, lips tightening as she moved away from the camera. The sound of heavy boots thudding downstairs followed. Nikki flung all her weight backwards, just as Nancy barked out an order. 'Kill her.'

The current from the cattle prod zapped Nikki on the chest as she propelled backwards landing on the floor, and the chair broke beneath her. Unable to move, but still conscious, Nikki saw Gordon approach with a machete in his hand. Nancy piped up behind them. 'I'll finish Tess.'

As the blade descended towards her throat, Nikki was glad her mother and sister were there for her kids. A tear dribbled down her cheek and she tried to roll away, but her entire body was numb. She closed her eyes and waited. Nothing!

She opened her eyes again in time to see Marcus, droplets of blood flying from his head wound, arms wrapped round Gordon's chest, dragging him backwards. The machete clattered to the floor at the same time as Nancy grabbed the cattle prod and fired it at Marcus, forcing him to let go as the electrical current hit his waist. The door crashed open and Saj, wearing body armour and followed by four SWAT team members, burst in.

'You took your fucking time, Saj,' Nikki said before passing out.

Chapter 74

Bruised, sore and battered, Nikki stood at the entrance to Nancy and Gordon's torture room. DS Springer had initially objected to her presence, until Archie had stepped in and, in his words, 'tied her proverbials in knots'.

The pool of blood where Marcus had lain made the air smell coppery. She looked at it for a long time. Marcus had saved her not once but twice and after cracking his head on the floor when he pulled Gordon off her, he'd sustained a fracture to the back of his skull, which in conjunction with the wound to his forehead had resulted in swelling on the brain. They had operated and he was now in an induced coma. Nikki couldn't help her thoughts returning to Margo and it took all her willpower to not allow those depressing images to dominate her mind.

Breathing in through her mouth, Nikki moved forward. Sajid was in the room, and like her, suited up, although most of the evidence had already been processed. Beyond the curtain rail, photographic equipment of the highest spec was dotted about; voice distorters, lighting, cameras, various lenses. The chair where Tess had breathed her last breath was empty, only the remains of the restraints and the accumulated bloodstains of years of torture remained. Like Khalid, Tess's head had been caved in by a crowbar. Although the machete, the crowbar and the cattle prod had been taken as evidence, the broken chair that Nikki had been strapped to was still there.

It was as if the room had been divided into two; a stage for Nancy and Gordon to act out their warped depravities and a sitting room for Nancy to work on her editing and recordings and then watch and rewatch her recordings time and again. The DVDs were her trophies. Nikki had no doubt in her mind that Nancy was the dominant one in the partnership, although she suspected that, like Rose West, she'd try to palm the organisation off on her husband and claim she was coerced.

For fifteen years, the pub had been her local. Gordon and Nancy had been her friends. How could she not have seen the evil in them when they served her pints? How could she have been duped?

But what preyed on her mind even more was Jacko's part in all of this. On hearing of his sister's death and confronted by what Nikki had heard, he'd broken down and confessed to being aware of what was happening since Khal's death. Tess had taken to stalking Khal and when he'd not left The Mannville Arms after a lock-in on the night he disappeared, she'd sneaked in through the back of the pub and followed them downstairs. When she'd seen what was happening to Khal, she'd taken a few photos and then hopped it without either Nancy or Gordon realising.

Later, she'd blackmailed them, not for money, but for access to their victims on occasion. Tess, it seemed, like to torture almost as much as Gordon did. According to Jacko, in Tess's warped brain it was better for Khal to be dead than for him to be with Nikki. He'd covered up for his sister all this time, but in recent years, he'd been able to control her better by subduing her with drugs. It was the death of Nancy's father in prison that provided the temporary hiatus in their activities.

The discovery of Khal's remains had been a catalyst not just for Gordon and Nancy to revert to their previous behaviours, but also for Tess. Jacko blamed their upbringing and had begged Nikki to understand ... to forgive. Nikki had walked away and allowed the uniforms to arrest him. She'd never understand that. Her own upbringing had been far from easy and yet here she was struggling to keep her city safe. As for forgiveness ... she wasn't there yet and maybe never would be. When she'd heard he'd tried to kill himself, the numbness in Nikki's heart hadn't budged. She'd been glad he hadn't succeeded. He deserved to rot in prison for a long time. Death was too easy a solution for Jacko.

Sajid came and stood next to her. 'They'll never get out, you know that, right?'

Nikki nodded. She couldn't summon satisfaction yet, but the fact that they'd been caught relieved a miniscule amount of her anger. There was justice in that, but not fairness ... if life was fair, there wouldn't be over twenty families out there only just on the road to closure for the loss of their loved ones. There wouldn't be all those people out there minus a son, a daughter, a partner or whatever. And why? Because Nancy's dad had infected her mum with the HIV virus and then been imprisoned for rape? Because her mum's illness had prevented Nancy from going to university and Nancy couldn't bear to see other people with the chances she'd missed? Because she'd wanted to punish her parents over and over again? Because Gordon had been a sick fuck who got off on torturing people? Because those two sick souls had connected ...? Because Jacko chose to protect his sister rather than his best friend and loads of innocent victims? Because Tess needed help she never got?

'You okay, Nik?'

'I'm fine.' Summoning a tight smile, Nikki was aware that she hadn't convinced Saj one little bit. 'They found Tyke's body this morning ... in the tunnels near the Interchange entrance. Looks like Nancy and Gordon didn't quite have time to dispose of him in the new car park.'

Nikki tried to summon up some sympathy and failed. 'Yeah

well, at least that's four scrotes off our streets. Franco, Deano and Big Zee are all up for various counts of murder. All the hair and bones and stuff that Gracie found combined with all the statements means Bradford's streets are a little bit cleaner this morning.'

Wishing she could feel ecstatic about that, Nikki walked into the middle of the room, her eyes fixed on one area. The shelf of DVDs had been catalogued and, although they still had to be watched, they had revealed a total of twenty-four victims in all, with Tess being the final one ... well, at least she hoped she was the final one. It didn't bear thinking about if she were to lose Marcus too.

Moving directly to the shelves, Nikki reached out her gloved hand and trailed it along, until she came to Khal's one. 'I want to watch this.'

'Aw, Nik, no. Don't do this to yourself, please don't.'

'That bitch told me Khal knew about Charlie. I need to see if that's true. Set it up. The equipment's all here. Archie says it's been processed. Let me watch.' She held Saj's gaze, conscious that he might well refuse her request, but then shook his head and took the DVD from her. 'Just the end bit. Just the last request bit, okay?'

Nikki frowned. 'You watched it?'

''Course I did. Hoped if I told you what was on it, that would be enough. Should have known better.'

Saj forwarded the recording and then paused it. 'You ready?' And when Nikki nodded, he pressed Play.

Epilogue

Three Weeks Later

The weeks since everything had blown open had been filled with chaos ... chaos and hospital visits and funerals. Nikki had gone to as many of the funerals as she was able to. The DVDs had been scoured and multiple excavation sites all over the city were being worked as they spoke. As each body was recovered and repatriated with their families, Nikki's spirits lifted – just a little.

The Muslim section of the cemetery was often filled with families paying their respects to their dead relatives. With flowers, liberally displayed, it was a colourful backdrop to the busy road that ran parallel. Nikki, her only experience being with Hindu cremations, had got Sajid's help to organise the funeral for Khal. And with the help of a Muslim funeral director, the funeral had gone smoothly. Nikki and Charlie, with their family and friends forming a protective barrier around them, paid their last respects and ignored the press vultures that had descended. For a moment Nikki felt a pang that Jacko wasn't there too.

In complete contrast, DS Springer strutted about like a peacock trying to claim the kudos for herself. The only problem with that was that Nikki and Marcus were the only two with visible injuries

369

and Nikki was the one burying her bigamist husband. To all intents and purposes, Springer had closed the case, but everyone knew it had really been Nikki. Still, Springer was the one who'd coordinated the excavations, interfaced with the media and conducted all the interviews. Nancy had demanded that Nikki interview her but both Nikki and Archie had refused. 'No pandering to damn serial killers on my watch ... she can sing for her proverbials,' had been his exact words.

What was more important for the press than giving a grieving family space to lay their loved ones to rest, was their desire to splash images of Nikki over their front pages. Although this time, her colleagues at Trafalgar House viewed her in a friendlier light than when she'd caused the downfall of one of their own. Still, Nikki could barely stop herself from lashing out at them. Marcus, with an interestingly shaved head, had been deemed well enough to accompany them to the cemetery and his arm round her shoulders felt good. She could have done it without him, but right now, she was pleased he was with her.

Since they'd caught Nancy and Gordon and arrested Jacko, and while Marcus was in a coma, everything had been beige for Nikki ... beige and heavy and full of effort. She hoped that laying Khal to rest would enable her and Charlie to move on. She could never regret her relationship with him for he had given her one of the three most perfect things she had in her life. He'd taught her two things; it was good to trust, for it could bring joy, but he'd also taught her not to ever trust completely.

Back in Willowfield Terrace, Nikki was glad to kick off her shoes and snuggle on the couch with Marcus at her side. A tiny smile played on her face as she watched Sunni on his laptop, the two girls arguing with Haqib over which Netflix show to watch, her mum pottering about making chai and Anika helping their mum. She gave Marcus's hand a little squeeze. Her external bruises had faded and she wasn't sure the internal ones ever would. Time would tell, but for now, she was happy to be alive.

Her hand slipped up to her neck. Her fingers drifted lightly along her scar and paused at the nick she'd earned in the cellar under The Mannville Arms.

*

Desperate to find out how Nikki gets her life back on track? If you want to be the first to know about the next gripping D.S. Nikki Parekh case, sign up to Liz Mistry's email list here:

po.st/LizMistryNewsletter

Acknowledgements

Getting a book ready for publication is always a combined effort and I have been blessed to have had such an amazing team of people behind me, cheering me on, offering practical advice and keeping me on the right track.

The team at HQ Digital are fantastic and my editor Belinda Toor is indefatigable. Her input has made *Last Request* a much better read. My amazing beta readers have also helped me to up my game with their pithy comments and invaluable advice; thanks to Anne Hampson, Craig Gillan, Dee Groocock, Emma Truelove, Lynn Hampson and Toria Forsyth-Moser. The Awesome Authors (you know who you are) have contributed in vast amounts to both my sanity and my ability to laugh. My writing group at Leeds Trinity University were there at the inception of *Last Request* and were influential in helping to mould Nikki into the character she is today; thanks to Andrea, Kathleen, Jo, Sam, Stephanie and Suzanne.

Throughout the writing process, my family are always my greatest source of support. They drag me through the bad days and ride with me through the good ones. Love you, Nilesh, Ravi, Kasi and Jimi.

372

However, the biggest thanks must go to all those absolutely amazing online book group members, readers and bloggers out there who share the book love on a daily basis. Without your support and enthusiasm, writing wouldn't be half as much fun ... so HUGE THANKS!

Want more?
To be the first to hear about new releases, competitions,
99p eBooks and promotions, sign up to our monthly
email newsletter.

Sign up at po.st/HQSignUp

Dear Reader,

Thank you so much for choosing to read *Last Request*.

The basic concept for *Last Request* has been jiggling around in my head for many years. The idea of someone disappearing without trace, leaving behind a loved one is an intriguing concept that opens up such a range of questions for a crime writer: *Was their disappearance voluntary? If so, why? What might prompt someone to leave their life behind with no word? What were they escaping from or running to? Who did they leave behind? What was their story? How do they survive not knowing where their loved one is?*

All those questions clamoured in my mind, and I couldn't decide whose story I wanted to tell – was it the person who disappeared or the people left behind, or a combination of both?

However, until DS Nikki Parekh landed on the page, I didn't feel I could resolve that issue, nor did I feel I had a character worthy of delivering that particular story. As soon as Nikki appeared to me, I knew *she* was the one and the premise for the story became clearer. I wanted to create a gutsy female character, and Nikki fits the bill. Having children of dual heritage myself, I suppose I subconsciously based Nikki on my daughter, who coincidentally is a bit feisty herself. That, though, is as far as the similarities go.

Set in Bradford, *Last Request* delivers an inclusive range of characters and, I hope, reflects Bradford.

I hope you enjoy reading *Last Request* and getting to know Nikki, her friends and her family. If you did, I'd love it if you left a review … a few words is enough, but if you want to write more then that's great too.

Best wishes,
Liz Mistry

Dear Reader,

We hope you enjoyed reading this book. If you did, we'd be so appreciative if you left a review. It really helps us and the author to bring more books like this to you.

Here at HQ Digital we are dedicated to publishing fiction that will keep you turning the pages into the early hours. Don't want to miss a thing? To find out more about our books, promotions, discover exclusive content and enter competitions you can keep in touch in the following ways:

JOIN OUR COMMUNITY:

Sign up to our new email newsletter: po.st/HQSignUp

Read our new blog www.hqstories.co.uk

🐦 *: https://twitter.com/HQDigitalUK*

f *: www.facebook.com/HQStories*

BUDDING WRITER?

We're also looking for authors to join the HQ Digital family!
Please submit your manuscript to:

HQDigital@harpercollins.co.uk

Thanks for reading, from the HQ Digital team

DIGITAL

H | Q

If you enjoyed *Last Request*, then why not try another chilling thriller from HQ Digital?